I0831731

ON THE TRAIL OF THE BLACK

ON THE TRAIL OF THE BLACK

Tracking Corruption

Edited by

Bibek Debroy

Kishore Arun Desai

RUPA

Published by
Rupa Publications India Pvt. Ltd 2017
7/16, Ansari Road, Daryaganj
New Delhi 110002

Sales Centres:

Allahabad Bengaluru Chennai
Hyderabad Jaipur Kathmandu
Kolkata Mumbai

ISBN: 978-81-291-4922-0

First impression 2017

10 9 8 7 6 5 4 3 2 1

Dedicated to
Narendra Modi
Prime Minister of India

Contents

Introduction

The history of corruption is synchronous with the history of mankind itself. One can easily find mention of various shades and forms of corruption even across ancient texts. It's not commonly known that one of the earliest mentions of corruption can be found in the Ramayana. Here is an interesting story[1] from the Uttara Kanda of the Valmiki Ramayana.

'After returning to Ayodhya, Rama began to rule. Vashishtha, other sages and advisers and ministers helped him rule well. Every day, Lakshmana's job was to go outside the court, to check and see if there was anyone with a complaint. Normally, there weren't any such complainants. Rama's rule was such that there wasn't any disease. The earth yielded plenty of food. Evil disappeared, fearing the king's wrath. Such was Rama's rule that there was no evil at all.

'On one such day, Lakshmana found that there was no one outside the court. "Go back and look again," said Rama. Lakshmana returned to the main gate and found a dog barking away. "What do you want?" Lakshmana asked the dog. "If you have something to tell the king, come with me". "I can't come with you," said the dog. "Dogs are not allowed inside temples, palaces and the houses of Brahmins. Those are the residing places of gods like Agni, Indra, Surya and Vayu. We aren't allowed there."

'But Rama gave special permission to the dog to approach the court. The dog had marks of a beating on its head. "What is your problem, dog?" Rama asked. "A Brahmin named Sarvarthasiddha was looking for alms and has beaten me without any provocation," replied the dog. On Rama's orders, the Brahmin was summoned. "Why have you beaten this dog?" asked Rama. "I was hungry and was roaming around, looking for alms," replied the Brahmin. "This dog was on the road, blocking my way. I asked him to move, but he didn't. So I beat him," replied Sarvarthasiddha. "I'm guilty. Please punish me. If I am punished, I will no longer have to fear about going to hell."

'Rama consulted his advisers and ministers like Bhrigu, Angirasa, Kutsa, Kashyapa and Vashishtha. Their advice was unanimous. According to the shastras, a Brahmin shouldn't be punished. "But you have promised," said the dog. "You promised to set right my complaint. Please make this Brahmin the kulapati of Kalanjara."

'A "kulapati" was a small ruler. His job was to feed ten thousand sages and study under them. Kalinjara or Kalanjara is in the Bundelkhand region. This seemed fair, because Sarvarthasiddha wasn't exactly being punished. The Brahmin was sent off to Kalanjara, riding on an elephant.

'"You have given him a boon instead of punishing him," remarked the ministers. "Not quite," responded Rama. "Ask this dog." On Rama's instructions, the dog related his story.

'"I used to be the kulapati of Kalanjara," said the dog. "I served gods and Brahmins and spent my time ensuring everyone's welfare. I ate after everyone else had eaten. I shared my property with everyone else. But having been a kulapati, I am now destined to this dog's life. That Brahmin is cruel and quick to anger. He will now become a kulapati and the next forty nine of his descendants will spend their lives in hell. No one should accept the post of a kulapati. If you want to make certain that an individual and his friends, sons and animals go to hell, make him a kulapati."'

That's how the story ends. But what does it convey? Though it is not stated explicitly in the Ramayana, the point being made is that power and wealth had corrupted the kulapati system so much that becoming a kulapati became a curse rather than a blessing. No amount of good that one did as a kulapati could sufficiently compensate for the sins of corruption—the burden of which was borne by generations to come. The story also means that corruption must have been a known evil even during the times of the Ramayana; indulging in which was equated with damnation.

Despite such well-entrenched beliefs, corruption survived time and it continues to remain prevalent even today. Such permanence can't be attributed to sheer providence. Corruption is driven by human nature, the fundamental levers of which haven't changed significantly over time. Need and greed for power, rank, money etc. still outweigh the need to abide by values, ethics and law. It is easy for people to compromise with the latter in blind pursuit of the former and most societies and individuals have succumbed to the temptation of power and wealth over morality and ethics. And this possibly explains why corruption could not only survive, but thrive as well, across millennia.

Before exploring this subject any further, it's important to first define the term 'corruption'. Many interpretations exist, depending on whether one takes a broad view on corruption or a relatively focused view. Consider Kautilya's interpretation of corruption for instance. This is what Kautilya's *Arthashastra*[2] has to say on corruption:

> A government officer, not caring to know the information… and neglecting to supervise the dispatch of work in his own department as regulated, may occasion loss of revenue to the government owing to his ignorance, or owing to his idleness when he is too weak to endure the trouble of activity, or due to inadvertence in perceiving…or by being timid when he is afraid of clamour, unrighteousness, and untoward results, or owing to selfish desire when he is favorably disposed towards those who are desirous to

> achieve their own selfish ends, or by cruelty…or by making use of false balance, false measures, and false calculation owing to greediness…

As can be seen, Kautilya took quite a broad view of corruption. Effectively, he makes it the duty of public officials to protect government revenues and then treats any behavioural vices that impact their efficiency to do so as corruption. Carelessness, inefficiency, negligence, weakness and indifference of public officials directly led to loss of revenues for the government and hence were part of the gamut of corrupt activities. Clearly, this is one end of the spectrum in which corruption is interpreted. The trouble with this interpretation is that it enhances the overall subjectivity in demarcating what activities can be classified as corruption and what can't. Further, this view is not in sync with the way one understands corruption in today's context. For instance, it won't be correct to label inefficient and lazy public officials as corrupt in present circumstances.

In contrast to the above, there's a more focused view on corruption at the other end of the spectrum. The World Bank defines corruption as using public office for private gain. As per this definition, any action undertaken by a public official that leads to a private gain (money, property, undue favours etc.) would classify as a corrupt action. However, this definition takes into account activities undertaken mostly by those who use 'public office', that is government officers, public representatives or elected/nominated leaders who occupy public positions. Though corruption is well-understood in the context of public offices, taking into account the current circumstances, using private office for private (individual) gain is also not uncommon. A more contemporary and relevant interpretation of corruption should therefore include activities undertaken in private or non-public offices besides public offices. Yet another point of view relates to the interpretation of corruption under Prevention of Corruption Act (PCA), 1988. While the PCA does not clearly define corruption, it stipulates penalization for a host of corrupt activities committed by public servants. In this regard, Section 13(1)(d)(iii) of PCA is noteworthy. It states, 'A public servant is said to commit the offence of criminal misconduct if he, while holding office as a public servant, obtains for any person any valuable thing or pecuniary advantage without any public interest.' This makes it difficult to delineate activities that should not be termed as corruption. For instance, in case a public servant makes an honest error or genuine mistake in judgment, he or she may find it difficult to justify how that action upholds 'public interest'. Despite honest intentions, risk of getting those mistakes treated as 'criminal misconduct' would always loom. In this manner, the PCA's interpretation of corruption could be considered somewhere between Kautilya and the World Bank's interpretation.

Coming back, despite a range of interpretations presented above, using public/non-public office for private gain seems to be the most commonly understood definition of corruption. The same has been largely followed in this book. While this is not a strict or uniform definition across various chapters, it is one that has helped us draw reasonable boundaries to maintain focus and consistency.

Why This Book?

The paragraphs above outlined the broad contours within which corruption has been interpreted in this book. Obviously, corruption is a subject that is perennially vital and topical. But the question is whether this subject merits a comprehensive coverage in the form of a book. Does it really warrant this much of attention and public discourse?

Corruption is so deeply rooted in our daily lives that it has become routine to expect it. A businessman expects that he may be needed to pay bribe to various government authorities. He even makes provisions for it in the expenditure budgets. An auto driver or a roadside vendor expects that he may be needed to pay 'kharcha paani' to policemen. In fact, recognizing the widespread incidence of corruption, Kaushik Basu, former Chief Economic Adviser to the Ministry of Finance, had even argued to make some kinds of bribes legal.[3] In his 2011 paper, Basu proposed declaring the act of giving bribes to get one's legal entitlements (referred by him as 'harassment bribes') as legitimate. But interestingly, that's just one side of the story. In the above examples, a possibility always exists that the businessman or auto driver/roadside vendor may also be on the other side of the law. For instance, the businessman may deliberately want to pay bribes to evade due taxes or get certain things done the 'easy' way or get away with rules or requirements. This brings us to the next interesting aspect. Is the common man often willing to pay bribe to get away from rules or just to get a preferential access to some services? Many otherwise morally upstanding and ethical individuals may not hesitate to pay the Railway ticket checker some additional money for a berth in case they do not have reserved seats. Why would the common citizen consider this form of corruption as bad if it is in fact facilitative?

To quote economist Samuel Paul, 'Such practices (read corruption) continue because large segments of the population seek personal favors and benefits rather than policy shifts and system reforms from their elected representatives and other public leaders. Laws may have been passed against such practices but many people pay scant attention to them… When people get used to such practices, they tend to rationalize their conduct instead of questioning their legitimacy and morality. They may protest and march on the streets demanding an end to corruption but in their personal lives do not mind paying of taking bribes. Once such practices are widespread, it is difficult to root them out.'[4] As an example, Paul further mentions that in the middle of the 2011 anti-corruption movement led by social activist Anna Hazare, a member of his team was accused of getting paid for false travel bills. The member justified it publicly by saying that the money was used for a good cause! Possibly, this normalization of corruption in everyday lives may have desensitized many towards the long-term damage this evil causes.

That said, corruption is such an exploitative disease, which, if not fixed in time, can ruin the prospects of our country. This is what Kofi Annan, former Secretary General of the United Nations says about the impact of corruption: 'Corruption is an insidious plague that has a wide range of corrosive effects on societies. It undermines democracy and the rule of law, leads to violations of human rights, distorts markets, erodes the quality of life and allows organized crime, terrorism and other threats to human security to flourish... Corruption hurts the poor disproportionately by diverting funds intended for development, undermining a Government's ability to provide basic services, feeding inequality and injustice and discouraging foreign aid and investment. Corruption is a key element in economic underperformance and a major obstacle to poverty alleviation and development.'[5]

While the impact of corruption on the overall socioeconomic progress of a country is multifarious, let's attempt to examine the possible impact of corruption on poverty alleviation and development. One way to look at this aspect is to study some of the biggest scams that have rocked India in the last few years. The following table shows the quantum of the scams, in other words alleged loss to the exchequer, caused by just a select sample of recent scams:

Scams	Year	Reported magnitude (₹ Crore)
Foodgrains in Uttar Pradesh	2010	2,00,000
Coal scam	2009	1,86,000
2G spectrum	2008	1,76,645
Belekeri Port in Karnataka	2010	60,000
Commonwealth Games	2010	36,000
Total		6,58,645

Source: B. Debroy & L. Bhandari. 2012. *Corruption in India: The DNA and the RNA*. New Delhi: Konark Publishers Pvt. Ltd; Secondary research

Now, contrast this with the Union budget allocations in year 2016–17 for three of the most important social sectors—health, education and food subsidy.

2016–17 Budget components	Allocation (₹ Crore)
Health	~41,000
Education	~72,000
Food subsidy	135,000
Total	2,48,000

Source: Union government data; Secondary research

It is evident from the data above that the magnitude of even a few scams is roughly thrice of the total amount that the government allocates on these critical sectors. One can imagine that even if a portion of this loss had reached government coffers, the benefits transferred to the most vulnerable sections of the society could have been significant. And this is just the financial side of the story. This does not take into account corruption's impact on other crucial pillars of governance such as quality and efficiency of service delivery. If one considers these as well, then the overall adverse impact of corruption on the governance and public delivery framework of the country would be significantly worse.

Coming back, our country is in a sweet spot currently. We are the world's fastest growing major economy. Important macro indicators, such as fiscal and revenue deficits, foreign exchange reserves etc. are comfortable and improving consistently. More than 65 per cent of our population is less than 35 years of age. The government of the day is also taking several reformative measures to ensure that the fruits of development and policy actions are particularly shared across the poor and needy. In short, today there is every reason to be positive and hopeful about the bright future of this country. But, if our public service delivery systems continue to be corroded by corruption, then rapid and inclusive growth for the country can't be achieved. We can't afford such a scenario. Hence, it is imperative and timely to dissect the fundamentals of corruption—what, why and how—and devise what needs to be done to conquer this powerful opponent. This is precisely what this book attempts to achieve.

On the Trail of the Black

We have titled the book *On the Trail of the Black* as it traces the elusive footprints of corruption across a multitude of sectors. Notice here that we are using the word 'Black' in the title instead of 'Corruption'. Corruption has an inherent linkage with black money. While it is not the only source for generation of black money, it is surely one of the largest and most important. From that perspective, the broader idea is that pursuit of corruption reflects the pursuit of black money as well.

This book attempts to give the reader a vantage point to grasp the cumulative and cascading impact of corruption on the common citizen. There are sixteen chapters in the book and all of them together cover the cross-sectoral prevalence of corruption in a comprehensive manner. Each chapter has a focused scope and aims to put forward concrete actions/steps to uproot corruption within its chosen focus. This action agenda is devised by following a broadly consistent fact-based diagnostic and analytical approach across chapters.

The first chapter quantifies the size of black economy and its macroeconomic impact, even as similar exercises by experts in the past have failed to arrive at a broader consensus due to the lack of credible data. Sonal Badhan highlights that the terms 'black economy', 'shadow economy', 'parallel economy', 'illegal economy' are often used interchangeably, but they don't mean the same thing. She also points out that black economy leads to several undesirable impacts such as loss of government revenue, underestimation of economic activity and productivity and suboptimal fiscal and monetary policy actions.

In Chapter 2, Aparajita Gupta digs deeper into the most crucial legislation against corruption—the Prevention of Corruption Act, 1988. In doing so, she analyses the broader scheme of this law and loopholes that help the dishonest escape and prevent the honest from taking decisions. Provisions under section 13(1)(d)(iii) are particularly debated. She also discusses key features of the Prevention of Corruption (Amendment) Bill, 2013, and outlines specific suggestions to plug the lacuna in the legal framework.

In Chapter 3, Suparna Jain reviews the role of the executive in combatting corruption through the institutional framework of the Central Vigilance Commission (CVC) and the Central Bureau of Investigation (CBI). While this framework exists, several practical shortcomings with respect to their powers, accountability, jurisdiction and need for sanctions/approvals render it ineffective in dealing with corruption.

In the next chapter, Swati Saini analyses the intent and commitment of the political class to create effective systems while responding to the demands of civil society actions. Taking the recent Lokpal Bill debates, she highlights the divide in the political class between sections who are pro status quo and those in favour of reforms to end this evil.

In Chapter 5, Shashvat Singh analyses the role and impact of civil society actions in the battle against corruption. Besides the commonly known outcomes such as the Right to Information (RTI) and Lokpal Bill, he argues that several other civil society initiatives such as Citizen's Report Cards (CACs), Zero Rupee Note, and campaigns like '*Aaj se khilana bandh, pilana shuru*' have provided a voice to a large section of people against corruption.

In the next chapter, Bibek Debroy delves into corruption in land and real estate sector—probably the biggest and most prominent contributor to this evil. The author underlines the fact that 'Corruption = Monopoly+Discretion-(Accountability + Integrity +Transparency)'. Extending this principle, he articulates a series of reform measures that reduce monopoly and discretion of land and revenue departments and increase their accountability, integrity and transparency. Some of the key policy suggestions include implementing actions such as rapid computerization of land records, re-engineering land use policies, reforming stamp duty regime, repealing the Urban Land Ceiling Regulation Act (ULCRA), reforming the Rent Control Act, introducing e-governance in local administration and tax payments, creating computerized fiscal cadastres and rationalizing property tax designs.

Investing in property (movable, immovable, tangible or intangible) through benami transactions has been a dominant modus operandi of the corrupt to hide black money.

In Chapter 7, Suparna Jain and Aparajita Gupta analyse statutes prohibiting benami property transactions and outline regulatory measures to hit this form of corruption.

In Chapter 8, Dhiraj Nayyar argues that demonetisation has created a unique space for overhauling the legacy rot in the country. This historic exercise has provided the opportunity to destroy systemic corruption and its enablers—black money, cash-dominated transactions, adversarial tax administration, etc. Building upon various steps taken by the government, Nayyar puts forward an action agenda to further the less-cash movement and taxation reforms to take on powerful lobbies and disrupt the corruption network.

In Chapter 9, Kishore Desai outlines important strategies to counter corruption in electoral finances—increase transparency by making election-related funding and expense statements of both parties and candidates public and rolling out a campaign that targets behaviour change amongst the masses. He also proposes creating a digital platform, where financial malpractices can be reported by people easily and directly to the concerned authorities. Further, by facilitating substitution of cash with digital modes and creating mechanisms for time-bound scrutiny of financial accounts and action against defaulters, the states can cleanse electoral finances, thereby hitting electoral corruption at its root.

In Chapter 10, Maninder Kaur Dwivedi dissects corruption in agriculture, procurement of produce and the public distribution system (PDS). In doing so, she calls for a need to relook policies such as farm loan waivers, tax exemptions to income from agriculture and Minimum Support Price (MSP) mechanism to tackle corruption.

Misinvoicing, as per estimates, cost the country more than $40 billion in 2008, clearly indicating the large quantum of this problem. Shambhavi Sharan, in Chapter 11, details the basics of trade misinvoicing—its meaning, incentives and channels for misreporting invoices. The author also articulates measures that should be taken to curb this malpractice.

In Chapter 12, Alok Kumar, Kheya Melo Furtado, Sneha Palit and Alok Kumar Dubey analyse the rampant corruption in health and nutrition services and its impact on efficient service delivery, the importance of which cannot be over-emphasized. They build the case for implementing measures that would plug systemic leakages and inefficiencies, link investments with outcomes, enhance use of technology and fix accountability within the governance framework.

In Chapter 13, Bhavana Kohli discusses corruption in the higher education sector with a focus on cases related to grant of recognition/approvals by regulatory bodies. She outlines a series of measures, some of which include reducing regulations, facilitating a shift towards self-disclosure by institutions on a centralized public portal, making inspections limited and random, minimizing scope of subjectivity in regulations and increasing focus on performance outcomes.

In Chapter 14, Anna Roy and Ritika Aghi build a case for overhauling the public procurement framework. They support enacting a new public procurement law and setting up a public procurement department with an effective independent oversight mechanism. Further, the authors also support standardization of tender documents and increased use of e-procurement.

But given the scale and complexity of the procurement issue, one should naturally expect different viewpoints to address this challenge. In Chapter 15, Bibek Debroy and T.V. Somanathan articulate an alternative approach, thus making this debate meaningful and enriching. They argue that a new procurement law will do more harm than good in the Indian context and instead what is required to cleanse the system is more flexibility and infusion of trust.

The final chapter, 'Cooperative Corruption', seeks to explore the basics of individual corrupt behaviour. Ranveer Nagaich examines how corruption is perpetuated by behaviour and social interactions. He argues that due to a prevailing culture of corruption, interests of individuals and society get misaligned and this eventually encourages corruption.

Summing up, this book is an attempt to address the plague of corruption that invades our country, which drags us one step back every time we take two steps forward. The time is ripe for finally ridding India of this menace from its very roots as we witness a rare convergence of public opinion and will of the highest decision-makers.

A conducive environment now prevails for taking tough, but much needed, actions. We hope that various ideas and recommendations, put together in this book, create a thought-provoking framework needed to decisively uproot corruption and black money—a significant priority for people and policymakers alike.

Bibek Debroy
Kishore Arun Desai

References

1 B. Debroy. 2008. *Sarama and Her Children*. New Delhi: Penguin.
2 B. Debroy & L. Bhandari. 2012. *Corruption in India: The DNA and the RNA*. New Delhi: Konark Publishers Pvt. Ltd.
3 K. Basu, 'Why, for a class of Bribes, the Act of Giving a Bribe should be treated as Legal', Working Paper, March 2011.
4 S. Paul (ed.). 2013. *Fighting Corruption: The Way Forward*. New Delhi: Academic Foundation.
5 Foreword to 'United Nations Convention Against Corruption'.

1

Black Economy and its Macroeconomic Impact

SONAL BADHAN

India's demonetisation exercise last November brought the focus back to corruption, black money and the size of the black economy. The term 'black economy' is often used interchangeably with 'shadow economy', 'parallel economy' or 'illegal economy'. At the outset, it must be clarified that neither the unorganized sector, nor the cash-driven sector in general equate to being called a black economy. Broadly speaking, black economy derives its meaning from the nature of activities that result in illegally as well as legally earned income that is under or unreported to tax authorities, legally or illegally income earned in India but exported out for the purpose of tax evasion and income which is legally earned but gets left out of inclusion into the national income.

The first instance includes income earned from smuggling, drug trafficking, betting, prostitution, etc. In the second category, income from under-reporting of profits, over-invoicing of input costs, under-invoicing exports, undervaluing property prices, etc. is included. Money laundering and money stashed in foreign bank accounts form part of the third category. Though the fourth category in itself does not constitute black economy, it does account for underestimation of national income and provides channels for tax evasion and circumventing government regulation.

Another misconception is equating black economy to the unorganized sector. A Confederation of Indian Industry (CII) report[1] by A. Srija & Shrinivas V. Shirke cites the National Commission for Enterprises in the Unorganized Sector (NCEUS) definition for the unorganized sector as, '...all unincorporated private enterprises owned by individuals or households engaged in the sale and production of goods and services operated on a proprietary or partnership basis and with less than ten workers.' It further points out, 'Informal workers being spread both in the organized and unorganized sector' are defined as '...those working in the informal sector or households, excluding regular workers with social security benefits provided by the employers and the workers in the formal sector without any employment and social security benefits provided by the employers.'

The above definition can be explained with the example of a local grocery store (kirana) that employs less than twenty delivery boys or helps and makes a net profit which falls below the minimum threshold level of taxable income. Further, the owner pays his delivery boys a small amount so that their income also falls below the threshold level of taxable income. In this scenario, both the owner and his employees are neither evading taxes, nor conducting any illegal economic activity. The only illegal activity that occurs here is non-registry of the business and non-compliance of filing income tax returns (which is required to be filed proving that there are no tax liabilities) with tax authorities.

Next, imagine an unincorporated private enterprise that hires less than twenty permanent employees and some additional employees on contractual/daily wage basis to do the same job. While the owner has effectively employed more than twenty employees, he is circumventing government regulation to remain a part of the unorganized sector, and saves on his costs, such as providing social security to all his employees. According to government rules, any company/factory employing more than twenty workers has to register itself with social security authorities for the welfare of its employees. If the owner does not report his taxable income/profits to the tax authorities at all, then the income generated becomes a part of the black economy. Overall, the presence of this sector at best underestimates the national income, but to conclude that all income generated in the unorganized sector forms part of the black economy would be wrong.

The above instances also prove that all cash economy is not black economy. In the first example above, if all transactions are cash based, it does not mean illegal trade or tax evasion. Businesses can operate using cash, however, moving to a formal banking system would only add efficiency to their operations and help the government keep a check on black money. No doubt transacting in cash facilitates generation of black income, but it cannot be termed as the reason behind the existence of a black economy.

Black economy does not imply only illegal economy or shadow economy, but contains parts of both. Unorganized or the informal sector can be termed as a part of the shadow economy and at best can be attributed for the underestimation of national income.

Generating Black Money

Illegal means of earning income include extortion, smuggling, trafficking and betting etc. The real challenge lies in detecting generation of black money in legal businesses. These methods vary from sector to sector, for example, in real estate it might take the form of benami properties, while in the public sector it takes the form of bribes and kickbacks. In the private sector, depending upon the size of the firm, methods such as evading custom or excise duties, over-invoicing input costs, under-reporting or non-reporting of profits, using tax treaties for money laundering, etc. are used.

After the economic liberalization of 1991 and subsequent opening up of the country's capital markets, money laundering has emerged as yet another way of generating black income. People have made wrong use of India's tax treaties with other countries. India has a Double Taxation Avoidance Agreements (DTAA) with other countries to incentivize foreign investment into our own country by providing clear rules on taxation of cross-border transactions. The DTAA helps in cases where a taxpayer resides in one country and earns income in another. A number of companies then spring up in low tax regime countries and use their DTAA with India to route their black money back into the country and avoid paying taxes on capital gains. For example, Mauritius is a low tax regime country with a DTAA with India. A business can be registered in Mauritius with a subsidiary in India. This company, while effectively operating in the Indian market and profiting from it, can evade paying taxes here by using the DTAA. By being a resident of Mauritius, the company's owner can claim exemption from taxes in India and pay low or zero taxes in Mauritius. This was one of the biggest loopholes in the treaty, which has now been fixed by the Ministry of Finance in 2016–17.[2]

Drivers of Black Economy

So what drives people to undertake such activities? What makes existence of a parallel economy or black economy more rampant in developing nations than in developed nations? When people see poor enforcement of law, easy acceptance of the culture of bribing, complicated tax structures which make flouting of government norms look simpler and cheaper, they indulge in unlawful activities that generate black income. Manual bookkeeping of business accounts, existence of a huge non-banking credit market and the presence of a large informal sector contribute to the growth of the black economy.

In 'Why Do Developing Countries Tax So Little'[3], Timothy Besley and Torsten Persson insist that larger the size of the informal economy, the smaller will be the share of income taxes in revenue. This could either be because income earned is small and non-taxable or because it can easily go unreported. This is also a reason why countries with a large informal sector (largely in developing countries) have lower shares of taxes in the gross domestic product (GDP) at smaller per capita income.

Running low on revenue from taxes, governments are generally unable to deploy adequate staff in the tax departments, or adopt technologically advanced means to track offenders and get them punished by the law. This leads to evasion of trust in people's mind. In 2014, a study on Behavioural Economics and Taxation, commissioned by the European Commission[4], concluded that 'higher institutional quality is associated with an increased intrinsic motivation to pay taxes (and) trust in governments and tax authorities can help to maintain a high level of compliance.'

Size of the Black Economy

In 1984, the National Institute of Public Finance and Policy (NIPFP) studied the available estimates of black economy at that time and critically reviewed their methodology. It also looked at the methodologies from the point of view of suitability to the Indian economy. They submitted a detailed report to the Ministry of Finance in 1985. In 2012, the Ministry of Finance published another study on estimates of black economy, quite ironically titled, 'White paper on Black Money'. The report, which was tabled in the Lok Sabha on 21 May 2012, highlighted, among other aspects, the amount of black money that has flowed out of the country. The report cites some interesting figures provided by foreign central banks/think tanks.[5] According to data provided by the Swiss National Bank (Central Bank of Switzerland), 'Its spokesperson stated that at the end of 2010, the total liabilities of Swiss Banks towards Indians were 1.945 billion Swiss Francs (about ₹9,295 crore or US$2 billion). The Swiss Ministry of External Affairs confirmed these figures when a reference was made by the Indian Ministry of External Affairs to them.' Upon analysing the Swiss bank data it concludes that in 2010 'deposits of Indians in Swiss banks constitute only 0.13 per cent of the total bank deposits of citizens of all countries. Further, the share of Indians in the total bank deposits of citizens of all countries in Swiss banks has reduced from 0.29 per cent in 2006 to 0.13 per cent in 2010… From these figures, it can be safely concluded that the common belief that Indians hold the maximum deposits in Swiss banks is not correct.'

Next, the report analyses an IMF study from 1990 and data from various reports by Global Financial Integrity (GFI), a Washington, DC-based non-for-profit organization, on illicit financial outflows from India. It then compares it with foreign direct inflows (FDI) inflows to gauge the money that returned to India. According to the IMF report[6], approximately $20–$30 billion left India between the years 1971 and 1986. This number was updated to $88 billion between the years 1971 and 1997.[7] The logic behind these estimates is that 'India's official balance-of-payments accounts do not record a number of hidden foreign exchange flows between India and the world economy.' Thus, whatever capital flows into the country must either finance the current account deficit (which defines the relationship between saving and investment) or get added to foreign exchange reserves. The capital, which doesn't get accounted anywhere, is assumed to be the capital flight.

The other report which discusses the issue of capital flight is a GFI report, where the organization provides estimates for 'illicit outflows' from a country, which refers to the 'money that is illegally earned, transferred, or utilized. If it violates laws or regulations in its origin, movement, or use, it merits the label'.[8] According to their December 2015 report[9], it is estimated that $19.4 billion worth of illicit outflows took place from India in the year 2004, which increased to a staggering $47.2 billion in four years (2008) and further to $70.3 billion by 2010. After hitting a peak of $92.9 billion in 2012, the 2013 estimate stood at $83 billion. Cumulatively, India has witnessed an illicit outflow of $510 billion between 2004 and 2013. Comparing these numbers globally, India ranked 4th in the world in terms of top sources of illicit outflows, after China, Russia and Mexico.

In addition to these official studies, the most credible data on the size of the black economy is available in *Corruption in India: The DNA & the RNA*[10]. The authors estimate private earnings of public official (percentage of sectoral GDP) for each sector for the year 2010–11. These sectors include agriculture, unregistered manufacturing, trade, railways, public administration, banking and insurance. Referring to micro-level studies, they evaluate data for bribes paid to officials, water, fuel and power theft, hafta for unorganized sectors, hoarding-related bribes in agriculture storage, bribery in loans and leakages from government programmes. Their estimates indicate that private earnings of public officials range from 0.1 per cent in agriculture, fishing, trade, communication, and banking and insurance (as percentage of their respective sectoral GDP), to 5 per cent in mining and quarrying, electricity and gas and water supply. At the national level, the gross figure is estimated to be 1.26 per cent in 2010–11.

Table 1. Illicit Financial Outflows from Top 10 Source Economies, 2004–13 (in million nominal $ or %)

Rank	Country	2004	2005	2006	2007	2008	2009	2010	2011	2012	2013
1	**China, Mainland**	81,517	82,537	88,381	107,435	104,980	138,864	172,367	133,788	223,767	258,640
2	**Russian Federation**	46,064	53,322	66,333	81,237	107,756	125,062	136,622	183,501	129,545	120,331
3	**Mexico**	34,239	35,352	40,421	46,443	51,505	38,438	67,450	63,299	73,709	77,583
4	**India**	19,447	20,253	27,791	34,513	47,221	29,247	70,337	85,584	92,879	83,014
5	**Malaysia**	26,591	35,255	36,554	36,525	40,779	34,416	62,154	50,211	47,804	48,251
6	**Brazil**	15,741	17,171	10,599	16,430	21,926	22,061	30,770	31,057	32,727	28,185
7	South Africa	12,137	13,599	12,864	27,292	22,539	29,589	24,613	23,028	26,138	17,421
8	**Thailand**	7,113	11,920	11,429	10,348	20,486	14,687	24,100	27,442	31,271	32,971

9	**Indonesia**	18,466	13,290	15,995	18,354	27,237	20,547	14,646	18,292	19,248	14,633
10	**Nigeria**	1,680	17,867	19,160	19,335	24,192	26,377	19,376	18,321	4,998	26,735
Total of Top 10		262,994	300,565	329,526	397,912	468,623	479,289	622,435	634,524	682,086	707,765
Top 10 as % of Total		56.5%	57.3%	60.6%	56.9%	56.6%	64.2%	68.7%	63.0%	65.8%	64.9%
Developing World Total		465,269	524,588	543,524	699,145	827,959	747,026	906,631	1,007,744	1,035,904	1,090,130

Source: 'Illicit Financial Flows from Developing Countries: 2004–2013', Global Financial Integrity Report, December 2015.

In his paper, 'Estimation of the Size of the Black Economy in India, 1996–2012'[11], Arun Kumar insists that 'the size of the black economy is projected on the basis of the share of the services sector and trade in gross domestic product, with the crime rate representing the extent of illegality.' He explains that the service sector is largely responsible for the creation of black money because 'the methods of making black incomes are based on a manipulation of accounts (Kumar 2006), and that leads to generating black incomes through trade, finance, transportation, and so on, which are all services.' The secondary sector and agriculture play a very small role. This is because small amount of output under-reporting leads to large black income in the secondary sector. Hence, the output is under-reported and cost of production of the unreported output is adjusted by mispricing services. Also, since agriculture income is non-taxable, this sector, while is used to circulate or misreport black incomes, is not responsible for generation of black income as such.

Using the fiscal approach to estimate black incomes, Arun Kumar generates a time series data for the share of black income in national GDP from 1996–2012. Estimates show that between 1996 and 2012, the share of black economy almost doubled from 32.05 per cent to 62.02 percent (see chart below). In absolute terms, the size of black economy rose by more than thirteen times between the year 1996 (₹4,54,919 crore) and 2012 (₹6,272,061 crore).

In 'Estimation of Unaccounted Income Using Transport as a Universal Input: A Methodological Note,'[12] the authors follow the principle of 'global indicator approach' in which a universal input (i.e. some input which is consumed across sectors) is used to estimate the amount of unaccounted income. Most commonly used 'universal input' is electricity consumption. Here, the authors attempt to use 'road freight transport' as the universal input. While justifying the choice of this input, they argue that transport is used by all sectors and that its services are always supplied when demanded. Therefore, by measuring the supply (using data from transport authorities, local surveys, fuel consumption) one can estimate the revealed demand for the transport services. They estimate the share of unaccounted GDP (in total GDP) to be 30.05 per cent in 2009–10, 26.6 per cent in 2010–11 and 25.4 per cent in 2011–12 (all of them calculated at 2007–08 prices).

Figure 1. Estimated Size of the Black Economy, (% share of Official GDP)

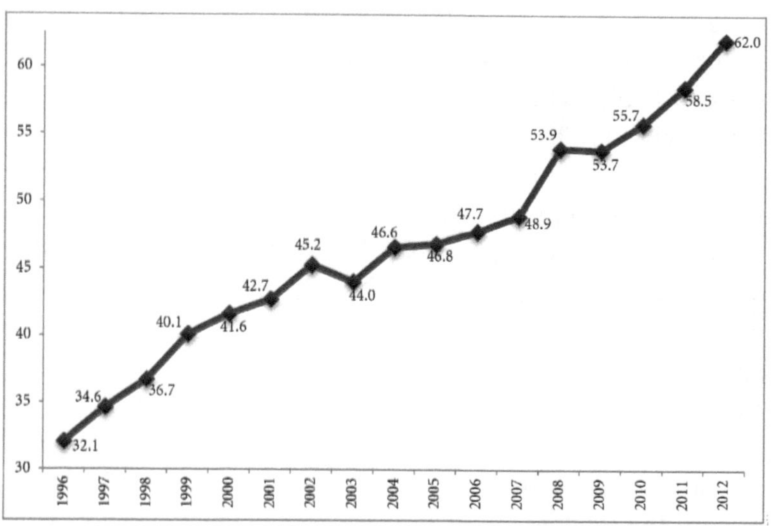

Source: A. Kumar. 2016. 'Estimation of the Size of the Black Economy in India, 1996–2012', *Economic & Political Weekly*, LI(48), pp. 36–42.

Real Impact Beyond Numbers

Authors Friedrich Schneider & Dominik H. Enste in their study[13] on shadow economy refer to a number of papers to explain the consequences of a shadow economy on official economy. They find that the impact of black economy on the overall economy is ambiguous. Patrick K. Asea (1996) concludes that, 'The underground economy, responding to the economic environment's demand for urban services and small-scale manufacturing, adds to the economy a dynamic and entrepreneurial spirit and can lead to more competition, higher efficiency, and limits on government activities. The informal sector may also contribute to the creation of markets, increase financial resources, enhance entrepreneurship, and transform the legal, social, and economic institutions necessary for accumulation.'

Another very common argument made in favour of the positive impact of shadow economy is that income earned there will ultimately boost consumption in the economy. An empirical study by Schneider in 1998 found that 'over 66 per cent of earnings in the shadow economy are immediately spent in the official sector, with positive effects for economic growth and for indirect tax revenues.' Dilip K. Bhattacharyya showed that, 'for the United Kingdom (1960–84), the hidden economy had a positive effect on consumer expenditures of nondurable goods and services, and an even stronger positive effect on consumer expenditures on durable goods and services.'

On the other hand, Norman Loayza finds strong empirical evidence based on his study on Latin American countries (1996) that, 'if the shadow economy increases by one percentage point (of GDP)—ceteris paribus—the growth rate of official real GDP per capita decreases by 1.2 percentage points'. He reasons that 'negative correlation between the informal sector and public infrastructure indices, while public infrastructure is the key element for economic growth'. He concludes that 'a substantial reduction of the shadow economy leads to a significant increase in tax revenues and therefore to a greater quantity and quality of public goods and services, which ultimately can stimulate economic growth.'

Paolo Mauro (1995) finds 'a significant negative correlation between a corruption index and the investment rate or rate of GDP growth... A one-standard deviation improvement in the corruption index is estimated by Mauro to increase the investment rate by about 3 percent.'

Closer home, Arun Ghosh, in his paper, 'Black Money and its impact on savings and Investment'[14], states that while the presence of a black economy underestimates the national GDP figures, it has no such impact on numbers that reflect our gross national savings. In fact, he goes on to argue that in case of high presence of a black economy, savings numbers are more reliable than GDP numbers. He first explains how the Central Statistics Office (CSO) estimates investments and saving, and then concludes that any saving made, either by the government or corporates or households must be in the form of financial assets. The saving made out of black income must get reflected in the 'total additional currency held by households'. This data on currency in circulation are maintained by the RBI and the possibility of error in this data is miniscule. A note from the author cautions that in this argument hoarding of gold and silver is not included, as hoarding neither affects capital formation nor economic activity. Hoarding does affect the balance of payments (BoP) but not the savings–investment data in particular. Thus, he finally concludes that, 'There can be no savings in the black market in addition to savings recorded in one or other of the various financial instruments which are sought to be captured in the official estimates of saving... For, black market transactions are also made in currency, and as we have seen, our estimate of saving in the form of currency is probably the most dependable of estimates of diverse national accounting aggregate.'

Lastly, Arun Kumar, in his paper[15] presents some more

linkages between the presence of black economy and its impact on the official estimates and thus on our policymaking decisions. Broadly, his study argues that, our BoP data are substantially influenced by activities of smuggling, trade misinvoicing and capital flight. Next, it is argued that in cases where a large shadow economy exists, input–output ratios get inaccurately measured. Underestimation of output also results in underestimated capacity utilization and factor productivity. For consumption, it is said that it tends to include both the one made out of white and black incomes. Only the propensity to consume differs, which is more in case of black income. Expenditures are mainly made on items like consumer durables, housing, entertainment, children's education abroad and visits abroad. Fiscal deficit of the government is impacted by the large supply of black income in investments that drive interstate rates and increase the interest burden of the government. Lastly, the author points out that due to capital flight, remittances which do not come back to the country, prove to be a loss to the forex reserves of the RBI. Additionally, assets held abroad by Indians using their black income mean a double whammy to our macroeconomy. We not only lose tax revenue from the income evaded/not reported, but it also negatively impacts out BoP statement.

It is amply evident that the only positives from the existence of black economy include higher rates of consumption and maybe increased competition in the informal sector, the negatives range from loss of revenue, underestimation of GDP and productivity, inaccurate figures for trade balance, high fiscal burden to policy mismatch, and growth of corruption.

It interesting to note here that the last 'official' study undertaken on behalf of the Ministry of Finance was in the year 1984–85, by NIPFP. According to *The Hindu*[16], the previous UPA government had, in March 2011, commissioned a study on black money to NIPFP, National Council of Applied

Economic Research (NCAER) and National Institute of Financial Management (NIFM). They were expected to complete this study within eighteen months, i.e. by September 2012. When asked about this in the Rajya Sabha on 5 May 2015, Finance Minister Arun Jaitely said, 'Reports received from these institutes are under examination of the Government.' [17] In May 2014, the current National Democratic Alliance (NDA) government announced 'setting up of a high-level Special Investigation Team (SIT) to help unearth black money stashed away abroad'.[18] Its report is yet to be made available in the public domain.

In order to arrive at consistent and comparable estimates, it is very important to narrow down the standard definition of black economy. It is equally important to undertake rigorous econometric studies to find out the methodology of estimating the size of the black economy that best suits the Indian economy. To make this possible, we must also strive to improve the quality of our existing data and broaden its overall scope. This would largely imply gathering more data on the existing informal economy by leveraging technology and promoting financial inclusion in the economy. The more successful we are in trying to formalize the informal sector, the easier it will become to track the growth of the black economy.

References

1 'An Analysis of the Informal Labour Market in India', October 2014.

2 See the following Press Information Bureau notifications: Government Decides to Amend Income-Tax Act 1961; Cabinet approves Agreement and the Protocol between India and Cyprus for the Avoidance of Double Taxation; India and Mauritius sign the Protocol for amendment of the Convention for the Avoidance of Double Taxation; India and Singapore Sign a Third Protocol for

Amending the Double Taxation Avoidance Agreement (DTAA).

3 T. Besley & T. Persson. 2014. 'Why Do Developing Countries Tax So Little?', *Journal of Economic Perspectives*, 28(4), pp. 99–120.

4 Till Olaf Weber, Jonas Fooken & Benedikt Herrmann. 2014. 'Behavioural Economics and Taxation', European Commission.

5 White Paper on Black Money, Ministry of Finance, 2012, http://finmin.nic.in/sites/default/files/WhitePaper_BackMoney2012.pdf

6 M. Rishi & J.K. Boyce. 1990. 'The Hidden Balance-of-Payments: Capital Flight and Trade Misinvoicing in India, 1971-1986', *Economic & Political Weekly*, July, pp. 1645–48.

7 N. Chipalkatti & M. Rishi. 2001. 'External Debt and Capital Flight in the Indian Economy', *Oxford Development Studies*, 29(1).

8 'Illicit Financial Flows: Analytical Methodologies Utilized', Global Financial Integrity.

9 'Illicit Financial Flows from Developing Countries: 2004–2013', Global Financial Integrity.

10 B. Debroy & L. Bhandari. 2011. *Corruption in India: The DNA & the RNA*. New Delhi: New Delhi: Konark Publishers.

11 A. Kumar. 2016. 'Estimation of the Size of the Black Economy in India, 1996–2012', *Economic & Political Weekly*, LI(48), pp. 36–42.

12 S. Mukherjee & R. Kavita Rao. 2017. 'Estimating Unaccounted Income in India-Using Transport as a Universal Input', *Economic & Political Weekly*, LII(7), pp. 107–15.

13 F. Schneider & D.H. Enste. 2000. 'Shadow Economies: Shadows, Causes and Consequences', *Journal of Economic Literature*, XXXVIII, pp. 77–114, http://www.econ.jku.at/members/Schneider/files/publications/JEL.pdf

14 A. Ghosh. 1987. 'Black Money and its impact on savings and Investment', *Economic & Political Weekly*, 22(32).

15 A. Kumar. 1999. 'The Black Economy: Mission Dimension of Macro Policy-Making in India, *Economic & Political Weekly*, 34(12), pp. 681–94.

16 'Study on the quantum of Black money yet to be completed', *The Hindu*, 18 June 2014.

17 Rajya Sabha, Unstarred Question No.1006, 5 May 2015.
18 'SIT to go after black money', *The Hindu*, 28 May 2014.

◆

Sonal Badhan is a former Young Professional of NITI Aayog's Economics, Finance and Commerce cell.

2

Corrupt'shun' Laws

APARAJITA GUPTA

> The means may be likened to a seed, the end to a tree; and there is just the same inviolable connection between the means and the end as there is between the seed and the tree.

In these words by Mahatma Gandhi, he insists that the means are as important as the ends sought to be achieved. In short, the ends cannot justify the means. That he was a staunch believer of this idea can be gauged from the suspension of the Non-Cooperation Movement due to violence at Chauri Chaura in 1922. But such strong adherence to such solid ideals is rare to find today.

This is proved by the prevalence of rampant corruption which, as a phenomenon, is a painful reality all over the world. India, too, is no exception. Those indulging in corrupt activities argue that the ends justify their means and make the otherwise slow process of service delivery efficient. But in law, it is not as much about economic efficiency as it is about legality in issues like corruption. Mindful of this, Indian lawmakers have, time and again, brought forth laws to keep a check on the growing corruption in the country. In fact, the need to prosecute corrupt officials was felt even when India was not an independent nation. Accordingly, the Indian Penal Code, 1860, contained a chapter titled 'Offences by Public Servants' to tackle the corrupt among them. With the Second World War, one noticed not only destruction of life and property but also of morals. Corruption in public life assumed greater proportions in light of the shortage created by the War.[1] An ordinance promulgated during the War, called the Criminal Law (Amendment) Ordinance, 1944, broadly dealt with corruption and confiscation of property. This is one of the few permanent ordinances.[2] However, as corruption prevailed even after the War, legislators had to enact the Prevention of Corruption Act, 1947. Interestingly, this was passed before India got independence and so it was assented to by the Governor General on 11 March 1947. Therefore, at the time of independence, we already had a special law to handle corruption in the public sphere. This law was amended by the Criminal Law Amendment Act, 1952, and Anti-Corruption Laws (Amendment) Act, 1964.

Along with this, there was also a need to protect public officials from false allegations that prevented them from discharging their official duties. Therefore, the makers of the Constitution of India drafted safeguards for certain officials. Article 309 of the Constitution empowers the appropriate legislature to make laws on recruitment and conditions of service for those in the public services and appointed to posts in connection with affairs of the Union/State. Article 310 clarifies that those in service of the Union or State hold office during the pleasure of the president or governor, respectively. Next, Article 311 assures security of tenure to government servants and lays down safeguards against arbitrary dismissal or removal of officers or reduction to a lower rank.[3] This particular Article has been a controversial one. While some argue for its repeal[4], some others want an amendment[5] or want to revisit the issue[6] and still others favour its retention. In spite of this controversy, the intention behind this constitutional safeguard was to protect honest and righteous officers.

Thus, a fine balance was sought to be established between prosecuting the dishonest and protecting the honest so that governance took the front seat. Whenever this balance is in danger, the legislature springs to action to maintain the equilibrium. This is evident from the enactment of the new Prevention of Corruption Act, 1988 (hereinafter referred to as the PCA) to replace the earlier law of 1947. As per the Statement of Objects and Reasons, the new law was enacted to increase the effectiveness of anti-corruption laws existing at that time. This was sought to be achieved by strengthening provisions and expanding its field of operation. Further, it was brought into force to 'consolidate and amend the law relating to the prevention of corruption and for matters connected therewith.'[7] Today, this is the basic law for penalizing the corrupt in India.

Additionally, there are numerous other laws that have a bearing on corruption. These include the Indian Penal Code, 1860; Delhi Special Police Establishment Act, 1946; Prohibition of Benami Property Transactions Act, 1988; Prevention of Money Laundering Act, 2002; Central Vigilance Commission Act, 2003; Right to Information Act, 2005; Whistle Blowers Protection Act, 2011; and the Lokpal and Lokayuktas Act, 2013, to name a few.

Prevention of Corruption Act, 1988: The Present

Scheme of the law

The PCA repealed and replaced the pre-Independence Prevention of Corruption Act, 1947. The new law was built on the earlier one, aimed at strengthening the noose around corruption. This law was amended by the Lokpal and Lokayuktas Act, 2013. At the outset, it would be helpful to understand the scheme of the PCA and the key provisions. It defines essential terms like 'public duty' and 'public servant'. It is important to note here that 'public servant' defined in this PCA is wider in scope than its definition under the Indian Penal Code, 1860.[8] In a law regulating corruption, many would feel that it would not be asking for too much if one expects to find a definition of corruption. But a perusal of the law will disappoint them. It does not define the words 'bribe', 'corruption' or even 'corrupt activities'. But it lists certain corrupt activities along with their penalties in Chapter III, 'Offences and Penalties' (Sections 7–16).

Section 7 punishes 'Public servant taking gratification other than legal remuneration in respect of an official act'. Section 8 makes it an offence for one involved in 'Taking gratification, in order, by corrupt or illegal means, to influence public servant'. According to Section 9, it is also an offence if one is in the process of 'Taking gratification, for exercise of personal influence with public servant'. Section 11 says public servants can be punished if one finds a 'Public servant obtaining valuable thing, without consideration from person concerned in proceeding or business transacted by such public servant'. Finally, Section 13 makes 'Criminal misconduct by a public servant' an offence.

For trying offences under PCA, special judges are to be appointed.[9] Further, it mentions the rank of police officers authorized to investigate offences under this law[10]. One of the most important and controversial provisions is Section 19 which mandates that prior sanction is generally necessary for prosecution of a public servant. In keeping with the purpose of this law, PCA allows raising of an adverse presumption in specific circumstances for trial of certain offences. This law also protects the bribe-givers from prosecution so that they can make statements against accused public servants.[11]

While this law has been an important tool to fight corruption, there are certain issues that may not be immediately apparent, yet are a cause of concern.

Legal Loopholes: Delight for the Corrupt

As pointed out earlier, PCA does not define 'corruption'. It is interesting to note that even the United Nations Convention against Corruption does not define this term. What the PCA does is that it penalizes certain listed corrupt activities. Now the problem here is that some other activities are excluded despite their adverse effects on public interest. The 2nd Administrative Reforms Commission (ARC) drives home this point in its 4th Report titled 'Ethics in Governance'. It has identified four cases which fall outside the purview of this law due to its restrictive scope:

1. '...gross perversion of the Constitution and democratic institutions, including, wilful violation of the oath of office.'
2. '...abuse of authority unduly favouring or harming someone, without any pecuniary consideration or gratification.' The Commission feels that the underlying motives could be personal prejudice, partisan interests and nepotism.
3. '...obstruction or perversion of justice by unduly influencing law enforcement agencies and prosecution.'
4. '...squandering public money, including ostentatious official life-styles.'

The restrictive nature of the law only checks corruption by public servants, and punishes private individuals only if they try to bribe the public servant[12] or indulge in abetment[13]. A pertinent and recent example of conviction of private individuals under this law is the highly publicized case on disproportionate assets of Late Tamil Nadu Chief Minister J. Jayalalithaa (State of Karnataka v Selvi J. Jayalalitha & Ors[14]). The Supreme Court held Sasikala Natarajan (a private individual) guilty under this law. In yet another instance, the Supreme Court covered private individuals through its interpretation of 'public servant' under the PCA in Central Bureau of Investigation, Bank Securities and Fraud Cell and Others v Ramesh Gelli and Others.[15] Here it was held that officers of a private bank, which was licensed by the RBI, perform a public duty and hence are covered under the phrase 'public servant' under the PCA. But some questions still remain unanswered on the issue of private corruption. For instance, what happens to corruption within the private sector in situations where there is no interface with a public servant? Many public services which were earlier within the exclusive domain of public officials are increasingly being entrusted to non-government agencies and many Non-Governmental Organizations (NGOs) rely on substantial government aid.[16] This has caused some to strongly argue for inclusion of these agencies within the scope of this law.[17] Differentiating between public and private corruption may be important but punishing both is necessary.

Another loophole in the PCA is that it does not differentiate between 'coercive' corruption and 'collusive' corruption.[18] While coercive corruption is where the bribe-giver is forced to pay bribe and get a service, collusive corruption occurs when the bribe giver and the taker are on the same side like in cases of executing substandard work.[19] So the question arises whether the two can be equated. As per the 2nd ARC, collusive corruption needs to be strictly checked. The Commission recommended that the PCA should specify the offence of 'collusive bribery', shift the burden of proof in such cases to the accused and impose a punishment, which is double of what is imposed in other forms of bribery. An interesting argument in case of coercive corruption has been presented by former Chief Economic Adviser to the Government of India, Kaushik Basu, who defines bribes given to get one's legal entitlements as 'harassment bribes.'[20] He argues that those giving harassment bribes should be given full legal immunity under the law as this will reduce instances of bribery since interests of the two players would diverge after the payment of the bribe.

Often, courts through their interpretations, have made conviction under the PCA difficult. Recently, the Supreme Court, in Krishan Chander v State of Delhi[21], has held that proof of demand of illegal gratification is necessary in addition to acceptance or recovery of the amount under Sections 7[22] and 13(1)(d)[23] of the PCA. Such a ruling highlights one of the problems of securing conviction in corruption cases.

Apart from the fact that some dishonest people escape prosecution due to these legal loopholes, the honest fear being prosecuted if they take decisions. Imagine a scenario where a public servant takes a decision without any extraneous or personal considerations. Yet, in future, it is found to be unintentionally benefitting a private party against public interest. Is this covered as corruption under the law? It is, and was even highlighted in the Economic Survey 2015–16 as an obstacle for civil servants in taking quick and firm decisions. Section 13(1)(d)(iii) of the PCA is relevant for this purpose. It states that, 'A public servant is said to commit the offence of criminal misconduct if he, while holding office as a public servant, obtains for any person any valuable thing or pecuniary advantage without any public interest.' A plain reading of this provision makes it amply clear that mens rea, or presence of a guilty intent, need not be proved to establish this offence as the aim of this provision was to be a catch-all offence for the corrupt in difficult cases.[24] As words like 'corruptly' or 'wrongfully' or words showing an improper motive are not used, the provision tends to penalize instances of error of judgment made in good faith.[25] It is problematic to equate the genuine errors in decisions and acts of corruption.[26] Unwillingness of civil servants to divest public enterprises or sell land, tendency to challenge fair and reasonable arbitration awards or decisions of lower courts and raising tax disputes founded on audit objections despite tax authorities not agreeing with auditors are just effects, as clearly highlighted in the Economic Survey 2015–16. The cause is the fear of producing pecuniary gain without public interest.

Another dimension is related to confiscation of property that was corruptly acquired. The provisions of the PCA are inadequate as they allow confiscation only in cases of conviction for an offence.[27] For example, public servants holding assets disproportionate to their known sources of income may dispose of or hide their assets by the time they are prosecuted and convicted. Making a strong case for forfeiture of such properties, the Law Commission of India has noted that, '...merely sending the corrupt holders of public office to jail is no remedy; it is no solution. It doesn't really hurt them. Unless their ill-gotten assets are forfeited to the State, the canker of corruption cannot be really tackled'.[28] Therefore, some suggest confiscation of such properties even pending prosecution.[29] On the same lines, the Law Commission of India, in its 166th Report in 1999, proposed a law in the form of the 'Corrupt Public Servants (Forfeiture of Property) Bill'. The bill empowers the Central Vigilance Commissioner to carry out the forfeiture. It is interesting to note that some states like Bihar and Odisha have laws in place on this issue. The Bihar Special Courts Act, 2009, allows for moving an application for confiscation of property of corrupt officials irrespective of whether the Special Court has taken cognizance of the offence or not.[30] This law, along with a similar one in Odisha, has been upheld by the Supreme Court.[31]

Next, the 2nd ARC had brought out the fact that there is no provision on compensation to the aggrieved party.[32] To remedy this, the Commission recommended that the PCA should have a chapter which provides for making good the loss caused by a corrupt public servant to the state or citizens and make him/her liable for damages. It then went a step ahead and recommended the enactment of a law similar to the False Claims Act in the US to allow civil society and citizens to go to courts for recovering of corruption proceeds and even get a share, if successful.

In an attempt to tackle some of these burning issues, the Prevention of Corruption (Amendment) Bill, 2013, (hereinafter referred to as the Bill) was introduced in the Rajya Sabha on 19 August 2013. Apart from amending the PCA, the Bill seeks to amend the Criminal Law (Amendment) Ordinance, 1944, the Delhi Special Police Establishment Act, 1946, and the Prevention of Money Laundering Act, 2002. After its introduction, the Bill was referred to the Department-related Standing Committee on Personnel, Public Grievances, Law and Justice, which gave its report on 6 February 2014. Based on these recommendations, an informal and improved version was circulated to the Law Commission of India. After analysing the same, the Law Commission gave its 254th Report titled, 'The Prevention of Corruption (Amendment) Bill, 2013', in February 2015. One of the major issues that the Law Commission pointed out was that the Bill was drawing heavily from the UK Bribery Act, 2010, which was problematic because the latter was made in a different setting and covered both public and private acts of corruption which was not the case in India.[33] Based on these recommendations, amendments to the Bill were circulated in 2015. This Bill was also referred to the Select Committee of Rajya Sabha, which presented its report on 12 August 2016 to the Rajya Sabha. At the end of the report, the Select Committee attached a revised version of the Bill. The Bill is still pending and an analysis of the same is relevant.

Prevention of Corruption (Amendment) Bill, 2013: The Future

A look at the Statement of Objects and Reasons appended to the Bill makes its legislative intent clear. It mentions that India's ratification of the United Nations Convention against Corruption in 2011, international practice on the issue and judicial decisions made it imperative to amend the PCA. Broadly, the Bill seeks to cover all aspects of passive bribery, create an offence to punish bribe-givers (checking the 'supply side of corruption'[34]), penalize bribery of a public servant by a commercial organization, punish abetment of all offences, mandate prior approval for investigation, extend protection to people who have ceased to be public servants, lay down the criteria and procedure for sanction of prosecution and make provisions for confiscation of property.

A comparison of the PCA and the Bill (after the 2015 official amendments) brings forth some issues. To begin with, the Bill, on the recommendation of the Law Commission, has introduced a phrase—'undue advantage'—and defined it. It has still not defined the term 'corruption' as the government feels that if a close definition is given, offenders may misuse it.[35] But the Standing Committee had recommended that the government should look into the matter and include definitions of 'corruption' and 'corrupt practices'.

Unlike the PCA, the Bill provides an exception where a public servant will not be liable for taking bribe. This is in case the public function is not dishonestly performed.[36] However, the Bill does not defines what it means by performance of public function dishonestly which could cause interpretational issues later.[37] Clarity of such a law, or for that matter any law, is non-negotiable.

The Bill creates two new offences. First, it penalizes the act of giving bribe directly or indirectly.[38] This is a step forward from the PCA which covered bribe-givers under the provision on abetment.[39] But the Bill does not differentiate between 'coercive' and 'collusive' bribery, which was suggested by the 2nd ARC. The Select Committee has questioned lack of protection to coercive bribe-givers.[40] Further, the Bill states that people who offer bribe after informing a law enforcement authority or investigating agency, to assist these agencies, shall not be liable for giving bribe.[41] The Standing Committee had recommended that those who report the incident after paying bribes in normal cases need not be protected but for those who report after paying bribes in compelling situations, the court may decide. It also suggested that the Right of Citizens for Time Bound Delivery of Goods and Services and Redressal of their Grievances Bill, 2011, should be enacted to check instances where a common man has to bribe to get his entitlements. The Select Committee had recommended that if the bribe-giver reports the case to the police or the law enforcement agency within seven days of paying the bribe, he may be provided immunity from criminal prosecution. It also stated that 'offer' of bribe should be excluded from the provision to penalize bribe-givers as it felt that mere offering of bribe should not be an offence unless the same is accepted or demanded.

Based on the Law Commission's recommendations, the Bill now has illustrations to clarify that acts of giving bribe for performance of both improper (like bribing for getting a licence over other bidders) and proper public functions (like bribing for timely processing of routine application) are covered.[42] This is a commendable addition.

Second, the Bill penalizes persons in charge of commercial organizations if a person associated with such organizations bribes a public servant.[43] This will help check the supply side of corruption. It also mentions that the central government shall come out with guidelines to help commercial organizations prevent people associated with it from bribing public servants after the Law Commission recommended the same. The Bill includes 'charitable services' within its definition of the term 'business' to tackle instances of bribery by the private sector. But the Select Committee had suggested that charitable services should be excluded from the ambit of this law. On the other hand, the 2nd ARC had argued for inclusion of those non-governmental agencies under the PCA which received substantial funding. It held that, '...any institution or body that has received more than 50% of its annual operating costs, or a sum equal to or greater than ₹1 crore during any of the preceding 3 years should be deemed to have obtained "substantial funding" for that period and purpose of such funding.' Excluding the NGOs may not be in the best interest of the spirit of this law, as all those discharging public functions must be made to shoulder the same responsibility of not indulging in corruption.

An analysis of the PCA and the Bill shows that categories of criminal misconduct have been reduced to two,[44] with two acts, earlier treated as criminal misconduct, being added to the provision mentioning the offence of taking bribe. Experts feel that this reclassification has reduced the maximum sentence for the two offences, which are now part of the provision on taking bribes.[45] This is because criminal misconduct under the PCA was punishable with an imprisonment ranging from four to ten years[46] but for the offence of taking bribe, the imprisonment can extend only from three to seven years.[47] This raises concerns.

Next, the provision covering a public servant who 'obtains for any person any valuable thing or pecuniary advantage without any public interest' has been removed. This was covered as a kind of criminal misconduct under the PCA. But this change happened in light of the apprehensions and concerns of honest officers.

Originally, the Bill had introduced a requirement to prove intention in cases where the public servant possesses pecuniary resources or property disproportionate to his known sources of income.[48] Such a requirement was not present under the PCA. Such a provision would have made it even more difficult to prosecute the accused. So the Standing Committee recommended that such an additional burden of proving the intention must be removed. Finally, the Bill has incorporated the suggestion.

Another new provision in the Bill mandates prior sanction to be taken from the Lokpal or Lokayukta before investigation of public servants, except in cases of on-the-spot arrest.[49] This adds another layer of protection for public servants in addition to the existing provision mandating prior sanction for prosecution. On one hand it can be argued that this would safeguard honest officers, but on the other one can argue that it adds an obstacle in catching the corrupt officers. Some Supreme Court cases also throw light on this issue. In Dr. Subramanian Swamy v Director, CBI & Anr.[50], the Supreme Court had struck down Section 6A of the Delhi Special Police Establishment Act, 1946, which mandated prior sanction for investigation of senior officials, holding it to be unconstitutional. It held that, 'The protection in Section 6A has propensity of shielding the corrupt'[51]. But, in Anil Kumar & Ors. v M.K. Aiyappa & Anr.[52], the Supreme Court had held that an application seeking a direction to the police to investigate cannot succeed without a prior sanction. Experts view this as turning the 'sanction to prosecute' into 'sanction to investigate' going against larger bench decisions.[53] Such diverging interpretations tend to complicate matters. On the point of sanction for investigation, some argue that if there is no investigation, then there would be no credible evidence, then what would be the basis for the sanction for investigation?[54] The 2nd ARC went to the extent of recommending that prior sanction for prosecution should not be necessary in cases of public servants caught red-handed or in cases of disproportionate assets. The Commission stated that the aim was to keep a check on malicious or vexatious complaints to harass honest officers. But this process of obtaining sanction was problematic since it often led to delays in prosecution due to the delay in getting the sanction and, in many cases, the accused was discharged or acquitted due to non-application of mind by the sanctioning authority.[55] Assuming that these problems may hamper the process of prior sanction for investigation also, adding this additional layer raises genuine concerns. Further, the process can get delayed due to vacancy in the office of Lokpal and Lokayukta.[56]

With respect to the provision on 'Previous sanction necessary for prosecution', the Bill has extended the protection to former public servants unlike the PCA.[57] Further, a time limit of three months, extendable by a month, has been prescribed for the sanction for prosecution.[58] The Bill also prescribes a time limit for trial, unlike the PCA. It states that the Special Judge should try to complete trial within two years from filing of the case which can be extended, after recording reasons, to a maximum of two more years.[59] Prescribing such time limits is really the way forward. But abiding by the same is the main challenge.

The Bill also introduces a provision on attachment of property.[60] In the 2013 version of the Bill, there was an entire chapter titled, 'Attachment and Forfeiture of Property'. But the Law Commission reasoned that such detailed provisions under the chapter would complicate matters as there were separate provisions on the same under the other three laws. These are the Criminal Law (Amendment) Ordinance, 1944, Prevention of Money Laundering Act, 2002, and the Lokpal and Lokayuktas Act, 2013. Now, the Bill has a single provision on the issue to make matters simpler.

In the PCA, for offences of taking bribe, abetment and habitual offence, presumption was to be raised against the accused unless contrary could be proved.[61] But in the Bill, the provision has been modified so that such a presumption would be raised only in cases of a public servant being bribed.[62] So the burden of proof is on the accused only in cases where the accused is the bribe-taker. Some analysts question this differential treatment arguing that the Bill tries to treat the bribe givers and takers in a similar manner when it comes to punishment, so why have a different burden of proof?[63]

Some experts have also pointed out that though one reason behind introducing the Bill was to bring the PCA in line with the United Nations Convention against Corruption, the latter's provisions covering bribing foreign public servants, private sector entities accepting bribes and compensation for those aggrieved by corruption are not part of the Bill.[64]

Thus, the Bill has introduced many important provisions. Further, it has accepted many recommendations of the Law Commission and introduced illustrations below provisions that have brought in the much-needed clarity.

The Way Forward

There is no doubt that the PCA is an important piece of legislation which strengthened the existing legislative framework to tackle corruption. Over the years, it has been interpreted by courts in India to catch the corrupt and protect the honest public servants. Yet maintaining this balance has been difficult. Additionally, with multiple challenges in a growing society, the PCA in its present form was found to be inadequate. To address these issues, the Bill was introduced in 2013 and it has been pending for almost four years now. These four years saw it being referred to multiple committees and even a commission. Each of them have given fruitful comments and analysed the Bill in depth. The present version of the Bill introduces a mix of provisions. While some strengthen the existing law, some others raise pertinent questions.

To safeguard the spirit of the anti-corruption law, some of the following suggestions may be incorporated. On the issue of forms of corruption, the Bill should differentiate between coercive and collusive corruption and protect coercive bribe-givers. Here, it needs to be kept in mind that proving whether the corruption is coercive or collusive will be difficult. So there is a need to evolve a mechanism where both the parties in collusive corruption are severely punished, but the bribe-giver in coercive corruption is protected. Pursuing the idea of full legal immunity for those giving 'harassment bribes' may be helpful to keep a check on coercive corruption. Further, those reporting bribery after paying the same may be protected if reported within a short span of time.

Another suggestion is to remove a unilateral 'offer' of bribe from the provision to penalize bribe-givers as the offence should involve acts from both sides. In the Bill, a disturbing fact noticed was that by reclassification of offences, the maximum punishment for some offences has been reduced. This may send a wrong signal and must be avoided. One of the most controversial additions has been the requirement of prior sanction for investigation. This will delay the process and seems to be an unnecessary additional cover. We already have a prior sanction for prosecution to prevent vexatious cases. Further, there is a need to have a similar burden of proof for both the bribe-taker and bribe-giver.

Lastly, it would be a good idea to incorporate two more provisions in the Bill. One on compensation for those aggrieved by corruption and the second to enable civil society and citizens to go to courts for recovering corruption proceeds and take a share if they are successful. This will take care of the interests of victims of corruption and attract the civil society to participate in the fight against corruption.

While the above suggestions will take care of the letter of the law, a lot will depend on its implementation to give effect to its spirit. Only when both work in tandem will we see a real difference in the fight against corruption. But this would only be an external control. The menace of corruption cannot be weeded out till we don't develop strong internal controls. Only a right balance of external and internal control can help us realize the dream of a corruption-free India 'where the mind is without fear and the head is held high'.

References

1 'Ethics in Governance', 4th Report, 2nd Administrative Reforms Commission, Government of India, 2007, p. 58, http://darpg.nic.in/sites/default/files/ethics4.pdf, accessed on 22 March 2017.

2 'The Prevention of Corruption (Amendment) Bill, 2013', 254th Report of the Law Commission of India, 2015, p. 1, http://lawcommissionofindia.nic.in/reports/report_no.254_prevention_of_corruption.pdf, accessed on 14 March 2017.

3 'Ethics in Governance', 4th Report, 2nd Administrative Reforms Commission, Government of India, 2007, p. 90.

4 Ibid, p. 97.

5 'Report of the Committee on Civil Service Reforms (Hota Committee)', Government of India, 2004, p. 24, http://darpg.gov.in/sites/default/files/Hota_Commitee_Report.pdf, accessed on 9 March 2017.

6 'Report of the National Commission to Review the Working of the Constitution', Ministry of Law & Justice, Government of India, 2002, http://lawmin.nic.in/ncrwc/ncrwcreport.htm, accessed on 3 February 2017.

7 Prevention of Corruption Act, 1988, http://lawmin.nic.in/ld/P-ACT/1988/The%20Prevention%20of%20Corruption%20Act,%201988.pdf, accessed on 10 January 2017.

8 'Ethics in Governance', 4th Report, 2nd Administrative Reforms Commission, Government of India, 2007, p. 59.

9 Section 3, Prevention of Corruption Act, 1988.

10 Section 17, Prevention of Corruption Act, 1988.

11 Section 24, Prevention of Corruption Act, 1988.

12 Sections 8 and 9, Prevention of Corruption Act, 1988.

13 Section 12, Prevention of Corruption Act, 1988.

14 Criminal Appeal Nos. 300-319 of 2017 in the Supreme Court of India, decision dated 14 February 2017, http://www.thehindubusinessline.com/multimedia/archive/03132/Disproportionate_A_3132784a.pdf, accessed on 3 March 2017.

15 (2016) 3 SCC 788. This is a decision of the Supreme Court of India dated 23 February 2016, https://dtf.in/wp-content/files/SC_Judgment_dated_23.02.2016_-_CBI_Bank_Securities__Fraud_Cell_Vs._Ramesh_Gelli_and_Others.pdf, accessed on 15 March 2017.

16 'Ethics in Governance', 4th Report, 2nd Administrative Reforms Commission, Government of India, 2007, pp. 71–72.

17 Ibid.

18 Ibid, p. 63.

19 Ibid.

20 Kaushik Basu, 'Why, for a Class of Bribes, the Act of *Giving* a Bribe should be Treated as Legal', 2011, p. 4 http://www.kaushikbasu.org/Act_Giving_Bribe_Legal.pdf, accessed on 6 March 2017.

21 (2016) 3 SCC 108. This is a decision of the Supreme Court of India dated 6 January 2016, http://indianlawcases.com/ILC-2016-SC-CRL-Jan-4, accessed on 15 March 2017.

22 'Public servant taking gratification other than legal remuneration in respect of an official act', Prevention of Corruption Act, 1988.

23 'Criminal misconduct by a public servant', Prevention of Corruption Act, 1988.

24 Economic Survey 2015–16, Ministry of Finance, Government of India, pp. 48–49, http://indiabudget.nic.in/es2015-16/echapvol1-02.pdf, accessed on 22 February 2017.

25 Ibid.

26 'Report of the Committee on Revisiting and Revitalising Public Private Partnership Model of Infrastructure', Ministry of Finance,

Government of India, 2015, p. 43, https://infrastructureindia.gov.in/documents/10184/0/kelkar+Pdf/0d6ffb64-4501-42ba-a083-ca3ce99cf999, accessed on 3 March 2017.

27 'The Corrupt Public Servants (Forfeiture of Property) Bill', 166th Report of the Law Commission of India, p. 5, http://lawcommissionofindia.nic.in/101-169/report166.pdf, accessed on 22 February 2017.

28 Ibid, p.6.

29 Draft National Anti-Corruption Strategy, Central Vigilance Commission, 2010, p. 10, http://www.cvc.nic.in/NationalAntiCorruptionStrategydraft.pdf, accessed on 10 February 2017.

30 Section 13, Bihar Special Courts Act, 2009, http://www.lawsofindia.org/pdf/bihar/2010/2010Bihar5.pdf, accessed on 22 February 2017.

31 Yogendra Kumar Jaiswal v State of Bihar, (2016) 3 SCC 183. This is a decision of the Supreme Court of India dated 10 December 2015, http://164.100.107.37/FileServer/2015-12-10_1449731938.pdf, accessed on 22 February 2017.

32 'Ethics in Governance', 4th Report, 2nd Administrative Reforms Commission, Government of India, 2007, p. 69.

33 'The Prevention of Corruption (Amendment) Bill, 2013', 254th Report of the Law Commission of India, 2015, pp. 3–4.

34 http://pib.nic.in/newsite/PrintRelease.aspx?relid=119941, accessed on 23 February 2017.

35 '69th Report of the Department-Related Parliamentary Standing Committee on Personnel, Public Grievances, Law and Justice', 2014, p. 24, http://www.prsindia.org/uploads/media/Corruption/SCR-%20Prevention%20of%20Corruption.pdf, accessed on 15 March 2017.

36 Clause 3, Prevention of Corruption (Amendment) Bill, 2013.

37 'Legislative Brief: The Prevention of Corruption (Amendment) Bill, 2013 and proposed 2015 amendments', http://www.prsindia.org/uploads/media/Corruption/LB-%20Prevention%20of%20Corruption%20%28A%29%20Bill%202013%20-%202015%20

amendments.pdf accessed on 14 March 2017.

38 Clause 3, Prevention of Corruption (Amendment) Bill, 2013.

39 Section 12, Prevention of Corruption Act, 1988.

40 'Report of the Select Committee of Rajya Sabha on the Prevention of Corruption (Amendment) Bill, 2013', 2016, Para 6.12, http://www.prsindia.org/uploads/media/Corruption/Select%20comm%20-Prevention%20of%20Corruption.pdf, accessed on 16 March 2017.

41 Clause 3, Prevention of Corruption (Amendment) Bill, 2013.

42 Clause 3, Prevention of Corruption (Amendment) Bill, 2013.

43 Ibid.

44 Ibid.

45 'Legislative Brief: The Prevention of Corruption (Amendment) Bill, 2013 and proposed 2015 amendments', http://www.prsindia.org/uploads/media/Corruption/LB-%20Prevention%20of%20Corruption%20%28A%29%20Bill%202013%20-%202015%20amendments.pdf accessed on 14 March 2017.

46 Section 13, Prevention of Corruption Act, 1988.

47 Clause 3, Prevention of Corruption (Amendment) Bill, 2013.

48 Clause 6, Prevention of Corruption (Amendment) Bill, 2013.

49 Clause 8B, Prevention of Corruption (Amendment) Bill, 2013.

50 (2014) 8 SCC 682.This is a decision of the Supreme Court of India dated 6 May 2014, http://acbmaharashtra.gov.in/legal/judgment1.pdf, accessed on 15 March 2017.

51 Dr. Subramanian Swamy v Director, CBI, (2014) 8 SCC 682.

52 (2013) 10 SCC 705. This is a decision of the Supreme Court of India dated 1 October 2013, http://supremecourtofindia.nic.in/pdf/SupremeCourtReport/2013_v9_piv.pdf, accessed on 16 March 2017.

53 A. Bhattacharya & B. Chugh, 'The Catch-22 of "No Investigation without Sanction" and "No Sanction without Investigation": A Critical Analysis of Anil Kumar v M.K. Aiyappa (2013)', Live Law, 22 February 2017, http://www.livelaw.in/the-catch-22-of-no-investigation-without-sanction-and-no-sanction-without-investigation-a-critical-analysis-of-the-law-laid-down-in-anil-

kumar-v-m-k-aiyappa-2013/, accessed on 16 March 2017.

54 Yogendra Yadav, 'Time to blow the whistle', *The Hindu*, 12 December 2016, http://www.thehindu.com/opinion/lead/Time-to-blow-the-whistle/article16793830.ece accessed on 16 March 2017.

55 'Ethics in Governance', 4th Report, 2nd Administrative Reforms Commission, Government of India, 2007, pp. 65–66.

56 'Legislative Brief: The Prevention of Corruption (Amendment) Bill, 2013 and proposed 2015 amendments', http://www.prsindia.org/uploads/media/Corruption/LB-%20Prevention%20of%20Corruption%20%28A%29%20Bill%202013%20-%202015%20amendments.pdf, accessed on 14 March 2017.

57 Clause 10, Prevention of Corruption (Amendment) Bill, 2013.

58 Ibid.

59 Clause 2, Prevention of Corruption (Amendment) Bill, 2013.

60 Clause 9, Prevention of Corruption (Amendment) Bill, 2013.

61 Section 20, Prevention of Corruption Act, 1988.

62 Clause 11, Prevention of Corruption (Amendment) Bill, 2013.

63 'Legislative Brief: The Prevention of Corruption (Amendment) Bill, 2013 and proposed 2015 amendments', http://www.prsindia.org/uploads/media/Corruption/LB-%20Prevention%20of%20Corruption%20%28A%29%20Bill%202013%20-%202015%20amendments.pdf, accessed on 14 March 2017.

64 Ibid.

◆

Aparajita Gupta is a Young Professional under Bibek Debroy at NITI Aayog.

3

The Role of the Executive

SUPARNA JAIN

The word corrupt is derived from the Latin word 'corruptus' meaning 'to break or destroy'. The World Bank defines corruption as 'the abuse of public office for private gain' while Transparency International defines corruption as 'the abuse of entrusted power for private gain. Both these definitions, though slightly variant, underscore the common message of private gain through misuse of power which flows from public office. In India, however, none of the statutes that monitor corruption define the term. But, all of them define the role of the executive in monitoring and curbing corruption.

The executive plays a critical role in maintaining public order and rule of law in the state, a key aspect of which is keeping a check on corruption. This is as critical as defending the state from external aggression or securing its integrity and unity.

Executive Arms Combating Corruption

The Central Vigilance Commission (CVC) and the Central Bureau of Investigation (CBI) are the two cornerstones of the existing institutional framework overseeing corruption at the central level. The role of the CVC is advisory is nature while the CBI plays an investigative role.

The CVC

The CVC is an independent agency directly responsible to the Parliament, vested with powers to enquire or cause enquiries to be conducted into offences alleged to have been committed under the PCA. It is entrusted with the task of overseeing vigilance administration and implementing government policies against corruption by certain categories of public servants of the central government, corporations, companies, societies and local authorities, owned or controlled by the central government and overseeing and implementing policies relating to vigilance administration.

The CVC was constituted by the Government of India through a resolution dated 2 November 1964 on the recommendations of a Parliamentary Committee under the chairmanship of K. Santhanam to review the existing instruments with a view to prevent corruption in central services and suggest steps for effective anti-corruption measures. The committee recommended conferring powers on the CVC, similar to those under Sections 4 and 5 of the Commission of Enquiry Act, 1952, so that it could undertake an enquiry into transactions where public servants were suspected of having acted improperly or in a corrupt manner. The committee envisaged the CVC to deal with complaints of failure of justice or oppression or abuse of authority suffered by the citizens, though it realized that it may be difficult to attribute them to any particular official or officials. It therefore recommended that the CVC should have the power to enquire into and investigate into complaints against acts or omissions, decisions or recommendation, or administrative procedures or practices on the grounds that they are: (i) wrong or contrary to law, (ii) unreasonable, unjust, oppressive or improperly discriminatory (iii) in accordance with a rule of law or a provision of any enactment or a practice that is or may be unreasonable, unjust, oppressive or improperly discriminatory or (iv) based wholly or partly on a mistake of law or fact. However, these suggestions were not accepted by the government as it was felt that vesting such a vast canvas of functions would over burden the CVC and consequently make it ineffective. The committee also recommended giving the CVC a statutory backing—a suggestion which was bypassed by the Parliament.

The 1964 resolution defined the CVC's function as undertaking an enquiry or to cause an enquiry or investigation to be made into any complaint of 'corruption, misconduct, lack of integrity, or other kinds of malpractices or misdemeanour on the part of a public servant, including members of the All India Services even if such members are for the time being serving in connection with the affairs of a state government'. It also clarified that the CVC would not be subordinate to any ministry/department and will have the same measure of independence and autonomy as the Union Public Service Commission.

Between 1964 and 1993, the CVC functioned with a low profile. In 1993, post the Bombay blasts, amidst alleged charges of corruption involving politicians and general perception of criminalization of politics that the central government constituted a committee known as the Vohra Committee to take stock of all available information about the activities of crime syndicates/ mafia organizations who allegedly had developed links with and were being protected by some government functionaries and political personalities. The committee recognized the nexus between criminal gangs, police, bureaucracy and politicians and recommended creation of a nodal agency under the Ministry of Home Affairs for collation and compilation of all information received from the Intelligence Bureau (IB), CBI and Research and Analysis Wing (RAW).

The CVC was strengthened in 1997 after the Supreme Court's judgement in the Vineet Narain case, popularly known as Jain

Hawala case. The Court observed that inertia on the part of the investigating authorities was a common phenomenon whenever the alleged offender was a powerful person. Realizing the need for safeguarding the investigating agencies from extraneous influences, the Court examined the structure of the CVC and suggested steps to insulate the agencies from external influence. It directed giving a statutory status to the CVC, gave detailed guidelines entrusting the CVC with the responsibility of exercising superintendence over the CBI's functioning and laid down the process for appointment Central Vigilance Commissioner.

The Law Commission also reviewed the Court orders and came out with a detailed report with recommendations on strengthening the CVC and a draft CVC Bill. However, it took six years to follow the court directions of giving statutory backup to the CVC.

With the enactment of the Central Vigilance Commission Act in 2003, the CVC acquired statutory authority and superintendence over the functioning of CBI in cases handled by it under the PCA. The CVC was also empowered to review the progress of investigations conducted by the CBI and the applications pending with the competent authorities for grant of sanction for prosecution for offences alleged to have been committed under the PCA. The CVC also exercises superintendence over the vigilance administration of the various organizations under the central government. The Lokpal and Lokayuktas Act, 2013 (1 of 2014) has recently amended some provisions of CVC Act, 2003.

One of the key issues relating to the functioning of the CVC is the limitation of its role as a mere adviser. It relies on the CBI for investigation and only oversees the bureaucracy; and ministers and members of Parliament are out of its purview. Presently, the recourse available to the CVC in case its advice is not taken is to reflect such cases in its annual report, which is placed before both the Houses of Parliament. The intention behind this was that such cases are deliberated and debated in the Parliament so that the authorities concerned are pulled up and held accountable for their (in)action. Unfortunately, as is witnessed, there has been hardly any discussion on the annual report of CVC in the Parliament.

Another weakness of the CVC is its lack of jurisdiction over the legislature, the judiciary and the state government. Though it is the apex anti-corruption body of India, it does not have an investigation wing. The CVC can undertake enquiries in addition to the cases referred to it by the CBI through the chief vigilance officers (CVOs). However, there is lack of clarity in the role of the CVOs. In case of public sector enterprises, the CVOs are not authorized to investigate. Further, there are issues relating to limited manpower amongst CVOs and ill-structured vigilance department.

The CBI

The CBI was established in 1941 as the Special Police Establishment (SPE), tasked with domestic security. After World War II, the need for a central government agency to investigate cases of bribery and corruption by its employees was felt. Therefore, the Delhi Special Police Establishment Act was brought into force in 1946. This Act transferred the superintendence of the SPE to the Home Department and its functions were enlarged to cover all departments of the Government of India. The jurisdiction of the SPE was also extended to all the union territories and could also be extended to the states with the consent of the state government concerned. In 1963, it was renamed as the Central Bureau of Administration on the basis of the recommendations of the Santhanam Committee.

It is interesting to note that the CBI has been created through an executive resolution. Initially, only offences relating to corruption by central government employees fell within its purview. Subsequently, with the formation of a large number of public sector undertakings (PSUs), the employees of these undertakings were also brought under its scanner. Similarly, with the nationalisation of banks in 1969, public sector banks and their employees also came within the CBI's ambit. From 1965 onwards, the CBI has also been entrusted with the investigation of economic offences and crimes such as murders, kidnapping, terrorist attacks, on a selective basis.

Over the years, much deliberation has been done on the shortcomings of the CBI and the reforms needed to overcome these. In 1978, the L.P. Singh Committee recommended the 'enactment of a comprehensive central legislation to remove the deficiency of not having a central investigative agency with a self-sufficient statutory charter of duties and functions'. The 19th Report of the Parliamentary Standing Committee in 2007 and the 24th Report of the Parliamentary Committee in 2008 have emphasized the same. In 2011, a Select Committee of the Rajya Sabha to look into the Lokpal Bill also suggested drastic reforms to the CBI in order to ensure its independence.

The issue of CBI's autonomy once again came before the Supreme Court in the Coal Block Allocation case in 2013. The Court rapped the government for having failed to ensure functional autonomy to the CBI and asked the government to 'come out with a law to insulate the agency from external influence and intrusion'. Accordingly, the then Prime Minister, Manmohan Singh, constituted a Group of Ministers (GoM) to consider the matter. The GoM recommended that a panel of retired judges would monitor CBI investigations to prevent external interference. In addition, it also recommended an increase in the financial powers of the CBI director, and a new mechanism for the appointment of the Director (Prosecution), a Law Ministry appointee, at present. However, these reforms were heavily criticized on grounds of being merely on-surface changes.

Broadly, the areas where reforms are sought in relation to CBI are as under. Foremost is revisiting the functioning of CBI as a Special Police Establishment under the Delhi Special Police Establishment Act of 1946. This has been discussed in detail by the Padmanabhaiah Committee in its report. The 2nd ARC report has also expressed concern about the power of CBI to investigate criminal cases only with the consent of state governments. The Commission has opined that a law should be enacted using the powers of the union government under the Constitution to define the constitution of the CBI, its structure and jurisdiction.

Another issue relating to functioning of the CBI, like all police force, is vacancy in the sanctioned strength. In addition to this, one of the key areas where reforms are needed in the functioning of the CBI is its autonomy. The CBI's lack of autonomy can be traced to its rules for the appointment of its director and limitations on its jurisdiction. The Supreme Court, in the 2013 Coal Allocation case, referred to the CBI as a 'caged parrot speaking in a master's voice'. It strongly recommended autonomy for the CBI to function free from the control of the executive. In this, one suggestion was to make the CBI accountable to the Lokpal. Accordingly, at the time of the enactment of the Lokpal and Lokayukta Bill, a Select Committee was appointed by the Rajya Sabha, which made several recommendations for strengthening the CBI. They include:

a) the appointment of the CBI director will be through a collegium comprising the Prime Minister, leader of the Opposition in the Lok Sabha and Chief Justice of India;
b) the power of superintendence over CBI in relation to Lokpal-referred cases shall vest in the Lokpal;

c) CBI officers investigating cases referred by the Lokpal will be transferred with the approval of the Lokpal;
d) for cases referred by the Lokpal, the CBI may appoint a panel of advocates (other than government advocates) with the consent of the Lokpal. Out of these suggestions, all the recommendations were accepted by the Cabinet except one that required the approval of the Lokpal to transfer CBI officers investigating cases referred by the Lokpal.

Handling Corruption Cases

All complaints relating to misconduct or corruption are filed with the CVO or with the CVC. The CVC, upon examination, registers it and on the basis of its nature either sends it to the concerned department or to the CBI for investigation. Additionally, it can also take on the complaint for enquiry suo moto. In cases where the case is forwarded to the CBI, the agency sends its final report to the CVC through the CVO, which is then sent to the concerned department or the competent authority to take action. The concerned department decides on whether to file charges or drop action on the basis of the evidence for prosecution. In cases where there has been a criminal offence and there is enough evidence for prosecution, the concerned department or the competent authority files the case in the CBI special courts to launch criminal proceedings. In some cases, the CVC, if it deems fit, may itself file a complaint directly before the special court and act as the complainant.

The following flowchart captures the process.

The Process of Handling Corruption Cases

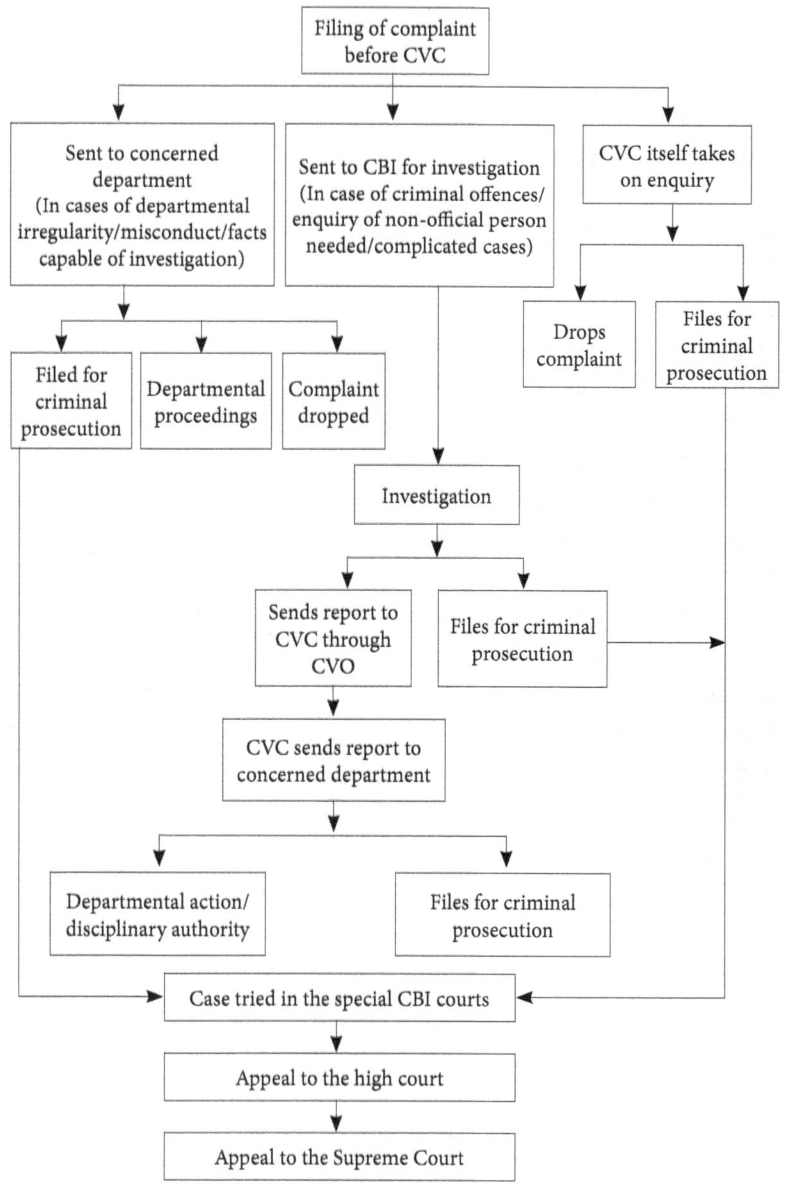

Bottlenecks in Resolution

Bottlenecks at the Departmental Level

As discussed in the previous section, all complaints for corruption first pass through the CVC. As per a 2015 based study[1] conducted by the CVC, the process of finalization of a vigilance case by the CVC itself takes eight years. On an average, there is a delay of about two years in conducting and finalizing the preliminary investigation for making the First Stage Advice (FSA), on the basis of which the decision is taken on the fate of the complaint.[2] Thereafter, the concerned government department takes about five months to finalize the FSA. If a probe is set up, the enquiry officer takes at least fifteen months to complete his investigation. Findings also reveal that the average delay on part of enquiry officers is significant and to the tune of about 1.3 years, and if this delay is clubbed with investigation at first stage, it goes up to 3.4 years.

The report observes that at least 5,000 corruption cases are referred to the CVC every year. Out of these, on an average, there are about 1,200 cases[3], which are of Second Stage Advice (SSA). Many of these cases turn out to be 'false' and 'flimsy' and the standard prolonged delay impacts the career opportunity of the officer or staff under the scanner.

Bottlenecks at the CBI level

It has been estimated that between 2006 and 2016, the CBI completed investigation in 7,217 cases under the PCA. Of these, 3,615 (50.1 per cent) ended in prosecution, 2,178 (30.2 per cent) ended in prosecution as well as Regular Departmental Action (RDA), while 636 cases (8.8 per cent) ended in only RDA. As many as 671 cases (9.3 per cent) were closed without any action. Since 2006, trial was complete in 6,533 cases under the PCA where the investigation was done by the CBI. As many as 4,054 cases (62.1 per cent) ended in conviction of the accused, while 2,095 cases (32.1 per cent) ended in acquittal.[4] As per CVC annual report 2014, there were as many as 9,243 cases pending in various courts at the end of year[5].

The delay in trial is clearly a major bottleneck. The major cause of delay in the trial, as identified by the 2nd ARC, is the tendency of the accused to obtain frequent adjournments and challenge almost every interim order in the high court and later in the Supreme Court with the aim of obtaining a stay of the trial.[6]

Nonetheless, the CBI case disposal rate seems high, particularly when compared with the CVC data. However, it is crucial to note that cases investigated by the CBI can proceed for trial only after receiving sanction from the relevant government under the PCA.[7] As a result, the number of cases that go in for trial is affected by the sanctions received and the time taken in giving such a sanction. Further, with the recent enactment of the Lokpal and Lokayuktas Act, 2013, another layer of approval from the Lokpal/Lokayukta has become mandatory before the CBI can probe a corruption matter. As per Supreme Court orders in the case of Subramanian Swamy v Manmohan Singh[8], the government is supposed to take a decision on sanction of prosecution within a period of three months. However, it has been observed that many such cases remain pending for sanction from the government even after four months. It has been estimated that on 31 August 2010, as many as 342 requests for sanction under the PCA were pending with various authorities of the central and state governments. Of these, 182 requests had been pending for more than three months, out of which thirty cases had crossed the twelve-month mark.[9]

One of the key aspects in the delay in obtaining sanction

by the CBI is crimes committed by ruling party politicians, or by those who can influence the ruling party. Cases where the CBI has shown either reluctance to take up investigations against ruling party politicians or, when forced to do so, adopted dilatory tactics. It has often been alleged that CBI is used by the party in power to harass and intimidate political opponents and favour members or supporters of the ruling party. A veteran CBI officer has claimed in an interview that 'the conviction rate of CBI is actually quite poor if you were to look specifically at cases involving senior politicians or business houses... Even in ordinary corruption cases, we often find that the witnesses turn hostile, and the investigation officers get transferred out.'[10]

Another important bottleneck in resolution of cases is lack of specialized CBI courts. This issue was recognized by the Supreme Court in 2003[11] when it directed the government to establish special courts in different states. On the basis of this order, it has been claimed that specialized CBI Courts have been set up. In 2013, the then Minister of State for Personnel, Public Grievances and Pensions, V. Narayanasamy said in response to a written question that there were forty-six courts of special judges and ten courts of special magistrates functioning exclusively for the trial of CBI cases all over the country[12]. Subsequently, in 2015, in response to a Lok Sabha query, Jitendra Singh, the present Minister of Personnel, Public Grievances and Pensions, stated that the government had set up eighty-six additional special courts in various states to expeditiously dispose of the PCA cases.[13] In a recent interview, CVC Commissioner K.V. Chowdary observed[14] that over 3,000 cases chargesheeted by the CBI are pending before various courts for more than three years, owing largely to the vacancy of judges in the special courts for CBI cases. He mentioned placing a request before the Chief Justice of India to issue suitable directions to high courts to fill up vacancies in special courts and create more courts, if needed.

Chowdary said that around 75,000 complaints were received by the CVC every year. After filtering down anonymous and irrelevant petitions, around 3,500 are found worthy of enquiry. Action is recommended to initiate formal proceedings for 500 to 600 cases, but by the time all formal proceedings are completed (prior to the legal proceedings in court), it takes seven to eight years.

Bottlenecks at the High Court and Supreme Court Level

One of the key problems hampering ruling in corruption cases by the courts is reservation of judgement. Recently, judgements in two cases that involved highly important questions of law were delivered more than a year after the judgement was reserved. In the 2G spectrum case, the court took 433 days to deliver its judgement after having reserved it.[15]

However, as observed in the 2nd ARC report, 'although the judges trying corruption cases under the Prevention of Corruption Act have been declared as Special Judges, they have been saddled with numerous other non-corruption cases with the result that trials in corruption cases get delayed'.[16]

Another aspect affecting Court rulings in corruption cases is the size of the matter. It has been observed that the court decision in big-ticket corruption cases takes years for a final order and prosecution.

Despite the pendency in decision-making by the judiciary, one striking factor is the evolving role of higher judiciary in taking up corruption matters suo moto using the remedy of continuous mandamus[17] to monitor investigations by directions to the CBI. It has also been observed that the Court has refused to award damages for misfeasance even though Indian constitutional law provides for such damages, while making frequent use of mandamus. Arguably, this contradiction suggests the Court's attempt not to overreach in its endeavour to secure the rule of law.

In 2015, the Supreme Court called[18] for a 'zero tolerance' approach towards corruption and advised the courts not to get swayed by mercy and forgiveness while awarding punishment to the corrupt. However, given the bottlenecks in the system at various levels, major institutional overhaul is needed before zero tolerance can be implemented in effect.

References

1 http://www1.worldbank.org/publicsector/anticorrupt/corruptn/cor02.htm#note1

2 https://www.transparency.org/what-is-corruption/

3 For instance, the key statute governing corruption, The Prevention of Corruption Act, 1988, defines only the offences which are punishable.

4 At the state level, anti-corruption bureaus fill the role of the CBI.

5 Vineet Narain v Union of India, (1998) 1 SCC 226

6 161st Report on Central Vigilance Commission and Allied Bodies by the Law Commissionof India.

7 http://www.thehindubusinessline.com/news/group-of-ministers-will-ensure-cbi-has-functional-autonomy-chidambaram/article4723820.ece?ref=relatedNews

8 In cases where there is a departmental irregularity or any misconduct on the part of the public servant or the complaint includes any facts which are capable of investigation, the complaint is sent to the concerned department.

9 These are offences which are punishable the Delhi Special Police Establishment Act or complicated cases where truth cannot be ascertained without making inquiries from non-official persons.

10 See "Report on Study of Existing Pattern of Prolonged Disciplinary Proceedings and Suggestions for Remedial Action; 28.7.2015, Central Vigilance Commission, New Delhi; Section 3

11 The study was conducted by a three-member CVC team of Keshav Rao and Nitish Kumar (both CVC Directors) and M.A. Khan, Under Secretary. The brief of the panel was 'Study of Existing Pattern of Prolonged Disciplinary Proceedings and Suggestions for Remedial Action'.

12 Based on the average SSA tendered by Commission between 2009 and 13.

13 http://www.firstpost.com/india/one-in-three-corruption-cases-against-central-govt-officials-probed-by-cbi-ends-in-acquittal-3012418.html

14 See http://www.cvc.nic.in/ar2014.pdf; page 89, para 6.11.

15 See Second ARC Report Volume 4; Ethics in Governance; para 3.2.5.2; page 70.

16 Section 19 Prevention of Corruption Act, 1988

17 (2012) 3 SCC 64

18 http://humanrightsinitiative.org/publications/police/cvc_cbi_some_developments_a_brief_history.pdf

19 http://www.thehindu.com/opinion/lead/Always-its-master%E2%80%99s-voice/article14022796.ece

20 Criminal Appeal Number 88–93 of 2003.

21 http://www.thehindubusinessline.com/news/over-6800-corruption-cases-pending-trial-in-special-cbi-courts/article4504733.ece; last accessed on 4/10/2017

22 http://www.loksabha.nic.in/Members/QResult16.aspx?qref=21881

23 http://www.thehindu.com/news/cities/Coimbatore/cvc-blames-vacancies-in-cbi-courts-for-pendency-of-cases/article8235474.ece

24 http://www.livemint.com/Politics/AaR91YL6KuVo3ZcN3q3JfO/Delayed-justice-When-judgement-day-arrives-too-late.html

25 See Second ARC Report Volume 4; Ethics in Governance; para 3.2.5.4; page 70

16 Mandamus ('We command') is a judicial remedy in the form of an order from a superior court to any government subordinate court, corporation or public authority to do (or forbear from doing) some specific act which that body is obliged under law to do (or

refrain from doing)—and which is in the nature of public duty, and in certain cases one of a statutory duty.

27 https://timesofindia.indiatimes.com/india/No-mercy-for-the-corrupt-says-SC/articleshow/48863669.cms

◆

Suparna Jain is an advocate engaged as Officer on Special Duty, Legal, at NITI Aayog.

4

The Elusive Search for the Lokpal

SWATI SAINI

'The five-decade struggle and yet no success' summarizes India's relationship with the Lokpal. Most blame political leaders, arguing that they have left no stone unturned in suppressing the Lokpal struggle. Nonetheless, although the need to have a strong and effective institution of the Lokpal has been felt for quite some time, one question stays unanswered; is India actually prepared for the Lokpal? The first Lokpal Bill, which was proposed by Shanti Bhushan in 1968, was accepted in the 4th Lok Sabha the following year. Labelled as weak and not serving its intended purpose, the bill was revived many times thereafter. However, even now after forty-nine years, the Lokpal is not free from criticism. To exemplify, the most recent criticism links the ineffectiveness of the Lokpal with the current government's irresponsible attitude of not appointing a Lokpal on time.

In view of the intense debate generated by this contentious issue, it is imperative to understand various aspects, including the definition of the Lokpal, its exercise of quasi-judicial powers or delegation of these powers to its subordinate officers, the efficacy of a single Act for both the Centre and state and inclusion of the prime minister within the jurisdiction of the Lokpal, among others.[1]

Evaluating Anti-corruption Laws

If Acts such as the Indian Evidence Act, 1872, the PCA and the Right to Information Act, 2005 (RTI Act) were so powerful then why do we need a Lokpal? In other words, have such laws really helped in punishing the acts of corruption and thus contributed to a powerful and well-defined legislative system? The PCA attempted to unify all laws on offences by public servants within one statute (i.e. the Prevention of Corruption Act, 1947, the Criminal Law Amendment Act, 1952, and Sections 161 to 165-A of the Indian Penal Code with modifications), incorporated stricter penalties and widened the definition of 'public servant'.[2] These amendments contributed to some extent towards making of a well-defined legislative system. In this regard, Shantaram Naik, member of the Rajya Sabha, representing the Congress, compared the provisions of the Lokpal with the PCA, suggesting that the Lokpal cannot tackle corruption the way PCA did. Scrutinizing his comment, the continuous rise in the cases registered by the CBI against public servants under the PCA can be perceived in two ways. First, the effectiveness of the PCA in finding corrupt public servants has increased over the years. The Act has definitely been the first of its kind to take exemplary steps, including expanding its coverage, bolstering its provisions and enhancing implementation. However, even after enactment of such a powerful Act, public servants continue to commit corrupt acts, leading to an increase in their ilk. If the PCA was so successful in combating corruption, then why is India not corruption-free? Thus, should the PCA be categorized as a power-*'ful'* law or rather a power-*'less'* law? Among the several identified critiques, Finance Minister Arun Jaitley[3] pointed out that the PCA belonged to the pre-liberalization era and therefore there is a need to relook the provisions of Section 13 of the

Act that defines what constitutes criminal misconduct by a public servant and the penal provisions for the same. He argued that due to the fear of penal action even for honest decisions the Act became a big impediment to effective functioning of government functionaries and officials. Further, the PCA does not adequately cover punishing corrupt acts of private parties, except to a limited extent through Sections 8, 9 (that deal with persons accepting gratification to use their influence on a public servant in the conduct of an official act) and 12 (dealing with abetment, pursuant to which a person offering a bribe could be punished). Thus, the provision on bribe offering and other similar corrupt practices by a private person still lacks adequacy. Further, it needs a more defined framework to handle the cases of 'collusive corruption', where the private person may be the creator and the public servant may have rejected the bribe. However, even after being incorporated in the 4th report of the 2nd ARC, the matter has not been resolved. In this light, BJP MP Arjun Ram Meghwal pointed that he hadn't noticed a dip in corruption levels, even though the PCA was in existence since 1988. To conclude, despite the PCA, India is still struggling to find a way to end corruption.

The RTI Act, 2005, was another popular initiative to achieve transparency and accountability within the public sector. The law permits any person of Indian origin to ask for the information they desire from public servants. One cannot deny the several RTI success stories, such as the Adarsh Society Scam, where RTI advocates, Yogacharya Anandji and Simpreet Singh, exposed the nexus between the political class and military officials. An RTI during the Commonwealth Games revealed diversion of funds by the Delhi Government from social welfare projects to private consumption. However, the Act has also been criticized for being inefficient on the grounds of transparency and accountability, especially due to inadequate infrastructure and personnel for running Information Commissions. Also, it was criticized for exempting the organization or person on whom the RTI has been charged, from revealing information on many grounds. To elaborate, Sections 8(1)(e) and 8(1)(j) of the RTI Act have provided for the provision of exemptions from disclosure. Further, Section 11 also makes it easier to exempt the person under question from disclosure of such information. To conclude, the RTI can be a more effective tool of transparency and accountability after amending its Section on 'exemptions from disclosure of information' by reducing the scope. Also, there needs to be a balance between 'too less' and 'too much', in the scope of 'any exemption from disclosure of information'.

Thus, although most anti-corruption laws are well-drafted, their implementation has been faulty. These laws face the issue of insufficiency of actors willing to report and penalize corrupt acts. In this regard, India Against Corruption pointed out that anti-corruption laws still face crucial deficiencies, which eventually protect the corrupt, rather than punish them. For instance, there was much argument about taking prior permission from an officer or minister in charge of the same department before commencing investigations or prosecution into any case. Nonetheless, it cannot be ignored that the officer or minister may be directly or indirectly involved in that case. Furthermore, it was argued that permission of the home secretary is required for phone tapping or interceptions during investigations. However, seeking such prior approvals from a member of the government might alert the public servant under question and may give him ample time to take necessary action to protect himself. However, on the other hand, keeping the Lokpal independent of a central body can face implementation challenges. Nonetheless, Delhi Chief Minister Arvind Kejriwal suggested empowering the bench of the Lokpal to tap phones without any prior reference or authorization from any entity.

Lokpal—The Lone Warrior?

The efficacy of the Lokpal to combat corruption single-handedly has not yet found a convincing reply. In this regard, Congress MP Rahul Gandhi called for a more representative and accessible democratic system, by mentioning that the Lokpal alone cannot be a substitute to combat corruption. He proposed that the Lokpal should be converted into a constitutional body like the Election Commission of India (ECI), as just making laws and institutions have not proved to be enough. In other words, a more autonomous, constitutional and permanent body authorized for administering corruption is needed. The question that then arises is—was the CVC not set up in 1964 as an autonomous body without the control of any executive authority to monitor all vigilance activities under the central government of India and thus address governmental corruption? It cannot be denied that the CVC delivered many of its promises. For instance, it released the Draft National Anti-Corruption Strategy, which highlights drawbacks in India's legislative framework. Nevertheless, the CVC does not have direct powers to scrutinize and, thus, must depend on the CBI for investigating alleged offences committed by officials under the PCA. To point, the need to take prior sanction of an appropriate authority, before scrutinizing the case of an offence by a public servant is a serious constraint as such sanctions would result in time lags. In other words, if the already autonomous, constitutional and permanent bodies, such as the CVC, have not lived upto the expectations, then how would redesigning the Lokpal, as a more autonomous, constitutional and permanent body make a difference? Would giving more charge to the CVC to function as an ombudsman in India with more autonomy, not be a more intelligible solution? In this light, Rahul Gandhi reinforced the recommendation made by the Santhanam Committee that suggested that the

CVC, which is already an autonomous body free of control from any executive authority to monitor all vigilance activities under the central government, should function as an ombudsman in India, taking cognizance of cases of maladministration as well as corruption. Nonetheless, the Government of India rejected this recommendation claiming that there should be a separate agency to look into the grievances of citizens against administrative corruption.[3]

CBI's Functional Autonomy

There has been a general conflict with respect to CBI's interest in the Lokpal, which is the apex body for investigating criminal intelligence information. The Congress's Sukhendu Sekhar Roy argued that although the CBI asks for greater functional autonomy, it also suggests that the Lokpal can exercise general superintendence on anti-corruption matters through the CBI director. Further, S. Semmalai, of the AIADMK party, said that even though the CBI was keen to work with the Lokpal, it did not want to be subordinated by any institution.

However, has the CBI been successful in its endeavours as an independent body for the past many years? The demand for CBI investigation from all over India to resolve important cases arises from the fact that the institution functions unfettered and uninfluenced by the government or any other outside party. It is only in some sensitive political cases, that the interference of the government is permitted, as pointed by CBI officers. Thus, to conclude, it is necessary to maintain CBI's independence to probe into cases of corruption against public functionaries. However, Anna Hazare's team of India Against Corruption asked for a disruption in the operations of the CBI by demanding its vivisection and subsequent merger of the CBI's anti-corruption wing with the Lokpal. On the one hand, it would definitely be better for the CBI and the Lokpal to act in tandem to combat corruption. While on the other hand, it may disturb the ongoing operations of the CBI. Further, there needs to be a mechanism to check that the CBI does not report to the government and rather functions independently after converging with the Lokpal. It could report either to the Parliament or the Supreme Court. The second alternative is to build a Lokpal investigation wing, which is independent of the CBI. This idea was initially recommended by the L.P. Singh Reform Committee in 1978 and Parliament Standing Committee on Personnel, Pubic Grievances Law and Justice in 2008.[4] However, this exercise would require considerable time and resources to build infrastructure. Also, it could result in coinciding of jurisdiction, conflict of interest and lack of synergy.

The Prime Minister and the Lokpal

The Prime Minister or the principal minister and head of the government, like any public functionary, should fall under the purview of the Lokpal, simply because, the PM is also a public servant. However, on the contrary, as the PM's office handles many national policies and issues, such as Energy, Defence and Security, which cannot be disclosed to the public, Lokpal could prove to be a much dangerous weapon in such cases, especially, as many interest groups working against the country, such as terrorists and Naxalites, could use the Lokpal to extract inside information and use it for destabilizing India, which needs to be protected. In this light, Shailendra Kumar[1] of Samajwadi Party argued that one can understand the sensitivity of the office of the PM and therefore it is logical to keep the office out of the ambit of Lokpal. However, the question that then arises is, where to draw a line? In other words, if the PM is completely exempted from the ambit of the Lokpal, it might make the other public officers feel they are being given an unfair treatment, or it might tempt the PM to pursue corrupt acts, thinking he can get away with it. To this the minister added, outside the sensitive issues, such as, Energy, Defence and Security, the PM may be brought within the ambit of the Lokpal. Pinaki Mishra[1], representing the Congress, agreed to the same with the reasoning that the Indian Parliament when enacting the PCA did not give the PM any immunity from prosecution then why should Lokpal leave out the PM.

However, it cannot be assumed that the ministries attached to Energy, Defense and Security would not be involved in any scandals. On the contrary, since these sectors are classified as sectors of high economic importance, should they not require a stricter scrutiny? To this, Mishra[1] argued that the PM has very often held important economic portfolios such as Defense, Telecom, etc. nonetheless, the ministries attached to these sectors have been involved in numerous scandals. Therefore, there is no reason to grant the PM who in our Parliamentary System is '*only first among equals*', any immunity from the Lokpal's scrutiny, *while the PM holds office.*

Inclusion of NGOs, Corporate Houses and Media

Should NGOs, corporate houses and media be included under the jurisdiction of the Lokpal as insisted by Lok Janshakti Party leader Ramvilas Pasvan? However, the point to note is that if the Lokpal was created only to check the acts of public functionaries, then why include organizations that may not be of public nature under its ambit? Will this not lead to ambiguity in its scope? In this light, social activist Nikhil Dey, suggested that any NGO, private sector or corporate body that takes on a task of public nature should be incorporated in the Lokpal. This can be through a public-private partnership (PPP) model or performing a task for the government where the organization receives financial aid from the government. Furthermore, with respect to mandatory disclosure of assets, debts and liabilities of senior management personnel at NGOs, several Board members who hold their positions only in honorary capacity, not taking any remuneration for their work may be demotivated to join or remain as a Board member. Anu Aga, Rajya Sabha member and an active member of several boards, argued[5] that many valuable NGOs have lost distinguished board members who object to the loss of privacy due to such a provision. Nonetheless, if politicians have been included under the jurisdiction of the Lokpal, then why should any member of an NGO, corporate house and media, who is directly or indirectly connected with the government, be immune to the institution? Is it only politicians who need to be checked for corruption? It is a common belief these days, that most politicians are corrupt. This might be a concern for many politicians who are struggling to fight that public image. Lalu Yadav[1], former Chief Minister of Bihar, expressed that such public image has created a feeling of hatred towards politicians. This has personally affected his political appearance in Bihar. The moot question is why are politicians so disproportionately targeted for criminal inspections? A study of the manner in which differing forms of corruption are deemed to be concentrated at different levels with varying degrees of dominance would help understand the question better.[6] Unfortunately, public scandals in the last twenty years have been majorly linked with politicians and ministers. Nonetheless, it might be worth mentioning that beyond political and administrative corruption (that includes persons like higher public authorities, officers, police officers, clerks, peons, etc.), there are other forms of corruption, such as professional corruption that includes a mixture of frauds in medicines, hygienic items, eatables and spices, stones in cereals, animal fats in ghee, kerosene in petrol etc. Thus, there is a dire need to broaden one's perspective and understand that terms 'public servant' and 'corruption' are not analogous. Prominent BJP leader and a member of the Rashtriya Swayamsevak Sangh, late Balwant Apte argued that most people believed that everybody in the government is corrupt. However, such presumption could never help in eradicating corruption because the entire approach here is based on disbelief and lack of trust. Therefore, there is a dire need to begin with a new approach, which is based on the principle of trust. Otherwise, despite the system spending a large amount of time and energy in appointing the Lokpal, which can implement the mechanism as desired, there will always be the festering issue of trusting the team's loyalty and integrity.

Investigation and Prosecution Wings

One school of thought, headed by lawyer and activist Prashant Bhushan, argues that since the Lokpal is directed to punish corrupt acts of public officers, it is advisable to keep the investigation and prosecution wings, the most important elements of the Lokpal, independent of the government. Nonetheless, such a desire seems ambitious as it requires a powerful investigation wing that is manned by experienced professionals, and would further require copious time and resources. Also, since it will be independent of governmental control, it might be difficult to keep a check on the development and progress of the Lokpal's investigation wing. To summarize, it cannot be denied that without the support of the government, the Lokpal may not function successfully.

Lokayuktas in the States—The Federal Dilemma

Lokayukta, or in other words, the Lokpal at the state level, would also investigate cases of corruption and maladministration against public officers. However, if there is one Lokpal handling the same function at the Centre, would it not result in duplication of roles and confusion in jurisdiction if the Lokayukta performs the same role at the state level? Interestingly, the role and power of the Lokayukta may vary from state to state. For instance, while some states may have the power to investigate the chief minister, other ministers and MLAs, other states can only limit their scope to civil servants, judges and the police. Also, Lokayuktas may face several implementation issues, such as limited autonomy, prosecution powers, personnel and funds. Finance Minister Arun Jaitley has said, 'One possible option is that one can legislate on areas where the legislature has jurisdiction. Where one finds that the central—legislature has no jurisdiction, there are two options—either that part should be left to the states or under Article 252, with the consent of two states, the central legislature can bring an enabling law compatible with the constitutional scheme'.

2017 and Still No Institution in Place

The most recent impediment related to the issue of absence of a leader of Opposition. It was required that the largest political party in opposition must have at least 10% of the total members in the House to get the leader's position. However, as none of the political parties could manage to achieve that mark, it could not be implemented. To this, Shanti Bhushan and Gopal Shankaranarayanan[7] asserted that the Centre is using this argument as a mere ruse to delay making the Lokpal functional. Nonetheless, in a short gap of time, although a solution was arrived to deal with the unavailability of a leader of Opposition, the Lokpal still stands defeated.

Have anti-corruption laws helped fight corruption? Several laws, such as the Indian Evidence Act, 1872, the PCA, the RTI Act and now, most recently, the Lokpal have been drafted with periodic revisions to punish corrupt acts of public servants. One school of thought understands the effectiveness of a law by the number of criminals imprisoned or cases successfully closed over the years. If the number has increased, then the law is considered effective. Another school of thought argues that if there has been an increase in the number of cases registered, then the law has only been effective in its implementation, but failed to teach public servants that they should adopt transparency and honesty, and any act against such principles is unacceptable.

These laws have only targeted public sector corruption, ignoring the corruption in the private sector or acts of authorities whose public character cannot be clearly defined, like private schools, colleges and religious institutions.

However, for the common man little or no change in the country's overall corruption levels and lack of economic growth and development indicates that the laws have failed to meet their promise. Year after year, every politician promises to show the common man a corruption-free India, in exchange of his vote. Nevertheless, the situation remains the same.

To summarize, India still needs to go a long way in drafting and implementing anti-corruption laws. The laws should be so powerful that first, they are efficient in their investigations and second, deter public officers from pursuing a corrupt act.

References

1 Political debate, 'Department related Parliamentary Standing Committee on Personnel, Public Grievances, Law and Justice: 48th Report on the Lokpal Bill, 2011', 27 May 2017, http://rajyasabha.nic.in/rsnew/48th_lokpal_report.pdf

2 B. Premalatha. 2016. 'Public Servant Definition under Prevention of Corruption Act 1988 - Evolution Scope and Challenges', *Journal of Legal Studies and Research*, 2(4).

3 'Draft – National Anti-Corruption Strategy: Central Vigilance Commission', http://cvc.nic.in/NACSSummary.pdf;
B.K. Lenin, 'Administration of Central Vigilance Commission: A Critical Analysis', http://manupatra.com/roundup/328/Articles/Administration%20of%20Central%20Vigilance.pdf

4 'Functioning of the Lokpal and the CBI: Need for Synergy', http://cbi.nic.in/articles/pdf/FunctioningofLokpal.pdf

5 'NGOs Want Board Members Out of Lokpal Act's Ambit', 26 May 2017, https://thewire.in/53931/ngo-board-members-lokpal-act/

6 A. Sanchez. 2012. 'India: the next superpower?: corruption in India', http://eprints.lse.ac.uk/43449/

7 'SC to govt: Appoint lokpal at earliest, absence of Leader of Opposition no reason to delay', *The Times of India*, 1 October, 2017 http://timesofindia.indiatimes.com/india/sc-to-govt-appoint-lokpal-at-earliest-absence-of-leader-of-opposition-no-reason-to-delay/articleshow/58407438.cms

◆

Swati Saini is a Young Professional with NITI Aayog.

5

Civil Society Rises against Corruption

SHASHVAT SINGH

The government's move to demonetise currency notes in November 2016 brought to the fore the issue of rampant corruption leading to the generation of black money. This menace further leads to many offences, including terror financing and money laundering.

It is not for the first time that the public consciousness was awakened. Getting rid of the malaise of corruption has, time and again, formed the core plank of local, state and national elections. Several movements have emerged and faded—some for the lack of leadership, others for the lack of consistency and yet others for degenerative public memory and energy that fails to last long.

Civil society has always come forward to voice its concerns on the depth of corruption, and set forth ideas to combat the problem. It is imperative to delve deeper into civil society movements aimed at not merely highlighting the issue, but also to generate public awareness to counter the problem. It is also important to analyse the concrete outcomes of enhanced civil society action.

Though a 'sum of interrelations' in the words of Karl Marx, the society is made up of individuals who, once they realize their power, have the ability and capacity to bury the undesirable and sow the seeds of betterment. Civil society may be referred to as a group of individuals conscious of an idea and willing to take action for the collective good. Members of a civil society form a link between the masses that are tied up with their day-to-day affairs and the government, which, more often than not, loses touch with those who elevated them to the corridors of power. If channelized effectively, civil society could be used to bridge the ever-widening gap between the government and the governed.

A civil society comprises formal NGOs as well as informal associations of citizens. Recent times have witnessed both these forms coming forward to bring about or demand positive changes in the Indian society and polity. This is a desirable phenomenon as a strong and proactive civil society exerts pressure on the state so that the latter does not exercise unbridled power over its citizens.

The 2011 agitation against corruption led by Anna Hazare is still fresh in the memory. Fresher still is the memory of the 2014 Lok Sabha election campaign where corruption was a major issue. Many observers considered it as the major reason for the ouster of the incumbent government. The year 2015 saw a fledgling political party, born out of a civil society movement against corruption, forming the government in the nation's capital with an overwhelming majority. And, with the aid of social media, the civil society has been able to create a platform for people to collectively raise their voice against corruption.

RTI Movement: A Defining Change

Even seventy years after India's Independence, corruption, camouflaged in various forms, had been flourishing unabatedly when the idea of the right to information emerged from the realms of the civil society.

The demand for a 'right to know' was not new, but the methods involved and the proposals made were innovative each time the issue cropped up. The Supreme Court, as the guardian of the Constitution and protector of the rights of the people, identified the citizens' right to know. Thus was born the RTI movement, the seeds of which were sown in 1987 and which grew out of the struggle of the Mazdoor Kisan Shakti Sangathan (MKSS) for transparency and accountability in village accounts in Devdungri, Rajasthan. Initially, the movement was centred on raising concerns related to fair daily wages, and survival and justice for the most marginalized sections of the population. It later spread to other regions, with its scope expanding to cover and reach broader sections of the population. The momentum to the movement was fuelled further by citizens' groups, social activists, media, academics, with support from small sections of the government and judiciary.

This demand for change when the prevalent scenario had become a norm was triggered by the fact that the state had become a maximalist one with hold over factors and resources for economic and social development. It soon became opaque and unaccountable; the dark clouds of corruption engulfed the system and the masses begun to choke. The distance between the common citizen and the government had widened beyond measure. It was only inevitable that the bubble burst, giving birth to the movement for RTI.

The RTI movement overlapped with the passage of constitutional amendments aimed at decentralization, liberalization of the Indian economy, widening economic disparity and failure of government schemes aimed at emancipation of the marginalized sections of the population.

What started from the hinterlands of Rajasthan where poor farmers and daily wage labourers met for Jan Sunwais (public hearings), gradually expanded its reach to the state capital Jaipur and thereafter, reached the heart of New Delhi. These Jan Sunwais were a medium for the people to bring out discrepancies in muster rolls and wages and corruption in constructions and development work. The first phase of the movement had begun and adequate care was taken to ensure that these Jan Sunwais were organized as open meetings in public spaces at central locations so as to ensure accessibility for all. This was also symbolic in more ways than one as it gave a sense of transparency and the confidence of being heard. As such, increased participation was witnessed and a consequent legitimacy was obtained from the support of the people.

Slowly, the movement moved from open spaces to people sitting in dharnas outside the government secretariat in Jaipur. The first outcome was securing the right to photocopy government documents. With this also came the confidence to push for legislation at the national capital, leading to the formation of the National Campaign for the Peoples' Right to Information (NCPRI) in 1996. The NCPRI was entrusted to oversee the drafting of and backing for an RTI legislation, and mobilize public support for the movement.

The intelligentsia joined in and meetings, seminars and conventions began to be conducted in different parts of the city. Network and alliances were sought with NGOs, international bodies and the media. The movement captured diverse spaces with alliances being formed between citizens of different locations, brought together by the long-standing demand for information and accountability by all. The movement initially focussed on the need for considered deliberations with people's participation along with the objective of building solidarity in carrying the movement forward, and creating awareness by mobilizing and reaching out to the masses and garnering support for the proposed legislation.

The movement was led by a diverse leadership comprising IAS officers, social activists and experts in fields such as rural development. Leadership and ideas was also received from lawyers, retired judges, journalists, environmentalists, academicians and human rights activists, all of whom gave the movement the requisite brain and balance. While it was important to have such leadership, it was equally vital for voices of the rural masses to be heard along with their urban counterparts. For the RTI movement not to be limited to the echelons of power, it was imperative to mobilize the grass roots and seek active citizen participation.

Creativity was at its peak with attention-grabbing slogans such as '*Hamara Paise, Hamara Hisaab*'; '*Hum Janenge, Hum Jiyenge*'; 'No RTI, No Vote'; 'Save RTI' and '*Ghoos ko Ghoonsa*' being used to take the idea to the masses and connect with them. Innovative methods of sharing information through slogans on walls and pamphlets, Panchayat-like meetings, youth camps and Majdoor Kisan Melas were employed. The medium of art and culture was also used, for example, organizing folk theatre, puppet shows, songs and nukkad nataks. Campaigns and dharnas were also organized along with signature campaigns, rallies by students, candlelight vigils, film screenings and live RTI radio.

However, this journey towards an effective RTI regime was marred by challenges. Difficulties emerged right from the beginning when civil society members had to be convinced to be brought on board. Internal strife had to be resolved through strong and prolonged negotiations and the text of the proposed bill was written and re-written so as to ensure that nothing non-negotiable was left out. The bill was, thereafter, intensely debated.

This powerful movement finally achieved success in October 2005, when the Parliament passed the RTI Act with the objective to 'provide for setting out the practical regime of right to information for citizens'. The Act empowers citizens to ask for information from any public authority, and has made it mandatory for the said authority to reply expeditiously or within thirty days.

Not soon after the enactment of the legislation, repeated attempts at stalling the implementation of the Act were witnessed. The media has played a major role in bringing such instances to light, leading to strong protests and criticisms by the general public. This is also reflective of a wide alliance that had been consolidated over the years. Social media platforms have also played a major role in awakening the consciousness. The spillover effects of such wide-ranging participation and the influence of the movement has been witnessed in instances of multilateral donor agencies putting up conditions for grant of loans being dependent on the setting up of transparency regimes.

The RTI movement brought forth a defining change within the boundaries of parliamentary democracy without questioning it. In fact, it helped strengthen the foundations of democracy. The RTI also strengthened other schemes such as Mahatma Gandhi National Rural Employment Guarantee Scheme. Though the burden of the political and administrative classes increased, they could not devise any legitimate excuse to counter the many benefits the Act had aimed to achieve. However, there have been various instances of RTI activists being murdered. Issues have also arisen owing to lack of prescribed timelines for settling cases pending with the chief information commissioner. While we have come a long way, more needs to be done.

Anti-corruption Movement: Galvanizing the Masses

The anti-corruption movement owes its origin to the demand for having the office of the Lokpal to monitor and deal with corruption in India. In 1968, the first Lokpal Bill was introduced in the Parliament. It was passed in the Upper House, but its passage in the Lower House remained pending. With time, subsequent versions of the Bill were introduced in the Parliament, but they never saw the light of day. The civil society regarded this as a complete disinterest of lawmakers in passing the Lokpal Bill.

On one hand, the Parliament was unable to pass an anti-graft bill, while on the other, instances of corruption in the top echelons of power were constantly making headlines, leading to simmering civil society discontent. This disillusionment of the civil society erupted in 2011 in the form of the anti-corruption movement (India Against Corruption) led by Anna Hazare. That year, Hazare went on an indefinite hunger strike in the national capital, demanding that the civil society draft of the Lokpal Bill be passed by the Parliament.

The anti-corruption movement was not just a reaction to the 'big' corruption of that time. The 'petty' corruption experienced by the public on a daily basis also formed the reason for this agitation. The movement ultimately aimed for the legislation to be drafted by a committee comprising government representatives and civil society members and hence was christened, Jan Lokpal Bill. The Bill aimed at creating independent institutions at central and state levels to receive complaints against erring government officials, and with powers to punish them after a thorough investigation that was to be completed within a stipulated time.

Anna Hazare's request for involving civil society members in the drafting of this Bill was turned down by the government, which forced the crusader to begin his 'indefinite fast' on 5 April 2011 at the iconic Jantar Mantar in New Delhi. His campaign received support from a number of celebrated people from the fields of spirituality, civil service, sports and entertainment. Though the opposition parties of the time rendered their support, Hazare decided not to share his platform with them. The fast awakened the public consciousness throughout the country. The government was forced to table the anti-graft legislation in the Parliament. It also agreed to include civil society members in the committee that was to be formed to draft the Bill.

However, strict government action on a similar protest by a yoga exponent about two months later rocked the boat. Hazare protested against this police action and said that the Jan Lokpal legislation be passed by the Parliament before India celebrated its sixty-fifth independence day in 2011. He warned of beginning a fast on 16 August if the government failed to deliver.

However, Hazare was to receive further setbacks in the coming months. Much to his chagrin, the Union Cabinet decided to keep the offices of the prime minister, higher judiciary and members of Parliament outside the purview of the Lokpal. This development impelled Anna to go ahead with his fast. On the morning of 16 August, Hazare and his associates were remanded to judicial custody and imprisoned for a week. This action not only invited opposition censure but was enough to send a shock wave across the country, leading to protests by civil society and the masses. Such an unprecedented response from the citizens compelled the government to release the anti-graft crusaders, thereafter Hazare began his fast at Ramlila Maidan. This resulted in the Parliament, in principle, agreeing to his demands. Thus Hazare suspended his fast with the hope that a strong Lokpal was soon going to be reality in India.

However, by December 2011, not much action had been taken by the Parliament, leading to another round of fasts by Hazare and his associates. But the remarkable change here was the presence of the opposition on the same platform. Heated debates on the subject were witnessed in the Parliament during that year's winter session. Yet the Bill could not be passed even in the budget session of 2012.

In the summer of 2012, Anna Hazare decided to take the protest further with renewed vigour. However, public interest and participation in the movement appeared to be waning. This forced the Gandhian to break his fast abruptly but he vowed to continue his fight to usher in transparency in the political system. Soon,

'Team Anna', comprising Hazare and his associates, headed for disintegration, with Arvind Kejriwal and his supporters deciding to reform the political system through the means of the ballot.

Though it could be said that the anti-corruption movement fizzled out without achieving its objective, it played an important role in galvanizing the masses against the menace of corruption in contemporary times. The action to get the Lokpal Bill passed caught the attention of the burgeoning middle class in India. A vast majority got interested in it, unlike other social movements, as the ills of corruption affect people from all socio-economic sections of the society.

The coverage by the national and international media went on to fuel the momentum and brought the issue of corruption to the centre stage. Social media crusaders also played an important role in creating awareness and generating support for the movement. Thus, the issue of corruption and its menacing proportions attracted the unprecedented attention of not just those sitting in state capitals, but also of those inhabiting thatched roof houses in far-off villages of the country.

The prominent places in the national and state capitals, district headquarters and village panchayats became the venues for people to register their protest, besides on social media. Non-resident Indians were not to be left behind. Though they were away from their motherland, when it came to freeing her from the ills of corruption, they took to streets in the countries of their residence and drew the attention of their neighbours and the local media. The reputation of the country was at stake in the international arena. This further built pressure on the government 'to act'.

Some leading social activists, however, were in disagreement with the scheme of the movement, since the beginning. Few even considered the imagination of an extra-constitutional Lokpal as a threat to democracy. As a result, different versions of the Jan

Lokpal Bill came out. The anti-corruption movement also failed to garner the support of the ongoing people's movement in the country.

Though opponents in Parliament agreed to the issue highlighted by the anti-corruption movement, parliamentarians, cutting across party lines, were seen lamenting the challenge posed by the movement to the House's wisdom. The anti-corruption movement was immensely different from the RTI movement in terms of tone and tenor. While the RTI movement aimed at working within parliamentary democracy, the anti-corruption movement went against the existing political and administrative set-up and was an attempt towards overhauling the system.

Inherent Strength of Civil Society Action

In 2007, a civil society organization (CSO) called Public Affairs Centre India came up with an exercise called Citizens' Report Cards (CRCs), to review the performance of the Citizen's Charter initiative of the government, launched a decade ago. It was a unique exercise that gathered the systematic feedback of end users on the performance of various agencies delivering public services.

The review found that government agencies did not effectively implement the Citizen's Charter initiative. It was an exercise just limited to drafting a document. The agencies lacked severely in reforming their service quality to bring transparency and accountability in their system. Moreover, many of them did not even adhere to the standards set in their own charter. The review also indicated that an overwhelming percentage of end users were in the dark about the existence of the citizen's charters.

The CRC exercise has many advantages. The feedback obtained through the CRC could be used by agencies to improve the quality and adequacy of the services provided by them. Moreover, if government agencies remain immune to the findings, the CSOs could utilize the CRC findings to nudge them to perform better. Thus, CRC plays a critical role in improving the quality of service delivery by public agencies and has reduced avenues for corruption in the provisioning of such services.

Another initiative by the civil society that has made a significant impact in highlighting and combating corruption is called the Zero Rupee Note (ZRN). This initiative was launched in 2007 by a CSO called 5th Pillar. Zero Rupee Notes are distributed among common folks to make them aware of their right for a corruption-free governance system. These notes carry the pledge, 'I promise to neither accept nor give bribe' and are meant to be handed over to public servants who demand bribes for performing their jobs, with an aim to create a feeling of guilt in them and make them introspect. As of 2016, over three million of these notes have been distributed across India.

Tata Tea, India's largest tea manufacturer, launched a marketing campaign called '*Aaj se khilana bandh, pilana shuru*' in 2009. The objective of this campaign was in similar vein, as of other civil society initiatives tackling corruption, to highlight the issue of corruption and urge the citizens to fight against it. Tata Tea also came out with a 'Jaago Re Corruption Index' to gauge the perception of people on corruption and quantify it. Likewise, the internationally marked 'Anti-Corruption Day' on 9 December was promoted as a national activity in India by the corporate entity.

On 15 August 2010, a CSO, Janaagraha, launched I Paid A Bribe (IPAB) website (ipaidabribe.com) with an objective to provide an online platform to encourage Indians to share their bribe-giving experiences. The IPAB collects bribe reports and builds a repository of corruption-related data across government departments, using a crowd-sourcing model. Such a collation helps governments and advocacy organizations to deal with the menace of retail corruption. The website enlists various success stories of the IPAB initiative. The stupendous success of the website encouraged the founders to launch its Hindi version in 2013. In about seven years of its existence, the IPAB has received around ten million visits, recorded over 47,000 bribe reports amounting to over ₹280 crore from more than 600 cities and towns in India. It has also been scaled to twenty-five countries, with twelve more in the process of launching their own IPAB sites. Hailed globally as an innovation to wage a war against 'petty' corruption, IPAB is also taught as a case study at Harvard Business School.

Transparency International India (TII) is another leading anti-corruption NGO in the country. Established in 1997 by a Gandhian, S.D. Sharma, it works with central and state governments, CSOs, corporates, academia, media and common citizens to reduce instances of corruption. The various programmes through which the initiative pursues its mission include India Corruption Study, raising awareness among people about good governance, promoting Integrity Pact among PSUs and corporates to fight corruption in the field of public contracting, awarding journalists for excellence in exposing corruption, engaging with other CSOs with parallel themes and bringing out publications. To promote access to justice among the vulnerable and marginalized, it offers free legal advice and assistance through its Advocacy and Legal Centre.

Pahal is an initiative to reach out to those at the 'bottom of the pyramid' in the rural areas. It helps to empower marginalized rural masses to demand and access their entitlements and public services with the knowledge and use of good governance tools such as the RTI, social audit, revived gram sabhas, Citizen's Charter and e-governance.

Corruption is not unique to India. But the manner in which it has seeped into the bloodstream of the nation, becoming acceptable and abhorred at the same time, is distinctive. Indians have been creative in devising ways to propagate corruption, while simultaneously being creative in creating mechanisms to counter the problem. For every three steps in the wrong direction, we have accumulated the courage to take one in the right. Though, of late, there has been no news of scams, the dark clouds of corruption still loom large. The government, along with the awakened collective consciousness of the masses, is taking measures to get rid of corruption and move towards becoming a progressive country.

The public, cutting across economic and ethnic lines, voices its concerns when it directly witnesses the ugly face of corruption. It rises in protest itself or begins to support those who are protesting, once the humiliation and exploitation due to corrupt practices breaches their tolerance limit. However, some distinction exists in the way the middle class and lower income groups respond to corruption. The former prefers abolition of doles and welfare schemes, while the latter wants these means to continue with a desire that they receive their genuine entitlements.

Another aspect that deserves mention is that the state is likely to agree to the demands of the civil society, provided it does not challenge the wisdom and authority of the state, though there may be instances of initial reluctance. The successes of the RTI movement and IPAB initiative, and unwillingness of the state in agreeing to all the demands of India Against Corruption, lend credibility to the preceding argument.

Clearly, action by an empowered civil society could lead to incredible consequences. Otherwise, who could dream that the stiff resistance by a bureaucratic state would cave in, and the residents of Devdungri would get access to the government records way before the enactment of an RTI law. Though the anti-corruption movement failed to get an anti-graft law, no one can deny that the same movement created pressure on the lawmakers to pass it this time. Civil society movements and actions against corruption have gone a long way in creating a sense of empowerment in the general public.

In the words of Ayn Rand, 'The roadmap to tackling corruption has been strewn with difficulties. It has been the collective effort of every single entity and individual who had the courage to join hands in the fight against corruption for us to reach where we have. It is from the inviolate integrity of such minds that the achievements thus far have come. It is to such entities and individuals that the nation owes its survival.'

Notes

1 D. Bhatnagar & A. Rathore. 'Mazdoor Kisan Shakti Sangathan'.

2 B. Debroy & L. Bhandari. 2012. *Corruption in India: The DNA and the RNA*. New Delhi: Konark Publishers Private Limited.

3 D. Goswami & K.K. Bandyopadhyay. 2007. *The Anti-Corruption Movement in India*

4 Guha, R. *India After Gandhi: the History of the World's Largest Democracy.* New York: HarperCollins.

5 A. Rand. 1996. *The Fountainhead.* New York: Signet.

6 M. Sengupta. 'Civil Society and Anti-Corruption Initiatives in India: Towards a Citizens' Perspective', in *Routledge Handbook of Corruption in Asia,* Ian Scott & Ting Gong (eds.). 2016. London UK: Routledge, pp. 196–208.

7 R. Singh. 2014. 'Civil Society and Policymaking in India: In Search of Democratic Spaces', Oxfam India.

8 S. Sondhi. 2000. 'Combating Corruption in India: The Role of Civil Society'.

9 P.K. Varma. 2013. *Chanakya's: New Manifesto to Resolve the Crisis within India.* New Delhi: Aleph Book Company.

10 'Tata Tea launches new 'Jaago Re' campaign, on corruption,' *Business Standard*, 20 January 2013, http://www.business-standard.com/article/management/tata-tea-launches-new-jaago-

re-campaign-on-corruption-109082600064_1.html

11 'ipaidabribe.com: A website that encourages Indians to share their bribe giving experiences', *The Economic Times*, 2 December 2012, 'http://economictimes.indiatimes.com/industry/tech/internet/ipaidabribe-com-a-website-that-encourages-indians-to-share-their-bribe-giving-experiences/articleshow/17443931.cms

12 India Has A 'Zero Rupee Note' And It Is To Be Given To Corrupt Officials Who Ask You For A Bribe', http://www.indiatimes.com/culture/who-we-are/india-has-a-zero-rupee-note-and-it-is-to-be-given-to-corrupt-officials-who-ask-you-for-a-bribe-252089.html

13 http://www.janaagraha.org/i-paid-a-bribe/

14 http://www.transparencyindia.org/

◆

Shashvat Singh is a Young Professional in the Infrastructure (Connectivity) vertical at NITI Aayog.

6

Single Black, Double Black: Land and Real Estate

BIBEK DEBROY

The expression 'black money' is used indiscriminately. One of the early studies on India's black economy was conducted by NIPFP in 1985 for the Ministry of Finance.[1] This made two points that should be obvious, but are not always appreciated in the discourse and debate. First, there are three different senses in which the word 'black' is used and they are not synonymous. The act that leads to the generation of income may itself be illegal, that is, a crime may have been committed. Because of that act of illegality, this can be called 'double black'. Alternatively, the activity that leads to the generation of income may not per se be illegal, but relevant taxes may not have been paid. This belongs to the 'single black' category. In addition, there is the macroeconomic notion of 'black' being something that has not been captured in any measurement of national income. India is still an economy that is informal and unorganized. Though it is possible to draw a distinction between the terms 'formal' and 'organized'[2], for our purposes, they can be regarded as interchangeable. Formalization is positively correlated with economic development. Having said this, there is not much point citing figures on the extent of formalization, since that is a function of the indicator used. However, a high share of the informal sector means that there are imperfections in data collection and, consequently, national income numbers can be under-estimated.[3] But informal is not the same as double black or single black. A high share of informal in national income is not the same as a high share of black in national income. In addition, national income is the annual value of goods and services produced in an economy. There must be a component of value addition. Transfer payments do not bring in value and, therefore, do not figure in national income computations. Many instances of bribery and corruption, cited commonly, are transfer payments. Also, there is a difference between creation of new black income, which is a flow, and the existing stock of black wealth, which is a stock. It is pertinent to move beyond macroeconomic estimates and focus on one particular segment—land and real estate.

In 2008, the Centre for Media Studies (CMS) and Transparency International jointly brought out 'India Corruption Study', with a specific focus on BPL (below poverty line) households.[4] This covered eleven public services, one of which was land records/registration. Across these eleven services, in terms of prevalence of corruption, land records/registration was second, right after police. According to the study, 'Land records form the basis for assignment and settlement of land titles. As a part of administration, land records are maintained at the village, tehsil and district levels. Record of Rights (ROR) serves as the legal title to the land for the cultivator. Certified records are needed to obtain credit and to transact (sale/purchase/mortgage) in land more quickly, safely and cheaply. At the State level, the work relating to Land Administration is handled by the Revenue Department. The Department of Registration looks after the registration of the sale/purchase land. At the taluk or tehsil level, the officer in charge of maintenance of land records is called the Tehsildar in most States. At the circle level, the functionary in charge is called Revenue Inspector, Circle Inspector or Kanungo, who usually supervises the work of Village Accountants (VA).

The Village Accountant, who is in charge of a single village or a group of villages, forms the base of the land administration. The villagers usually approach the Village Accountant/ Revenue Inspector for obtaining a copy of land records and to undertake a field visit to speed up the process of mutation. The public approaches the circle/tehsil level office for obtaining land records (ROR), file petitions for partition of land and mutation requests. Owners visit the office of the revenue department for the purpose of paying land revenue. Certificates such as Caste Certificate, Income Certificate, Residential Certificate, Birth and Death Certificate and Legal Heir certificate are issued by the Revenue Officials on request by citizens. For the registration of land, people approach the Sub-registrar office. People from all sections, including BPL households, visit the revenue and registration department to avail the land related services.'

Strictly speaking, the Revenue Department should only be concerned with land records (required for obtaining bank loans, mutations, partitions, inheritance and sales). Services like income and caste certificates should have nothing to do with the department. But they have been unnecessarily bundled with other services. Why did bribes have to be paid? 'For the BPL households, too many procedures especially for doing mutation and land registration implied ambiguity in getting the work done and which means scope for corruption. For more than one-fourth of the BPL household, procedural complexity leading to confusion and delay was another problem.'

What does one do to reduce these kinds of corruption? Some version of the Robert Klitgaard formula will inevitably crop up.[5] The original formula stated, C = M+D-A. Corruption = Monopoly+Discretion-Accountability. The United Nations Development Programme (UNDP) refines the formula a bit more.[6] Corruption = Monopoly+Discretion-(Accountability+Integrity +Transparency). For land revenue departments, corruption will decline if the department's monopoly declines and there is greater accountability, integrity and transparency, with reduced discretion. One of the early reports on the undesirable effects of controls and subsidies was the one by the Dagli Committee.[7] In the segment of housing and construction, it particularly looked at rent control legislation, the now repealed Urban Land (Ceiling and Regulation) Act, municipal laws and building plans. More important than these sectors was the broad philosophical thrust of the committee. 'Among the many sources of black money generation, the regime of controls has been an important one… An important point of note is that quite apart from the fact that controls where not effective have not benefited the consumer, an important consequence is the loss of revenue for Government arising from the difference between the actual price and the invoice price, the latter having to be limited to the price permitted under the control system. It is for this reason that the Committee has recommended non-discretionary controls to the extent possible… Quite frequently, the control laws are too complex to be understood by the common man and this has led to the generation of black money.' Even though there was no formula, the points were all covered. Perhaps there is only one additional issue. All the points mentioned cover improvements in the supply side of land-related services. Though demand and supply are not neat silos, behavioural changes on the demand side can act as a countervailing force and curb corruption.

Major Reforms

The Ministry of Rural Development had a centrally sponsored (with 100 per cent Union government funding) scheme, Computerization of Land Records (CLRs). There was a separate centrally sponsored scheme, Strengthening of Revenue Administration and Updating of Land Records (SRA & ULRs).

In 2008, these were spliced into the Digital India Land Records Modernization Programme (DILRMP), with components of computerization of land records, surveys/resurveys and computerization of registration. Once implemented fully, as by-products, there will be automated and automatic mutation, integration between textual and spatial records, inter-connectivity between revenue and registration and a replacement of the present deeds registration and presumptive titling system with conclusive titling and title guarantees. Table 1 shows the statewise physical progress of DILRMP as of 16 March 2016.[8]

Table 1. Statewise Physical Progress of DILRMP

Activity	States/Union territories that have completed the activity
Computerization of land records (31 States/UTs)	Andhra Pradesh, Chhattisgarh, Gujarat, Goa, Haryana, Himachal Pradesh, Karnataka, Madhya Pradesh, Maharashtra, Odisha, Punjab, Rajasthan, Sikkim, Telangana, Tamil Nadu, Tripura, Uttar Pradesh, Uttarakhand, Dadra & Nagar Haveli, Daman & Diu, Puducherry, Bihar, Jharkhand, Kerala, Assam, Manipur (partial), West Bengal (partial), Andaman and Nicobar (partial), Chandigarh (partial), Delhi (partial), Lakshadweep (partial)
Computerization of property registration (30 States/UTs)	Andhra Pradesh, Assam, Bihar, Gujarat, Goa, Haryana, Himachal Pradesh, Jharkhand, Karnataka, Kerala, Maharashtra, Madhya Pradesh, Odisha, Punjab, Rajasthan, Sikkim, Tamil Nadu, Telangana, Tripura, Uttar Pradesh, Uttarakhand, West Bengal, Chandigarh, Dadra Nagar Haveli, Delhi and Puducherry, Daman and Diu, Manipur (partial), Andaman & Nicobar (partial), Lakshadweep (partial)

Integration of land records and property registration (11 States/UTs)	Andhra Pradesh, Gujarat, Haryana, Himachal Pradesh, Karnataka, Maharashtra, Odisha, Tripura, Telangana and Puducherry (partial), West Bengal (partial)
Stoppage of manual issue of Record of Rights (RORs) (18 States/UTs)	Chhattisgarh, Gujarat, Goa, Haryana, Karnataka, Madhya Pradesh, Maharashtra, Andhra Pradesh, Odisha, Punjab, Sikkim, Tamil Nadu, Telangana, Tripura, Uttar Pradesh, Uttarakhand, West Bengal (partial) and Puducherry
RORs on the Web (22 States/UTs)	Andhra Pradesh, Chhattisgarh, Gujarat, Goa, Haryana, Himachal Pradesh, Karnataka, Madhya Pradesh, Maharashtra, Odisha, Punjab, Rajasthan, Tamil Nadu, Telangana, Tripura, Uttar Pradesh, Uttarakhand, Dadra Nagar Haveli, Puducherry, West Bengal, Bihar, Jharkhand
Bhu-naksha customization done (15 States/ UTs)	Assam, Bihar, Chhattisgarh, Haryana, Himachal Pradesh, Jharkhand, Madhya Pradesh, Maharashtra, Nagaland, Odisha, Rajasthan, Sikkim, Tripura, Uttar Pradesh, Mizoram
Digitally signed RORs (7 States/ UTs)	Goa, Karnataka, Andhra Pradesh, Telangana, Uttar Pradesh, Tripura, Rajasthan
Integration of Bhunaksha with ROR and as a service to the public on the website (5 States/ UTs)	Madhya Pradesh, Chhattisgarh, Tripura, Odisha, Jharkhand
Linking with Aadhaar (5 States)	Andhra Pradesh, Telangana, Haryana, Tripura, Maharashtra Provision in the software for capturing Aadhaar-Himachal Pradesh

Capacity building (19 States/UTs)	Gujarat, Sikkim, West Bengal, Puducherry(UT), Uttarakhand, Odisha, Haryana, Himachal Pradesh, Maharashtra, Tripura, Arunachal Pradesh, Rajasthan, Nagaland, Mizoram, Andaman & Nicobar, Lakshadweep, Uttar Pradesh, Bihar and Andhra Pradesh

Admittedly, this is work in progress. But there have been improvements in several states. For instance, in the land records modernization strand, one can mention Bhoomi (Karnataka), HALRIS (Haryana Integrated Land Records and Registration), Mee Seva (Andhra Pradesh), the cadastral survey in Gujarat, survey and settlement in Jammu and Kashmir, modern record rooms in Rajasthan, Bhu-naksha in Chhattisgarh, Haryana, Madhya Pradesh, Himachal Pradesh and Uttar Pradesh and Him Bhoomi in Himachal Pradesh.[9]

A few important points need to be made about land markets:[10] (1) Land laws are primarily a State subject and there is a bundle of land rights, of which, ownership is only one. (2) There is a titling issue, which establishes who owns the land. (3) There is a separate land mapping/record-keeping issue, where land is clearly identified in transactions concerning land and/or property. (4) The cadastral surveys are old and dated and there are multiple agencies involved in the same. (5) In general, there are multiple and uncoordinated government agencies concerned with land records—Revenue Department, Survey and Settlements Department and Registration Department. (6) The land titling system is presumptive and not conclusive. Hence, one can neither validate titles, nor is there a system of title insurance. Not all land-related transactions have to be compulsorily registered under the Registration Act of 1908.[11]

Land Titling

According to D.C. Wadhwa, one of the first people to highlight the issue[12], 'There are millions of small, illiterate, backward, poor farmers in our country whose only evidence of title to their holdings is the entry in the record-of-rights in land maintained by the state governments. But the entire exercise is drained of all significance if this entry in the record-of rights in land has only a presumptive value. If they are dispossessed of whatever little they have in the form of small pieces of land, which is happening in all parts of the country, the poor fellows are pitted against the might of the mighty and do not get back their lands. Rights in land also carry with them, as a necessary concomitant, the right to have those rights recorded in the records maintained by the government, as conclusive proof of their ownership. This is not happening with the result that the rights of the poor are being allowed to go by the state's default. In a welfare state, the state must protect those who cannot protect themselves. Under the system of conclusive title to land, the record maintained by the government is an authoritative record and the state accepts the responsibility for the validity of the entries in the record. The state guarantees title to land. This system does away with the need for investigation of title to land by the buyers.'

At that time, Professor Wadhwa had every reason to be pessimistic. However, on land titling, there is every reason to be a bit more optimistic now. The Union government committee[13] set up to indicate a roadmap for land titling states, 'Starting with One Man Commission under Prof. D.C. Wadhwa, titling has been talked in India, now and then from 1986 onwards though not on a serious scale and intensity. The first serious attempt by any Government in the country was by the Government of Andhra Pradesh, when they issued a Government Order promulgating it to be the policy of the State to introduce the

Torrens System and starting a pilot for it. They designed a comprehensive project, starting with resurvey and containing titling, legal reforms and administrative re-engineering. They also went ahead and drafted a law for bringing in the concept of titling in India that would later become the model for others including Government of India to follow. It was only in 2008 that the Government of India declared Torrens System to be the ultimate objective under the National Land Records Modernization Programme (NLRMP)[14]. Under this programme, the Government of India set up a committee to suggest legislation for the purpose of titling, apart from a Core Technical Advisory Group to look into other aspects of NLRMP. Meanwhile some other state governments also made an effort at it. The Rajasthan Government went and issued an ordinance for title certification in the year 2007 which later lapsed without much action under it. The Delhi Government also attempted to draft a law and stopped at that.'[15] The intention can be further gauged from the fact that, 'There are three principles which form the basis of a conclusive titling system i.e. Curtain, Mirror and Single Agency. The essence of the Curtain principle is that once a title is registered in the title register, a curtain falls on all the past transactions on the property and the past history or transactions cannot affect the rights of the current title holder, unless and until they are mentioned as restrictions on the current rights. In other words, the rights of the current title holder is indefeasible and cannot be questioned on the basis of defects, if any, created by past history. The essence of the Mirror principle is that the record related to land should always reflect a true and faithful picture of the realities on the ground. This is true of both cadastral and textual records. To ensure that the graphical records, textual records and registration records (related to any transaction in the property) are in tune with one another, it is essential that they are unified and a single agency maintains and operates it. Conclusive titling becomes guaranteed tilting once the element of insurance is introduced. In the guaranteed tilting model, the government not only keeps the records as per the principles of conclusive titling, but also compensates a person who incurs loss due to a wrong entry in the records.' Admittedly, the initiatives are incremental and it is still a work in progress. But in states like Haryana, Uttar Pradesh, Maharashtra, Chhattisgarh, Andhra Pradesh and Telangana, land records are already available online and are being linked to Aadhaar numbers. While a land titling Act is still pending at the level of the Union government, in 2016, Rajasthan became the first state to pass the Rajasthan Urban Land (Certification of Titles) Act.

Land Conversions

Land titling takes care of only one element of corruption associated with land. There is also the element of purchase of agricultural land and its conversion to non-agricultural use, inevitable in any process of development. While development requires such conversion, the problem lies in the non-transparency associated with the process. It is difficult to generalize, because laws vary widely from state to state, on the purchasing part. While some states stipulate that agricultural land can only be sold to farmers, others have no such stipulation. When there is such a stipulation, the farmer's certificate is subject to manipulation, quite apart from the phenomenon of it being bypassed through the leasing route. Once purchased, there is a 'change of land use' policy for converting agricultural land into residential or industrial land. Because there is inherent subjectivity in permitting such conversion, injecting transparency is more difficult.

Inside the Property Market

The White Paper on black money prepared by the Ministry of Finance in 2012[16] states, 'The real estate sector in India constitutes about 11 per cent of the GDP. Investment in property is a common means of parking unaccounted money and a large number of transactions in real estate are not reported or are under-reported. This is mainly on account of very high levels of property transaction taxes, commonly in the form of stamp duty. High transaction taxes in property are one of the biggest impediments to the development of an efficient property market. With tax rates of over 5 per cent being imposed as stamp duty on buying of property, which otherwise also involves high transactions costs in terms of search, advertising, commissions, registration, and contingent costs related to title disputes and litigation, the property market remains one of the most inefficient asset markets in India. As per the division of powers between the states and the centre, the real estate sector has largely been left to the state governments to regulate and tax. Even after the 73rd and 74th amendments to the Constitution of India which recognized local rural and urban bodies as the third tier of government, the power to legislate with respect to real estate properties and transactions therein remains with the states. …The role of the central government in reforms of the real estate sector is generally limited and advisory in nature. However, this has not prevented the Government of India from initiating steps to incentivize reforms. Its flagship programme, the Jawaharlal Nehru National Urban Renewal Mission (JNNURM), being implemented since 2005-06, aims to support urban infrastructural development by providing both monetary and non-monetary support, for reforms in different sectors of the local economy. It includes reforms of the stamp duty regime to restrict it to no more than 5 per cent. Some states have carried out this reform, but others are still persisting with very high stamp duty regimes. For states that are resource constrained, there is a case for identifying and implementing adequate revenue-neutral substitutes to facilitate the rationalization of stamp duties. There are many other pending reforms required for the emergence of an efficient competitive real estate market. These include repeal of the Urban Land Ceiling Regulation Act (ULCRA), reforms of the Rent Control Act that will balance the interests of tenants and owners and free properties of its distortions, revision of bye-laws to streamline the approval process for construction of buildings, development of sites, simplification of legal and procedural frameworks for conversion of land from agricultural to non-agricultural purposes, introduction of the Property Title Certification System in Urban Local Bodies, introduction of computerized process of registration of land and property, introduction of e-governance in local administration and tax payments, creation of computerized fiscal cadastres and rationalization of property tax designs. … The current provisions of the direct tax legislation provide for mandatory furnishing of the tax identification number by the buyer and seller of an immovable property if the value exceeds ₹5 lakh. Also, every registry of property is required to furnish annually information regarding transactions in immovable property if the value exceeds ₹30 lakh. However, as many registrar offices still operate on a manual system, there are a number of gaps and lapses in the reporting of such transactions. …One of the measures for deterring use of the real estate sector for generation and investment of black money could be the provision of deducting tax at source on payments made on real estate transactions and mandating it as a pre-condition for registering of the transacted property. The provisions of tax collected at source on the developers of the property can also be considered as a possible policy measure.'

As Table 2 shows, stamp duties vary widely from state to state.[17] They do indeed need to be reduced. Subsequently, from 1 June 2013, TDS (tax deducted at source) at the rate of 1 per cent has to be deposited by the buyer and deducted from the price paid to the seller, provided the immoveable property is not on agricultural land and costs more than ₹50 lakhs.[18]

The Real Estate (Regulation and Development) Act of 2016 has been passed.[19] The real estate sector is fragmented and unorganized, prone to cash transactions, which in turn, has a correlation if not with double black, then certainly with single black. At a broad brush level of generalization, the Real Estate (Regulation and Development) Act makes the sector more organized and less prone to cash transactions. An unorganized to organized sector transition also makes laws (and regulations) easier to enforce. There are new sections like 269ST and 271DA in the Income Tax Act, curbing the use of cash, including that for real estate transactions. The Benami Transactions (Prohibition) Amendment Act of 2016 has been passed. There is also the cleansing associated with the demonetisation exercise of 8 November 2016, both in terms of creation of new black income and destroying the stock of black wealth, cash and non-cash.

Estimation of Black Money

In addition to the study by the NIPFP, three more studies have been conducted on the estimation of black money. These include a revised version by the NIPFP submitted in 2013, one conducted by NCAER in 2014 and a study undertaken by the National Institute of Financial Management (NIFM), also submitted in 2014. These reports are now with a Parliamentary Panel. Whenever these reports are in the public domain, they will serve a limited utility because they will be outdated, unlike the many recent initiatives to curb single and double black in land and real estate.

Table 2. Stamp Duties in States

State	Stamp Duty and Registration Fee			Source
	Criteria	Stamp Duty	Registration Fees	
Andhra Pradesh	Sale Deed	4%	0.50%	Andhra Pradesh Government website (March 2014)
	Conveyance Deed (gift, mortgage, lease etc.)	5%	0.50%	
Maharashtra	Within Municipal Corporation boundary	5%	1%	Money Control website (Since April 2012)
	Within Municipal Council boundary	4%	1%	
	Within Gram Panchayat boundary	3%	1%	
Odisha	None	7%	2%	Odisha Government website (March 2014)
Tamil Nadu	None	7%	1%	Tamil Nadu Government website (March 2014)
Karnataka	None	5%	1%	Karnataka Government website (March 2014)
Goa	None	7%	1%	Goa Government website (March 2014)
Gujarat	None	3.50%	1.05%	Gujarat Government website (March 2014)

Rajasthan	General			5%	1%	Rajasthan Government website (March 2014)
	Female			4%	1%	
	Disabled			4%	1%	
Punjab	None			6%	1%	Punjab Government website (March 2014)
Haryana	Sale Deed	Within Municipal boundary	Male	7%	From ₹1 – ₹50,000 It is ₹100. From ₹50,001 – ₹1,00,000 it is ₹500. From ₹1,00,001 – ₹5,00,000 it is ₹1,000. From ₹5,00,001 – ₹10,00,000 it is ₹5,000. From ₹10,00,001-₹20,00,000 it is ₹10,000. From ₹20,00,001-₹2500000 it is ₹12,500. Above ₹25 Lacs it is ₹ 15,000.	Haryana Government website (March 2014)
			Female	5%		
		Outside Municipal boundary	Male	5%		
			Female	3%		
	Conveyance Deed	Within Municipal boundary		7%		
		Outside Municipal boundary		5%		
Uttar Pradesh	None			12.50%	2%	Uttar Pradesh Government website (March 2014)
Delhi	Male			5%	1%	Delhi Government website (March 2014)
	Female			3%	1%	
Madhya Pradesh	None			8%	1%	Madhya Pradesh Government (March 2014)

Chhattisgarh	None	7.50%	1%	Chhattisgarh Government website (March 2014)
Jharkhand	None	4%	3%	Jharkhand Government website (March 2014)
West Bengal	Within Municipal boundary	6%	1.10%	West Bengal Government website (March 2014)
	Outside Municipal boundary	5%	1.10%	
Manipur	None	4%	3%	Mizoram Government website (March 2014)
Sikkim	None	4%	3%	Sikkim Government website (March 2014)

Over the years, CMS has undertaken several studies on corruption in the delivery of public services, including the latest report in 2017 after demonetisation.[20] However, as pointed out by CMS, a caveat is in order. 'It is pertinent to mention that the "demonetization phase" as one may call the period starting 8 November, 2016 did not have much effect on the main findings of the study. Reason being the reference period for the study is "during last one year" prior to the survey and hence a major part of the reference period was before the "notebandi". Also, it is important to understand that the focus of all rounds of CMS-ICS since beginning (2000) is to capture corruption prevailing in G2C (Government to Citizen) phase i.e. at service delivery end, which is by and large observed to be petty (or retail) in nature, where the money paid as bribe, in majority of the cases, is not in the denomination of the currency (Rs 1000 and 500) barred for legal tendering since November 10, 2016. In short, demonetization phase has no or minimal effect on the findings of CMS-ICS 2017 on petty corruption.' CMS surveys cover ten public services and one of these is land/housing. The CMS methodology also covers perception, experience and estimation of corruption. Despite the caveat, Table 3, from CMS 2017, shows that citizens perceive demonetisation has reduced corruption. It must be underlined that November 2016 was only one piece in the broader jigsaw of institutional cleaning up, which includes land and real estate.

Table 3. Households' Perception of Corruption in Public Service during Demonetisation (in %)

State	Increased	Decreased	Remained same
Andhra Pradesh	28	40	32
Assam	7	67	27
Bihar	4	65	31

Chhattisgarh	4	73	23
Delhi	7	67	26
Gujarat	7	87	6
Haryana	13	53	34
Himachal Pradesh	-	38	62
Jammu & Kashmir	10	38	52
Jharkhand	11	63	26
Karnataka	11	61	28
Kerala	13	60	27
Madhya Pradesh	6	56	38
Maharashtra	25	50	25
Odisha	15	55	30
Punjab	6	44	50
Rajasthan	7	80	13
Tamil Nadu	6	56	38
Uttar Pradesh	20	60	20
West Bengal	40	33	27
All states average	12	56	32

References

1 'Aspects of the Black Economy in India', National Institute of Public Finance and Policy, 1985.

2 Such issues were discussed in various reports and working papers of the erstwhile National Commission for Enterprises in the Unorganized Sector, especially between 2006 and 2008.

3 See, for example, the 2001 Report of the National Statistical Commission (the Rangarajan Commission).

4 'India Corruption Study—2008: With Special Focus on BPL Households', Centre for Media Studies and Transparency International India, 2008.

5 R. Klitgaard. 1988. *Controlling Corruption*. Oakland, California:

University of California Press.

6 'Mainstreaming Anti-Corruption in Development', United Nations Development Programme, 2008, http://www.pogar.org/publications/ac/books/practicenote08-e.pdf

7 'Report of the Committee on Controls and Subsidies', 1979, better known as the Dagli Committee, after the Chairman, Vadilal Dagli.

8 http://dolr.nic.in/dolr/downloads/pdfs/DILRMP%20Physical%20Progress%202016-03-16.pdf

9 See http://dolr.nic.in/dolr/downloads/pdfs/revenue_ministers_document.pdf

10 Though written in a different context, that of credit generation and collateral, there is an excellent discussion in: K.P. Krishnan, V. Panchapagesan & M. Venkataraman, 'Distortions in land markets and their implications to credit generation in India', Indira Gandhi Institute of Development Research, February 2016, http://www.igidr.ac.in/pdf/publication/WP-2016-005.pdf

11 Section 18 of the Registration Act has instances where registration of documents is optional.

12 D.C. Wadhwa, 'Guaranteeing Title to Land: The Only Sensible Solution', Gokhale Institute of Politics and Economics, 2002, http://siteresources.worldbank.org/INTINDIA/Resources/dc_wadhwa_paper.pdf

13 'Land Titling – A Road Map: Report of the Expert Committee formed by Government of India', February 2014.

14 National Land Records Modernization Programme.

15 Ibid.

16 'Black Money', Ministry of Finance, May 2012, http://finmin.nic.in/reports/WhitePaper_BackMoney2012.pdf

17 This information is sourced from https://www.commonfloor.com/guide/stamp-duty-and-registration-fee-in-states-41750.html and may be slightly dated. However, the point about interstate variations and high stamp duties will remain.

18 Under Section 194-IA of the Income Tax Act.

19 However, most states are yet to notify rules under this Act. At the time of writing, 13 states and Union Territories have done so.

20 'CMS-India Corruption Study 2017', CMS, http://cmsindia.org/sites/default/files/Monograph_ICS_2017.pdf

◆

Bibek Debroy is Chairman of the Economic Advisory Council to the Prime Minister and Member of NITI Aayog.

7

Tackling Black Money through Benami Transactions

SUPARNA JAIN AND APARAJITA GUPTA

Post demonetisation, Prime Minister Narendra Modi, in December 2016, made a strong statement to operationalize the Prohibition of Benami Property Transactions Act, 1988, a law which, till date, has remained a paper tiger. He said, 'We will take action against benami property. This is [a} major step to eradicate corruption and black money.' This statement assumes significance owing to the size of the parallel economy in India. As per a World Bank study, 'Shadow Economies All over the World', India's parallel economy was around ₹15 lakh crore in 2010 and rose to around ₹28 lakh crore in 2013, as per another study conducted on the directions of the Government of India.[1]

Understanding Benami Transactions

A benami transaction means purchasing or holding of property in another person's name. Literally, the term benami means 'without name'. The key feature of these transactions is that there is no intention to benefit the benamidar, that is, the person in whose name the transaction is made. Though he has the title of the property in his name, the beneficial ownership of the property does not vest in him but in the real owner. The term ‘property’ covers movable, immovable, tangible and intangible property. Therefore, other than land and houses, shares, debentures, bonds, bank accounts, deposit receipts and negotiable instruments are capable of being held as benami.

The practice of holding benami properties has been prevalent since the early 1800s. However, the reasons for registering properties as such have varied across time. Before Independence, benami properties were purchased for evading taxation, defrauding creditors or family members and avoiding political and social risks.[2] Post Independence, though the same factors remained in force, the legislation relating to ceiling of land holdings by zamindars further incited landlords to secure their rights through benami transactions in the names of their tenants. Over the past few decades, these transactions have increased owing to corruption and black money, which is usually hidden for taxation purposes, by investments in real estate. This was also observed by the 2nd ARC which found that the wealth accumulated by corrupt officers is hidden either in benami accounts or spent in buying property in the names of others.[3]

British Law on Managing Benami Transactions

Way back in 1884, benami transactions were so widespread that it was noted that even a drastic law would not be able to uproot it.[4] Several cases came up before the Federal Courts and the Privy Council on issues relating to benami transactions.[5] The British followed two different approaches in managing this menace. Jurisprudentially, such transactions were not treated as illegal as purchase in a third person’s name was seen as one of the most common form of trusts.[6] The general (though not absolute) principle followed was when a person purchases property in the name of a third person, a ‘trust results’ in favour of the purchaser or his representative, and the beneficial interest in the property 'results' to the true purchaser. In 1915, this was clarified by Lord George Farwell who held that, 'So long, therefore, as a benami transaction does not contravene the provisions of the law, the courts are bound to give it effect. As already observed, the benamidar has no beneficial interest in the property or business that stands in his name; he represents, in fact, the real owner, and so far as their relative legal position is concerned, he is a mere trustee for him.'[7] In a subsequent case, the court held that a benamidar is not a trustee in the strict sense of the term. He has the ostensible title to the property standing in his name, but the property does not vest in him but is vested in the real owner. He is only a name lender or an *alias* for the real owner.[8] The court also distinguished between the a trustee under the English law and benamidar on grounds that a trustee is a legal owner of the property standing in his name and the cestui que trust is only a beneficial owner whereas in the case of a benami transaction, the real owner has got the legal title though the property is in the name of the benamidar. However, in another judgement the court gave a contradictory interpretation and held that a benamidar holds the property as a trustee for the beneficiary...as a legal owner; a beneficiary has the right to sue for possession against a trespasser.[9]

However, legally, way back in early 1800s, Regulation 11 of 1822 empowered the government to cancel and annul benami purchases made at a sale for arrears of revenue.[10] Subsequently, Act 12 of 1841 provided that any suit brought to oust a certified purchaser as aforesaid on the grounds that the purchase was made on behalf of another person and not the certified purchaser, would be dismissed even though the certified purchaser's name was used by agreement. In the latter part of the nineteenth century, the laws that were enacted recognized benami transactions as valid. They, however, built safeguards to avoid misuse of such transactions.

In this regard, the Transfer of Property Act, 1882, the pre-Independence law governing purchase and sale of property, is the key statute. Though the term benami is not used in this law, it recognizes such transactions and safeguards the rights of the actual owners, while at the same time making suitable provisions for protecting the rights of creditors in case benami transactions are made to deceive them. To elaborate, this law does not mandate that the 'transfer' *in favour of one person* may not be *in the name of another person*. Section 5 of this law states that 'transfer of property' means an act by which a living person conveys property, in present or in future, to one or more other living persons, or to himself, or to himself and one or more other living persons.' The right of the owner of the property is also recognized under Section 41 which provides that where, with the consent, express or implied, of the persons interested in immoveable property, a person is the ostensible owner of such property and transfers the same for consideration, the transfer shall not be voidable on the ground that the transferor was not authorised to make it: provided that the transferee, after taking reasonable care to ascertain that the transferor had power to make the transfer, has acted in good faith. This law provides that transfers of immoveable property made with intent to defeat or delay the creditors can be stalled by the creditors.[11]

The Indian Trusts Act, 1882, is another key statute that regulated benami transactions.[12] Section 81 of this law provided that where the owner of the property transfers or bequeaths it and it cannot be inferred consistently with the attending circumstances that he intended to dispose of the beneficial interest therein, the transferee must hold such property for the benefit of the owner or his legal representative. Similarly, Section 82 provided that where property is transferred to one person by another and it appears that such person did not intend to pay or provide such consideration for the benefit of the transferee, the transferee must hold the property for the benefit of the person paying or providing the consideration. Section 84 further provided that when a property is transferred to one person for a consideration paid or provided by another person, and it appears that such other person did not intend to provide such consideration for the benefit of the transferee, the transferee must hold the property for the benefit of the person who paid or provided the consideration. Section 94 stated that cases that do not come within the scope of any of the preceding sections are those where there is no trust but the person in possession of the property does not have the whole beneficial interest therein. In such cases, he must hold the property or the benefit of the person having such interest or the residue thereof (as the case may be) to the extent necessary to satisfy their demands.

Recognizing that benami transactions were being resorted to for dishonest purposes, subsequently, when the Code of Civil Procedure 1908 (CPC) was being enacted, the legislature put in provisions to discourage benami purchases. The CPC provides that no suit shall be maintained against the purchaser on the ground that the purchase was made on behalf of the plaintiff unless he can prove that the name of the said purchaser was inserted in the sale certificate fraudulently or without his consent.[13]

The Indian Penal Code, 1860 (IPC) also makes specific provisions for punishing fraudulent dealings with and disposition of property[14], including dealings intended to defeat execution[15] which are wide enough to cover benami transactions. A person who dishonestly or fraudulently removes, conceals or delivers to any person, without adequate consideration, any property, intending thereby to prevent the distribution of that property according to law among his creditors or the creditors of any other person, is punished.[16]

Post-Independence Legal Set-up

Post Independence, land ceiling laws in various states stepped up benami transactions. The abolition of the zamindari system and estates and simultaneous elevation of the tiller of the land as the owner thereof promoted numerous benami transactions. The land owners whose land holdings exceeded the ceiling prescribed under the agricultural ceiling reform laws permitted the land to be held by their labour without transferring the real ownership rights. This was particularly evident in the case of a Punjab chief minister whose family held numerous benami assets, and certain industrialists who took control of companies in someone else's name. Similarly, another study done in Gujarat in Borsad taluka revealed thousands of concealed tenancies.[17]

In 1956, a committee[18] on income tax reforms recommended that in order to deter benami transactions, the benami holder should be asked to disclose the name of the beneficial owner at the time of registration, and if he failed to do so, he should be treated as the beneficial owner in law. Subsequently, the 1st ARC and later the Select Committee on Taxation Law Amendment Bill, 1969, brought up the matter of prohibiting such transactions. In 1971, Taxation Laws (Amendment) Bill was introduced, which added a new section[19] to the Income Tax Act, 1961. It provided that no suit shall be instituted in any court to enforce any right in respect of property held as benami unless the claimant has either disclosed the property in question or the income therefrom in connection with his wealth tax or income tax assessments or given notice to the income tax officer of such property.

Accordingly, the issue was put forth before the Law Commission of India in 1973 by the Union government. The Law Commission carried out a survey with state governments, high courts, bar associations, chambers of commerce and 'other interested persons and bodies'[20] and sought comments on ways to deal with benami transactions. Interestingly, very few supported the alternative of declaring these transactions as an offence, as benami transactions were entered into for honest motives, not necessarily with the intention of evading taxes or defeating credit claims. It was felt that this was a deep-rooted habit and ought to be restricted rather than prohibited. However, it was also recognized that enforcement of prohibition would be difficult since such transactions would not be evident. The Law Commission supported this feedback and suggested that benami should cease to be a part of the Indian law. They accordingly suggested that the law should refuse to recognize the benami character of transactions, without making it an offence. This means that when a property is transferred, the benamidar would become the real owner. In effect, Section 66 of the CPC, which does not recognize involuntary alienations, would then extend to voluntary transfers as well. The Law Commission also recommended certain legal provisions to tackle benami transactions. The guiding consideration of the Law Commission in making recommendations was reducing litigation arising from such transactions.

Fifteen years after the Law Commission's report, an ordinance based on these recommendations was passed in 1988. The ordinance took in all the suggestions of the 1973 report except for one deviation: it made its implementation retroactive. Therefore, the ownership of all existing benami property was to be passed on to the benamidar. This became a subject of intense protest on grounds that such transactions were previously permissible under law and the state could not snatch such rights to ownership of property.

Subsequently, the provisions of the ordinance were again brought before the Law Commission. The report supported the Ordinance and was in favour of making the law retroactive. Unlike the 1973 report, the 1988 Law Commission Report also supported prohibition of benami transaction and treating such transactions as an offence. It also suggested creating a dispute resolution mechanism and empowering recognized NGOs to complain before such bodies, which were to be empowered to investigate, with the support of legal aid authorities, and award compensation to the complainants in case the complaint was found to be frivolous. They suggested either creating a tribunal for this purpose or appointing liaison officers attached to the Gram Nyayalayas at the rural level and similar machinery at the urban level.

Following the ordinance and the Law Commission recommendations, the Benami Transactions (Prohibition) Act was finally passed in September 1988, a few days prior to the enactment of the Prevention of Corruption Act, 1988 (PCA).

Prohibition of Benami Property Transactions Act, 1988

Scheme of the law

The Prohibition of Benami Property Transactions Act, 1988, originally called the Benami Transactions (Prohibition) Act, 1988, was passed with a view to 'prohibit benami transactions and the right to recover property held benami and for matters corrected therewith or incidental thereto.'[21] This law replaced the Benami Transactions (Prohibition of the Right to Recover Property) Ordinance, 1988, and repealed Sections 81, 82 and 94 of the Indian Trusts Act, 1882, Section 66 of the CPC and Section 281A of the Income Tax Act, 1961.

The Act defines certain important terms. 'Benami transaction' has been defined as 'any transaction in which property is transferred to one person for a consideration paid or provided by another person.'[22] Further, it defines 'property' as 'property of any kind, whether movable or immovable, tangible or intangible, and includes any right or interest in such property.'[23]

It prohibits people from entering into benami transactions and specifies that violators will be punished with imprisonment (to a maximum of three years) or fine or both.[24] However, this has two exceptions. First, the Act allows a person to purchase property in his wife's or unmarried daughter's name.[25] In such cases, it presumes, unless contrary is proved, that such property has been purchased for their benefit. Second, it does not apply to securities held by a depository as a registered owner under the Depositories Act, 1996, or participant as an agent of a depository. This provision also specifies that offence of entering into benami transactions is a non-cognizable and bailable offence.

The next provision imposes a prohibition on the right to recover property that is held as benami and prevents the use of such a defence.[26] There are two exceptions to this prohibition. The first is a case where the property is held in the name of a person, who is a coparcener in a Hindu undivided family, and it is held for the coparceners' benefit. The second case is where the property is held in the name of a person who is a trustee or a person standing in a fiduciary capacity and it is held for the benefit of another person for whom the former is a trustee or stands in such capacity. Section 5 clarifies that all benami property shall be subject to acquisition by an authority and adds that no amount shall be paid for the same. This law does not affect certain laws like those relating to transfer for an illegal purpose.[27]

Legal Loopholes

Although this law was passed with the intention of checking a major problem, it also had certain loopholes. It is interesting to note that there was a dispute on whether the Act, especially its Section 4, is prospective or retrospective in nature. The Supreme Court of India, in Mithilesh Kumari and Anr. v Prem Behari Khare[28], had held the Act to be retrospective in nature. But later, this case was overruled in R. Rajagopal Reddy (dead) by L.Rs. and others v Padmini Chandrasekharan (dead) by L.Rs.[29], where the Court held that the Act only had prospective effect. So this problem seemed to have been sorted out. But many other problems still persisted.

The Standing Committee on Finance (2015–16), in its 28th Report, titled 'The Benami Transactions Prohibition (Amendment) Bill, 2015', conducted a detailed study of this law. It also identified the problems in the Act that made it necessary to amend it. According to the Standing Committee, the law suffered from four major infirmities: (1) powers of the civil court had not been conferred on the authority; (2) there were no provisions to vest the confiscated property in the central government; (3) there was a need to define an appropriate appellate structure and bar civil court jurisdiction against actions of the authorities under this law; (4) there was a need to provide for matters of procedure like its administration, notice of hearing to concerned parties, service of notice and orders, competent authority's power on gathering of evidence, to name a few.

Therefore, the Standing Committee noted that on account of all the problems in the law, rules could not be formulated without having a comprehensive law repealing the existing one.[30] Thus, a bill was drafted to amend the law.

Benami Transactions Prohibition (Amendment) Bill, 2015

The Benami Transactions Prohibition (Amendment) Bill, 2015, was introduced in the Lok Sabha on 13 May 2015. It was then referred to the Standing Committee which gave its report on 28 April 2016, following which the government proposed amendments to the Bill on 22 July 2016. Finally, the Bill was passed by both the Houses of Parliament and got the presidential assent.

A look at the number of provisions in the Bill and the Act raises an obvious question. While the Act has only nine sections, the Bill raises this number to seventy-two. This is puzzling. The Standing Committee began its report with an explanation that initially a new draft was prepared which would replace the Act. It contained a provision that any benami transaction between 1988 and the date when the proposed law comes into force, would be covered by the new law. But the Ministry of Law opined that such a provision would go against Article 20[31] of the Constitution of India and therefore could not be incorporated. This would have meant that benami transactions between the said period would have gone unpunished. To prevent such a situation, the Ministry of Law suggested that to cover the benami transactions of the said period, it was advisable to amend the Act rather than replace it by a new one.

Among the important provisions of this Bill, it changed the title of the Act to Prohibition of Benami Property Transactions Act, 1988. It modified the definition of 'benami transaction' and increased the exceptions. The modification has brought clarity to the definition by incorporating the following three kinds of transactions:

- 'transaction or an arrangement in respect of a property carried out or made in a fictitious name; or
- a transaction or an arrangement in respect of a property where the owner of the property is not aware of, or, denies knowledge of, such ownership
- a transaction or an arrangement in respect of a property where the person providing the consideration is not traceable or is fictitious'. [32]

The Bill now defines a 'benamidar' and a 'beneficial owner', reducing ambiguity. Further, it defines 'property' and 'benami property' separately. Both these definitions include the proceeds from such property. The expanded definition of property covers 'property in the converted form'. The Bill also defines 'transfer' and 'fair market value'. The latter has been defined so that it is easier to compute the fine as a percentage of the fair market value of the property.

The Bill has divided the law into several new chapters. The first one deals with preliminary matters. The second one is titled 'Prohibition of Benami Transactions'. The third chapter has provisions on authorities like the Initiating Officer, Approving Authority, Administrator and the Adjudicating Authority. The fourth chapter looks at attachment, adjudication and confiscation of property. The fifth one has provisions on the Appellate Tribunal and the sixth deals with Special Courts. Then there is a chapter on offences and prosecution and the last one has miscellaneous provisions.

There are some important changes in the provisions of the Act. Section 5 of the Act has been amended by giving the power to the central government to confiscate property. Section 6 has been amended to prohibit retransfer of property by the benamidar. The Bill now gives a detailed account of the authorities under the law along with their composition, qualifications of members and terms of service. The adjudicating authority has been given the power to regulate its own procedure and it shall be guided by principles of natural justice and not the CPC. Further, the authorities have been given the same powers as those vested in the civil courts in certain matters. Provision has also been made to seek the assistance of certain officers for enforcement of the law. These officers include income tax authorities, Customs and Central Excise Department officers, officers under Narcotic Drugs and Psychotropic Substances Act, 1985, Reserve Bank of India (RBI) officers, police personnel, officers under Foreign Exchange Management Act, 1999, and Securities and Exchange Board of India (SEBI) officers to name a few.

In the Bill, the Initiating Officer has been given the power to issue notice for attachment of property, where such officer, 'on the basis of material in his possession, has reason to believe that any person is a benamidar in respect of a property.'[33] In case the officer fears alienation of property, he has the power to provisionally attach the property after taking previous consent. A new provision has been added for adjudication of benami property where the adjudicating authority can pass orders holding the property to be benami and confirming attachment or holding it not to be benami and revoking the attachment. The adjudicating authority also has the power to provisionally attach properties other than the one referred to it by the Initiating Officer. It can also pass the order for confiscating the benami property. After such an order, the confiscated property shall vest in the central government, absolutely free from all encumbrances. Further, there will be no right of compensation in lieu of the confiscation. The Bill has given the power of receiving and managing confiscated properties to an administrator.

Next, an Appellate Tribunal is sought to be created to hear appeals against the order of the adjudicating authority. This Tribunal is not bound by the procedure laid down in the CPC and can regulate its own procedure and the principles of natural justice. Further, the Bill bars the jurisdiction of civil courts. From the decision of the Appellate Tribunal, one can appeal to the high court.

In order to have quick disposal of cases under this law, the Bill provides for designating certain Courts of Session as Special Courts. It stipulates that these Special Courts shall endeavour to conclude the trial within six months from the time the complaint has been filed.

The punishment for benami transactions has been increased to imprisonment for a maximum of seven years from three years. The minimum punishment is an imprisonment for a year. In addition, one will also be liable to pay a fine which may extend to 25 per cent of the fair market value of the property. Prosecution in respect of certain offences cannot be instituted without previous sanction of the Central Board of Direct Taxes (CBDT). Further, the offence under this law is still non-cognizable. Another important provision is that the central government has been given the power to exempt any property of a charitable or religious trust from the application of this law.

Thus, the Bill has covered the issue holistically. But its provisions have raised some concerns. These were identified by the Standing Committee in its report and it gave valuable recommendations.

Recommendations of the Standing Committee

The Standing Committee analysed the Bill and made recommendations to make the law against benami transactions stronger. Its first recommendation was to replace the expression 'out of known source of income' used in the definition of 'benami transaction' with 'out of known sources.' This is because loan funds may also be used for purchasing property and the same would have been excluded from the law as it doesn't amount to income. It added that after 'known', 'and legal' should be added to save only bona fide transactions.

Next, some representatives raised concerns over the Bill's impact on rural and urban properties. For rural areas, the Standing Committee recognized the reality of cash transactions and poor state of land records which may make it difficult for even the bona fide owners to prove their title and bona fides. To help such genuine people, it recommended that the Initiating Officer should carry out a thorough and serious enquiry before the issue goes to the adjudicating authority. To enable a detailed enquiry during which genuine owners could prove their bona fides, it recommended that the time period for the same be extended from thirty days to three months. In light of the practice in urban areas, it recommended that in cases where transfer of immoveable property is through the following means: '(i) a registered Agreement to Sale (ii) a registered irrevocable General Power of Attorney (GPA) and (iii) a registered Development Agreement on payment of stamp duty in accordance with law applicable thereto', the same shall not be deemed to be benami. In case of transfers through Power of Attorney or possession of property using a Power of Attorney and a Sale Agreement, it suggested that enough time should be given to legitimate holders of such instruments and owners under valid agreements (even if unregistered) to legitimize their ownership rights through an appropriate amnesty scheme. Next, it suggested that in cases where lenders pay the consideration under a financial arrangement, the same should be excluded from the definition of 'benami transactions'.

Since 'land' is a state subject under the 7th Schedule of the Constitution of India, some have argued that right to confiscate the benami property should be with the state government. On this issue, the Standing Committee asked the government to study it constitutionally. During the consultation, the Ministry of Finance had mentioned that the power to make law on benami property came from Entry No. 97 of the Union List which deals with, 'Any other matter not enumerated in List II or List III including any tax not mentioned in either of those Lists.' Here, it needs to be mentioned that this issue was also brought before the Law Commission of India[34] at the time of enactment of the original law in 1988. The Commission was of the view that though the power to make laws and regulate 'land', as per the state list, vests with states, 'transfer of property' (other than agricultural land) is covered in the Concurrent List.[35] Therefore using the legal doctrine of 'pith and substance'[36] they recommended that the subject would be covered under the Concurrent List and the

Parliament can legislate on the subject.

Next, the Standing Committee cautioned that the Bill should not go against Tribal Land Acts (administered by the State) in Tribal Areas and Scheduled Areas mentioned under the Constitution. The Standing Committee was of the view that adequate provisions should be added to address the extra territoriality of the Bill. It found that the Bill was silent on whether its provisions extended to benamidar, beneficial owner and people standing in fiduciary capacity or property located outside India.

On the issue of right to representation, the Standing Committee felt that such a right which is present for those filing an appeal before the Appellate Tribunal should also be there for people filing an appeal before the adjudicating authority. It also recommended that the qualification of the chairperson of the Appellate Tribunal should mandate an experience of at least five years as a high court judge.

In keeping with the times, it recommended that consequential amendments should be made to the Transfer of Property Act, 1882, and Registration Act, 1908. These include provisions for making online registration mandatory for all immoveable property, linking certain details like Aadhaar and Permanent Account Number (PAN) of all those party to the transaction and registration authorities sharing data with central agencies. It also emphasized the need to digitize land records and regularly update them, which has been implemented by land revenue departments of states like Haryana, Uttar Pradesh, Maharashtra, Chhattisgarh, Andhra Pradesh and Telangana to name a few.

In the end, it said that since the purpose of the Bill was to curb domestic black money generation (as mentioned by the finance minister in the 2015 Budget speech), the same should be mentioned in the Statement of Objects and Reasons. Further, it recommended the inclusion of 'prevention of corruption and tracking of tainted money' as supplementary objects. These were some of the major recommendations of the Standing Committee, which the government considered and incorporated in the Bill.

Benami Transactions (Prohibition) Amendment Act, 2016

The Benami Transactions (Prohibition) Amendment Act, 2016, clarifies that cases of transfer of property where certain conditions are satisfied shall not be considered as benami transactions. These conditions include payment of stamp duty and registration of contract. Next, the recommendation on replacing 'out of known source of income' with 'out of known sources' has been accepted. The confiscated property still has to vest in the central government. The recommendation on qualification of the chairperson of the Appellate Tribunal was also accepted. These are some of the changes that were made. Further, the Prohibition of Benami Property Transactions Rules, 2016, came into force on 1 November 2016, with a clear message—the amended law is in place to deal with the people who would have turned to benami transactions post demonetisation on 8 November 2016. Hopefully, with these measures and implementation of the strong law, people indulging in benami transactions will be forced to think twice.

References

1 http://www.business-standard.com/article/economy-policy/black-money-estimated-at-30-of-gdp-113011300067_1.html

2 These are the four key reasons identified by the Federal Court in Punjab Province v Daulat Singh, AIR 1942, FC, 38, 40.

3 'Ethics in Governance', 4th Report, 2nd Administrative Reforms Commission, Government of India, 2007, p. 77.

4 K.K. Bhattacharya, 'Joint Hindu Family, (Tagore Law Lectures) (1884-85)', Report 57, Law Commission of India, pp. 469–70.

5 See Gopeekrist Gosain v Gunga Persaud Gosain (1854) 6 M.I.A 53; Bilas Kunwar v Desraj Ranjit Singh (1915) I.L.R.37 Allahabad; AIR 1915 P.C. 96; Punjab Province v. Daulat Singh, AIR 1942, FC 38.

6 Dyer v Dyer (1788) 2 Cox 92.

7 Bilas Kunwar v Besraj Ranit Singh, AIIR 1915 PC 96.

8 Pitchayya v Rattamma AII 1929 Mad 268, 269.

9 Gur Prasad v Hansraj AIR. 1946 Oudh 144, 145.

10 See Sections 18 and 19 of Regulation 11 of 1822.

11 Section 53 of the Transfer of Property Act, 1882.

12 The provisions of this statute regulating benami were repealed post enactment of the Prohibition of Benami Property Transactions Act, 1988.

13 Section 66, Civil Procedure Code, 1908.

14 Sections 421–424, Indian Penal Code, 1860.

15 Sections 206 and 207, Indian Penal Code, 1860.

16 See Section 421, Indian Penal Code, 1860

17 As observed in the 130th Law Commission Report.

18 Nicholas Kaldor Committee.

19 Section 281 A, Income Tax Act, 1961

20 See 57th Law Commission Report, 1973.

21 Long Title, Prohibition of Benami Property Transactions Act, 1988.

22 Section 2(a), Prohibition of Benami Property Transactions Act, 1988.

23 Section 2(c), Prohibition of Benami Property Transactions Act, 1988.

24 Section 3, Prohibition of Benami Property Transactions Act, 1988.

25 Ibid.

26 Section 4, Prohibition of Benami Property Transactions Act, 1988.

27 Section 6, Prohibition of Benami Property Transactions Act, 1988.

28 (1989) 2 SCC 95. This is a decision of the Supreme Court of India dated 14 February 1989 available at https://www.legalcrystal.com/case/653625/mithilesh-kumar-anr-vs-prem-behari-khare, accessed on 29 March 2017.

29 AIR 1996 SC 238. This is a decision of the Supreme Court of India dated 31 January 1995 available at https://www.legalcrystal.com/case/641664/r-rajagopal-reddy-dead-l-rs-vs-padmini-chandrasekharan, accessed on 29 March 2017.

30 'Benami Transactions Prohibition (Amendment) Bill, 2015', 28th Report, Standing Committee on Finance (2015–16), April 2016.

31 Article 20: '(1) No person shall be convicted of any offence except for violation of a law in force at the time of the commission of the act charged as an offence, nor be subjected to a penalty greater than that which might have been inflicted under the law in force at the time of the commission of the offence. (2) No person shall be prosecuted and punished for the same offence more than once. (3) No person accused of any offence shall be compelled to be a witness against himself.'

32 Clause 4, Benami Transactions (Prohibition) Amendment Bill, 2015.

33 Clause 9, Benami Transactions (Prohibition) Amendment Bill, 2015.

34 130th Law Commission Report..

35 See Entry 6 in List III, 7th Schedule to the Constitution reads: 'Transfer of property other than agricultural land; registration of deeds and documents'.

36 When the question of determining whether a law refers to a particular subject (mentioned in one list or the other), the court looks to the substance of the matter. Thus if the substance falls within the Union List, then the incidental encroachment by the law on the State List does not make it invalid. (see notes to Article 246 under Constitution of India by P.M. Bakshi).

◆

Suparna Jain is an advocate engaged as Officer on Special Duty, Legal, at NITI Aayog.

Aparajita Gupta is a Young Professional under Bibek Debroy at NITI Aayog.

8

Demonetisation and Tax Reforms

DHIRAJ NAYYAR

Corruption has taken such deep roots in India that it would be impossible to eliminate it in a single stroke. No government or leader, however powerful, can halt corruption in its tracks. That is partly because it would take multiple policy initiatives to even begin to curb corruption. But it is also because vested interests, with direct and indirect links to the polity and machinery of the government, which have become strong and symbiotic over decades, have a powerful incentive to preserve the existing, rotten system for it delivers an impressive prosperity and unparalleled influence for them. It would take a bold, brave and radical decision to attack the powerful vested interests at their very foundation. And so, when history of our times is eventually written, 8 November 2016 will occupy an important place as the day Prime Minister Narendra Modi announced his decision to demonetise 86 per cent of India's currency in the form of making all high-value notes of ₹500 and ₹1,000 illegal tender. Cash is the preferred instrument of exchange for those who wish to leave no paper or electronic trail of their illicit activities. By making the store of value redundant, demonetisation caused spectacular disruption in the business of the corrupt.

The critics of demonetisation are wrong if they argue that the exercise affected in equal measure those who had not engaged in any illicit activity. For the honest, demonetisation caused temporary discomfort because currency became scarce for two months. But their money would still be their money, stored in bank accounts. There was no confiscation involved. But for those with black money, there was either deadweight loss (if they chose to destroy their illicit cash) or a heavy price (read tax and penalty) to pay if they declared it by depositing it in banks. It is difficult to imagine any other single policy measure that disrupted the activities and fortunes of all corrupt citizens in the way demonetisation did.

Beyond the Short-run

It is a folly to view the impact of demonetisation in the short-run alone, notwithstanding the oft-invoked quote from economist John Maynard Keynes, 'In the long run, we are all dead.' The history and trajectory of nations is not determined by a matter of a few weeks or months. In the short-run, it is difficult to deny that the withdrawal of 86 per cent currency from circulation hurt a majority in a country that is still used to transacting in cash, and where bank coverage, the use of plastic money (i.e. credit cards), the penetration of Internet and the spread of smartphones is still not near universal. Of course the poor and deprived were affected more than the rich who had access to other modes of payment. They were also employed in the informal sector which suffered a bigger temporary blow than organized businesses. The obvious outcome of the squeeze on economic activity in general was on GDP growth, which witnessed a minor slowdown. But, all of the adverse short-term outcomes (and these are genuinely short-term, a matter of a quarter or two at most) must be weighed against the gains which may accrue in the long-term before a final judgment is made on demonetisation.

Serious gains can be made in terms of economic growth by

curbing corruption. Rampant corruption does nothing for the ease of doing business, dissuading honest entrepreneurs, possibly driving the best of Indian entrepreneurship overseas and the best of overseas entrepreneurship to other emerging economies. It certainly raises the costs of doing business (above an already costly environment given the low quality and high prices of key infrastructure) and uncertainty for investors deterring investment in the long-run, which is the main driver of sustainable growth. India's GDP will grow faster and in a sustainable manner if the system is cleaned of its excesses and illegalities.

The corollary is that an economic system that has been eaten away by corruption is unlikely to deliver sustained high growth and prosperity. Demonetisation happened at an inflexion point in India's political economy. It was a point at which choices made by the political leadership and economic policymakers would determine whether India would finally begin to grow at double digits and catch up with China and the Asian Tigers or it would continue to trundle along in stops and starts and remain an emerging economy for a long time. In 1991, India's economy had reached breaking point. A failed tryst with statist economics over four and a half decades—a policy trend which began post Independence but accelerated in the late 1960s and early 1970s just when other nations in Asia changed track to open economies—had left the country at the brink of bankruptcy. There is little doubt that corruption had seeped into the system but it was not the causal reason for India being on the verge of default. A complex web of regulations and excessive interventions by the government had destroyed the incentives for efficient, productive economic activity. Corruption, at best, ensured the longevity of that system as a tiny clique of businessmen and officials/politicians prospered even as the rest of the country remained poor and very middle class.

The economic liberalization that began in 1991 under the

government of P.V. Narasimha Rao used the necessity of the crisis to dismantle some of the worst elements of India's socialist past, ending industrial licencing, drastically cutting rates of tariff, permitting foreign investment and beginning to create institutions for a new market economy (SEBI was a prime example). The process of liberalization was carried forward by the succeeding United Front government (which cut the top income tax rate to 30 per cent, a rate which stands till today) and the NDA government (which liberalized critical sectors like telecom and carried out strategic disinvestment of public sector companies). The market-oriented economic reforms between 1991 and 2003 yielded rich dividends, albeit with a lag. Between 2003 and 2008, India grew at near double digits every year. There was a temporary dip after the global financial crisis in 2008, but in 2010 and 2011, India was again growing at 8 per cent plus per annum. If India had sustained that growth for two more decades, poverty would have been eradicated. However, we could not sustain that growth even till 2012.

The return of a new licence raj between 2004 and 2012, which unleashed a virulent strain of crony capitalism threatened to not just stall growth but also bring into question in the public eye the legitimacy of the post-1991 market economy, which despite its flaws had delivered more prosperity to a larger number of Indians than ever before.

The fact is that the leviathan government had never completely exited from its role in exercising control over the economy. Only the turf had changed. The avenues for corruption had grown and the quantum of what could be illegitimately grafted had multiplied. The government no longer had the power to issue licences for setting up factories, but it discovered that it still had the power to give out licences for critical natural resources, like spectrum or coal or other critical minerals. As the sovereign, the government would always have control over the distribution of natural resources but whether it chooses to do so in a discretionary manner or via open competitive bidding is its choice. Liberalization had never driven corruption away even if it had closed some avenues. The rapid growth post liberalization and the resultant prosperity ensured that the very natural resources which may not have commanded much value in the pre-1991 economy now attracted huge rents and rent-seeking. In addition, the need for a massive infrastructure upgrade, whether in airports or roads, which required a public–private partnership (PPP) in the absence of sufficient finances and capacity for execution with the government, also unleased a strain of crony capitalism where profits were often private but losses socialised, and passed on to the government. The rampant crony capitalism of the decade between 2004 and 2014 is well documented in the form of the telecom spectrum scam[1], the coal block allocation scam[2] and the numerous controversies surrounding PPP projects[3].

When the scams began to unravel in the public eye towards the end of 2011, there was a spilling over of public anger and mass revulsion against corruption. The initial rise of the India Against Corruption movement (which subsequently gave birth to the populist Aam Aadmi Party) cornered the government. As investigations into wrongdoings began, a paralysis set into decision-making. A sentiment of fear scared away investors. The economy, which was growing at 9 per cent per annum decelerated to just 4.5 percent per annum in a matter of two years. This time, unlike in 1991, it was not socialism which was sending the economy into a tailspin, but a lethal strain of crony capitalism which was bred on exorbitant corruption and loot of national resources.

Such a scenario provided a fertile ground for a populist backlash against the market economy. The 2014 general elections were a pivotal political moment. Fortunately, the strongest, and ultimately victorious, campaign was led by then Gujarat Chief

Minister Narendra Modi. Among politicians, he was unique in having a reputation for total integrity combined with a pro-market policy outlook, which was evidenced in his long stint as Gujarat's chief minister. His historic mandate—the first single party majority in thirty years, based on his own probity and competence—prevented an upsurge against the private sector as a whole, the kind which was being fuelled by the populist India Against Corruption movement. To his credit, Modi was always careful to distinguish between people who wanted to do business honestly—he has consistently been pro-market—and those who sought to game the system—he has shown little inclination to be pro-business persons.

However, for the populace at large and genuine entrepreneurs to regain faith in the market economy and capitalism sans cronies, Prime Minister Modi would have always had to take decisive action. Demonetisation was the radical policy measure which helped restore the faith of the common Indian in the 'system'. It renewed belief that the system could be cleansed without overthrowing the gains which had accrued from liberalizing the economy to market forces over the years. That is the reason demonetisation found public support despite the short-term pain it caused. In the process, it has also laid the foundation of the next round of pro-market reforms that will ultimately lead India to a double-digit growth rate for a sustained period.

It is now feasible for the government to pursue genuinely pro-market policies like improving India's Ease of Doing Business ranking, removing barriers to trade and investment, encouraging start-ups and permitting bona fide failures of business through the mechanism of a new bankruptcy law. Capitalism only thrives when competition weeds out the inefficient from the efficient However, it does not survive and thrive if those who fail are consistently bailed out by the government. The argument in favour of fair capitalism and against crony capitalism must continue to be made. After his courageous step on demonetisation, Prime Minister Modi is the one politician who can make that argument with even greater credibility than before.

Cleaning Public Services

The elimination of corruption which manifests as crony capitalism is necessary to sustain a healthy, rapidly growing market economy but it is not sufficient. At India's stage of development and per capita income, simply allowing the free market to function efficiently may not be enough. The government will continue to play a pivotal role in terms of providing critical public services and redistributing resources to the poor. This is a crucial complement, probably even a foundation, to functioning and fair capitalism.

Over three decades ago, former Prime Minister Rajiv Gandhi said that for every rupee intended to reach the common man from the exchequer only 15 paise actually reached the beneficiary. It is perfectly reasonable to argue over that statistic, but evidence suggests that a significant amount of government spending intended for the poor, through a plethora of welfare schemes, simply leaks away, leading to a loss to the exchequer and the common citizen. The gains are to countless intermediaries, petty bureaucrats, touts and local politicians who ensure that money is siphoned off, at every stage, on its way down an elaborate government machinery from New Delhi to state capitals to districts to blocks to villages and then to the final beneficiary. Just as demonetisation hurt crony capitalists and their conduits in government, it has hurt and disrupted all the middlemen who had enriched themselves by siphoning cash out of a leaky system.

For India's most vulnerable, mostly away from the gaze of the national media, corruption has been a steady killer. Corruption in important government schemes like the MGNREGA, Public

Distribution System (PDS)[4] and the National Rural Health Mission (NRHM)[5] become life-and-death issues for the poor who are totally dependent on them for basic income, essential food and critical healthcare. Though the rampant corruption in these schemes does not make headlines of the kind cronyism does (2G scam or coal block scam), but they steadily erode the credibility of the government and the legitimacy of a political economy that must be based on the rule of law and fairness. It is, therefore, unsurprising that the strongest support for demonetisation has come from the poor even though the temporary shortage of cash hit them the most.

A Move Away from Cash

It is a well-known fact that India is a highly cash-dependent economy, much more than advanced economies and emerging economies.[6] A move away from cash transactions to digital transactions would reduce avenues for corruption and other illicit activities like tax evasion. The move away from cash will happen over time, but demonetisation may have provided a hard nudge in that direction. Again, the timing of demonetisation is particularly opportune. If people are to move to digital transactions, there needs to be an infrastructure that facilitates the same. Five years ago, the foundations did not exist. But a combination of technological advancement, government policy and market forces has laid the foundation for a massive push for digital transactions. The most fundamental is Aadhaar, a combination of government policy, technology and entrepreneurship within the government apparatus. The fact that one billion Indians have a unique identity number authenticated by their biometrics opens up limitless avenues to move away from cash and curb leakages and corruption in the system. Of course, for Aadhaar to make a difference, Indians needed to have bank accounts. The success of Prime Minister Narendra Modi's Jan Dhan Yojana has ensured that 98 per cent of India's households have access to at least one bank account. Apart from Aadhaar and Jan Dhan accounts, the extensive penetration of mobile phones and smartphones has played a key role. In 2010, only 20 million Indians had smartphones. This number has grown to 200 million at present and is estimated to rise to 700 million by 2020. The growing penetration of phones has been aided by continued competition in the telecom services sector, with data services being cheaper than ever before. Demonetisation will speed up technological innovation (in the form of mobile applications like BHIM), which will enable financial transactions to be conducted easily, smoothly and securely.

Demonetisation has prompted many ordinary Indians to experiment with digital transactions. The emerging architecture of digital finance will also give a major fillip to the government's attempts to move all benefits to the poor away from the leaky system India has at present to a better targeted, foolproof system of cash/benefit transfers. It is true that the government had been working on the potential of the JAM (Jan Dhan accounts, Aadhaar cards and Mobile numbers) trinity for the transfer of benefits well before demonetisation was even in the planning stage. But the speeding up of technological innovation and the change in the transaction habits of a very significant majority of Indians will undoubtedly give a fresh impetus to the JAM-based benefits transfer plan. Needless to say, it will thwart the ambitions of those whose vested interest lies in preserving the existing system.

Beyond Demonetisation: Tax Reform

The most vociferous criticism of the demonetisation exercise is that it was a failure because, in value terms, almost all the currency that was demonetised returned to the system. According to the RBI's annual report, 98.96 per cent of the ₹1,000 and ₹500 denomination banknotes that had been invalidated were returned.[7]

It certainly defied most estimates and expectations which had assumed that a significant amount of black money would be destroyed and thus would not return to the system. But this is not a failure of demonetisation. In fact, it actually shows the failure and rottenness of the system as it existed before the exercise. Corruption had become so rampant and entrenched that people were able to launder their money back into the formal banking system with the connivance of bank officials. More importantly, just because the money has found its way back into bank accounts doesn't mean that it has become legitimate. It only means that the government has to work harder to make those in possession of unaccounted money pay, quite literally, in the form of taxes and penalties. Some may do it voluntarily under the Pradhan Mantri Garib Kalyan Yojana. For others to comply, it may require penal action. Of course, once snared into the tax net, whether by force or voluntarily, hitherto tax evaders will have to pay tax every year in the future as well.

The burden of ensuring this has fallen on the tax administration system, which will be seriously tested since in the past it has hardly distinguished itself as a bulwark of either honesty or efficiency. Indeed there is plenty of evidence to suggest that very few people pay income tax in India. Of the 125 crore Indians only 1.5 per cent (1.9 crore) pay income tax. On a macroeconomic scale, India's tax to GDP ratio, which is 17.5 percent of GDP, is not only much lower than the Organization for Economic Co-operation and Development (OECD) average of 35 per cent, but also lower than in other emerging economies like Brazil (34 per cent), South Africa (27 per cent) and China (22 per cent). Worst of all, India's ratio of direct taxes (paid only by the well-off) to indirect taxes (paid equally by all) is 35:65, whereas the OECD average is the precise opposite. The regressive tax structure has burdened the poor unfairly.

Demonetisation has created the enabling environment to correct these anomalies. But it requires the tax administration to be able to pin down the wrongdoers without harassing those who pay their taxes. Every year, there is pressure on the tax administration to deliver on certain revenue targets. Given the tight fiscal situation, this is but obvious. It is easier to squeeze more out of those already in the tax net, and requires more effort to target those outside.

To achieve this, a comprehensive reform of the system of taxation and tax administration is necessary. The long history of taxes and their administration in India has been more about enforcement than compliance. The perversity of extraordinarily high tax rates (the peak marginal tax rate was 97 per cent in the 1970s) created disincentives for compliance and incentives for evasion. It also created collusion between evaders and tax officials and a culture of harassment as tax authorities amassed huge power. Instead, if India would have created a system of reasonably low tax rates, the incentive for compliance would have been high.

But it isn't high rates of direct tax alone which created distortions. There have existed a host of exemptions for particular categories of persons or corporates which provided ample opportunities for rent-seeking and corruption. While tax rates have greatly moderated over the 1990s and 2000s, the regime of exemptions has remained complex. It is to the credit of the government of Narendra Modi that there is now a commitment to further reduce tax rates (at least on the corporate side) from a peak of 30 per cent to 25 per cent, while removing exemptions over a few years. On the income tax side, the 2017–18 Budget resisted the usual political temptation of increasing the exemption limit opting instead to lower the rates for the lower taxable slab from 10 per cent to 5 per cent. The guiding principle of removing exemptions is to widen the tax net as much as possible because lowering rates creates a culture of compliance and limits the discretionary powers of tax officials.

The acutely adversarial nature of tax administration has other antagonistic consequences. The creation of uncertainty for investors and individuals is one. The infamous retrospective tax amendment of 2012 which sought to reverse an adverse court verdict in the Vodafone case destroyed the credibility of an already uncertain Indian tax environment. The litigious nature of the tax administration[8]—which despite losing cases at the tribunal level insists on filing appeals which go all the way to the highest court—causes unnecessary harassment and uncertainty while again creating opportunities for corruption and rent-seeking. While it is unlikely that any government will repeat the fiasco of the retrospective amendment, there is a need to rationalize the litigation by the tax administration. Only particularly egregious cases should be fought on appeal; in the rest, the tax administration should accept tribunal verdicts.

It is imperative to use technology to reduce the direct interface between the taxpayer and the tax administration. The entire process of filing tax returns should be computerized and completed online. The process of scrutinizing tax returns must be done using technology and advanced data analytics with little or no human discretion. The post-demonetisation scrutiny of bank accounts with anomalies will be done using technology and advanced data analytics. It is the perfect opportunity for the tax administration to show its reformist side.

The system of indirect taxes, which has also been a den of corruption and rent-seeking, will be dramatically overhauled with the implementation of the Goods and Services Tax (GST) from July 2017. The fact that a single tax will replace multiple and cascading taxes, will improve compliance. Also, since GST is imposed at the point of consumption rather than at the factory gate will reduce avenues for corruption and rent-seeking. Further, the strong IT infrastructure that will form the backbone of administering the GST will make evasion, and its corollary of collusion with tax officials, much more difficult. The reform of indirect taxes is therefore at a much more advanced stage than direct taxes. It would have helped if the GST had fewer exemptions and fewer rates (ideally a single rate) at the time of its introduction, but given India's federal structure and political economy, the best cannot be the enemy of the good.[9] Hopefully, the system will migrate to fewer exemptions and rates of tax and lower tax rates overall in the years to come.

India has a relatively high threshold for tolerating corruption. While voters, from time to time, have punished perceived or real corruption on the part of politicians and governments by ejecting them from office, there has been little in terms of radical reform of the system which sends a decisive message of zero tolerance to the corrupt. That demonetisation was a radical measure is not disputed by many. The real debate is around its efficacy as a measure to curb corruption and other illicit activities like tax evasion.

There is a danger in passing a final judgement on demonetisation too soon. It may not be necessary to wait for the proverbial long run before seeing an impact. The net of the tax authorities will soon entrap those who have laundered unaccounted cash into their bank accounts. Over a reasonable period of time, the sources of illicit funds, whether corruption or tax evasion, will be known. Action against the dishonest in the form of penalties or jail terms will be a strong deterrent for those contemplating corruption and illicit activities in the future.

In a single stroke of the pen, the drive against corruption

was elevated to a completely different level on 8 November. The exercise also provided a platform for sustainable growth, efficient delivery of essential services and, eventually, prosperity to all Indians. It also underscored the tremendous appetite of people for drastic steps against corruption. It is unlikely that the war against corruption will end with demonetisation. The battle will spill over to other spheres like tracing benami property and reforming the real estate sector which is a major hub of corruption. Other steps like electoral reform are also under way. The probability of more anti-corruption measures being implemented is higher than ever before.

References

1 See http://indiatoday.intoday.in/story/what-is-the-2g-scam-all-about/1/188832.html

2 See http://www.business-standard.com/article/companies/7-things-you-wanted-to-know-about-coalgate-113101500366_1.html

3 A committee under economist Vijay Kelkar was set up by the present government to sort out the logjams in PPP projects. See http://pib.nic.in/newsite/PrintRelease.aspx?relid=133954

4 For a summary on the corruption in mega schemes see, Surjit Bhalla, 'PDS or NREGA: Corruption Must Go On, *The Indian Express*, 1 November 2014, http://indianexpress.com/article/opinion/columns/no-proof-required-pds-or-nrega-corruption-must-go-on/

5 On the NRHM scam, see, 'Rs 5,000-cr NRHM scam resurfaces once again, *Business Standard*, 23 September 2015, http://www.business-standard.com/article/politics/rs-5-000-cr-nrhm-scam-resurfaces-once-again-115092300853_1.html

6 A report in the *Business Standard* quotes comparative statistics compiled by CLSA. See, http://www.business-standard.com/article/economy-policy/infographic-68-of-transactions-in-india-

are-cash-based-116111400495_1.html

7 Gopika Gopakumar, 'RBI says 99% of demonetised ₹500, ₹1,000 returned to banking system'; *Hindustan Times*; 31 August 2017, http://www.hindustantimes.com/business-news/rbi-says-99-of-demonetised-rs-500-rs-1000-returned-to-banking-system-after-pm-modi-s-surprise-move/story-jPFYdNpNw5nuEYcFNunknI.html

8 An estimated ₹5.5 crore was stuck in litigation in 2016. See, http://economictimes.indiatimes.com/tax-savers/tax-news/tax-litigation-income-tax-department-to-write-to-over-2-59-lakh-taxpayers/articleshow/53286921.cms

9 See Chapter 5 of the report of the Finance Commission on an ideal GST, http://fincomindia.nic.in/TFC/Chapter5.pdf

◆

Dhiraj Nayyar is Officer on Special Duty and Head of the Economics, Finance and Commerce vertical at NITI Aayog.

9

Reforming Electoral Finances

KISHORE ARUN DESAI

It will not be unfair to state that elections are the biggest driver of corruption and black money in the country today. At a recent conference[1] organized by the Association for Democratic Reforms (ADR), Dr S.Y. Quraishi, former Chief Election Commissioner of India, remarked, '...elections have become the root cause of corruption in the country...after winning elections, the politician-bureaucrat nexus indulges in "recovering the investment" and that is where corruption begins.' Politicians seek significant funds to invest in ticket distributions and campaigning. However, since elections are a regular feature in the country, the cycle of investing and scouting money never stops. And more often than not, the sources of these funds and the activities on which these are expended are not transparent. Thus, both candidates and political parties end up embracing this toxic cocktail of corruption and black money.

Corruption in elections is primarily driven by the perception that money influences outcomes. For instance, during campaigning, many politicians distribute cash, liquor, pressure cookers, or other gifts to voters. The hypothesis being that a voter's behaviour can be influenced by such illegitimate gestures. Similarly, parties may ideally want to allocate constituency tickets based on a mix of non-monetary factors—candidate winnability, caste/religion mix of the constituency etc. Despite this, the influence of 'financial contributions' from potential candidates around ticket allocations cannot be completely ruled out. Commenting on this aspect, the Law Commission of India, in its 255th Report on Electoral Reforms[2], notes, 'It is now well established that money plays a big role in politics, whether in the conduct, or campaigning, for elections. The Election Commission of India, in its guidelines issued on 29 August 2014, recognized that "concerns have been expressed in various quarters that money power is disturbing the level playing field and vitiating the purity of elections..." These are not mere theoretical debates but are actual problems afflicting the electoral process in India.'

While the law lays down boundaries to prevent electoral corruption, there are some gaps in this framework that are routinely misused by politicians. Limitation in policing and enforcing laws further enhances the problem. This situation disturbs the level playing field of the electoral battle and more importantly vitiates the sanctity and integrity of the overall ethical fabric of the country. When people see lawmakers turning into lawbreakers, it sends a wrong signal. This possibly has a multiplier effect on the overall levels of corruption in the country.

Defining Electoral Corruption

The term 'electoral corruption', as generally used, comprises a significant spread of corrupt practices within the electoral system. Section 123 of the Representation of People Act 1951 (RPA 1951) defines 'corrupt activities' in the context of elections. This includes a host of serious challenges, such as bribery, interference with free exercise of electoral rights, publishing false statements, hiring of conveyance for voters, booth capturing and so on. In day-to-day conversations, one also mixes related issues—presence of criminal elements in politics, horse trading, nexus between politicians and bureaucracy and so on—with the larger malaise of electoral corruption. While these perspectives are valid, with so many issues pooled together into the basket of electoral corruption, it would effectively be impossible to stay focused on matters which demand attention on priority basis. The issue of corruption within electoral financing is being widely acknowledged as one of the most serious issues hampering reform of the country's electoral process. Considering the seriousness and priority of this issue, corruption within electoral financing deserves maximum attention.

Legal Framework—Regulations Governing Electoral Finances

In an urge to win elections, both political parties and candidates constantly endeavour to raise and invest money. However, legitimacy of finances—sources of such funds and areas on which they get spent—is questionable. Expenses are often much more than the legal limits and, at times, on illegitimate activities as well. Significant portion of funds are raised from unknown sources. Hence, law and regulations get routinely compromised. The legal framework for electoral finances is derived through relevant provisions of the RPA 1951, Conduct of Election Rules 1961 (Election Rules), Companies Act 2013 and Income Tax Act 1961 (IT Act 1961). Table 1 summarizes the key provisions:

Table 1. Laws Regulating Election Finance in India

Area/Topic	Key provisions within existing regulations	Applicable law
Limits on expenditure	• Between ₹54 lakh and ₹70 lakh for parliamentary constituencies and ₹20 lakh and ₹28 lakh for assembly constituencies, depending on the size and population of constituencies. • The above limits include party and supporter spending towards a candidate's campaign. • Excludes expenditure incurred by 'leaders of a political party' for travel for propagating the party's programme. Excludes expenditure by parties or their supporters incurred for generally propagating the party's programme as long as no specific candidate is mentioned (given that the focus of Section 77 (of RPA 1951) is on 'candidate' and not party).	• Section 77 of RPA 1951; Rule 90, Election Rules, 1961, as amended by Conduct of Elections (Amendment) Rules, 2014
Disclosure of expenditure	• For candidates: True copy of account of election expenses of every contesting candidate lodged with the District Election Commissioner within thirty days of election of returned candidate.	• Sections 77 and 78, RPA 1951; Parts VIIA, VIII Election Rules, 1961
Limits on contribution	• No limits on individual contributions. • No limits on corporate contributions as well (as per latest proposals included in the Finance Bill 2017. Prior to this bill, corporate contributions in every financial year were allowed up to 7.5 per cent of their average net profits during the three immediately preceding financial years. • Corporate contributions to parties or electoral trusts entitled to deduction from total income. • Ban on foreign contribution to candidate or political party. • No limits on political party accepting contribution.	• Section 29B, RPA 1951 • Section 182(1), Companies Act 2013 • Sections 3 and 4, Foreign Contribution (Regulation) Act, 2010

Disclosure of contribution	• By party: Report detailing all contributions above ₹20,000 received from any person or company submitted in each financial year to the Election Commission. • By company: Profit and loss account will detail the total amount contributed and the name of the party to which contribution is made in every financial year.	• Section 29C, RPA 1951 • Section 182(3), Companies Act 2013. • Section 13A, S. 80GGB and 80GGC, IT Act
Public funding of election campaigns	• No direct state subsidy Partial in kind subsidy in the form of: (a) free allocated air time on state-owned electronic media (since 1996) to parties based on their past performance. (b) Free supply of copies of electoral rolls and identity slips of electors to candidates.	• Sections 39A, 78A and 78B, RPA 1951 (introduced by the 2003 amendment)
Penalties	• Both civil and criminal in nature and affect. • For candidate: Disqualification from being a voter or standing in elections if convicted of corrupt practices or failure to lodge election expenses (three years). • For party: Loses IT exemptions. • Company: Fines and imprisonment.	• Sections 8A, 10A, 11A,123(6), RPA 1951 • Section 182(4), Companies Act 2013 • Section 13A, IT Act

Source: 255th Report on Electoral Reforms, March 2015, Law Commission of India, para 2.3; and secondary research

The following are the key inferences from the above:

- While there is an upper limit to how much a candidate can spend in his/her election campaign, there are no spending limits for political parties. Besides, the ECI, in its recent guidelines dated 29 August 2014, has directed political parties not to spend amounts exceeding ₹20,000 in cash (with some exceptions).
- Candidates are required to disclose true accounts of election expenses to the District Election Commissioner

and assets and liabilities to the ECI.

- Political parties are required to disclose contributions only above ₹20,000 received from any person or company submitted in each financial year to the ECI. Any contribution below this cap may stay undisclosed. Further, political parties are also required to submit statements of expenditure to the ECI and file annual income tax returns/audit reports with income tax authorities within a prescribed time from the date of the completion of the election.
- The law also provides penal provisions, both civil and criminal in nature and affect, in case of non-compliance.

As can be seen above, while there are some obvious gaps, the law still does lay down reasonable boundaries to create transparency in electoral finances. Despite all these stipulations in place, electoral corruption has not abated. Cash and black money are rampantly pumped into elections, by both candidates and parties. Accountability of politicians to disclose their true election-related finances has not improved and instead financial management has probably become more opaque.

Key Drivers

There are several reasons for corruption in electoral finances. These include the role of money in the electoral value chain, loopholes in the legal framework and limitations in policing and enforcing laws.

Role of Money in the Electoral Value Chain

There is an inherent space for 'money power' in the way elections work. The electoral value chain can be broadly seen to comprise three distinct milestones/phases: ticket distribution, campaigning and post-result. Both political parties and candidates make expenses—some legitimate and some illegitimate in each of these phases. For this, they need significant funds.

But where does the funding typically come from and on what areas do these funds get spent?

Figure 1. Typical Sources of Funds and Areas of Expenditures for Political Parties

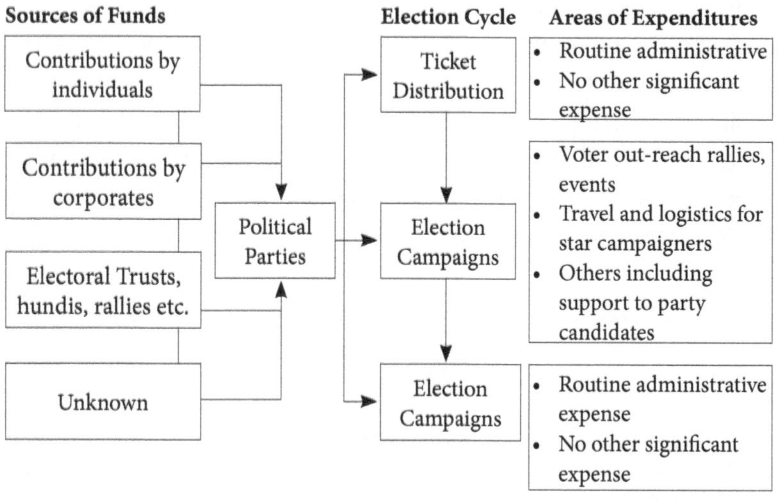

Figure 1 captures the typical sources of funds for political parties and areas of expenditure across the value chain. Given that political parties are not 'business entities', they raise funds through contributions from individuals or corporates. The other sources include electoral trusts, collections during political rallies, etc. However the biggest source of funds is corporates and individuals with high net worth. Similarly, on the expenses side, the largest source of expenditure is campaigning, which includes travel costs for star campaigners, leaders, workers, logistic costs for rallies, advertising and marketing activities, door-to-door outreaches, etc. Parties also provide financial support to few candidates in their campaigns. Parties also incur routine administrative expenses for other milestones in the value chain, including ticket distribution and post-election costs.

Figure 2 captures the typical sources of funds and areas of expenditure relevant to candidates. A bulk of funding for candidates is typically their own funds. However, sometimes a large portion of such funds may come from unknown sources. Parties may also contribute a portion. However, on the expenses side, candidates end up incurring significant legitimate and illegitimate expenditures. Legitimate expenses include expenses for genuine outreach to voters—organizing rallies, door-to-door visits, marketing campaigns, hoardings, pamphlets, radio or other modes. Illegitimate expenses include expenses on 'ticket contributions', 'voter bribery' or even attempting to 'bully' voters in favour of the candidate.

Figure 2. Typical Sources of Funds and Areas of Expenditures for Candidates

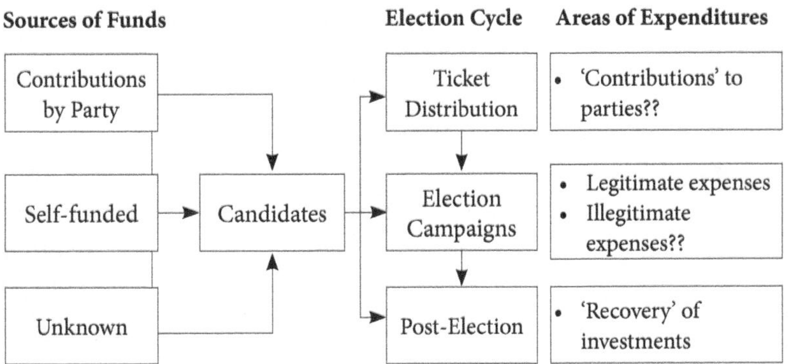

The above flowcharts essentially show that money is needed at each step in the value chain. But more importantly, money power has the potential to influence outcomes at any stage. Candidates believe that both voters and key decision-makers in political parties can be influenced through money. And this possibility drives corruption.

Parties, on the other hand, pump money to derive electoral advantages. The Law Commission of India articulates the Supreme Court's view on influence of money in politics. Its report[3] on electoral reforms notes, '...money is bound to play an important part in the successful prosecution of an election campaign. Money supplies assets for advertising and other forms of political solicitation that increases the candidate's exposure to the public. Not only can money buy advertising and canvassing facilities such as hoardings, posters, handbills, brochures etc. and all the other paraphernalia of an election campaign, but it can also provide the means for quick and speedy communications and movements and sophisticated campaign techniques and is also a substitute for energy in that paid workers can be employed where volunteers are found to be insufficient. The availability of large funds does ordinarily tend to increase the number of votes a candidate will receive. If, therefore, one political party or individual has larger resources available to it than another individual or political party, the former would certainly, under the present system of conducting elections, have an advantage over the latter in the electoral process.'

Like candidates, even political parties believe that electoral success is linked to the amount of money pumped into the process. This unholy impact of money on outcomes across the electoral value chain inherently makes candidates and parties embrace corruption.

Loopholes in the Legal Framework

The legal framework that governs electoral financing has some gaps that parties and candidates take undue advantage of. These include:

- Political parties are only required to disclose contributions above ₹20,000. Parties argue that a number of individuals across the country contribute in very small denominations. They assert that it is therefore logistically impossible for parties to disclose all contributions. While there may be some merit in this argument, this loophole is unfortunately used in a way that parties raise bulk of their funds from unknown sources.

  The graph below indicates that during the period 2004–05 to 2014–15, national parties raised funds totalling to about ₹9,280 crore. Seventy per cent of this funding (i.e. about ₹6,600 crore) is from unknown sources. For regional parties, the same figure stands at 60 per cent (₹1,220 crore from unknown sources out of a total funding of ₹2,090 crore). The loophole facilitates easy supply of black money where large contributions can be broken down to smaller denominations.

Figure 3. Funds raised by National and Regional Parties over the period 2004–05 to 2014–15 (₹ Crore)

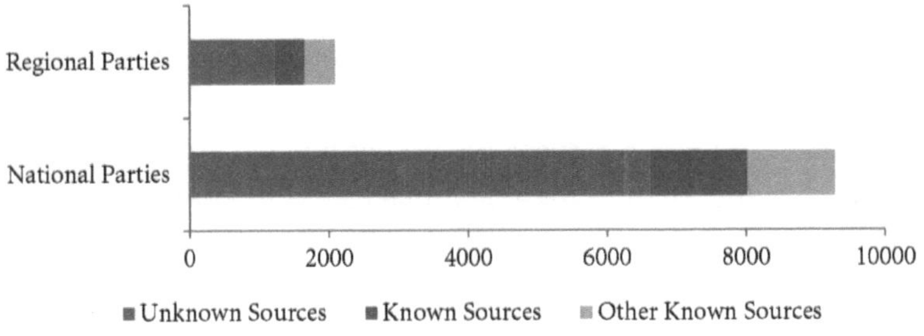

Source: Association of Democratic Reforms

- The law provides exemption from income tax for donors who contribute to political parties. This provision has been created to incentivize donors to disclose their contributions in case parties fail to do so. Despite this, donors prefer to stay anonymous. They want to avoid any association with a particular party or a set of parties due to the fear of unwarranted scrutiny post elections. Thus, while parties may have their reasons to not disclose funding sources, even individual donors do not come forward to make political funding more transparent.
- On the expenditure side, there are no limits to expenditures by parties. Hence, their expenditures are not monitored by authorities. This opens up space for parties to do some clever financial engineering and a lot of money gets disguised under vague heads. Candidates belonging to parties that are financially strong derive direct electoral advantages through this disguised party spending.
- However, authorities monitor expenditures of individual candidates during the election period. Besides, candidates are also required to submit their assets and liabilities statements to the ECI. Hence, most of the corruption that takes place is on account of either false disclosures (i.e. not reporting true accounts of funds and expenses) or practical limitations in detecting illegitimate activities undertaken by candidates.

A recent report[4] by ADR on 'Impact of Black Money in Elections and Politics' states that for the 2014 Lok Sabha elections, the average expenditure declared by candidates was only ₹40.30 lakh (59 per cent of the allowed limit). Now, contrast this with the following. Unofficial media reports estimate that a total of around ₹30,000 crore was spent in the 2014 Lok Sabha elections by both candidates and parties combined. Political parties disclosed that they spent ₹1,589 crore, meaning the balance (about ₹28,400 crore) was spent by candidates.

Similarly, another ADR report[5] indicates that in the 2009 Lok Sabha elections, national parties declared that they provided funding support to 138 members of Parliament (MPs). However, on their part, only 78 MPs declared having received aid from their parties. Such observations clearly substantiate the above-mentioned challenges.

Limitations in Policing and Enforcing Laws

The third factor that drives electoral corruption is that there are practical limitations in policing and enforcing laws. Elections are a continuous affair in the country. While the relevant authorities—ECI and Income Tax Department—do have access to financial accounts of parties and candidates, there are practical limitations in assimilating their disclosures and detecting grey areas. Similarly, even during elections, while the ECI does deploy shadow observers to monitor candidate expenditures, it is not possible to police majority of incidences as they happen discreetly. A recent pre-post poll study survey conducted by CMS estimated that about ₹5,500 crore were spent on campaigns for UP State Assembly elections in 2017. This included about ₹1,000 crore towards 'note for vote' with nearly *one-third* voters admitting to offers of cash or liquor. While the authenticity of these findings can be questioned, such illegitimate activities are not uncommon despite the best efforts of the ECI.

One of the major factors that further limit detection and policing electoral finance corruption is the dominant use of cash both in funding and in expenditures. Cash is the preferred mode for funding. Since cash does not leave an audit trail, donations to political parties also become an opportunity to invest black money. Similarly, on the expenditure side, while the dominant mode for parties' expenditure is through cheques, the absolute quantum that parties spend in cash is still significant. For candidates, cash is possibly the most preferred mode of expenditure.

Another related issue is that the recent Transparency Guidelines issued by the ECI have limited statutory authority. For instance, the guidelines require parties to file expenditure statements to the ECI within a limited time frame (seventy-five days post results for assembly elections and ninety days for Lok Sabha elections). Despite this directive, there have been several cases of non-compliance by political parties. An ADR report[6] titled, 'Funds Collected and Expenditure incurred by Political Parties in 11 years from 2004 to 2015', highlights several cases of non-compliance, particularly by regional parties. For such cases, the ECI finds it difficult to take appropriate actions against the non-compliant parties.

Ill-effects of Electoral Corruption

Electoral corruption vitiates the level playing field of elections. The Constitution envisages enabling fair and equal opportunities to all Indians to participate in the democratic electoral process. However, corruption provides a financial edge to rich candidates and the rich. In the 2014 Lok Sabha elections, 27 per cent[7] of all candidates were 'crorepatis' with average assets amounting to ₹3.16 crore. Commenting on this aspect, the Law Commission report also highlights Supreme Court's views in its 2014 decision in Ashok Shankarrao Chavan v Madhavrao Kinhalkar[8]: 'This view of ours is more so apt in the present day context, wherein money power virtually controls the whole field of elections and that people are taken for a ride by such unscrupulous elements who want to gain the status of a Member of Parliament or the State Legislature by hook or crook.' The lack of a level playing field also deters honest and genuine candidates from contesting elections. Even if they contest, the power of money reduces their winning possibilities. Finally, the public ends up voting for suboptimal representatives.

Corruption in electoral finances essentially creates a safe ecosystem for generating and disposing of black money. The above ADR report also provides that parties collected a total of ₹3,370 crore funds for assembly elections. Of this, 60 per cent was collected through cash. The same figure stands at about 45 per cent for Lok Sabha elections (₹1,040 crore in cash out of the ₹2,355 crore collected in total).

Figure 4. Mode-wise total funds collected by various political parties (2004–2015)

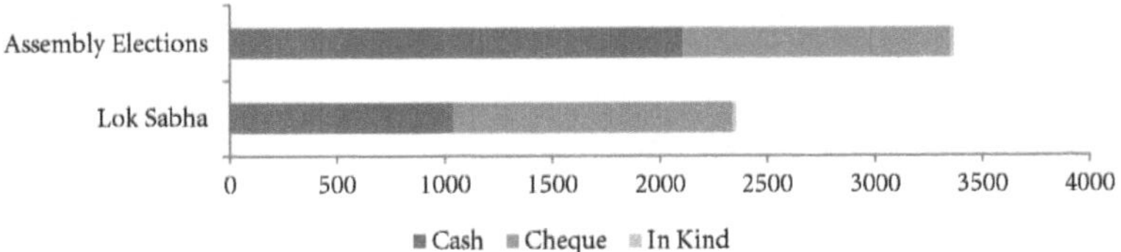

Source: Association of Democratic Reforms report on funds collected and expenditure incurred by political parties from 2004 to 2015.

The situation is slightly better on the expenditure side, while the absolute quantum of expenditure made in cash is still worrisome. As can be seen from Figure 5, cash accounted for around 10 per cent of the total expenditure made by parties in Lok Sabha elections during the period 2004–15 while the same for assembly elections was around 12 per cent.

Figure 5. Mode-wise total expenditure made by various political parties (2004–2015)

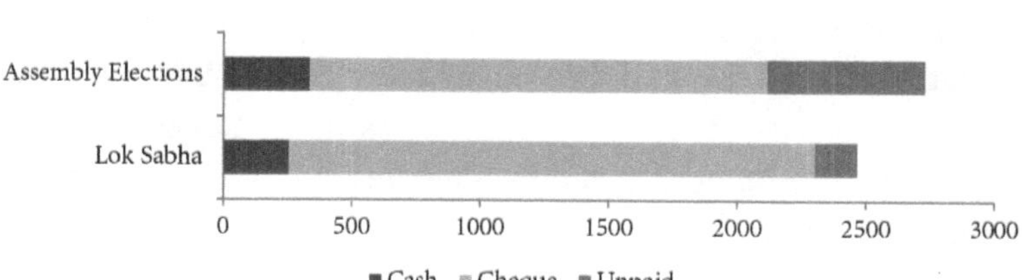

Source: Association of Democratic Reforms report on funds collected and expenditure incurred by political parties from 2004 to 2015.

Electoral corruption also influences public policies as it encourages a sort of quid pro quo between large donors (corporates or individuals with high net worth) and politicians. The Law Commission report states, '...election financing leads to two types of captures: the first involves cases where the industry/ private entities use money to ensure less stringent regulation, and the money used to finance elections eventually leads to favourable policies. The second involve cases of "deeper capture", where through their disproportionate and self-serving influence, corporations capture not just regulators, but also the views of ordinary citizens and what they think of as "public interest".'[9]

Possibly one of the most worrisome impacts of electoral corruption is the message it sends out to the common man. Seeing lawmakers rampantly indulge in malpractices dents the moral and ethical fibre of the society. People question the need and relevance of honesty and integrity. As a result, corruption becomes an acceptable norm in the Indian society—a way of daily life. This then percolates to other institutions like bureaucracy, government institutions and even private entities. In this context, electoral corruption could be seen as one of the biggest indirect drivers of overall corruption within our society.

A Multipronged Strategy

The Law Commission of India, in its report, has given a range of suggestions to plug the lacuna in the legal framework. On the other hand, the ECI has suggested some policy measures to tackle corruption in electoral finances in its December 2016 report titled, 'Proposed Electoral Reforms'.[10] While these expert committee reports are in the public domain, we need a holistic, multipronged strategy to address electoral corruption.

The reform of electoral financing can happen only if all the stakeholders—political parties, candidates, large donors, government institutions (Income Tax Department, ECI, etc.) and the public—extend genuine support on their respective parts. The government or ECI cannot address this challenge alone. The recommended approaches are thus a combination of policy measures and behavioural change strategies.

Increasing Transparency

As per the current guidelines, both parties and candidates are required to submit financial statements to relevant authorities. Parties submit statements of electoral funding and expenditure to the ECI and yearly audited financial accounts to income tax authorities. Candidates submit their assets and liabilities statements and true accounts of expenditures to the District Election Officer. However, these statements are rarely scrutinized or verified. Parties also take advantage of regulatory loopholes and, as a result, it becomes difficult for the concerned authorities to detect malpractices. There is significant under-reporting in expenditures. Sources donating funds cannot be traced (70 per cent of total funds received by parties comes from unknown sources). Cash dominates electoral finance management. It is, therefore, essential to create a framework which deters parties and candidates to continue the above malpractices. A three-pronged strategy is suggested:

a) Cap funding and expenditure limits on cash: The Finance Bill 2017 has already made a solid beginning in this regard. The bill proposes the maximum amount that a party can receive from any individual as ₹2,000. A similar cap of an appropriate amount should be set for cash expenditure as well.
b) Making public the list of donors and accounts of expenses and funding: The financial statements that parties and candidates submit should be collated in an online data repository. This data, or at least the relevant portions, should be made public. For instance, list of donors who are not specifically exempted from being disclosed (donors contributing in cash) should be a good start. Similarly, expenditure of parties and candidates on election-related activities beyond an appropriate cut-off can also be made public.
c) Innovative mechanisms such as electoral bonds for donors who prefer to stay anonymous: The Finance Bill 2017 has further introduced electoral bonds as an innovative mechanism to realize twin purposes—get cleaner funding and maintain anonymity of donors. Bonds should be seriously promoted by the government, especially for such large donors.

Invest in Behaviour Change and Create Framework for Reporting Malpractices

Electoral corruption hinges on the fundamental premise that money can influence outcomes. Parties or candidates indulge in malpractices because they have a basis to feel that money can help achieve desired results. So if the public starts looking down on cash, liquor or gifts while making their choices, a significant portion of such malpractices will automatically cease to exist. In this context, it is recommended that the ECI collaborate with the government to roll out a campaign that sensitizes the public to change its behaviour. There is a clear trade-off between short-term gratification (gifts or cash) and medium- to long-term benefits. Therefore, the overall negative consequences of voting under the influence of cash or gifts can be easily communicated. At the end, all of us want to elect representatives who work on our problems and can bring positive changes in our existing state of affairs. This campaign should also be complemented by an appropriate platform, using digital technology, where malpractices can be reported by people easily and directly to the concerned authorities. Both these steps together can make it difficult for candidates to stay undetected in case they keep indulging in financial malpractices.

Promote Digital Transactions

Post demonetisation, there has been a decisive emphasis towards substituting cash with digital options such as Universal Payment Interface (UPI), net banking, Unstructured Supplementary Service Data (USSD), e-wallets, etc. These options have been developed in a manner that even people in the remotest corners of the country can easily access the same. The prime minister himself is leading the nationwide campaign to incentivize digital economy. This ongoing push must be leveraged and funding and expenditures through digital means should be incentivized. For example, a Universal Payment Interface for specified accounts of political parties can be created. Similarly, candidates and parties should be nudged to make expenses in cheques or other digital modes.

Time-bound Scrutiny and Action against Defaulters

The above recommendations will have limited impact if a mechanism for time-bound scrutiny and action against defaulters is not created. As discussed earlier, reporting false financial statements and not adhering to timelines for submission of financial accounts are common practices. These practices are prevalent due to the lack of scrutiny and action in case of default or false submissions. Therefore, a two-pronged strategy is proposed:

a) Ensure time-bound scrutiny of financial statements: An expert government agency, such as the ECI or Comptroller and Auditor General of India (CAG), should facilitate scrutiny and appropriate verification of funding and expenditure statements submitted by parties and candidates. Similarly, income tax authorities should also scrutinize and process annual accounts submitted by parties in a time-bound manner. This may require augmenting the existing capacities and manpower of such institutions. All these steps will significantly help in enhancing detection of financial malpractices.
b) Actions in case of default: Parties are required to file their audited accounts and financial statements to authorities in a time-bound manner. A default in submission is rarely pursued. The Finance Bill 2017 reiterates the need for parties to file their returns within stipulated time frames. Appropriate penalty in the form of fines should be imposed in case parties default on this. There should be strict action in case of repeated defaults.

Towards a Clean Indian Polity

Corruption in electoral finances is clearly one of the biggest challenges of our electoral system. This issue has a legacy and is well-entrenched across the country. This form of corruption not only vitiates the purity and sanctity of the election system, it also harbours a breeding ecosystem for generating and disposing of black money. Still, the most unfortunate impact of electoral corruption arises from the message it sends to the society.

However, various actions can potentially create an environment where, in the first place, it would be quite difficult to indulge in malpractices. Even if someone indulges in corruption, the chances of time-bound detection and punishment would improve considerably. Thankfully, the agenda of cleaning up electoral finances is a significant priority for the current government. From time to time, the prime minister himself has publicly articulated his intent to implement steps that can uproot this form of corruption. But, for the above actions to create a long-lasting impact on ground, it is important that all stakeholders and, more importantly, people support this agenda and take up their respective roles—something similar to what was witnessed in the Swachh Bharat and the digital economy initiatives. Success may take some time, but eventually cleaner electoral finances would be the biggest lever to reform Indian polity—a desperate need to realize the true principles of democracy that the Constitution envisages.

References

1 http://adrindia.org/content/discussion-%E2%80%9Csimultaneous-elections-%E2%80%93-possibilities-and-challenges%E2%80%9D-26th-oct-wednesday

2 255th Report on Electoral Reforms, Law Commission of India, March 2015, paragraph 2.4.

3 Ibid.

4 http://adrindia.org/sites/default/files/Impact_of_Black_Money_in_Elections_and_Political_Activities.pdf

5 http://adrindia.org/content/circulation-unaccounted-money-activities-related-electoral-process-adr-submits-memorandum
6 https://adrindia.org/content/analysis-funds-collected-and-expenditure-incurred-political-parties-during-elections-11-0
7 255th Report on Electoral Reforms, Law Commission of India, March 2015, para 2.9.
8 255th Report on Electoral Reforms, Law Commission of India, March 2015, para 2.6.
9 255th Report on Electoral Reforms, Law Commission of India, March 2015, para 2.15.
10 http://eci.nic.in/eci_main/ElectoralLaws/HandBooks/PROPOSED_ELECTORAL_REFORMS_01052017.pdf

◆

Kishore Arun Desai is Officer on Special Duty with Bibek Debroy at NITI Aayog.

10

The Roots of the Agrarian Distress

MANINDER KAUR DWIVEDI

Agriculture has been the mainstay of the Indian economy since Independence. It employs about sixty crore people, which is almost half the population of the country. In 1960, agriculture contributed 42.6 per cent to the GDP which, in 2015, stood at 17 per cent, signifying faster growth in other sectors. The share of agriculture in GDP is abysmally low compared to the number of people engaged in animal rearing and growing crops. Also, the growth in agriculture in recent years has been only 3 per cent, lagging far behind the overall growth in the economy.

India has claimed self-sufficiency of foodgrains as an achievement since the Green Revolution in the 1960s. It was a remarkable development to shift from 'ship-to-mouth' stage when India depended on imports to a situation of large buffer stock holdings. However, the revolution and the subsequent turnaround remained restricted to wheat and rice. Paradoxically, the reversal from position of self-sufficiency to a net deficit and hence an importer has happened for corn, soya bean, oil seeds and cereals, among others. Yet this is neither a matter of public alarm nor discourse.

Falling productivity in a sector that absorbs the largest number of people in the country should be a matter of concern. It is often said that the large number of people engaged in agriculture is disguised unemployment as there are no other job opportunities. Even if so, people need to be gainfully engaged and their productivity enhanced. The sad state of affairs is due to causes that are more man-made than natural, where policy and schemes did not evolve with changing realities and continued addressing redundant issues.

The black economy or corruption in the sector is not easy to delineate as it is distributed. Perhaps it is better understood in terms of omissions and commissions in the set-up. There are loopholes, due to several reasons, which have continued or have simply become more gaping over the years.

Causative Factors Remain Unaddressed

The frequent discussions of reforms in the agriculture sector refer to ushering in a second green revolution, another white revolution or even a blue revolution. In reality, farming practices, availability of credit, infrastructure, technology, agricultural markets and processing facilities and laws related to leasing of land and insurance all limp along, in need of surgery and reconstruction. Through the decades, a standard response at the state level to the stagnation in the agricultural sector and its inefficiency has typically provided populistic cheap inputs. Successive governments vie with each other to subsidize water, electricity and fertilizer, even at the cost of near total environmental degradation, as has been seen in Punjab. It is simpler to give in to the farmer lobbies and not push either reforms or crop diversification as per the natural agroclimatic zone or set up procurement systems in areas more suited for grain cultivation. In spite of data and indisputable facts, the subsidies which erode the farms of sustainability have been perpetuated.

It is common knowledge that groundwater has depleted and dipped to alarming levels in Punjab, and that soil in parts of Punjab and Haryana is so heavily laden with pesticides and chemical fertilizers that it verges on toxicity. The 'cancer belt' in Punjab is poignantly well known with clear relation to the overuse of chemicals in agriculture. The populist response from the state has been to set up cancer hospitals and provide better train services to treatment centres in Rajasthan. Is it policy paralysis, policy of collusion or total lack of empathy that causative factors remain unaddressed? The subsidy on fertilizer to grow paddy-wheat as per season continues as before. To sustain the crops in degraded soil more and more fertilizers and pesticides are used as inputs, further accelerating the vicious cycle. The farmers know their actions are harmful, yet these are the only crops with assured market and purchase by the government. Till such time that they can be certain of return in value, there is no alternative of diversifying crops, of shifting to something more sustainable and less polluting.

Agricultural extension and diversification to more appropriate crops and marketing linkages may have been a rational solution. Yet this is practised only as lip service while things continued to remain the same. The very policy of free electricity to pump out fast-depleting water and government purchase of only paddy and wheat sends out conflicting signals that sustainable diversification is only for discussions.

Productivity of agricultural land has declined steadily due to small holdings as a result of fragmentation. This rules out investment in technology or economies of scale. State revenue laws impose a ceiling on the extent of agricultural land that can be held legally and leasing rules are strongly biased, making renting of land to consolidate fields difficult. The legal safeguards for farmers have not kept pace with the changes in the sector. So they block use of technology or mechanization, which requires scale and leads to high productivity.

Middlemen themselves are powerful lobbies which further restrict the actual flow of price support to farmers. Instead of curtailing their stranglehold, states like Punjab and Haryana have institutionalized the 'arthiya' system, with a formal arthiya commission as part of the procurements done on behalf of the central pool of foodgrain stock.

APMCs—Deepening the Crisis

Agricultural markets are fragmented, distorted and inefficient. The agricultural produce market committees (APMCs) restrict trade in vegetables and fruits. Simply put, within the territorial jurisdiction of an APMC, the farmer can sell his produce only in the mandi and a buyer can buy only from there, in the process, paying commission to the mandi. It may have been conceived of as a protective measure for the farmer to guard him from being fleeced by evil traders of corporates in days when price discovery was difficult. However, with progress in technology and communication, the APMC has become more restrictive and less protective, as it prevents a farmer from accessing competitive pricing and is also an obstacle to backward linkages for farm produce retail networks.

The net result is frequent manifestations of agrarian distress as farmers destroy tomato or potato crops, as they are unable to recover even the input cost. At the same time, imported fruits and vegetables crowd urban markets. The APMCs are controlled by agents with political clout. They add no value to the supply chain, yet charge commissions as high as 6–14 per cent. Onion shortages and price rise, which have resulted in major election defeats in the past, have been attributed to the dealings of the agents in the onion growing belt, hoarding to push up prices and cartelization to import. Unfortunately, whenever such episodes of scarcity happen, instead of making the system transparent and bringing in free trade, more regulation is introduced, with 'raids' on traders of the commodity to check the stocking position. The anti-hoarding laws are also double-edged as they prevent large-scale storage facilities from developing in the private retail space.

It is not so much the form of the fragmented markets or the APMC Act, but it is more of the implementation and facilitation available to farmers that impede their development. Bihar did not have an APMC Act in place, yet its farmers were not better off. Also, assured markets for wheat and paddy, as the entire stock brought by the farmer is purchased, have created a situation of complacency where the farmer does not look beyond finding higher or better varieties which may sell with better returns. The production has been limited to the varieties and qualities the government will purchase. Thus these markets, through their nature and layers of processes and commission agents, distort the demand–supply relation of a 'free market'.

The APMCs also offer no safeguard against gluts in markets from fluctuations in import duties, which are decided by another ministry. This directly impacts the farmers, as they are stuck with produce and no capacity to store, while the market is flush with cheaper world produce. This has, in the past, led to area under specific pulse cultivation shrinking to one half or lesser by the time of the next sowing season. Ideally, the APMCs should have evolved with time to factor in facilities like processing of produce, scientific storage, etc. so that it enables its registered farmers to withstand the deluge which is beyond their planning capabilities.

Suffering in Silence

The rot in the system is, time and again, crystallized and projected in extreme cases as news of farmer suicides. It is no longer just the drought-stricken farmers of Maharashtra,

Andhra Pradesh or Tamil Nadu who are unable to carry the burden of failed rains and mounting debts. In Punjab, the largest contributor to the national food stock, districts like Bathinda, Mansa and Barnala are a part of the 'suicide belt'.

The malaise in not only due to increasing input costs, fragmented holdings and short-sighted government policies, but also because of oft-repeated mala fide actions. Spurious fertilizers, pesticides and seeds lead to crop failures even in areas of assured irrigation. It is inconceivable that government supply of fake inputs is without collusion of local officials or politicians, as the government machinery is supposed to test and validate the quality of supply. So, while ineffective or duplicate inputs may make news, cognizance of such cases, investigation and penal action is so infrequent that it makes the risk worth taking for the delinquents. A policy solution could have been to equip and train farmers into making their own mulch, bio fertilizer, vermicompost, poultry waste compost or neem-based fertilizers or pesticides, with a view to reduce the dependence on market inputs. These are all solutions which have worked in pilots, are sustainable and have low cost. However, it would mean prioritizing the farmer above vested interests, which, as it was lacking, has resulted in such episodes in the first place.

Since farmers are unable to repay debts of moneylenders (who, in some cases, have been made a part of the system like arthiyas), there is no relief for these farmers after crop failures, even in populist loan waiver schemes, forcing them to take the extreme step. Loan waivers invariably favour those who are wilful defaulters and await election time for the bonanza, as opposed to those who repay the loan. The whole concept of waiver needs elucidation and differentiation about the target beneficiary. But suicide is the extreme expression of agrarian distress which is also covert, reflected only in falling productivity, reduced income and standard of living and migration to urban areas as unskilled labour. It is this silent suffering which policy and schemes do not reach due to the layers of rural economy beyond the formal sector, like the money lender or the corrupt local official.

Agriculture loans, which are cheaper than standard loans, are meant for 'farmers who are cultivating' and the moratorium is linked to crop maturity. Cooperative banks and regional rural banks, prone as they are to local and political pressure, advance many such loans to people who own land that is ploughed into other activity. Actual farmers either resort to loans from the state-propped middlemen, like the arthiyas, or from the informal channels, both of which are at high interest rates and waiver of these in cases of crop failure is impossible.

Agricultural Taxation

Income from agriculture does not attract income tax since the inception of income tax in India under the British rule in 1886. Since 1935, the right to levy land revenue, and as its corollary to levy tax on agricultural income, was with the provinces. After Independence, agriculture as a subject was placed on the state list, so only states can tax income from agriculture. The policy or subjective stand on taxing agriculture is an emotive and political issue; hence, states have generally ignored this potential source of revenue. But the fact remains that this is a big legal loophole which is used by people to evade taxation.

The Law Commission of India's 49th Report in August 1972 had examined the issue of assessees showing non-agricultural income as agricultural income, thereby evading tax legitimately payable on non-agricultural income. The question the Law Commission examined was whether it was permissible for the Parliament to amend the Income Tax Act, 1961, to provide that 'total income' as defined in the Act will include 'agricultural income' for the purpose of computing the rate of tax though no tax will be levied by the Centre on agricultural income. The commission had found that Parliament may levy tax on income other than agricultural income and provide for accounting agricultural income for the purpose of determining the rate of such tax on non-agricultural income.

Even after more than four decades of legal deliberation and recommendation, no action has been taken in this regard. So we continue to have scenarios where six to seven lakh taxpayers claim exemption of agricultural income to the tune of lakhs of crores. Amongst these are large agro-companies and seed firms, though it is intriguing why states do not deem them fit for taxation. The large reporting of agricultural income presumably provides camouflage to many innovative and resourceful tax evaders, as matching their land records and mandi sale papers is seldom carried out. Fake mandi receipts and documentation is easy to come by and difficult to disprove.

The level of evasion using agricultural income as a conduit can be made out from GDP figures juxtaposed against the reported agricultural income. In 2010–11, India's GDP was ₹78,77,947 crore, which included ₹1,319 crore from agriculture. However, income tax returns showed ₹2,000 crore and this when small and marginal farmers below the threshold limit would not have reported any income, agricultural or otherwise. In 2012–13, similarly reported agricultural income surpassed the GDP share of agriculture by 7.5 times. These figures are so high and the malpractice so widespread, that one can reasonably suspect some collusion of the local tax official or pressure on him to look the other way. Else, a focused campaign to verify and scrutinize such cases alone would be an effective deterrent to the perpetuation of this loophole.

At the policy level, a simple factoring in of the agricultural income for determining the rate of taxation will, at least, initiate transparency in this grey sector. A bolder step would be determining a threshold of agricultural income beyond which income tax will be applicable. If corporates pay 30 per cent income tax, then beyond some limit, agriculture, too, should be taxed. However, this would be a strong stand as it is fraught with the political risk of being labelled 'anti-farmer', though in reality all our agriculture policies are heavily biased towards the big farmer only. The K.N. Raj Committee had, way back in 1975, recommended tax on agricultural income. The Tax Administration Reform Commission under Parthasarathi Shome later reiterated the recommendation.

MSP and the Procurement Maze

Minimum Support Price (MSP) is announced every year for specific food items. Currently, MSP is available for twenty-four commodities, including cereals (paddy, wheat, barley, jowar, bajra, maize and ragi), pulses (lentil, gram, arhar, moong and urad), oilseeds (mustard, groundnut, toria, soya bean, Niger seed, sunflower, sesame, safflower); and copra, raw cotton, raw jute and Virginia flu cured tobacco. However, procurement at MSP is effectively done only for wheat and rice in limited states which have established systems for the same. Other minor cereals and pulses, like corn, bajra or jowar, are procured in smaller quantities at state level, but the process is neither stable nor reliable and changes from year to year. Cereals were systematically procured for the first time only last year. In all these complex procurement decisions, the choice of state and commodity is decided more by history of cultivation and easy availability, perhaps guided by inertia, rather than policy direction or planning to increase areas under pulses sustainably.

Wheat is procured from Punjab, Haryana and, of late, Madhya Pradesh. Lesser quantities have been procured from UP and Uttarakhand, but not enough to meet even the state's own demand. The government is the largest trader in wheat. All the wheat that comes to the mandis for sale to the central or state agencies is procured at MSP, while finer varieties that command a higher price go to private parties. Since wheat crop comes once a year, there is a deluge of grain in April–May and the buffer has to be maintained till the next crop.

Though paddy grows across the country, not all varieties are procured at MSP. States surplus in paddy, and consequently rice, which contribute to the central pool, are Punjab, Haryana, Uttarakhand, Odisha and Chhattisgarh. Paddy crop comes in multiple times a year and the period varies across states, so it is more spread out and presumably easier to manage from the point of logistics of supply chain management. However, despite growing almost everywhere, paddy procurement is limited to a few states. Punjab and Haryana have little requirement of paddy for local consumption and the crop is targeted at supplying for central buffer through MSP.

Transporting foodgrain is expensive. To give an illustration, one railway rake (containing 2,400–3,600 metric tonnes of grain) to be moved from Punjab or Haryana to Tamil Nadu costs ₹1 crore. This is only the cost of the railway freight, exclusive of the loading and unloading and transportation by trucks to and from the godowns at point of origin or destination. The Food Corporation of India (FCI) alone moves about 13,000 railway rakes a year, in addition to states moving rakes and trucks internally to transport foodgrains.

Now, if these costs are juxtaposed with the production figures across states, one wonders why procurement is not done to a larger extent locally, to minimize transportation. Assam, Bihar, Tamil Nadu and Chhattisgarh produce roughly the same quantity of paddy—between five to six thousand metric tonnes—yet only Chhattisgarh contributes to the central pool as a surplus state, while others remain in deficit and are supplied by transportation through long distances.

There are many reasons cited for incurring huge cost of operations by limiting the procurement operations to a few states, chiefly being that it is a state subject and the concerned states have to show initiative. Though production is sufficient in many states, deficit in foodgrains, the mandis or modalities of purchase are not established, so the produce is consumed by the farmer or sold locally.

Setting up procurement mechanisms to ensure MSP to the farmers, thereby improving rural economy, is not rocket science. Madhya Pradesh, Chhattisgarh and Odisha set up their procurement systems only in the last decade and a half but are already surplus states and even contribute to the central pool. In fact, it is heartening to note that wheat varieties in Madhya Pradesh command a premium price in private markets. West Bengal has been almost self-sufficient in rice procurement in the last couple of years. Whatever the cost of setting up systems and infrastructure, it would be less than the annual freight paid by FCI to Railways. There are other recurring costs like loading and unloading the railway rakes by using trucks and labour, transit and storage losses and preservation of the stock. A state agency employed for locally produced grains will be more accountable than a central agency which is further divided into state and zonal entities.

It is beyond logic why consuming states do not set up systems to be self-sustainable as this benefits their farmers directly. Assured sale at MSP automatically kicks in technology upgradation of farming inputs and investment to increase productivity. The oft-repeated complaints of having to eat Punjab–Haryana rice varieties, which are implied to be inferior to their local varieties, will also be automatically addressed. It would be an additional advantage to states that the local varieties which are preferred will be consumed as per the quality specifications acceptable to them. States can also encourage procurement of local grains like corn, jowar, bajra and kodu, which were the staple food before the advent of rice and wheat in the public distribution system (PDS). There will be states or areas not suitable for grain production, but these would be few and far between and could continue to be supported from the central buffer.

Punjab and Haryana contribute to the national buffer at the cost of degradation of the soil, depletion of groundwater and air pollution through crop stubble burning. The agroclimatic profile is not suited to growing paddy, but since the MSP benefits the farmer lobby, it has been continued despite awareness of the critical need for diversification. It would be logical to put in a ceiling limit to the quantity of paddy purchased from these states as production in other states picks up. Pulses as a second crop would be much more suitable, yet farmers do not cultivate them for lack of assured prices or markets. These have to be established along with support of agricultural extension, so that the diversification can proceed smoothly. Strangely, when pulses were purchased in 2015–16 for the national buffer, Punjab and Haryana were left out altogether, on the grounds that the acreage under pulses was less. Yet this assured purchase at MSP could have been a singular factor to shift from paddy to more appropriate pulses in the following season. It seemed like building the buffer of pulses was a knee-jerk exercise without serious planning into converting it into a sustainable practice.

Burgeoning Food Subsidy Bill

The entire budget of the FCI is borne on the central Budget as food subsidy. Since the rates at which FCI procures foodgrains and then sells to states are both fixed, the former is higher than the latter, the cost is to be met from the food subsidy. In addition, the entire cost of operations of maintaining the supply chain, from procuring to the consuming states/UTs and reimbursing various states/UTs for expenditure on permissible heads of accounts as well as the entire establishment cost of FCI is booked to food subsidy. Why the establishment cost (salaries, office expenses, travel, etc.) cannot be booked as such and continues under food subsidy is anyone's guess. The argument that it is miniscule compared to the cost of operations may sound plausible to some extent. However, it is also a fact that food subsidy is in arrears most of the time, but since operations have to carry on, FCI resorts to market borrowing, both secured and unsecured. When the subsidy tranche is released, it is used to pay interest. So the cost of operations also includes the interest payment on it. Hence, everything not related to the cost of foodgrains and operations should be budgeted under specific heads and not as food subsidy. This also leads to better fiscal oversight over expenditure, which otherwise gets subsumed in the overall food subsidy.

Given the burgeoning subsidy bill, focus should be on reducing operational costs of procurement, storage and transport. It would mean thrashing out high mandi tax, arthiya commission and other such levies imposed by procuring states, which are an exorbitant, opportunistic source of revenue for state governments, without the larger picture of sustainable agriculture. Encouraging procurement in Assam, Bihar, Jharkhand, Karnataka and Tamil Nadu will reduce operational costs.

Methods and Intermediaries

The procurement systems differ widely across the country, each with its own set of strengths and weaknesses. The older procuring states of Punjab and Haryana have the entrenched arthiya system, where the arthiya is paid MSP and a commission. How much of this passes on to the farmer is something state governments have refused to examine, as it will mean upsetting the applecart of a powerful vote bank. Chhattisgarh and Madhya Pradesh procure though Primary Agricultural Credit Societies (PACSs), which effectively ensure that farmers are paid directly for the produce through banking transactions. Other models like involvement of private players have been tried out with varying success. Chhattisgarh did an end-to-end computerization of its procurement, milling, storage and PDS about a decade ago, which has stood the test of time. It also involved business process reengineering, as the PACS and PDS shops were streamlined and criteria were laid down for the same. The system was transparent and efficient; it made the PACS viable and functional. The system is also replicable, the IT structure simply requiring recoding as it was built by the National Informatics Centre, yet all other states reinvented the wheel. Some did not venture further after studying the model as 'their PACSs were not as strong'.

Systems should benefit farmers, procure from them fairly and pay them at the earliest. Perhaps middlemen and arthiyas were required at a particular point of time, but IT-enabled services, direct payments and doing away with intermediaries must propel action and not just the maintenance of status quo.

Inherent Flaws in the PDS

The face of the PDS is the chain of ration shops that supply subsidized foodgrains to about 16 per cent of the population, though the civil supplies offices (CSOs) may dispute the coverage. The backbone of the PDS is the entire procurement machinery of the FCI or the concerned state, and the supply chain that feeds the ration shops. Problems with PDS abound, though at the same time there are states like Andhra Pradesh and Chhattisgarh which have set up exemplary methods of providing these entitlements. Here again, replicable good practices are slow to find imitation in other states.

The basic problem is the long supply chain, as for most of the country the foodgrains come from far off. There are storage and transit losses, like driage, which is a natural moisture loss. There are also leakages, inefficiencies and corruption that plague the process at every step. Practices like water spraying on wheat to increase weight as it is hygroscopic before dispatch to consuming regions, mixing good quality grain with downgraded stock, under-weighment, etc. are inherent in the system. At the PDS shops, under-weighment, inferior quality, faulty weights, over-charging and diversion to the market are common complaints. Diversion, recycling and admixing PDS rice with fresh milled rice not up to fair average quality specifications are common malpractices across the states where paddy is milled to rice. Recycling PDS rice purchased at subsidized prices as freshly milled rice after lifting paddy from the state has been a rampant malpractice, very difficult to prove unless the culprit is overconfident. It has only been established when the culprits made a mistake like using scooter or bike registration numbers as trucks plied in the work in the records. Adding PDS rice to below specification milled rice or conversely adding cheap broken stock to good-quality milled rice within specification limits to maximize returns are also common. It is often remarked that if conducted honestly there is no benefit or charm in the business of milling rice for the government.

Identification, Inclusion and Exclusion

The selection of beneficiaries itself is rife with unfair means. Bogus cards are a shortcut to be able to divert PDS supplies to the open market, while pocketing the large differential between the subsidized and open costs. Many dynamic officers who showed zeal in rooting out fake cards suddenly found themselves transferred or facing other charges, as such coteries yield enormous influence. Bogus cards have another corollary—exclusion of the truly deprived. So there are pockets of disadvantaged who have not been covered by the scheme or people who have migrated in search of work or otherwise and get excluded for such periods.

Quality and Service at Ration Shops

There are huge variations in these aspects across states. While some states have transparent procedures in place which facilitate delivery of foodgrains to customers, there are places where ration shops are dysfunctional. The resultant problems are faced by the people tagged to those shops which do not open, divert foodgrains or under-weigh and supply poor quality.

Agriculture, procurement, PDS and imposing duties are all functions carried out by different ministries and departments, the organic linkages between them getting lost somewhere as each views it from his own silo. It is not just a coordination failure or policy short-sightedness, but also an unwillingness to disrupt the vested interest lobbies. Delay in acknowledging problems or addressing them make those responsible culpable to the crisis in agriculture, be it farmer suicides, depleting groundwater, toxic soil and crops or large-scale malnutrition.

◆

Dr Maninder Kaur Dwivedi is an IAS officer of 1995 batch and has worked as an Adviser and Head of Department (Education) at NITI Aayog.

11

Mirage of Misinvoicing

SHAMBHAVI SHARAN

In the discussion about rampant corruption in India, one aspect of the economy still remains less scrutinized in a time of growing surveillance over corrupt and illegal practices. This aspect pertains to trade, wherein it functions as a vehicle for the movement of illegal capital from and to India. This movement is disguised through the practice of trade misinvoicing. This widespread and unchecked practice is growing as trade grows between economies. Not only does this practice allows traders to flout rules to make undue profits, it also allows these entities to transfer proceeds from illegal activities such as corruption, drug trafficking and others to move between borders.

It is important to understand the practice of trade misinvoicing as black money generated in India is either sent to other countries (considered as tax havens) or brought back into the country as legal proceeds through trade channels. It is also important for India because trade is an important pillar for the Indian economy, and with the pressure to sustain high growth to meet the demands of an ever-growing population, trade channels would need to be adequately unrestricted, to allow growth in exports and imports that can support domestic production.

Under trade misinvoicing, traders and private entities misreport either the quantity or value of the trade being undertaken, thereby tampering with the 'invoice' receipt. The invoices can be misreported both for imports and exports, and can either be over-reported or 'overvoiced' or under-reported or 'undervoiced'. It is primarily due to restricted trade and misaligned exchange rates that the practice first started in the country. But now, despite a market-determined exchange rate and less restrictions, traders continue to undertake this practice for a variety of reasons. Corrupt individuals have also joined the bandwagon to move their funds across borders, masked along with other kinds of misinvoicing done with the purpose of tax evasion or other types of private gain, not necessarily arising from corruption.

Trade misinvoicing is also the first aspect that is considered when it comes to estimating the level of global illicit financial flows (IFFs). In fact, as per data gathered by Global Financial Integrity (GFI)[1], of the $1 trillion in illicit flows leaving developing nations annually, over 83 per cent is due to trade misinvoicing. Further, Asia remains the region of the developing world with the most significant volume of IFFs, comprising about 38.8 per cent of the total flow from the developing world between 2004 and 2013. As India is one of the leading players in trade in Asia, the case for estimating and analysing the prevalent misinvoicing becomes even stronger.

Understanding Misinvoicing

As mentioned earlier, misinvoicing arises due to several reasons and depending on the case, the objective of the act and its subsequent consequences vary. Studies suggest that misinvoicing is not a recent phenomenon, but has garnered recent attention, owing to three key reasons.[2] Firstly, trade is increasingly becoming more relevant in understanding the economic growth of a country. Thus, globally, there has been an increased interest in improving the measurement of trading activities. Secondly, misinvoicing of trade can be estimated more precisely in comparison to other kinds of illegal economic activities, owing to the availability of 'mirror statistics', or the same kind of data being available in both nations under consideration, where the mismatch can be easily identified. Thirdly, and most importantly, various reports suggest that trade misinvoicing is a key vehicle to move unrecorded capital outside the country.

Several studies have been undertaken to frame a methodology through which trade misinvoicing can be detected and subsequently estimated. While it is easy to determine conditions under which misinvoicing can take place, it is difficult to establish the instances and extent of faking.[3] However, in recent times, trade misinvoicing has garnered more attention as it can be detected, as mentioned earlier, due to the availability of mirror statistics. These are statistics that are recorded independently by two separate authorities, at the time of leaving the source as exports, and at the time of arrival in the destination country as imports. While the import data are specified at the CIF value, the export data are recorded at the freight on board (FOB) value. 'Perverse discrepancies' arise when the value of imports is significantly higher or lower than the value of exports plus the cost of transport, insurance and duties (export at CIF value).

However, there can be other genuine reasons, beyond intentional misinvoicing, when such discrepancies are noted. These include the issue of inconsistent classification of products across countries, which arises over time due to genuine customs mistakes and differences in adopted conventions. For instance, an early research[4] on the subject suggested in the matter of undervoiced Turkish imports that some level of normal discrepancies arose due to international differences in the treatment of refinery ownership. Another way in which discrepancies may arise is if there is a lag between shipment and arrival in an importing country. It could be the case that goods cleared by customs of the exporting country at a certain year may not be reported by the customs of the importing country in the same year, either due to a large time lag or differences in the calendar followed in both countries (financial year versus calendar year). This may lead to gaps in the reporting of data, which in aggregate terms may falsely suggest misinvoicing. Lastly, inconsistencies in data may also arise because of inaccuracies in currency conversion calculations. If all these aspects are investigated, and yet the inconsistency between export and import data remains unexplained, then the plausible motivation for misinvoicing is looked into.

The associated four types of misinvoicing have also been explained to better understand the practice.

Export Over-invoicing

Export over-invoicing is a frequent phenomenon in countries which seek to promote exports by offering tax incentives. In India, export incentive schemes which are value-based or computed on the net foreign exchange earnings encourage over-invoicing of exports. One of the biggest ongoing reported cases of this kind of over-invoicing is that of Adani Group's exports of gold and diamonds to the UAE.[5]

In a bid to encourage exports from India, the Ministry of Commerce and Industry had introduced schemes and export benefits in early 2000s. One of these was the Duty Free Credit Entitlement (DFCE) scheme in 2003–04. Under this scheme, a status holder would receive financial benefits equal to 10 per cent of the total incremental exports achieved in 2003–04 over the exports in the previous financial year (2002–03), provided the incremental growth was at least 25 per cent. Apart from this, other export promotion schemes were introduced, including the Target Plus Scheme (TPS) in September 2004, which offered incentives to status holders varying between 5 and 15 per cent of the incremental growth in the turnover of exports. Initially, studded gold jewellery and polished diamonds were permitted to be included while calculating the FOB figure, and, therefore, towards claiming incentives under the TPS.

'For more than a decade now, the Directorate of Revenue Intelligence (DRI) has been investigating how a clutch of companies in the Adani Group allegedly evaded taxes and laundered money while trading in cut and polished diamonds and gold jewellery,' report Thakurta, Palepu and Jain. In fact, the DRI has issued a number of show-cause notices to these firms since 2007 on misusing the benefits under DFCE for this trade. 'The corporate conglomerate has been accused by the DRI of having allegedly evaded taxes and laundered money to the tune of around ₹1,000 crore,' they add further.

As per their report, DRI noted that the consortium companies mis-declared the FOB values of both cut and polished diamonds (CPD) and gold jewellery. This was first detected in 2003–04, when the total export turnover of the Adani group reported an increase of 1,181 per cent or a growth of more than eleven times. Thereafter, the trade policy was amended (through notifications issued in 2005 and 2006) to exclude studded gold jewellery and certain categories of diamonds from the list of items entitled to receive export benefits under the TPS. This led to a fall in the group's exports post 2005.

The case is still under investigation because the firms later allegedly indulged in a 'circular trading' process wherein old gold bars having 995 purity were imported from the UAE and then exported in the form of crude studded gold jewellery back to the UAE. According to reports, between September 2004 and February 2005, the firms in the Adani Group exported over 59,500 kg of studded jewellery valued at over ₹3,843 crore. The DRI argues that these export orders comprised gold bangles weighing anywhere between 100 grams and 240 grams and pendants weighing over 70 grams each, which is considered to be impossible using gold with 995 purity, owing to the inability of pure gold to hold precious stones. Moreover, DRI has further stated that the value of the goods was artificially inflated by including 'making charges'. Consequently, it has been estimated that the value of export incentives obtained by the Adani Group companies in this specific instance was more than ₹575 crore.

Sometimes, exports can be inflated not only to avail export benefits, but also to bring back illegal capital to India. One such case[6] was identified by the investigative teams of *The Economic Times* and Kotak Institutional Equities Research, which looked at exports to the Bahamas that witnessed a significant increase from $2.2 million in 2008–09 to $2.2 billion in 2010–11. This increase raised the question whether these trades were sham transactions done to bring back money stashed in secret accounts with offshore banks. This is because 'the mirror statistic of this number did not match the data on the Bahamas' global imports, which according to United Nations Conference on Trade and Development (UNCTAD) was $2.8 billion in 2010', reports Seth. India held only a 7.5 per cent share or $200 million value in the country's imports. This pegs the entailing discrepancy to about $2 billion. According to analysts, this increase is a ploy to bring back undisclosed money under the garb of cross-border trade because the country is known to be a tax haven. The process would have thus allowed exporters to allegedly over-invoice their export bills wherein the buyer may be fictitious, or a shell or front company of the Indian exporter. The motive for the same could be increased international scrutiny of unaccounted funds in foreign bank accounts amidst heightened debate in India about action against unaccounted overseas wealth. Later in 2011, the Finance Ministry asked for a combined probe by the Central Board of Direct Taxes (CBDT), DRI and the Enforcement Directorate

(ED) into the matter. However, no official investigation has yet been reported on the matter.

Both these cases of export over-invoicing suggest that the practice exists not only to avail trade-related benefits or evade taxes, but also as a route to simply move funds as the channel itself lacks sufficient scrutiny. Export over-invoicing has picked up after India became an export hub; thus, if one investigates export figures vis-à-vis the production figures, several discrepancies can be noted.

Import Over-invoicing

Research suggests that import over-invoicing is typically observed in product categories with low or zero import tariffs. Besides, inflating imports also allows producers to lower their domestic profits, thereby incurring lower taxation or receiving other government-related benefits.

An important example under this category is the recent case of over-invoiced imported coal from Indonesia.[7] In March 2016, the DRI alerted fifty customs offices in India to check for the case of over-invoicing of coal imports from Indonesia. According to the DRI, the electricity generating companies were allegedly benefiting from the high power tariffs by reporting inflated coal costs in their costs of production. The investigation of these coal imports took place between 2010 and 2015. 'The scam is conservatively estimated by government officials at no less than ₹29,000 crore,' report Thakurta and Malik. These included the likes of the Adani Group, Reliance Group, Essar Oil and Essar Power, JSW Steel and public sector firms such as Metals and Minerals Trading Corporation of India (MMTC) Limited, National Thermal Power Corporation (NTPC) Limited and the Tamil Nadu Electricity Board.

As per the investigations, the average price of Indonesian

coal (having a gross calorific value of 3,800 kCal/kg–4,200 kCal/kg) ranged between $38 and $49 per tonne on FOB basis, as per international prices. When freight and insurance charges were added, the CIF rate of Indonesian coal amounted to $55–$60 per tonne, while the invoices displayed inflation up to over $82 per tonne. Steam coal procured for power plants, entails a 2 per cent customs duty and a 2 per cent countervailing duty. However, the preferential trade agreement between India and Indonesia provides for concessional duties. This affirms the fact that over-invoicing does occur when trade barriers are reduced, despite allowing for market realization of prices. This further goes to show that misinvoicing, as it occurs presently, does not arise only out of misaligned exchange rates or restrictions. It is an intentional practice to further personal gain by misreporting data. In this case, not only was the price of coal overvalued in the received invoices, but the gross calorific value of coal was also declared incorrectly. Consequently, higher power tariffs were passed on to the end consumers who received electricity generated by inferior quality coal. This allowed producers to make undue profits.

Import Under-invoicing

Globally, import under-invoicing is considered the most prevalent form of trade misreporting on account of its immediate benefits. Since customs duties are typically determined based on the declared value of the article, undervaluation directly reduces tax payments. Just as over-invoicing occurs due to low import duties, the practice of under-invoicing of imports occurs due to high import duties. In fact, high import duties, often lead to the act of smuggling, which lowers import figures. This has been the case for gold in India, the commodity that faces large import duties. The Central Board of Excise and Customs (CBEC) has tried several interventions, such as raising the tariff value ($461 per 10 grams from $432 per 10 grams) and the base price on which the customs duty is determined, in a bid to prevent under-invoicing of gold. However, the practice of gold smuggling or under-invoicing continues to cater to the growing domestic demand for the commodity.

As per official data prior to demonetisation, the imported quantity of gold fell throughout 2016. However, at the same time, there was a rising trend for the provision of discounts for the purchase of gold during the same period. Reports suggested that gold sale at a heavy discount could be due to rising supplies from unofficial channels, either through misinvoicing or smuggling. For instance, it has been reported that between April 2015 and January 2016, Bengaluru customs department was able to uncover 28.97 kg of gold worth over ₹8 crore smuggled into the Kempegowda International Airport.[8] Thus, smuggling of gold continues to be on the rise in India owing to its high import duty of 10 per cent. And this, in turn, caters to the Hawala channels of money transfer, facilitating undetected transfer of capital from India.

Another commodity that faces rampant under-invoicing is steel. In fact, the industry was faced with dumping of cheap steel by countries such as China, Russia, Japan and South Korea. Korea, for instance, exported 64,913 tonnes of hot-rolled coil in October 2015 at $275 a tonne, much below its domestic selling price of $420 a tonne.[9] Meanwhile, China, the world's largest producer, consumer and exporter of steel, was consistently dropping its export price for India, from $385 a tonne in July 2015 to $311 in October 2015. At this point, a safeguard duty had been imposed on steel items. It was noted that prior to the levy of the duty, invoices suggested that Korea was exporting steel to India at a price of $308 a tonne, which was later reduced to $224–$247 a tonne in CIF value. This raised the question whether importers were avoiding paying extra on safeguard duty by under-invoicing the import. This later led to the government implementing a minimum import price in 2016, much higher than the global price for several items in steel. However, the demand for cheap steel imports remains strong in India as the country's engineering and auto components industries rely on these. This has now led to the fear of over-invoicing in steel where payments are made through Hawala transfers. However, another plausible conjecture could be that under-invoicing may still continue, this time by underquoting the quantity shipped, as exporting countries that are already producing enough steel to meet global demand may continue dumping to save their domestic industry. Nonetheless, it can be noted that wherever a restriction is created in trade, an illegal channel is sought to meet demand.

Export Under-invoicing

A recent example of under-invoicing of exports in India is the case of shipment of iron ore from the Bellary region in Karnataka to China.[10] The scam was uncovered by Karnataka Lokayukta Santosh Hegde in 2008 when he published a report on corruption in mining projects in Bellary. The scam entailed several violations on the part of Obulapuram Mining Company, owned by G. Karunakara Reddy and G. Janardhana Reddy, then ministers of the state. This included the encroachment of forest land, underpayment of royalties to the state and mining in a larger area than what was permitted.

However, the key motivation for this was the undervoiced exports to China to feed an infrastructure boom triggered by the Beijing Olympics.[11] Under-invoicing India's iron ore exports allowed the country to stay competitive for the Chinese demand. The Lokayukta report[12] says that 12.57 crore tonnes of iron ore was exported overseas from Karnataka between 2006 and 2010. Moreover, there was an evasion of customs duty by exporters through under-invoicing, typically during the period of ad valorem based customs duty. Export under-invoicing, as it exists today, is a tool to achieve global competitiveness, most notably in the infrastructure industries where the demand is high.

Main Motives

Trade misinvoicing is a complex and rampant practice, undertaken in several forms through varying motives[13], which include:

- First, firms engage in trade misinvoicing either to take advantage of tax-related benefits or evade high tariffs. Advantage of tax benefits usually occurs in the form of inflated exports. Also, this practice is meaningful only if the benefit from subsidies is greater than the black market premium or cost of acquiring foreign exchange on the black market.[14] Meanwhile, import under-invoicing often occurs in the case of high tariffs or custom duties. Such has been the case of steel in India, where to protect the domestic steel industry, the government is consistently trying to increase import pricing as under-invoiced imported steel continues to cater to the domestic demand. Recent research on global trade also suggests that tariff evasion is one of the factors that lead firms to intentionally misreport data.[15]
- The second major motive for misinvoicing is to circumvent bureaucratic hurdles. Such was the case for gold, which now enters into the Indian market through smuggling. UN research suggests that this motive is also linked to countries where there are high levels of corruption in the public sector. The case of illegal iron ore being mined from Bellary and leading to under-invoiced

exports is one prominent example of this motive. In fact, even the inflated coal imports were associated with public and private sector companies, which not only availed benefits from the government, but also passed on the price burden to consumers, thereby making illegal profits.

- The third motive is to circumvent currency-related controls. This often leads to the twin practice of export under-invoicing or import over-invoicing to enable capital flight. This market distortion enables a black market to flourish where exchange becomes more readily available. This was the prevailing case for India during the initial years of trade liberalization.

Changing Landscape

India's story in misinvoiced trade has seen a notable shift on account of change in trade-related policies over the last three decades. The changing landscape also points to India's role in the global level of trade misinvoicing.

During the period of exchange rate liberalization, Indian traders faced intense uncertainty about the future value of the rupee. Heavy misinvoicing activity was noted, especially for exports, due to misalignment of the Indian exchange rate. Recent academic research on the matter suggests a gradual shift from export under-invoicing during the initial trade liberalization years to export over-invoicing post the global financial crisis.

Starting from July 1991, the government first introduced a downward adjustment to the overvalued rupee against major international currencies. This was followed by the adoption of a dual exchange rate system in February 1992, where exporters were allowed to convert 60 per cent of their export proceeds at the free market rate, while the remaining 40 per cent was converted at the government set official exchange rate. It is in such a scenario that export under-invoicing is undertaken to safeguard earnings when there is an expectation of exchange rate depreciation. For instance, if the market rate is higher than the fixed exchange rate, traders would under-invoice their exports to receive a greater amount of domestic currency for the same amount of foreign exchange. The idea is that when the rupee further depreciates to equal the market rate, the under-invoicing would reduce. However, another reason for Indian exporters to under-invoice was to transfer capital outside the country as uncertainty was created by the currency devaluation. It was feared that the rupee may fall further until the exchange rate policy is made clear. According to a study[16], the dual exchange rate did attempt to reduce uncertainty and thereby helped in reducing export under invoicing from 7.3 per cent of total exports in 1991–92 to 1.7 per cent of total exports in 1992–93.

In April 1993, the government adopted full convertibility on the trade account by unifying the official exchange rate with the market one, and subsequently by August 1994, the full current account convertibility was achieved. During this period of 1993–94, uncertainty was back, and while the RBI tried to maintain the rupee–dollar exchange rate at constant levels, under-invoicing increased to 5.73 per cent of the total exports. After 1993–94, Patnaik and Vasudevan suggest that for a few years the market perception remained that the rupee would continue to depreciate. It was only in August–September 1995 that the RBI finally let go of the controls and the rupee fell sharply. This was accompanied by a reduction in the under-invoiced exports, which were a negligible 0.74 per cent of total exports in 1995–96. In all, the total under-invoicing between 1990–91 and 1996–97 amounted to $8.37 billion.

In the meantime, import over-invoicing was also taking place as a means to allow corporates to accumulate illegal balances overseas. The fundamental idea was that when there is a restricted capital account, the only means to transfer money to foreign accounts was through trade channels, as the current account had been recently liberalized. This was also the time of uncertainty and the fear of devaluation led to capital flight through over-invoiced imports. For the period 1990–97, the estimated over-invoiced imports were of the value $8.2 billion. In all, Patnaik and Vasudevan have estimated that about $16 billion worth of capital fled in the time of misaligned exchange rates.

As mentioned earlier, a black market economy for foreign exchange is usually associated with a regulated exchange rate. Reports suggest that the black market premium remained significant through the early 1990s assisting both inflated imports and deflated exports, but this market lost its significance when the rupee eventually depreciated.

Inflation in Recent Exports

Post liberalization, Indian exports saw slow growth in the first decade, and more fast-paced growth in the years thereafter, barring the year of the global slowdown. During the pre-financial crisis years of 2002–03 to 2008–09, exports grew at a rate of 24 per cent per annum. Post the crisis, Indian exports registered a growth rate of 37 per cent in 2010–11, much higher than the pre-crisis years. The exports were only set to grow faster in the coming years, and this led to an increased scrutiny over the given numbers. According to one study, the export surge in recent years cannot be attributed to over-invoicing arising out of export-led policies.[17] However, non-academic investigations into the matter reveal a different case altogether.

An instance where data showed discrepancies or unusual growth was that of the engineering industry exports, which reportedly grew by 80 per cent in 2011–12. *The Economic Times* investigated the surge reported for the copper industry, which grew at an astonishing rate of 350 per cent in 2010–11, over the previous year. Under this investigation it was noted that all the four points in the value chain of the copper industry, from importing copper scrap to smelting and subsequently production did not indicate that sufficient quantity of copper was produced to match the value of exported copper.[18] Neither did the reported increase in copper prices could explain how the value of copper exports grew from $1.8 billion in 2009–10 to $8.1 billion in 2010–11.

The subsequent investigation lacked a thorough research from DRI or any other regulatory authority. However, the case does indicate the possibility that export channels, now with less constraints, may be prone to over-invoicing, in view of the country's dependence on an export-led growth. And so, increased scrutiny of this trade channel will help in catching illegal capital returning to India or identifying entities making undue profits out of trade benefits.

Another research[19] points out that traditional literature has largely focused on trade misinvoicing arising out of economic instability or currency controls. But even though such conditions have ceased to exist in India, a sharp reduction in misinvoicing has not been witnessed. Other factors such as capital account openness, political instability, customs duties and interest rates have driven this practice in the developing as well as developed world. Hence, more studies are required to understand this practice being undertaken in India, and its association with corruption and black money.

India and the Global Scenario

A recent study has shown that capital flight, arising solely out of misinvoicing in trade, amounted to $186 billion between 1988 and 2012, with a peak of $40 billion in 2008.[20] If this peak is compared to the 2008 statistics ($828 billion) compiled by GFI of IFFs leaving developing countries, India held a share of 5 per cent. GFI's statistics for India's total IFF for 2008 itself is about $47.22 billion. Thus, the IFF coming through misinvoicing holds a share of 84.7 per cent. India's story goes with the global narrative that the predominant share of IFFs comes from the rampant practice of misinvoicing. According to GFI's estimates, the developing world lost $1.1 trillion in the form of IFFs in 2013, and this amount was reportedly greater than the combined FDI and net official development assistance received by the economies in that year. Thus, trade misinvoicing is not only taking away capital that could otherwise be utilized for economic activities, but also putting a dent in the growth achieved by these economies.

The ill-consequences of trade misinvoicing include the loss of revenue and stunted growth, and masking of revenue channels for illegal drugs and narcotics. The GFI report also suggests that trade misinvoicing has also assisted drug traffickers in shifting ill-gotten gains. For India, the ratio of total trade misinvoicing outflows to total trade with drug trafficking/transit countries is about 10 per cent. This follows the fact that India is a transit country for drugs where traffickers are more active. These traffickers are more likely to resort to trade-based money laundering in drug-transit countries than in drug-producing countries. Thus, India is not only a victim to this practice and its consequences, but also a key contributor. Similarly, these trade channels increasingly cater to terrorist financing. As a result, efforts undertaken by India to curb this practice would not only improve the domestic economic situation, but also have spillover benefits to other trading partners.

Combined Efforts to Reduce Misinvoicing

On the domestic front, the GST is a key step in reducing under-invoicing of exports arising due to evasion of payments in customs duty.[21] This is because under the GST regime, a goods and services tax network (GSTN) will be set up that would form the information backbone of the GST. The Central Board of Excise and Customs (CBEC) would, with the help of the GSTN, be able to track the sale prices of imported items, and check if the prices were under-declared by the importer. Further, the customs department's own IT system would also be linked to the GSTN to provide further information on the importer and the commodity to track misinvoicing more effectively. Besides, regular updating of the national import and export databases is essential to monitor trade channels and curb misinvoicing. In fact, real time, commodity-level world market pricing data should be made available to customs officials. This would enable them to determine under- or over-pricing of a certain commodity in comparison to its prevailing world market norm price.

On the global front, sharing of information between nations is important for not only estimating the quantum of misinvoiced trade, but also in nabbing big offenders. Misinvoicing has garnered the interest of the UN under its 16th Sustainable Development Goal—significantly reduce illicit financial and arms flows, strengthen recovery and return of stolen assets and combat all forms of organized crime by 2030. This can only be achieved through effective law and governance. As trade misinvoicing predominantly includes multinationals, efforts on revenue declaration, auditing and improving transparency would also deter companies from misrepresenting data. Lastly, the DRI, which already looks into commercial frauds such as trade-based money laundering, mis-declaration, under-invoicing and misuse of Foreign/Preferential Trade Agreements, must enhance its scope to include over-invoicing and other trade malpractices which cater to domestic corruption.

Going forward, more studies on plugging the holes of our present understanding of the practice of trade misinvoicing and the country's role in global IFFs through misinvoicing may help in understanding the severity of the problem. This knowledge will also help in estimating the level of damage that is caused to the country's domestic growth and prosperity. Together, all these steps would stop leakages in the trading system, and pave the way for more efficient trade practices and higher profit realization.

References

1 D. Kar & J. Spanjers, 'Illicit Financial Flows from Developing Countries: 2004-2013', Global Financial Integrity, December 2015.

2 V. Nitsch, 'Trade Misinvoicing in developing Countries', Center for Global Development Policy Paper 103, February 2017.

3 J.N. Bhagwati (ed.). 1969. *Illegal transactions in International trade*. Amsterdam: North Holland/American Elsevier, pp. 68–73.

4 J.N. Bhagwati. 1964. 'On the underinvoicing of Imports', *Bulletin of the Institute of Economics and Statistics (Oxford University)*, 27(4), November, pp. 389–97.

5 P.G. Thakurta, A.R. Palepu & S. Jain. 2016. 'Adani Group Accused of Evading ₹1,000 Crore Taxes in Diamond Trade', *Economic & Political Weekly*, 51(53), December 31.

6 Smriti Seth, 'Sudden surge in India's exports to Bahamas raises doubts', *The Economic Times*, 21 October 2011.

7 P.G. Thakurta & Aman Malik. 2016. 'How over-invoicing of imported coal has increased power tariffs', *Economic & Political Weekly*, LI(15).

8 P. Peter. 'Sly smugglers adopt innovative ways to sneak gold into Bengaluru', *The Times of India*, 13 February 2017.

9 S.P. Iyengar. 'Under-invoicing by exporters is new worry for steel industry', *The Hindu BusinessLine*, 17 December 2015.

10 'Fighting Corruption in India: A Bad Boom'. 2014. *The Economist*, Briefing (Print Edition), March 15.

11 Sudipto Mondal. 'Karnataka lost ₹1 lakh cr from 2006-2010', *The Hindu*, 17 June 2013.

12 N. Santosh Hegde. Report on the Reference made by the Government of Karnataka under Section 7(2-A) Of the Karnataka Lokayukta Act, 1984 (Part-II), 27 July 2011.

13 'Trade Misinvoicing in Primary Commodities in developing Countries: The cases of Chile, Cote d'Ivoire, Nigeria, South Africa and Zambia'. 2016. Report by United Nations Conference on Trade and Development.

14 J.N. Bhagwati. 1967. 'Fiscal policies, the faking of foreign trade declarations, and the balance of payments', *Bulletin of the Institute of Economics and Statistics (Oxford University)*, 29, pp. 61–77.

15 D. Kellenberg & A. Levinson. 2016. 'Misreporting Trade: Tariff Evasion, Corruption, and Auditing Standards', National Bureau of Economic Research, Inc.

16 I. Patnaik & D. Vasudevan. 2000. 'Trade Misinvoicing and Capital Flight from India', *Journal of International Economic Studies*, 14, pp. 99–108.

17 C. Veeramani. 2012. 'Anatomy of India's Merchandise Export Growth, 1993-94 to 2010-11', *Economic & Political Weekly*, XLVII(1), January 7.

18 R. Shah & J.S. Raja. 'Increase in FY11 Copper Exports Packs a Mystery', *The Economic Times*, 26 December 2011.

19 I. Patnaik, A. Sen Gupta & A. Shah. 2010. 'Determinants of trade misinvoicing', NIPFP Working Paper No. 75.

20 R. Jha & Duc Nguyen Truong. 2015. 'Estimates of Trade Misinvoicing and their Macroeconomic Outcomes for the Indian Economy', *Review of Economics & Finance*, 5, pp. 19–34.

21 R. Nair, 'GST to help in checking of under-invoicing of imports', *Livemint*, 20 July 2016.

◆

Shambhavi Sharan is a Young Professional associated with Professor Ramesh Chand, Member, NITI Aayog.

12

The Malady in Healthcare: Agenda for Action

ALOK KUMAR, KHEYA MELO FURTADO,
SNEHA PALIT, ALOK KUMAR DUBEY

Good governance is the sine-qua-non for the developmental process, while corruption is antithetical to good governance. In the absence of good governance, governments fail to deliver public services effectively, health and education services are often substandard and corruption kills opportunities and growth.[1] India has achieved rapid economic growth in the two decades since it embarked upon economic liberalization, and has pulled out millions of its citizens out of poverty. Yet, its performance on social sector indicators pertaining to education, health and nutrition has belied expectations for the level of economic progress. While there remains a case for enhanced government spending on health and nutrition, it is a fact that at the current levels of public spending, outcomes in health and nutrition are poorer than countries with similar or lower levels of economic development. For instance, we have created a workforce of 3.4 million front-line workers at the community level to address the twin issues of health and nutrition in addition to an elaborate super-structure of a supervisory cadre at the block, district, state and national levels, yet we fare worse than Bangladesh and Nepal on mortality and undernourishment indicators. Therefore, it appears that an efficiency question needs answers given that outcomes are not in line with investments. A partial answer to this question lies in the inefficacy of our delivery systems, a part of which may be due to the corrosive influence of corruption stemming out of a lack of accountability of these service providers, to the ordinary citizen.

Endemic Prevalence of Corruption

According to a recent Transparency International publication, India has the highest bribery rate among all countries surveyed in the Asia-Pacific region, with 69 per cent of the people accessing public services reporting having paid a bribe for the same.[2] Of greater concern, however, is the fact that India also reported the highest bribery rate of all countries (59 per cent) for accessing healthcare services in the public sector whereas the corresponding global average was 18 per cent. While there may be arguments about the robustness of the methodology employed by these surveys, the finding that there is a persistently high perception of corruption among those accessing public hospitals remains, although it is heartening to note that its prevalence shows a marginally declining trend over the years. Repeated surveys by different institutions measuring the public perception and experience of corruption over the period 2002–10 have documented the endemic prevalence of corruption in health service delivery.[3,4,5] Although, within India, studies report that the public perception of corruption is highest with the police services, followed closely by health and education sectors, the essentiality of healthcare and frequency of interaction of the people with the system, cause the maximum impact of corruption among the masses in this sector.[2] The forms in which this is manifested traverses the entire gamut of the mixed Indian health system, consisting public and private service providers.

Therefore, although the former accounts for a national average of 20-40 per cent of service delivery which is, in principle, low-cost (with a large proportion of free services), accessible and available to the most vulnerable of populations, it does not remain free of the scourge of corrupt individuals and networks that seek to exploit vulnerable population groups in the face of an absence of adequate social security.

Fixing Accountability

The foremost issue in public sector health delivery is the lack of accountability. This is translated firstly into large-scale absenteeism of government health workers, reportedly at 40 per cent in 2008,[6] and even recently reported as ranging from 28-68 per cent across states. While self-reported reasons include official duty and leave, unauthorized absence accounts for up to 18 per cent of absenteeism.[7]

Even when public sector primary care doctors do show up for work, the quality of care provided merits questioning the returns on investment in public funds for healthcare. Das et al.[8] report that the quality of care provided by qualified government doctors is no better than that of unqualified private sector doctors, who spend more time per patient and are more likely to ask essential questions required for a standardized treatment protocol. The likelihood to correctly diagnose and treat a patient was similar for public and private providers. While there was a positive correlation between prices charged by private doctors and the measures of quality of care provided, there was no correlation between the salaries of public doctors and the quality of care provided.

However, in the cited study, the same government doctors were found to provide better care in their private practices, thereby implying that the control mechanisms regulating provider behaviour is conspicuous by its absence. Therefore, while the lack and quality of human resources forms a major limitation to efficient delivery of healthcare services in the public sector, the low levels of effort and motivation seem to exist in a space that doesn't provide incentives to its staff to perform, neither disincentives not to, or to under-perform.

Informal Payments

Within the publicly delivered health services, those related to pregnancy and childbirth have always remained the focus of health policy in India, and account for the largest share of allocations under the flagship scheme of National Health Mission (NHM). Initiatives such as the Janani Suraksha Yojana (JSY) and Janani Shishu Suraksha Karyakram (JSSK) provide either cash transfers to women to ensure institutional deliveries or provide free services to the mother and a sick newborn up to thirty days after birth. However, recent estimations of out-of-pocket expenditure per delivery in public health facilities remain as high as ₹3,198 for India (including urban and rural areas), with rural deliveries also incurring high costs of an average of ₹2,947 per delivery.[9] These figures signal a failure of the core of public health service delivery, which is supposed to be free at the point of care, even for the minimalistic services related to pregnancy and childbirth. Evaluations of the JSY have reported that cash transfers are not received in full by the woman, and leakages occur owing to distribution of this amount among health workers who are responsible to ensure service delivery.[10] Since the introduction of JSY, institutional delivery rates have gone up. However, it is also true that households incur higher out-of-pocket expenses than they would if they had undergone home deliveries in addition to the corrupt and rude behaviour of health staff. There are reasons to be anxious about univocally promoting institutional deliveries, thereby defeating the purpose of their intention, and leading to hardship for families.[10,11,12] If women and their family members have to make informal payments in the flagship initiative of the government, then the extent of prevalence of this scourge could be very well imagined. Corruption may not only manifest itself in the rampant under-the-table payments made for supposedly free health services, but also in the lack of accountability of healthcare workers for the services they provide

BOX 1

Interviewer: 'How was it in the hospital?'
Lilam did not respond.
Interviewer: 'So you did not have an OK time in the hospital?'
Lilam: 'No.'
She did not look up from the pot she was scrubbing.
Interviewer: 'Why not?'
When Lilam looked up, she gave the impression she might be about to cry. She started to respond, hesitated, and then looked back down at her work.
Interviewer: 'Was it because of the pain, or the money, or something else?'
Lilam: 'There will be pain [when someone gives birth], it was because of the money.'
Lilam went on to explain that her husband fought with the staff to try to avoid paying them the money he had scrambled to borrow from neighbors before they left for the hospital. Eventually, he paid 480 rupees so that she could be admitted.
Interviewer: 'So what would happen if you said that you weren't going to pay?'
Lilam's mother-in-law: 'If you don't pay, they don't look at you, or admit you, or cut the cord. If you don't pay, they turn you out.'
Lilam's female relative: 'The hospital was built to help people, but if you don't pay, they run you off.'

Source: Extract from Coffey D. (2014)[10]

Unethical Practices in the Private Sector

The private-for-profit healthcare sector has witnessed an explosive growth in the last two decades. The private sector was responsible for 5–10 per cent of patient care at the time of Independence.[13] The initial Five Year plans provided policy space for the growth of the private-for-profit sector in the provision of curative and specialist services. This was meant to fill in the gaps in public service provision as a means to supplement government spending.[14,15] The measures aimed at increasing private sector provisioning of healthcare services included providing highly subsidized land, loans with low rates of interest, reduced costs for utility services and tax concessions.[13] These entitlements were often accompanied by clauses that required the private sector to offer a proportion of their services free of charge or at concessional rates to the economically disadvantaged sections of the population. However, these provisions did not achieve the intended objectives due to the absence of effective regulation that ensured compliance to contract conditions. Consequently, the private sector provides 60–80 per cent of healthcare and remains a critical provider of services.

Regulatory permissiveness and passivity have led to a proliferation of unethical provider behaviour in the delivery of health services. What was earlier confined to individual instances of first-hand stories of patients suffering at the hands of private providers has become pervasive enough to attract documentation. A plethora of published evidence is now available that captures this pernicious practice. For instance, the *British Medical Journal* reported a collection of instances of corruption in private medical practice covering the domains of medical education, cash referrals and kickbacks, financial relationships between doctors and private medical industry, and instances of scams in the NHRM.[16] Similarly, in their recent book *Dissenting Diagnosis*[17], practising doctors, Arun Gadre and Abhay Shukla present a disturbing insight into the reality of medical practice (both public and corporate) exposing the extent of the rot within the profession. They cite umpteen instances of unnecessary procedures, prescriptions and diagnostics, often resulting from the burden of targets set by large hospitals on doctors to enable them to be employed; greed induced kickbacks or commissions received for prescribing these services; and the hold that pharmaceutical companies have over doctors through 'freebies' and 'gifts' that require the doctors to in turn adhere to unethical demands of these companies through their clinical services.

Regulatory Failure: Guarding the Guardians

Professional councils were set up with the intention to serve as self-regulators of the practice of the medical and other allied professions. In theory, they were expected to maintain a judicious balance between the often diverging interests of medical professionals and citizens while ensuring that the standards of professional education and practice keep up with the evolving situation. However, in practice, they have degenerated into trade unions, where a caucus elected by an electoral college consisting of the very same regulated professionals, presides over an anarchy perpetuating the entrenched privileges of the professionals, at the cost of a hapless citizenry. These councils could maintain a semblance of credibility till 1991, but post the economic liberalization, with the opening up of professional medical education to the private sector and these councils becoming the final arbiters of permitting entry to private colleges, it did not take long for them to degenerate into cesspools of rent-seeking. They stopped attracting the best talents from the profession and we have repeatedly witnessed the unedifying spectacle of the heads of these councils being jailed and facing charges of bribery and corruption in various courts of law. The case of the Medical Council of India (MCI) is symptomatic of the malady afflicting these bodies. The Parliamentary Standing Committee on Health and Family Welfare consolidated the numerous reports of corruption and dereliction of functions by the MCI. It was constrained to observe that as a regulator '…MCI has repeatedly failed on all its mandates over the decades' and further that the challenges of a twenty-first century health and medical education system 'cannot be addressed with an ossified and opaque body like MCI. Transformation will happen only if we change the innards of the system. Game changer reforms of transformational nature are therefore the need of the hour and they need to be carried out urgently and immediately'. It listed exchange of money in the sanctioning of medical colleges, in increasing and decreasing seats, cases of ghost faculty and patients during inspections of medical colleges, and no action against such practices as well as the lack of transparency in the election process of the council members.[18] All in all, there is enough evidence to suggest that the body was no longer able to function since it had its authority undermined through systematic floundering of rules for monetary gain.[19] In a partial measure to ameliorate the situation, the Government of India has prepared a draft National Medical Commission Bill, 2016, set to replace to existing MCI established under the Indian Medical Council Act, 1956.

Actions at Multiple Levels

The 'trust' factor, so essential in healthcare, has unfortunately eroded in both public and private healthcare sectors. Underlying these behaviours are issues of design in health systems, market influences, incentives that govern provider behaviour and accountability, and governance mechanisms. All these factors remain interlinked and require actions at multiple levels to curb their influence. Adherence to standard treatment protocols and the quality of healthcare can be monitored and controlled when all such data are recorded in electronic formats and subject to periodic audits. The strengthening of health information systems, therefore, is vital to creating mechanisms for monitoring and quality assurance. Digitization of patient records and data availability to the extent needed (while protecting patient privacy) requires to be taken up on priority for both public and private sector health services. However, to ensure data provision by the private sector, effective methods of engagement with the sector are required to be developed by the government. Even today, no nationwide law has been affected that requires the compulsory registration of private sector health facilities with the government. Data sharing, therefore, remains a next level of complexity in private sector engagement by the government. One method of achieving this is to initiate a single-payer system in which the government can leverage its purchasing power to control quality of care, by both public and private sector. The ability of governing systems to hold providers accountable for health outcomes of patients may also be dependent on such a system and requires to be appropriately in-built to ensure that a certain level of accountability is built into the system without placing a burden on health providers. Provider payment methods may then be effectively designed as per the level of care, for example, capitation payments for primary and outpatient care and diagnosis-related group for secondary and tertiary care, as opposed to a fee for service payments, to control costs and disincentivize over-provision. However, here too the need for monitoring service provision is required to ensure there is no under-provision of services.

There are initiatives that are aimed at curtailing unethical practices. For example, a recent report describes a group of diagnostic laboratories in Bengaluru that have come together to offer laboratory tests at 40 per cent lower rates than the average market price for these tests.[20] This is seen as an effort to curb uncontrolled cost escalation in prices of tests and protect citizens from being compelled to avail of expensive services. In order to provide a space for the public to report cases of unethical practices experienced, websites such as www.medileaks.in provide a platform for healthcare professionals, patients and relatives to submit their stories so that patterns and trends can be identified and reported, serving as a repository of information on unethical medical practices.

Patient rights, measures for grievance redressal and visible action on these grievances by those in authority are paramount to ensure that the victimization of patients is arrested, especially where information asymmetry in addition to the essentiality of the health services places people in a uniquely vulnerable situation.

Nutrition

The Integrated Child Development Scheme (ICDS) is one of the world's largest supplementary nutrition and early childhood care programme that has been under implementation since 1975. Currently, it has a network of 1.4 million Anganwadi centres (AWCs) being operated by 2.5 million Anganwadi Workers (AWWs) and helpers and is availed of by 101 million beneficiaries.[21,22] It is aimed at addressing the vicious cycle of malnutrition, morbidity, mortality and reduced learning capacity. The Supplementary Nutrition Programme (SNP) is at the core of the ICDS with roughly half of the total budgetary allocation of ₹14,000 crore (2016–17)[23] having been dedicated to it.

Considering the fact that ICDS has been implemented over decades now, significant improvement in the nutritional levels is a natural expectation.

However, Figure 1 highlights the key nutrition indicators of children. The decline has been less than a percentage point per annum in stunting and underweight prevalence with no movement at all in wasting. The situation is similar with respect to prevalence of anaemia among women within 15-49 years of age with a near negligible decline from 55.3 per cent (from National Family Health Survey [NFHS] 3) to 53 per cent (NFHS 4). As is evident, absolute levels of malnutrition continue to remain high (we are worse off than many Sub-Saharan African nations such as Rwanda, Sudan, Sierra Leone and Chad) and the rates of decline remain disconcertingly low (we are worse off than Bangladesh and Nepal, in this respect). In fact, studies have gone so far as to find no or limited statistically significant causal impact of the presence of an AWC in a village on child anthropometric measures.[24]

Figure 1. Key Nutrition Indicators (children <5 years) in %

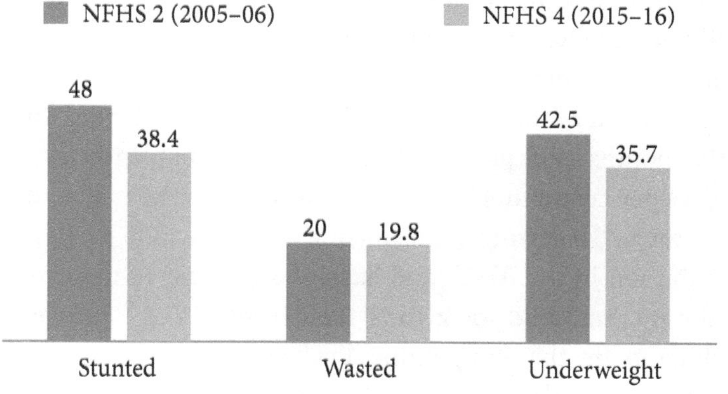

Admittedly, there are multiple determinants of population nutrition status. India is stuck in a vicious intergenerational malnutrition cycle which includes factors such as the poor social status of women in the family, low body mass index of mothers, limited initiation of breastfeeding following childbirth, failure to rely exclusively on breastfeeding in first six months of birth, inability to provide nutritious complementary food to infants after 6 months of age, incidences of diseases such as diarrhoea, fever and influenza during childhood, poor sanitary and hygiene practices and inaccessible healthcare services.[25] These factors perpetuate the poor nutritional status. Given this scenario, it would be impossible to isolate the impact of weak delivery systems riddled with corruption, inefficiency and lack of accountability on our inability to make a decisive impression in addressing malnutrition. Equally, it will be naive to deny the adverse impact of the corrupt practises upon the quality of service delivery.

Several studies and evaluations of the ICDS have attempted to examine its efficacy in terms of quality and adequacy of service delivery in which prevalence of corruption has been cited as a major impediment in the achievement of its desired outcomes, in addition to other reasons. For instance, the Rapid Survey on Children (RSOC) study shows that only 42 per cent of lactating mothers (mothers of children aged 0–5 months) received supplementary food from AWC. The proportion of children aged 6–35 months and 36–71 months receiving supplementary food was 49 per cent and 44 per cent, respectively. The major reasons cited for not receiving supplementary food include 'lack of food distribution in the AWC' and 'lack of awareness of the eligibility of the mother/child for getting food from AWC'.[26] Similarly, an evaluation by the Programme Evaluation Organisation (PEO) of the erstwhile Planning Commission highlighted issues regarding the programme design and its implementation such as inadequacy of required infrastructure; overburdened, underpaid and unskilled AWWs; and low effective coverage as compared to the official statistics[27] (a euphemism for leakages).

In the face of large-scale leakages under the ICDS, the Supreme Court took cognizance of the matter and was constrained to appoint commissioners to conduct investigation.[28] The report of the commissioners pointed towards non-functionality of several sanctioned centres[29] as summarized by the Court in its order as: 'The Report presents a gloomy picture both in regard to the operation of the sanctioned AWCS in some of the states like Uttar Pradesh, Bihar and Jharkhand and the position in those which are operational. Instances have been given in the Report where for months the supplies were not made to the children.'

Some of the common observations regarding corrupt practices in the SNP are further elaborated below.

Inflating Beneficiaries

Instances of proxy beneficiaries have been reported by evaluation studies as well as news reports. The Planning Commission study (2011) points out instances of manipulation in the official statistics relating to beneficiary coverage and functional AWCs. A recent investigation by the Vigilance and Anti-Corruption (V&AC) unit in Assam[30] found as many as nine lakh fake (ghost) beneficiaries (about 20 per cent of the total enrolment) and 390 fake AWCs. It is estimated that the scale of pilferage in this single case was to the tune of ₹150 crore over the last fifteen years. While this particular case came to light during scrutiny, such incidents are neither new nor uncommon. This is not helped by the fact that the financial provisions for SNP, i.e. ₹6 per child per day and ₹7 per woman per day [31] were fixed in 2011 and have not been revised since. In itself, the paltry provision is insufficient.

Moreover, they have not been indexed to food price inflation unlike the mid-day meal programme, thereby letting inflation gradually eat into the entitlements of the mother and child. This, among other reasons, pushes the field functionaries to take recourse to manipulating beneficiary data by recording a large number of ghost/proxy beneficiaries in the official records and the SNP supply chain.

Nexus with Private Contractors

The report of the Supreme Court commissioners points to a deep-rooted nexus of programme implementers and private contractors to siphon off funds meant for poor children and women.[32] Prohibiting the involvement of private contractors in nutrition supply, the Court ordered, 'Contractors shall not be used for supply of nutrition in Anganwadis and preferably ICDS funds shall be spent by making use of village communities, self-help groups and Mahila Mandals for buying of grains and preparation of meals.[33] It was envisaged that this order will break the contractor-politician-bureaucrat nexus, ensure transparency in the supply of nutritious food while simultaneously promoting rural employment and increasing community ownership. However, such is the strength of this unholy alliance that it remains immune to the majesty of the law as laid down by the order, and several state governments have found creative means to subvert it with complete impunity. The Court commissioners, in their follow-up reports, have alluded to such violations by the governments of Uttar Pradesh, Maharashtra, Gujarat and Karnataka.[34] In other states, where the orders have been complied with, the contractors have found innovative ways to use the women Self Help Groups (SHGs) as a front to carry on with business as usual without embracing any change as was envisaged by the Supreme Court.

Diversion of Food

Under SNP, freshly cooked meals and morning snacks are provided to children between 3 and 6 years of age, while 'take-home rations' consisting of micronutrient, fortified and energy-dense foods are provided to children aged 6 months to 3 years, pregnant women and lactating mothers.[35] The foodgrains are obtained from PDS shops. Instances of diversion of foodgrains procured under SNP are quite common. They fall under two categories: first, the superior quality is sold to private traders and low-quality supplements which are inedible to the extent that they are fed to the cattle rather than being retained for human consumption.

A study in Andhra Pradesh has highlighted how supplementary nutrition powder believed to be of superior quality is sold to dairy farmers who in turn use it to feed cattle.[36] On the other hand, several cases have come up indicating the substandard quality of the food provided. Samples in Maharashtra and Uttar Pradesh failed to meet the prescribed norms for nutritional standards and calorific content.[37]

Addressing Critical Challenges

Even though the scale, size and complexity of the problems appear formidable, despondency is not an option since a malnourished workforce is incompatible with the idea of an emerging India. Depending on their respective social capitals, different states have evolved different scalable solutions that are working fairly well in their context. Amongst them, we present the models pioneered by Odisha and Kerala in Box 2. However, there is an urgent need to check the corrupt practices and strengthen the entire system of service delivery at AWCs and its outcome monitoring.

BOX 2	
Kerala Model The Kudumbashree experiment in Kerala involves 2.15 lakh neighbourhood groups (NHGs) federated into Area Development Societies at the ward level, and Community Development Societies (CDS) at the Gram Panchayat/Municipality Level. Supplementary nutrition through the Nutrimix, viz. Amruthan which is a cereal based powder is created by micro-enterprises of women SHGs. Amruthan is produced by a common production protocol with high degree of quality control measures adopted. Each Nutrimix Unit supplies the Amruthan to the AWCs in its service area.	**Odisha Model** The key is to decentralize the procurement decisions regarding nutrition ingredients to the Panchayats. SHGs provide Chattua, a Ready to Eat (RTE) mix—packaged in colour-coded packets—to women and children every fortnight. A monthly procurement plan is made by the AWW and Ward member. The Jaanch Committee, formulated at every Revenue Village verifies and approves the plan and the money is accordingly transferred to the joint bank account of the AWW and Ward member. Any leftover cost is used to provide additional food material. A statement of expenses is prepared and verified by the Jaanch Committee and the vouchers are kept safe.

The models address one link in the chain of corruption, namely supply of Take Home Rations (THR) for pregnant and lactating mothers and children below the age of three. However, their universal replicability is also suspect since the capacity and vibrancy of women SHG movement show huge variations across states. While community oversight over nutrition programmes is a basic requirement to minimize, if not eliminate, the scourge of corruption from SNP, the challenge of building capacities is a non-trivial one. Use of technology will aid the process of social audit and Aadhaar seeding of Beneficiary Database would go a long way in addressing ghost beneficiaries and AWCs. Geotagged uploading of pictures of hot cooked meals being served at the AWCs and dedicated call centres to handle grievances relating to the delivery system would enable programme managers to monitor the SNP in a far more efficient manner. An option of a Direct Benefit Transfer (DBT) of an equivalent amount of cash to an Aadhaar-linked mother's bank account could also be considered in lieu of the in kind supplementary food so that the purchasing decision is delegated to the mother who is in the best position to safeguard the interest of her child. An investment in creating a universal Mother and Child Database duly recording the growth charts and access to health services on a real time basis using handheld devices by the front-line workers would be critical in fixing accountability frameworks for performance at all levels.

The deep-seated problem of corruption impacts achievement of desired outcomes that are vital for human development, and by extension, economic growth. India is at the crossroads of a large potential being transformed into achievements. However, if we are to harness our underlying potential, the sectors that have been traditionally left behind to competing priorities, need the impetus that is rightfully theirs. Health and nutrition are at the core of improving the quality of life of Indian citizens. Therefore, ensuring that all investments in these sectors can be efficiently converted into desired outcomes requires that the leakages and inefficiencies are rooted out. For this, good governance must pave the path for real national development. The road to good governance will require us to fix our accountability frameworks which in turn would crucially hinge upon our ability to leverage technology to empower our citizens. We believe that we have both the capacity and the intent, but are we willing to walk the talk?

References

1 https://www.ifac.org/global-knowledge-gateway/governance/discussion/good-governance-and-fight-against-corruption

2 People and Corruption: Asia Pacific- Global Corruption Barometer 2017, Transparency International, March 2017.

3 'Corruption in India', Transparency International India and ORG-MARG, 2002.

4 'India Corruption Study 2005', Centre for Media Studies and Transparency International India.

5 'India Corruption Study 2010', Centre for Media Studies.

6 'Provider Absence surveys in Education and Health: A Guidance Note', World Bank.

7 'Understanding Healthcare Access in India', IMS Institute for Healthcare Informatics, 2012.

8 J. Das, A. Holla, A. Mohpal & K. Muralidharan. 2016. 'Quality and Accountability in Health Care Delivery: Audit-Study Evidence from Primary Care in India', *American Economic Review*, 106(12), pp. 3765–99.

9 National Family Health Survey 2015–16 (estimate for last birth in the five years prior to the survey).

10 D. Coffey. Costs and consequences of a cash transfer for hospital births in a rural district of Uttar Pradesh, India. 2014. *Social Science and Medicine*, 114, pp. 89–96.

11 S.S. Gopalan & D. Varatharajan D. 2012. 'Addressing maternal healthcare through demand side financial incentives: experience of Janani Suraksha Yojana program in India', *BMC Health Services Research*, 12, p. 319.

12 P. Jeffery & R. Jeffery R. 2010. 'Only when the boat has started sinking: A maternal death in rural north India'. *Social Science and Medicine*, 10, pp. 1711–18.

13 P.H. Rao. 2012. 'The Private Health Sector in India : A Framework for Improving the Quality of Care' *ASCI J Management*, 41(2), pp. 14–39.

14 R. Duggal. 2001. 'Evolution of Health Policy in India'.

15 'National Health Policy'. Ministry of Health and Family Welfare, Government of India, 1983.

16 'Corruption in Healthcare, collection of articles'. 2015. *British Medical Journal*, http://www.bmj.com/campaign/corruption-healthcare

17 A. Gadre & A. Shukla. 2016. *Dissenting Diagnosis*. New Delhi: Random House India.

18 Department-Related Parliamentary Standing Committee on Health and Family Welfare: Report 92 submitted to the Rajya Sabha on 8 March 2016.

19 R. Baru & A. Diwate. 'Vyapam is the symptom, Criminalization of Medical Education is the disease', The Wire, 12 July 2015.

20 '45 diagnostic laboratories team up, slash prices of tests by 40%', Times News Network, 19 March 2017.

21 Annual Report 2016–17, Ministry of Women & Child Development.

22 Children (6 months to 6 years) and pregnant and lactating mothers.

23 This is only the contribution of the Union government, the states put in their matching share on a 50:50 basis for SNP and 40:60 basis for other components (20:80 and 10:90 for the Northeastern and Hilly states).

24 B. Maity. 2016. 'Interstate Differences in the Performance of Anganwadi Centers under ICDS Scheme', *Economic & Political Weekly*, LI(51).

25 Editorials. 2012. *Economic & Political Weekly*, XLVI(12).

26 Rapid Survey on Children (RSOC), Ministry of Women and Child Development and The United Nations Children's Fund (UNICEF), 2013–14.

27 'Evaluation Report on Integrated Child Development Services Volume I', http://planningcommission.nic.in/reports/peoreport/peoevalu/peo_icds_v1.pdf

28 http://www.sccommissioners.org/About/about.html

29 http://www.sccommissioners.org/CourtOrders/Orders/ICDS_071004.pdf

30 http://www.assamtribune.com/scripts/detailsnew.asp?id=nov0316/at050

31 Annual Report 2016–17, Ministry of Women & Child Development.

32 http://www.indiaenvironmentportal.org.in/content/367355/supreme-court-commissioners-report-on-supplementary-nutrition-scheme-under-icds/

33 http://www.sccommissioners.org/CourtOrders/Orders/ICDS_071004.pdf

34 In April 2001, the People's Union for Civil Liberties (PUCL), Rajasthan, submitted to the Supreme Court a writ petition seeking enforcement of the right to food. The PUCL contended in the appeal that the right to food is fundamental for the right to life enshrined in Article 21 of the Indian Constitution. The case has become public interest litigation and accordingly received a considerable number of interim orders. Among these orders is Interim Order dated 8 May 2002 which installed commissioners of the Supreme Court and stipulated their power to investigate violations of interim orders related to the case, and demand redress. http://www.sccommissioners.org/About/about.html

35 B. Maity. 2016. 'Interstate Differences in the Performance of Anganwadi Centers under ICDS Scheme', *Economic & Political Weekly*, LI(51).

36 D. Sinha. 2006. 'Rethinking ICDS: A rights based perspective', *Economic & Political Weekly*, 3689–94.

37 http://www.business-standard.com/article/economy-policy/india-sees-children-dying-as-2-bn-programme-proves-defective-112122302010_1.html

◆

Alok Kumar is a 1993 batch IAS officer of the UP cadre and currently heads the Health and Nutrition vertical at NITI Aayog.

Kheya Melo Furtado is a Research Assistant in the Health Division at NITI Aayog.

Sneha Palit is a Young Professional in the Women & Child Development Division of NITI Aayog.

Alok Kumar Dubey is a Research Assistant in the Women & Child Development Division of NITI Aayog.

13

Ignobility in a Noble Occupation: Corruption in Higher Education

BHAVANA KOHLI

सर्वेषामेव दानानां विद्यादानं विशिष्यते।
Of all gifts, imparting education is the best charity.

As this ancient Indian saying signifies, education has been traditionally seen as a charitable and noble occupation. A certain moral elevation is associated with it as it serves larger public interests. After all, individuals and nations develop, evolve and progress due to the knowledge and competencies acquired through education. The noble and charitable connotations associated with education do not imply that those in these occupations should have no material needs or desires—they are of course entitled to reasonable remuneration from their source of livelihood. However, the larger public good is expected to take precedence.

Our national policy framework and the rulings of our judiciary have taken positions in favour of education being kept away from profiteering and commercialization. Through multiple judgements[1], the Supreme Court of India has emphasized that education is a 'noble occupation' that should be carried out on a 'no-profit-no-loss' basis[2]. Moreover, with reference to Article 19(1)(g) of the Constitution that gives all citizens the right to carry out any occupation, trade or business, the Court ruled that education can only be considered as an 'occupation', and not as a 'trade' or 'business', as the latter two connote profit motives.[3] In case an educational institution generates a reasonable surplus of revenue, after its expenditures on salaries, infrastructure, facilities, maintenance, and so on, this surplus is expected to be reinvested to improve or expand the institution's educational activities. Also, it is noteworthy that our legal framework[4] defines employees of all universities, public or private, as 'public servants'.

While it is a debatable matter, the rationale of expecting educational activities to refrain from profit-making motives sounds reasonable. Nevertheless, one cannot help but wonder whether these expectations are utopian. When the country's medical sector can be corrupted to such shocking levels that human lives are compromised, it would be naïve to expect education to remain immune to profit-making taking precedence over public good. In reality, numerous people are involved in the education sector only with the motive of making money.

However, what is more serious is when public servants, who are duty-bound to ensure standards in this 'noble' activity, use their positions to compromise the standards of our educational institutions for illegal personal monetary gains. The importance of this public duty needs to be understood beyond a commonly held, superficial, short-term view. The quality of the country's human resource is liable to being impacted if its education system does not meet basic standards. The ramifications of granting undeserved approvals to higher educational institutions appear more grim if one realizes, for instance, that the lives of people (and perhaps our own) may be at stake with doctors trained at or with structures built by engineers trained at those institutions. Even at a micro level, granting undeserved recognition or approvals to a college amounts to playing havoc with unsuspecting young students' educational future, career and financial resources. That everyone regulating our education system engages in undeserved approvals is not the insinuation. Our regulatory bodies and innumerable public servants do a commendable job, in many ways, of regulating a system of mammoth proportions. Similarly, innumerable people run excellent educational institutions. But there are many persons who do engage in corrupt practices for personal gains, and lay knowledge is sufficient to infer that these people exist in sizable numbers in the education sector.

In view of the above, it is critical to focus on the issue of public servants engaging in corruption[5] for grant of recognition or approvals of higher educational institutions by regulatory bodies. In case of such approvals, both parties involved, that is representatives of regulatory bodies as well as employees of educational institutions, fall under the legal meaning[6] of 'public servants'.

There are certain key scenarios in which such corruption may occur. One category of cases involves the grant of approvals to undeserving institutions who do not meet the required standards. A second category is where an institution meeting required norms and standards is not granted the approval it deserves or delays are caused, unless its representatives pay the illegal gratification desired by officials of regulatory bodies. A third category relates to ambiguity or lack of objectivity in certain norms and requirements that allows discretion on part of the regulatory bodies to arrive at their own judgment on the institution's ability to meet a particular requirement.

There is indubitable evidence[7]—in the form of reports of high-level committees, CBI enquiries, judicial proceedings, press reports—of corruption in grant of approvals of higher educational institutions, particularly private institutions. Over the years, there have been numerous complaints that private institutions literally 'buy' recognition and approvals of their programmes by paying bribes to regulatory officials. A former president of the country's medical education regulator admitted during an investigation by a Parliamentary Standing Committee last year that there was rampant corruption in the grant of approvals to medical colleges. CBI officials reported that within a span of less than a year they investigated more than 200 complaints and found that forty-two private engineering colleges were granted illegal approvals. At one point, seventeen CBI offices were investigating more than 100 persons across India in these matters. Officials and representatives across the regulatory hierarchy—from inspection committee members to top leadership of these statutory bodies—have been charged with corruption. Bureau officials have reportedly found that some inspection committees from professional councils did not even visit the institutions' sites before submitting reports, while some knowingly visited the same site for three different colleges and approved the establishment of all three at the same location. In another case, according to CBI sources, an inspection committee submitted a report approving an engineering college at a particular site in Uttar Pradesh that was found to be a farmland. The nadir of the perceived credibility of our regulatory bodies was seen in recent years when the CBI charged the chairmen of certain professional councils for accepting bribes ranging from tens of lakhs of rupees to a couple of crores to grant approvals to private colleges.

Higher Education Landscape and Regulatory Framework

An understanding of how such corruption operates requires a deeper dive into our country's higher education landscape. Higher educational institutions in India are categorized as university-level institutions, colleges, and stand-alone institutions. University-level institutions include central and state public universities, institutions of national importance, and public deemed to be universities—all funded and managed by the government. In addition, there are state private universities and private deemed to be universities that are funded and managed by the private sector. Colleges may be funded and/or managed by the public or private sector, but every private college must be affiliated to a public university, which awards degrees to its students. Stand-alone institutions typically run diploma programmes (e.g. polytechnics and institutions awarding management, nursing or teacher training diplomas), and while they function outside the purview of universities, they do require recognition from the concerned regulatory body.

India has 760 university-level institutions, about 39,000 colleges, and almost 13,000 stand-alone institutions.[8] In the last couple of decades, there has been an exponential growth in the number of private providers of higher education. Now, the private sector dominates the higher education landscape, especially in 'lucrative' areas of professional education. The statistics are striking—65 per cent of deemed universities, 63 per cent of colleges and 66 per cent of stand-alone institutions are private unaided. If we include institutions that receive government aid but are privately managed, the private sector makes up over three-fourths of these institutions.

Every higher educational institution in India is expected to acquire recognition and various kinds of approvals from the country's statutory regulatory bodies. The University Grants Commission (UGC) is the apex statutory body to regulate and fund universities in India. In addition, there are at least thirteen statutory professional councils that regulate and/ or fund programmes in specialized fields of higher education, including the All India Council for Technical Education (AICTE) for fields such as engineering/technology/management; National Council for Teacher Education (NCTE) for teacher training; and the MCI for medical education. These regulatory bodies are established and empowered by Acts[9], to establish and maintain standards of teaching, examination and research. A university requires recognition and various approvals from the UGC as well as all concerned professional councils in whose fields it offers or seeks to offer programmes. This chapter focuses on regulation by the UGC and AICTE, with limited references and anecdotal evidence of medical colleges and teacher training institutions.

The recognition and approvals are based on whether an institution meets a diverse set of requirements and norms laid down by these bodies. These cover the minutiae of academic and non-academic infrastructure and facilities, faculty and staff, type and content of permitted courses and their nomenclature, et al. To assess institutions, regulatory bodies are empowered by their Acts to conduct inspections, which involve pre-fixed visits to the institution's campus by an inspection committee comprising empanelled academicians and government officials. Depending on the nature of approval required by a private institution, regulatory bodies charge processing fees (that is, 'legal' fee) ranging from tens of thousands to a few lakh rupees.

Apart from recognitions and approvals, higher educational institutions are required to get 'accreditation' or quality grading from two designated government bodies: the National Assessment and Accreditation Council (NAAC) for universities and colleges, and the National Board of Accreditation (NBA) for programmes of technical education.

Higher Education Framework—Catalyst of Corruption?

Corruption indicates problems in the system. Individual motivations or a so-called degradation of social values and morals are not the main causes, although these can be strong propellants. A key reason for corruption to thrive is the presence of certain features and loopholes that provide a conducive environment. These include excessive regulation, discretion in the hands of powerful authorities, lack of accountability, penalties that are too mild or too heavy and mismatch between demand and supply. On close examination, many such features can be identified in our country's higher education scenario and regulatory framework.

Absolute Concentration of Power

The UGC is the only regulatory body empowered to grant recognition and approvals to universities and colleges. Similarly, the AICTE is the only statutory council to grant approvals to technical education institutions; similar is the case with the MCI for medical education and NCTE for teacher education. Moreover, the same body decides the norms and requirements, assesses and inspects institutions with respect to these norms and requirements, and then grants approval based on its own assessment reports. Thus, there is complete concentration of power in these regulatory bodies. In market terminology, they enjoy monopoly. The same is the case with accreditation, where only NAAC can accredit universities and NBA can accredit technical programmes.

In case of public institutions, recognition is linked to the key issue of funding. It is only when a public institution is recognized by the concerned regulatory body as being 'fit', can it receive any government funding. The problem of corruption in regulatory approvals is rampant in the case of private institutions, which are self-financing. For these institutions, our regulatory bodies command enormous power because of the importance of their recognition and approvals for the institution to hold value. Regulatory bodies regularly identify 'unrecognized', 'fake', or 'blacklisted' institutions, and issue public notices advising persons to refrain from seeking admission in these as their degree or diploma would hold no value. Thus, regulatory approval and recognition is a necessity.[10]

When there is complete concentration of power in an authority to grant a necessity, it creates conducive environments for misuse of that power to engage in forms of 'blackmail'. Moreover, the one requiring the necessity is also willing to go to great extents to obtain it.

Excessive Degree of Regulation

The existing level of regulation of higher education in our country is excessive in many respects—the purposes for which approvals are needed, the minutiae that are assessed for each purpose, the frequency with which assessments are required, as well as the coverage of educational institutions.

The purposes for which approvals from UGC and professional councils are needed include starting new institutions; any change or expansion in existing institutions, including additional courses/programmes, change in student intake; conversion of a women's institution to co-educational; conversion of a degree to diploma programme and vice versa; and foreign collaborations or twinning arrangements.

The norms and requirements cover the minutiae of physical infrastructure, such as, land and building norms and area; number and carpet area of classrooms, laboratories and other rooms or open spaces; laboratory equipment; number of computers, printers; software and Internet requirements; library facilities including books and journals; academic and non-academic facilities; and hospital requirements, number of medical and paramedical staff, number of patients, etc. specifically for medical colleges. There are also strict norms regarding the nomenclature of degree/diploma programmes and courses. Further, there are specific requirements regarding the number and qualifications of faculty and staff. Norms also cover aspects of pay scales, admission, examinations, etc.

The long list of reasons for approvals as well as micro-level requirements makes any approval process quite cumbersome. Moreover, it is not a one-time or infrequent exercise. The frequency with which some approvals are required increases not only the cumbersomeness, but also the opportunities for corruption. For instance, after granting approval to a new technical college, the concerned professional council requires the institution to get the approval renewed every year. Moreover, if an institution misses getting renewal for a particular academic year, then the next time it applies, many of the processes and fees involved would be as if the institution was applying for fresh approval as a new institution.

All these procedures are followed for all institutions in the country's mammoth landscape of higher education, irrespective of whether an institution falls in the top layer of high performers or at the bottom. The aforementioned excesses in regulation provide plenty of opportunities for regulatory bodies to leverage their power in granting highly sought-after approvals.

Arduous Procedures with Multiple Authorities

In addition to the above, every approval process involves long procedures with multiple authorities. Recently, some regulatory bodies have made attempts to reduce the intricacies in their approval process. But what they label as 'greater ease, simplification, and transparency' still appears to be quite complex, time-consuming and with loopholes.

A run through the approval process[11] for a new technical institution by AICTE is revealing. An institution submits its application on AICTE's online portal as a 'single window application'. However, the procedures involved are multilayered, cumbersome and without deadlines for many of the required actions by authorities. The application requires several documents, including various project plans, reports, financial information, affidavits, approvals and certificates from various state and local authorities. It is then evaluated by several layers of committees—scrutiny committee, a probable re-scrutiny committee, expert visit committee, regional committee, executive committee and a standing appellate committee—each of which submits its own reports. In addition, 'comments' are received from the concerned state government and the affiliating university/board. The various committees consist of a mix of AICTE officials, empanelled academicians, advocates, architects, bureaucrats and representatives of the state government and affiliating university/board. Thus, there are multiple stages and involvement of multiple persons/authorities at every stage. One cannot help but wonder in amusement at how claims of having a simple, easy, 'single window application' may actually conceal multiple mazes prior to and beyond that single 'window'.

When processes are not convenient and time-bound, it increases the desire and incentive to offer bribes to fast-track one's case. The stakes are especially high in case of annual 'renewals', because here an institution that is already functioning with enrolled students requires renewal for it to run its next academic session.

Lack of Objectivity in Norms and Requirements

The lack of clarity and objectivity in parameters of assessment opens the door to discretion by regulatory officials. Such lacunae can be exploited to reach judgments that suit an official depending on motives or rewards involved. Many such examples exist in current regulatory norms or guidelines. Close examination of several documents and inspection reports of regulatory bodies reveals the use of subjective words such as 'adequate' or 'satisfactory' when referring to norms/requirements.

A glaring example of misuse of subjectivity in requirements was in the declaration of institutions as deemed to be universities.[12] Institutions that are awarded this status enjoy certain privileges, some of which are not permitted even for universities. They gain greater autonomy (academic, administrative and financial) and can open campuses outside India. It is no wonder then that many private colleges seek this status, thus making it a breeding ground of grant of undeserved approvals. Assessment by the Tandon Committee[13] revealed that out of approximately 130 deemed universities, one-third did not deserve this status. Their condition was so poor that it was beyond scope for correction. A regulatory provision that was identified by the committee as a key point of misuse was where 'de novo' institutions that engaged in teaching/research in 'innovative' and 'emerging areas' of knowledge could be granted deemed university status. Institutions selected under this provision were exempt from the requirement for A-grade accreditation over three cycles, as was in place for other institutions. The subjectivity involved in judging 'innovative' and 'emerging areas of knowledge' was exploited to grant undeserved approvals to new private players.

Lack of Transparency in Inspection and Approval Process

Lack of transparency is the cornerstone of corruption. In recent years, some regulatory bodies have taken initiatives to improve the level of transparency. For example, videography of inspection committee visits to the institution is now mandatory. Also, some inspection reports are now uploaded on the websites of regulatory bodies. The AICTE now claims to select evaluation committee members through an 'automated' process.

However, gaps continue to exist. First, videography helps only to a limited extent. During inspections, colleges are known to prop up students or hire persons on hourly basis to act as faculty, nurses, doctors and even patients. The MCI's former president admitted that the regulator was aware of rampant practices of fake faculty and patients during medical college inspections. A press exposé revealed that on the day of inspection of a medical college, the security guard of the college hospital was instructed to disregard the visitor restriction rules. He was to let in as many patients and attendants as possible so that the hospital appeared 'full'. In case of such inspections, videography is likely to be no better than no videography—the only difference will be that the 'actors' will be playing their 'roles' in front of a camera. Second, regarding availability of inspection reports on the regulatory body's website, only a few reports are available online—it is not an exhaustive searchable database. Further, on examining some of these reports, one finds the main section claims to provide various 'details' about the institution in the annexures, but the annexures are actually missing from the version uploaded online. Third, the AICTE's supposed automated selection of committee members also has a loophole. Their handbook says that under 'extraordinary circumstances' or if a member is 'unable to attend', the AICTE officials can 'manually choose' the members of the evaluation committee. Does this not open the door to human intervention again? Persons enjoying favour with a private player can be purposely selected as evaluators under the garb of extraordinary circumstances or inability to attend.

Recommendations for Reforms

The stories (or one should say the 'facts') of corruption in higher education and how the system is tricked are disheartening. Our country's higher education regulatory framework was conceptualized with the objective of maintaining standards of higher education, but to claim that standards are *not* being maintained in a dominant share of our institutions is not an exaggeration. The urgent need to re-examine the framework is obvious, as there are several loopholes and catalysts in the system. While no solution may be foolproof, the system can be tightened through a series of interlinked reforms to make corruption increasingly difficult.

Reduce and Grade Levels of Regulation

There is a need to reduce regulation on all previously discussed aspects. First, the purposes for which approvals are needed and the minute requirements assessed need to be re-examined. Those that can be done away with should be cut down. For example, currently, private colleges need to obtain approval for every small increase in student intake. A way around this could be that while approving a new institution, the regulatory body should assess its infrastructure, facilities, staff, etc. by taking into account scope for future expansion expected by the institution, say in the next two to five years.

Next, the current frequency with which approvals are required is not reasonable. It appears unnecessary to require an institution, which has been duly approved, to get into the process of renewing its approval in less than a year's time. Infrastructure and facilities do not change so quickly under normal circumstances. If the regulatory body suspects that institutions may play foul and cut down facilities soon after the initial approval, then other measures should be in place to address the concern—for example, convenient complaint mechanisms and public blacklisting of institutions for violations.

Another key area needing reform is that the same extent of regulatory requirements need not encompass *all* educational institutions in the country. A graded level of autonomy should be conceptualized, wherein institutions with a history of high performance (A grades during accreditation) should be granted academic, administrative and financial autonomy in some respects. These Level-1 institutions should be exempt from regulatory approvals in specified matters. The second level of institutions receiving moderate accreditation grades may be granted a lower degree of autonomy. Finally, institutions accredited with low grades should have a greater degree of regulation. Such low-rung institutions are likely to compromise standards and interests of unsuspecting students. There should be a provision where repeatedly receiving accreditation grades below a certain level should make the institution liable for closure.

Self-disclosure on Centralized Public Portal

Efforts must be made at the national level to increasingly shift towards self-disclosure by institutions on a centralized public portal. This should replace the existing system of multiple layers of committees in multiple bodies evaluating institutions on multiple parameters, without public access to the basis of their approvals. The centralized portal should be used by all bodies and stakeholders. It is critical to ensure a user-friendly interface, which displays all the indicators for an institution, like a checklist. Every institution's self-declaration should be accompanied by an affidavit, making them liable for prosecution for false declarations. The portal should also have the functionality for every regulatory body or other authority to perform actions/flag issues/grant approvals in a time-bound manner, next to an institution's self-declared information, with links to supporting documents uploaded online.

Another key benefit of such a portal would be to have all the information online and visible to everyone. Psychological research says that continuous surveillance or the *perception* of continuous surveillance is required for moral regulation to be effective. If such a portal can be effectively implemented, it would indeed achieve *perception* of continuous surveillance for institutions and regulatory bodies.

Penalties must be put in place for false declarations or violations of norms after approvals. Moreover, if such a centralized, publically visible portal (with all of an institution's details, approvals or lack of them, outcomes, accreditation grades, etc.) can be popularized for use by the public, then poor indicators will itself act as a 'penalty' for an institution and affect the number of students it could attract.

Limited and Random Inspections

Self-disclosed information may be fabricated. To check such situations, random inspections by regulatory bodies are important. The system should be particularly open to public complaints against institutions, so that violations can be more easily identified and inspections be conducted. The above-described centralized portal may have such a mechanism to flag on-ground violations.

In addition, inspections must be conducted at random with no prior information to the concerned institution. The existing Acts provide for institutions to be informed in advance about dates of inspection (UGC Act, 1956). This gives institutions ample time to plan their act and set the stage with props and actors to welcome the inspection committee.

Further, inspections must be transparent. The full report of each inspection (including annexures) should be uploaded on the centralized portal on the web page of the concerned institution.

Minimize Scope for Subjectivity

Overall, excessive regulation needs to be pared down; however, for regulations that are retained, norms/requirements must be based on clearly defined parameters, without scope for subjective judgments and discretion by regulatory officials.

Strict Timelines

Avoidance of delays and long-drawn-out procedures in regulatory processes is an incentive for private players to engage in corrupt dealings. Also, sometimes, government officials purposely cause delays to hint to the other party to offer illegal gratifications. It is important to have strict timelines for each body to perform its role/action—this would check lingering of matters and enhance accountability.

To effectively build timelines into the system, the centralized portal could have tickers that display the time taken by every agency/body/person to perform their action, along with clearly visible deadlines.

Disclosure of Outcomes

Existing assessment of higher educational institutions is driven by a focus on inputs, which is believed by some to fuel 'licence raj.'[14] There is a need to build a simultaneous focus on outcomes, which are a critical measure of an institution's performance—such as, number of students passing out with minimum desired competencies, placement rates, research output of universities, etc. Every institution should declare its outcome performance on the centralized public portal. Further, exit tests should be conducted by credible national bodies (e.g. UGC, professional councils) and the number of students clearing these annually should be declared by every institution on the centralized portal. Existing national-level tests such as the National Eligibility Test (NET) and Graduate Aptitude Test in Engineering (GATE) may be used to start with.

Permit External Reputed Accreditation Agencies

Once a regulatory body grants approval to an institution, quality evaluation should be done by other agencies. There is a need to build a credible framework of such accreditation agencies—both national and international. While there are several agencies (many of international repute) that accredit higher educational institutions, this practice is not popular in India because our regulatory framework only recognizes accreditation by bodies under UGC and AICTE, according them monopoly.

Ratings by established and credible agencies can be recognized by our regulatory bodies. However, it must be ensured that such new regulation does not lead to the entry of unreliable players, resulting in a racket of buying accreditation grades. Such a racket grew in India after the UGC brought in a scheme to award points for publications by faculty, for their appointments and promotions—this became the breeding ground for several shoddy journals whose sole objective was to publish substandard research in return for money. Accreditation should place weight on outcome indicators such as competencies of students passing out of the institution, placement record, employer ratings, etc.

Increase Public Focus on Institution's Performance Indicators

Public awareness should be built regarding the importance of checking an institution's indicators, including accreditation grades, before seeking admission. For this purpose, the proposed centralized portal can be popularized among students and the public at large.

Simple Online Complaint Mechanism

The centralized portal should have a quick and simple mechanism to flag issues and complaints of violations by institutions. The numerous regional offices of national regulatory bodies should be boosted to address these complaints and take speedy action, including inspections to confirm reports of false declarations. Updates about each action taken and its report should be displayed on the centralized, publically available portal on the concerned institution's web page.

One cannot take a simplistic view on regulatory control by conveniently painting it as an ill that drives corruption and that must be discarded. The role of regulatory bodies is important to maintain basic standards, which may otherwise be compromised by entities that do not give due weight to quality and public interests. Our regulatory bodies perform a mammoth task considering the size of our higher education sector, which has grown to become the largest in the world. Their efforts and initiatives must be appreciated. If there was no regulation in higher education, the sector may have been in a worse state and one of utter chaos.

However, the current state of the regulatory framework is also problematic—it has several features and loopholes that are being rampantly exploited for corruption. The sector has seen several new lows in recent years. Thus, there is an urgent need to identify the problems, plug the loopholes and reform the system altogether, where needed.

A classic theory of moral development predicts that a large proportion of people would reason out performing an unethical act if they knew they would get away with rewards, without any punishment or social disapproval. According to this theory, there are three levels of moral thinking. Moral thinking of people who operate at the initial two levels is largely guided by self-interest, gain of rewards, avoidance of punishment, or a desire for social approval. Only those who reach the third 'post-conventional' level have an internalized personal code of ethical principles. Various studies have estimated that only 5–20 per cent adults reach this third level. These figures are hard-hitting. If this is true, it indicates that most people would indulge in unethical and corrupt acts if the system allowed them opportunities to slip through and get away without punishment.

To bring any serious reform in the higher education system, the will of politicians and bureaucrats is essential—that is a Pandora's box in itself. One hopes that ignobility in this noble activity will be addressed and appropriate reforms will be implemented, sooner than later.

References

1 Unni Krishnan, J. P. & Ors. v State of Andhra Pradesh & Ors. (4 February, 1993). Cited as 1993 AIR 2178, 1993 SCR (1) 594, 1993 SCC (1) 645, JT 1993 (1) 474, 1993 SCALE (1) 290.

2 Modern Dental College and Research Centre & Ors. v State of Madhya Pradesh & Ors. 2 May 2016. Civil Appeal No. 4060 of 2009.

3 T.M.A. Pai Foundation & Ors. v State of Karnataka & Ors. 31 October 2002. Writ Petition (Civil) 317 of 1993.

4 Prevention of Corruption Act, 1988.

5 Corruption is legally defined as taking or attempting to take 'gratification' other than 'legal remuneration' in respect of an official act (PCA, 1988).

6 PCA, 1988.

7 Yashpal Committee. 2009. Report of 'The Committee to Advise on Renovation and Rejuvenation of Higher Education'; P.N.

Tandon Committee. 2009. 'Report of the Committee for Review of Existing Institutions Deemed to be Universities'; National Institute of Financial Management. 2012. Draft Report: Study on Unaccounted Income/ Wealth both Inside and Outside the Country. NIFM: Faridabad; Hari Gautam Committee. 2015. Review of University Grants Commission for restructuring and strengthening to address imperatives and challenges in Higher Education sector; Ministry of Finance. 2015. Recommendations of SIT on Black Money as Contained in the Third SIT Report. Press Information Bureau; M.K. Kaw Committee. 2015. 'Technical education in India: A futuristic scenario - Report of the AICTE Review Committee'.

8 Ministry of Human Resource Development. 2016. 'All India Survey on Higher Education (2014–15)'.

9 For example, University Grants Commission Act, 1956; All India Council for Technical Education Act, 1987.

10 The case of Indian School of Business (ISB), Hyderabad, is rare. Owing to it being established and run by internationally acclaimed academic and corporate institutions, ISB managed to create a global reputation among employers, despite having no AICTE recognition. But, if an ISB graduate applies for further studies in India, his/her management education may not be recognized on paper, for instance, as meeting an eligibility criterion for prior education.

11 All India Council for Technical Education - Approval Process Handbook, 2017–18.

12 'Deemed to be university' is a status granted to established institutions performing well in post-graduate teaching and research in distinctive fields of study, e.g. Indian Institute of Science. This declaration is made by the central government, and recommended by the UGC under Section 3 of the UGC Act, 1956.

13 P.N. Tandon Committee. 2009. 'Report of the Committee for Review of Existing Institutions Deemed to be Universities'

14 A common argument, to completely replace input-focussed regulation with outcome-based evaluations, is hard to concur

with. Several inputs are critical and must not be ignored. For instance, a college's building as an input has to obviously be evaluated (for structural stability, safety and such basic norms). Evaluation of such inputs can obviously not be replaced with evaluations of its consequent outcomes (such as accidents).

◆

Dr Bhavana Kohli is a Young Professional at NITI Aayog.

14

Navigating the Public Procurement Maze

ANNA ROY AND RITIKA AGHI

Public procurement remains one of the major functions of a sovereign state, accounting for a significant part of government expenditure and the GDP of any country. Corruption in public procurement can have a debilitating impact on public welfare since it not only amounts to misuse of public funds, but can also adversely affect the quality of goods and services provided by the state. Given its scale and varied nature, public procurement is prone to a greater risk of malfeasance and thus the importance of putting in place an ecosystem that helps in arresting the incidence of corruption and promotes transparency, competitiveness and efficiency. Post-Independence India gave commanding heights of the economy to the state, thus implying substantial public procurement. However, as a subject it did not receive the requisite attention. Unlike several other developed and developing countries, India does not, as yet, have a procurement law, a policy or a dedicated institution to deal with public procurement. It is thus not surprising that the country has witnessed a series of scandals concerning public procurement over the years. These developments have taken both direct and indirect toll on the economy where, at times, the indirect costs have been far more substantial. The current state of public sector banks with their high level of non-performing assets (NPAs) and the sharp reduction in credit flow are, in many ways, a result of malfeasance in public procurement in different infrastructure sectors. In the absence of timely action on part of the government, the judiciary has intervened on several occasions to address the systemic issues. In 2011, in the wake of major scams like the spectrum scam and 'Coalgate', the government had set up the Committee on Public Procurement. However, almost all the substantive recommendations of the committee are yet to be implemented. The present government has taken several steps to combat corruption in public life, including in public procurement, such as setting up of Government e-Marketplace (GeM). However, several major issues remain to be addressed. It is thus imperative for the government to take a holistic view and lay down a roadmap comprising a comprehensive strategy, including enactment of a modern procurement law based on United Nations Commission on International Trade Law (UNCITRAL) Model Law as well as setting up of a dedicated department for meeting the ever-growing challenge of public procurement.

Context

Traditionally, states have played a central role, both in governance as well as in the provision of public goods and services to their citizens. However, the role of the state has varied across countries, with the private sector having a greater share in provision of public goods and services in developed countries where market imperfections are fewer. Globally, governments still remain the largest buyers of goods and services in their respective countries.[1]

Procurement of goods, services or works by or on behalf of the government or its agencies is termed as public procurement.[2]

Goods include simple commodities like office supplies, equipment, furniture, books, vehicles and medical supplies as well as more complex items like defence equipment. Works normally imply civil works, like construction of buildings, highways, bridges, railways, etc. as well as their renovation, extension, maintenance and repairs. Services could be in the nature of advisory or physical services.

As public procurement involves use of public funds, governments are expected to carry it out efficiently and with high standards of conduct in order to ensure robust quality of delivery while safeguarding public interest. A sound public procurement process should aim at being efficient, competitive, legally tenable and amenable to innovative solutions, while taking environmental and social considerations into account.

In practice, however, public procurement remains very vulnerable to waste, fraud and corruption. In this context, a broader definition of corruption seems more appropriate against a narrow definition that describes it as a 'misuse of *public* power (by an elected politician or appointed civil servant) for private gain'. A wider definition would include any misuse of *entrusted* power (by heritage, education, marriage, election, appointment or whatever else) for private gain.[3]

Cause and Effect

The risk of corruption in public procurement is high for several reasons. Firstly, large sums of money are involved, thus making individuals more susceptible to corrupt practices. Secondly, the process is very complex and involves several stages, including assessment of needs, framing of selection process, formulation of contract terms, actual award, contract management, payment, etc. and each stage is prone to different kinds of corrupt practices. Undue influence in needs assessment or contract terms, rigging of the award process, fraud in bid evaluation, cartelization in bid process, conflict of interest in decision-making, etc. can undermine the procurement process and introduce malfeasance. Thirdly, involvement of several stakeholders also increases the incidence of corruption while diffusing accountability.

Given its importance, the subject has been researched widely over the years and several international bodies like the OECD, World Bank and Transparency International have been involved in analysing the reasons for corruption in public procurement, indicators for measuring corruption and ways to address the problem.

A recent OECD report states that the 'direct costs of corruption include loss of public funds through misallocation or higher expenses and lower quality of goods, services and works. Those paying bribes seek to recover their money by inflating prices, billing for work not performed, failing to meet contract standards, reducing quality of work or using inferior materials, in case of public procurement of works. This results in exaggerated costs and a decrease in quality. A study by the OECD and the World Bank shows that corruption in the infrastructure and extractives sectors leads to misallocation of public funds and provision of substandard and insufficient services. Indirect costs lead to distortion of competition, limited market access and reduced business appetite for foreign investors.'[4]

The OECD report goes on to quantify the impact of corruption and states that though it is difficult to measure its exact cost due to its hidden nature, it has been estimated that between 10–30 per cent of the investment in publicly funded construction projects may be lost through mismanagement and corruption. However, estimates of 20–30 per cent of project value lost through corruption are widespread. The Construction Sector Transparency Initiative (CoST) has estimated that 'annual losses in global construction through mismanagement, inefficiency and corruption could reach $2.5 trillion by 2020'.

The Indian Scenario

While there are no definitive estimates of the total size of India's public procurement, the OECD has estimated that it stands at about 30 per cent of the GDP[5], which means about ₹36 lakh crore against a GDP of ₹121 lakh crore in 2016–17. Even if a more conservative estimate is made, the scale of public procurement would still be enormous and so would be the impact of corruption in public procurement. As such, there can be little doubt that reform of public procurement deserves a very high priority in pursuit of good governance.

Corruption in public procurement has remained a constant feature of public life since Independence. With rapid economic growth and liberalization, the scale of corruption appears to have taken much larger proportions and has also become more complex. According to the Corruption Perception Index released by Transparency International in 2016, India ranks 79 out of 176 countries. In the indices for all past years, India has clocked a score lower than the average international score. The report goes on to state that, 'India's ongoing poor performance with a score of 40 reiterates the state's inability to effectively deal with petty corruption as well as large-scale corruption scandals.'

Major Corruption Cases

It would be relevant here to recount some of the major scandals in public procurement that have caused outrage over time. The first such scandal to hit independent India was the procurement of 155 jeeps worth ₹80 lakh from a foreign firm by V.K. Krishna Menon, the then High Commissioner to the UK, without allegedly following normal protocol. In 1958, the alleged irregularities in investment of ₹1.24 crore in companies owned by Haridas Mundhra, a stock speculator, led to the resignation of the then Finance Minister, T.T. Krishnamachari. In 1965, Odisha Chief Minister Biju Patnaik was forced to resign after it became known that he had favoured his privately owned company, Kalinga Tubes, in awarding a government contract. In 1974, grant of a new licence for manufacturing cars caused great furore as favouritism was alleged in respect of the then Prime Minister Indira Gandhi's son Sanjay Gandhi, who was the managing director of the licensee company. There were several other high-profile cases of corruption in award of licences and corruption was perceived to be rampant at all levels as virtually every activity was closely controlled by the government machinery.

Bofors Scandal

The Bofors case in 1987 became one of the biggest political scandals which exposed corruption and the nexus of middlemen in defence procurements. It was alleged that the Swedish firm Bofors AB paid ₹64 crore in kickbacks to top Indian politicians, including Rajiv Gandhi, the then prime minister, as well as key defence officials for winning a bid to supply 155 mm field howitzers.

Fodder Scam

In 1996, the alleged corruption involving embezzlement of about ₹950 crore in procurement of fodder led to the resignation of the then Bihar Chief Minister Lalu Prasad Yadav, followed by his subsequent conviction on charges of corruption. In this case, embezzlement of funds that started at a small scale in the form of some government employees submitting false expense claims grew in magnitude to involve politicians and businesses over time, leading to the formation of a full-fledged mafia.

Commonwealth Games Scam

In 2010, India hosted the Commonwealth Games on which the government spent about ₹70,000 crore. Preparations for the Games came under intense media glare and reports of mismanagement, delays and irregularities became part of daily news. Though the Games concluded with no major adverse incidence, the quality of infrastructure created as well as the accompanying corruption, delays and mismanagement put a question mark on India's ability to host international events. Subsequently, large-scale irregularities and corruption were revealed in a number of contracts awarded for the Games.

Uttar Pradesh NRHM Scam

In 2012, a major siphoning of funds from NRHM in the Health Department of the Uttar Pradesh government came to light. It was alleged that around ₹10,000 crore meant for healthcare in rural areas was diverted by politicians and officials. It assumed deadly proportions with murders of several high-ranking health officials and mysterious deaths of several others associated with the case.

2G Scam

A major scandal relating to the allocation of licences for telecom spectrum came to be known as the 2G scam. It involved allocation of spectrum at rates much lower than the prevailing market prices, which resulted in windfall gains for select players. Issuance of 120 licences on a single day in 2008 at a price discovered six years ago drew attention from several quarters leading to a detailed investigation by the CAG. It was alleged that the allocation of spectrum involved glaring procedural irregularities, subversion of the basic tenets of price discovery and lack of due diligence, fairness and transparency, leading to grant of licences to eighty-five ineligible companies. It was estimated by the CAG in its 2010 report that the scam resulted in a loss of about ₹1.76 lakh crore to the exchequer.[6]

The Supreme Court nullified the aforesaid spectrum allocation, thus affecting several domestic and foreign companies as well as their lenders. This destabilized the telecom industry, affected its operations and growth prospects, compromised India's reputation among foreign investors and led to criminal prosecution of several politicians and bureaucrats.

Coalgate

The coal block allocation scam, popularly also known as the 'Coalgate' of 2012 revealed irregularities in the allocation of captive coal mines. The inability of PSUs to meet the coal requirements for power generation had led to part denationalization of the coal industry followed by allotment of about 200 coal blocks to public and private enterprises without any auction or bidding process, thus resulting in an enormous loss to the exchequer and corresponding unjust enrichment of private entities.

The CAG report of 2011 highlighted several irregularities and stated that 'there were no objective parameters to decide the allocation of coal blocks for allotees amongst the eligible bidders'.[7] Instead of adopting the approved policy for competitive bidding, the allocations were made on recommendations of a Screening Committee through government dispensation. Financial loss on account of this scam was pegged by the CAG at ₹1.86 lakh crore, which makes this the biggest scam in India till date. Subsequently, the Supreme Court quashed these allocations declaring the entire process as arbitrary and illegal. The cancellation led to large-scale socio-economic implications, including job losses as well as financial losses to investors and lenders besides delaying the production of coal, thus hurting the entire economy.

DND Tollway

In October 2016, the Allahabad High Court decided that no toll shall be collected from commuters using the Delhi-Noida Direct (DND) flyway project. The court observed that the agreement between the UP government and Noida Toll Bridge Company Ltd (NTBCL) was a 'glaring example of misuse of power by a public authority'. The Supreme Court, while refusing to stay the high court order, has asked the CAG to verify the total cost of the project as well as the claim of the concessionaire that it has not yet recovered its expenses. The DND flyway was among the first few projects executed under the PPP model in India. Awarded in 1997, it was a blatant example of conflict of interest as the project adviser, the concessionaire and the lender were all sister concerns. The agreement not only guaranteed a high rate of return, it also virtually gave away the tolling rights in perpetuity to the concessionaire.[8]

Evolution of Growth Strategies

Corruption in public procurement can be better appreciated in the context of the underlying economic growth models, the prevailing policy and regulatory and institutional regime over time.

Pre-1991: Pre-Liberalization Period

India, post Independence, was largely an agrarian economy with a very narrow industrial base. Iron and steel, cotton and jute were the only industries where the private sector had some presence.

Realizing the importance of rapid industrialization for spurring economic growth, the government relied on expanding the industrial sector. Given the market limitations and low capacity of the private sector, the controlling and commanding heights of the economy were assigned to the public sector. The state not only assumed the entrepreneurial role taking complete control of industries which were considered critical for the economy, but also owned and operated businesses in sectors like hospitality, food and beverages, aviation, etc. This led to proliferation of public sector undertakings (PSUs) leaving only a few areas of non-strategic nature to the private sector.

The period from 1956 to 1980 came to be known as the 'licence-permit-quota-raj' where the state retained the right to determine all manufacturing activities, including what is produced, how much is produced, where it is produced and who will produce, besides reservation of items for small manufacturing enterprises. While India succeeded in developing a diverse industrial base during this period, it failed to achieve rapid economic growth. Its annual growth rate stagnated at around 3 per cent, famously termed by economist Raj Krishna as the 'Hindu rate of growth'. The licence raj adversely affected the efficiency and competitiveness of industrial units which resulted in stagnant industrial growth and rising unemployment. Dominance of government in economic activity led to a burgeoning public expenditure while low economic growth resulted in low growth in revenues, worsening the fiscal deficit.

Reforms initiated in the 1980s to open up the economy were piecemeal in nature and failed to achieve the desired results. While showing occasional spurts, the growth trajectory remained subdued. Moreover, the 'command and control' economy continued to prevail in various forms, especially in the infrastructure sector where the state was responsible for provision as well as operation of assets and services.

The command and control mode of the Indian economy substantially increased the quantum of public procurement, with major procurements being undertaken by the government and its PSUs, such as for construction of dams, highways, railways, etc. and setting up of heavy industries. A complex quagmire of red tape created by the licence raj provided a fertile breeding ground for corruption to flourish. Corruption in grant of licences and permits was alleged to have permeated to all levels of the government with demands of bribe being made for even routine official work. Then there were allegations of favouritism and corruption at the highest levels in award of contracts.

Post-1991: Era of Liberalization

In May 1991, the growth rate was negative, foreign exchange reserves were reduced to only about $1 billion and the government debt rose to almost 62 per cent of the GDP. Highly restrictive policies on foreign trade led to a deteriorating balance of payments (BoP) position. The Gulf War of 1991 further worsened the already weak BoP position. Disintegration of the Soviet Union implied that India lost its main trading partner while the wave of liberalization that occurred in the erstwhile communist bloc during the same period gave hope of far-reaching reforms. Compelled by domestic stress and buoyed by global instances of liberalization, India embarked on an era of economic reforms which saw opening up of major sectors to various forms of private participation.

The reforms ushered in the 1990s witnessed several changes in the policy and regulatory framework governing various spheres of economic activity. However, opening up of several sectors to private participation required clear rules and procedures to be laid down in order to guide public procurement in the changed regime. Absence of such rules and procedures led to several major scams relating to allocation of natural resources such as spectrum and coal for the provision of infrastructure services like telecom and power as well as in the award of long-term contracts for construction and operation of infrastructure projects. Malfeasance was equally widespread in procurement of various infrastructures projects and services.

Legal Framework

Unlike several developed and developing countries, India does not have a comprehensive public procurement law. Instead, procurement in the central government is governed by the General Financial Rules (GFR), 1963 (amended in 2005 and 2017), and the Delegation of Financial Powers Rules (DFPR), 1978, issued by the Ministry of Finance. The GFR does not have the status of legislation and its violations do not attract severe penalty, especially for suppliers of goods, works and services. States have their own rules and guidelines for procurement. Though a few states like Tamil Nadu, Rajasthan and Karnataka have enacted their own procurement laws, these are far from comprehensive.

The PCA

The Prevention of Corruption Act, 1988, is the legislative tool for dealing with corruption in public life.[9] The Act covers offences under three broad categories, viz. trap cases in which corrupt public servants, middlemen etc. are caught red-handed taking bribes; abuse of official position which targets corruption at higher places; and disproportionate assets. The Act has proved to be highly ineffective in dealing with the menace of corruption amongst public officials. There are protracted delays and the conviction rate is poor. On the other hand, it often results in harassment of officers and slows down the decision-making process, thus affecting good governance. At any rate, this Act only provides for punitive action. It does not lay down the norms, principles and processes that public officials must follow while engaging in public procurement. Typically, these are complex matters that should form a part of comprehensive procurement legislation.

In the absence of a procurement law, sole reliance on a rule-based regulation limits the legal recourse for punishing irregularities. Moreover, there is no uniform and comprehensive policy framework that deals with various aspects of this complex subject. There remains a lot of discretionary power with officials to interpret various rules. Lack of standardized documents and processes also adds to the discretion and tends to undermine the tenets of an efficient and transparent procurement system. The absence of effective oversight and dispute resolution mechanisms further exacerbate the situation. The overall procurement scenario in India can thus be described as suboptimal.

Enabling Framework for Private Participation

After the advent of private participation post the 1991 economic liberalization, it took more than a decade for policies to be crystallized and a comprehensive framework to be put in place for procurement of projects in the PPP mode, which gradually emerged as the preferred mode in sectors like highways, ports, airports and power. The enabling framework included streamlined appraisal and approval mechanisms as well as standardized documents for bidding and award of projects. A prominent feature of the PPP architecture was the adoption of model documents such as Model Concession Agreements, Requests For Qualification (RFQ), Requests For Proposal (RFP), etc. The objective was to secure optimal sharing of risks and rewards while ensuring bankability of projects coupled with efficient delivery of services at costs to be determined through a fair, transparent and competitive process. It is noteworthy that in a study[10] commissioned by the Asian Development Bank (ADB), the Economic Intelligence Unit (EIU) of *The Economist* (UK) commended this PPP architecture while rating it among the best, by international standards.

The above initiatives, especially the standardization of documents and processes, helped in the rapid rollout of PPP projects that resulted in India being recognized as the largest recipient of PPP investments during 2008–12, as reported by the World Bank. According to the data published by the erstwhile Planning Commission, the total investment in infrastructure during the 11th Five-Year Plan period (2007–12) aggregated $480 billion, which constituted 7 per cent of the GDP as compared to 5 per cent during the Tenth Plan period (2002–07). In particular, private investment increased from about 22 per cent of the total investment in infrastructure during 2002–07 to about 37 per cent during 2007–12, which implied a threefold increase in absolute terms.

Crony Capitalism in PPP

Soon the PPP process came under the influence of crony capitalism with the dilution of some norms and principles. Moreover, the absence of due diligence by various stakeholders constituted an open invitation to malfeasance. This led to the withdrawal of foreign investors from the competitive arena while allowing aggressive bidding by domestic players who were confident of manipulating the system to suit their requirements. This ultimately resulted in a large number of unsustainable projects which were mainly financed by public sector banks. The growing malfeasance in PPP projects would have been substantially contained if the banks had displayed a modicum of due diligence expected from a prudent lender. However, the system was blatantly abused by unscrupulous bidders and bankers for gold-plating projects in order to siphon off funds, thus making the projects financially unviable.

By way of illustration, take the highways sector where the banks financed a large number of projects at gold-plated costs (when compared with costs projected by the National Highways Authority of India [NHAI]) on the basis of estimates provided by the lenders' engineer (whose fees was actually paid by the private concessionaire implying a patent conflict of interest). In the absence of an effective due diligence culture, the banks financed huge amounts while the stake of private sector entities became negligible. Such padded costs could not have been sustained on the strength of project revenues, and eventually triggered defaults in debt service. As for NHAI, while waiving off some critical conditions and overlooking the padded costs, it virtually enabled the concessionaires to siphon off large sums of money. As a result, the banks ended up losing enormous sums of money as reflected in their mounting NPAs. This malaise also prevailed in other infrastructure sectors in different forms.[11]

In the case of PPP projects in the airport sector, flawed bid processes and contract terms coupled with 'cost plus' determination of tariffs led to inflated investments accompanied by a steep rise in user charges for the Delhi, Mumbai, Bengaluru and Hyderabad airports.[12] Similarly, flaws in the tariff regime and bid documents associated with PPP projects in the port sector have led to exploitation of users.[13]

Acute problems have also been observed in power sector projects procured by various state-owned companies under the guidance of the Union Power Ministry. In most of these cases, public sector banks lent huge amounts for generation projects that did not have enforceable Fuel Supply Agreements (FSAs).

With a fixed revenue stream, the concessionaires were required to assume long-term fuel pricing risk, which constituted a perfect recipe for financial disaster and eventually led to increasing failure of projects. Several gas-based projects have thus been languishing for want of gas supplies at sustainable prices and their accumulated losses are already irreversible. The recent judgment of the Supreme Court that disallowed the compensatory tariffs sought by two mega projects to offset the increase in fuel prices demonstrates the nature and extent of this malaise.

Impact of Malfeasance

Public procurement encumbered by malfeasance can have long-term repercussions for the economy as well as the public. Besides compromising the quality of services, it can lead to a significant increase in costs, which in turn can affect the entire economy in the medium- and long-term. For example, comparatively expensive power can adversely affect the economy for a long period of time, thus contributing to the high costs that typically lead to the growth trap in middle-income economies.

A more direct and visible impact of crony capitalism is evident in the case of public sector banks which are reeling under a huge volume of NPAs and showing little sign of recovery for the past several years. Credit flow has thus been adversely affected, which in turn has sharply slowed down the pace of investment in the economy while depressing the growth potential as well as generation of employment and incomes. The direct and indirect consequences of corruption in public procurement can hardly be overemphasized.

Initiatives to Address

To address corruption in public procurement, a GoM was

constituted in January 2011 under the chairmanship of the then Union Finance Minister to consider measures for tackling corruption in various spheres of national activity. One of the terms of reference of the GoM was to consider legislative, administrative and other measures to tackle corruption and improve transparency in public procurement. The GoM set up the Committee on Public Procurement (COPP) to suggest measures to ensure full transparency; legal, institutional and systemic measures to strengthen public procurement practices; and the best domestic and international practices for fair and equitable treatment of suppliers, promotion of competition as well as ethics and probity in public procurement.

The COPP

The report submitted by the COPP noted that despite the enormous scale of public procurement, the regulatory and institutional framework remained incomplete and weak. It had, therefore, failed to provide a sufficient basis for ensuring transparency, accountability, efficiency, economy, competition and professionalism. The COPP also noted that India appeared to be lagging behind on many of the parameters in the OECD matrix that enable a quick assessment of the state of procurement, such as a legislative framework, model documents, general conditions of contract, procedures for contracting, multi-year planning and integration with budget, timely procurement and payments, conflict of interest, quality control and performance evaluation, contract administration, dispute resolution, appeals, etc.[14] The COPP made a number of substantive recommendations, most of which are yet to be implemented. As such, little progress can be claimed on any significant reform in public procurement or on the aforesaid matrix of OECD for evaluating the state of public procurement.

Drive against Black Money

One of the planks on which the present NDA government came to power was the eradication of corruption. In fact, one of the first decisions that the government took after coming to power was to constitute a SIT to bring back black money from off-shore safe havens. The government has also taken several other initiatives to address the problem of corruption in public procurement. On the launch of the GeM initiative, Prime Minister Narendra Modi stated that, '...the government is committed to curbing corruption. One of the key aspects of this objective is to minimize government's human interface. Accordingly, public procurement is being transformed by leveraging technology such as online market places and e-tendering.' The GeM is a one-stop portal that facilitates online procurement of goods and services required by various government departments and PSUs, and aims at replacing the existing system of rate contracts. State governments are also being encouraged to adopt GeM.

A Comprehensive Procurement Law

In his Budget speech for 2015–16, the Union Finance Minister had conveyed the government's commitment to legislate on India's public procurement system as a part of its continuing reforms in public financial management. The legislation is still awaited and needs to be formulated and enacted on high priority.

It is noteworthy that in order to help states in modernizing their respective procurement laws, UNCITRAL had circulated and commended a 'Model Law on Public Procurement' in 1994. A revised version of the same was circulated in 2011. The Model Law contains procedures and principles aimed at achieving value for money while eliminating abuses in the procurement process, and for promoting objectivity, fairness, participation, competition and integrity. It classifies different types of procurements and provides guidance on the principles and processes associated with each of them.

The UNCITRAL states that a comprehensive law is required since procurement, by its nature, involves discretionary decision-taking at all levels. It represents a substantial portion of the GDP and total government spending and necessarily involves a risk of abuse; potential losses could be significant affecting important sectors like health, education and infrastructure, in turn having a major impact on economic performance and development. Such a law will enable the evolution of a modern procurement system that will achieve value for money and avoid abuse, using modern commercial techniques, such as e-procurement and framework agreements. So far, twenty-three countries have enacted laws based on the UNCITRAL Model Law while several developed countries already had comprehensive procurement laws of their own. The need for India to enact a comprehensive procurement law on the above lines can hardly be over-emphasized.

Department of Public Procurement

Public procurement is a complex subject that continues to evolve and throw up newer challenges. Besides a comprehensive law, it requires a plethora of policies, rules, regulations, guidelines, processes, procedures and standardized documents as well as an institutional structure for addressing the above needs and exercising oversight, besides building capacity. An efficient dispute resolution mechanism is equally important.

Burdened with their respective objectives and lacking in procurement-related expertise, individual departments and organizations of the government can hardly measure up to the demands imposed by the complexities of procurement, including the ingenious and all-pervasive presence of corruption. Setting up of a Procurement Division in the Ministry of Finance should be regarded as a weak and inadequate response to the need for a full-fledged organization equipped to address the complex challenges of public procurement. A dedicated department with the sole function of dealing with public procurement is needed for ensuring formulation and implementation of efficient and effective public procurement policies, rules, regulations and standard documents. It would have to function as the reference department for all procurement-related matters, providing overall direction to procurement policy as well as leadership in the development of a uniform and simplified procurement system for adoption by all procuring departments.

A notable example of a dedicated institutional apparatus is the Office of Federal Procurement Policy (OFPP) in the United States, which is headed by an administrator who is appointed by the President and confirmed by the Senate. It provides overall guidance for government-wide procurement procedures with the aim of promoting economy, efficiency and effectiveness in the procurement processes. The OFPP is entrusted with the overall procurement policy direction and six specific statutory functions: (a) establish a system to coordinate and standardize procurement regulations; (b) establish a method for letting interested parties participate in the development of procurement regulations; (c) monitor the government's reliance on the private sector for needed goods and services; (d) promote and conduct procurement research; (e) establish a procurement information system to meet the needs of Congress, the executive branch, and the private sector; and (f) promote programmes for recruitment, training, career development and performance evaluation of the procurement personnel.

Oversight Mechanism

An effective oversight mechanism is presently not in place. Both the CVC and CAG perform only ex-post facto review. An efficient procurement system should have the checks and balances necessary to address any irregularity before it causes irreparable damage to the economy, especially through ex-post judicial reviews leading to major upheavals as was witnessed upon cancellation of spectrum licences and coalmine allocations by the Supreme Court. These cases should serve as a lesson for ensuring that timely executive action henceforth minimizes the possibilities of such judicial interventions.

Conflict of Interest

There is an apparent lack of appreciation relating to the serious problems arising out of conflict of interest. The case of the DND flyover demonstrates the consequences of conflict of interest. In another case of a large central sector PPP project, the legal advisers of the government who drafted the contract agreements, switched over as advisers of the concessionaire immediately upon signing of the concession agreement. In yet another case reported recently, an infrastructure project ran into rough weather as a director of the selected company was also an adviser in the concerned ministry. To safeguard public interest, the government should issue clear rules on how to define and address conflict of interest which has the potential of compromising the entire procurement process.

Standardization of Documents

As noted above, standardized documents in the case of PPP projects had enabled a fast, efficient and hassle-free rollout of projects in different sectors over the past decade. The government should consider mandating more such model documents in the remaining areas. Each such document should be evolved through expert assistance and must be accompanied by extensive consultations with independent experts and stakeholders.

E-procurement

Technology can be effectively leveraged towards improving efficiency and transparency in public procurement. Though GeM is an important initiative taken by the government in this regard, it is restricted to routine procurements and not designed to handle more complex two-stage procurement processes involving prequalification. There is a need to introduce e-procurement of goods, services and contracts through bidding systems that involve evaluation of both technical and financial proposals. In addition, the Internet may also be used to make e-disclosure mandatory and to graduate to comprehensive end-to-end e-procurement solutions in a calibrated fashion.

Make in India

'Make in India', a flagship initiative of the government needs to be integrated with public procurement. Given the enormous size of public procurement in India, the purchasing power of the government should be leveraged not only to augment the manufacturing capacity, but also to procure indigenous goods at economic prices. In this context, it is especially important to focus on defence equipment where India enjoys the dubious distinction of being the largest importer of defence equipment. By using its purchasing power, the government should be able to attract the world's best companies to set up shop in India. This has been successfully demonstrated by the award of two locomotive contracts, aggregating about ₹40,000 crore, to top international firms who will manufacture state-of-the-art locomotives in India for supply to the Indian Railways. It is time to leverage the power of public procurement to ensure production and supply of efficient economic goods and services from within India.

Widespread corruption in public procurement has resulted in substantial losses to the exchequer, generation of black money, stranded assets leading to overall deceleration of growth and delivery of substandard goods, services and works. While there are no studies that have attempted to quantify the impact of corruption in public procurement in India, it can be safely assumed that it is not only substantial but pans over several decades of lower growth and welfare. Delay in addressing these issues would not only result in lower growth and welfare, it would also attract greater judicial outreach that would show the government in poor light, besides causing a debilitating effect on economic development. Therefore, a robust public procurement framework is an essential prerequisite for sustained growth aimed at meeting the growing aspirations of the people as well as their legitimate expectations from the government in terms of better delivery of public goods and services.

References

1 As per the Organisation for Economic Co-operation and Development (OECD), the quantum of public procurement in European Union (EU) countries ranges from 15–20% of the GDP.

2 Includes central as well as state governments, subordinate organizations of the government, PSUs, autonomous organizations and local bodies.

3 B. Baesens, V. Van Vlasselaer & W. Verbeke. 2015. *Fraud Analytics Using Descriptive, Predictive, and Social Network Techniques*. New Delhi: Wiley.

4 'Preventing Corruption in Public Procurement', Organisation for Economic Co-operation and Development, 2016.

5 https://www.oecd.org/gov/ethics/Going_Green_Best_Practices_for_Sustainable_Procurement.pdf

6 CAG Report, 2010, Union_Performance_Civil_Allocation_2G_Spectrum_19_2010

7 'Performance Audit of Allocation of Coal Blocks and Augmentation of Coal Production', CAG Report No. 7 of 2012–13, Ministry of Coal.

8 See 'Concession for the Delhi Noida Bridge' published by the erstwhile Planning Commission in 2007 (under PPP Section on the website–Case Studies/Papers) http://planningcommission.gov.in/sectors/ppp_report/4.Case%20Studies/6.Concession%20for%20Delhi%20Noida%20Bridge.pdf

9 The first direct and consolidated law on corruption was the PCA, 1947, enacted to supplement the IPC. In 1988, a new PCA was passed, repealing the 1947 Act and Criminal Law Amendment Act, 1952.

10 'Evaluating the environment for public-private partnerships in Asia-Pacific: The 2011 Infrascope', a report by The Economist Intelligence Unit.

11 'Sub-prime Infrastructure: Crony capitalism in Public Sector Banks', August 2015, *prime_Infrastructure_Crony_capitalism_in_Public_Sector_Banks.pdf*

12 See case study titled 'Bidding process in Delhi Mumbai Airports', published by the erstwhile Planning Commission in 2007, (under PPP Section on the website–Case Studies/Papers) *http://planningcommission.gov.in/sectors/ppp_report/4.Case%20Studies/1.Bidding%20Process%20delhi%20mumbai%20Airport.pdf http://planningcommission.gov.in*

13 See case study titled 'Concession for Nhava Sheva International container Terminal' published by the erstwhile Planning Commission in 2007, (under PPP Section on the website–Case Studies/Papers) *http://planningcommission.gov.in/sectors/*

ppp_report/4.Case%20Studies/7.Concession%20for%20port%20 terminal%20JNPT.pdf, http://planningcommission.nic.in

14 Report of the Committee on Public Procurement, 2011.

◆

Anna Roy is an Indian Economic Services officer currently working as an Adviser and Head of Department (Industry, Data Management & Analysis) at NITI Aayog.

Ritika Aghi is a former Young Professional at NITI Aayog.

15

Procurement Principles: Statute or Process?

BIBEK DEBROY AND T.V. SOMANATHAN

The more corrupt a state, the more numerous the laws.
—Publius Tacitus, Roman historian

This quote from the author of several texts, including *Annals*, is not quite correct. We indeed have a clause about a corrupt state and another one about plurality of laws. But there was no obvious causation in Tacitus. One could equally well translate this as, 'The more numerous the laws, the more corrupt a state.' However, the correlation is not in doubt. This is worth noting, because quite often, there is a presumption that the solution to every problem under the sun is to pass a piece of legislation.

The definition of public procurement according to OECD is, 'Public procurement refers to the purchase by governments and state-owned enterprises of goods, services and works. As public procurement accounts for a substantial portion of the taxpayers' money, governments are expected to carry it out efficiently and with high standards of conduct in order to ensure high quality of service delivery and safeguard the public interest.'[1] As a template, the recommendations of the OECD Council on public procurement are beyond reproach.[2] Problems arise when one starts to flesh out the template.

The 4th Report of the 2nd ARC had a long section on 'systemic reforms in government procurement' and the recommended principles for reform were not remarkably different from that in the OECD template.[3] This report has several sections that deserve to be quoted at length. For instance, 'A World Bank estimate pegs the total value of public procurement at all levels and by all agencies put together in the country at around $100 billion representing 13 per cent of the total budget and over 20 per cent of the GDP.' Or, 'The Santhanam Committee had as early as in the 1960s observed that we were told by a large number of witnesses that in all contracts of construction, purchase, sales and other regular business on behalf of the government, a regular percentage is paid by the parties to the transaction, and this is shared in agreed proportions among the various officials concerned'. A Confederation of Indian Industry (CII) study of 1999 involving 210 private sector firms found 60 per cent of the firms confirming 2–25 per cent of the contract value to be the price payable to secure a government contract. The World Bank assessment of December 2003 referred to above also found that 'both the officials and contractors, who were interviewed, confirm to its prevalence; but while the officials believe that it does not exceed 5 percent of the contract price, the contractors assert that the amount may be as much as 15 per cent to cover all branches of government and is built into the price.' An undated report by United Nations Office on Drugs and Crime (UNODC) on public procurement in India[4] states, 'At the global level, public procurement spending accounts for about 15 per cent of the world's GDP. In India, estimates of public procurement vary between 20-30 per cent of GDP. There are ministries in the Government of India where approximately half the total budget is spent on public procurement alone.'[5] Several figures on India originate in a country procurement assessment report that was undertaken by the World Bank in 2003.[6]

Two propositions can be accepted as given. First, there is a substantial amount of public procurement in India. Second, there is corruption associated with public procurement. However, many high-profile scandals or controversies do not relate to procurement, and instead relate to the sale or disposal of valuable rights by the government: spectrum, oil exploration (at the central level), liquor vending, sand mining (at state level), fishing, tree-cutting (at local level).

Institutional and Legal Framework

If one intends to address the corruption issue, one needs to understand the institutional and legal framework under which public procurement takes place. The 2nd ARC report, cited above, states this succinctly. 'The institutional and legal framework for procurement derives from the Constitution of India. Article 298 authorizes the Union and State Governments to contract for goods and services and requires the executive to protect the fundamental rights of all citizens to be treated equally. Article 299 of the Constitution deals with contracts on behalf of the Union and State Governments, and Article 300 with suits and proceedings thereon. The broad framework for contracts is regulated by the Contract Act, the Sale of Goods Act, the Arbitration Act, the Limitation Acts and the recent Right to Information Act, 2005. There is no Union law governing procurement in India. The policies, procedures, guidelines and delegation of authority relating to procurement are issued by the Government of India primarily through the finance ministry, supplemented by orders of each Ministry/Department. The Directorate General of Supplies and Disposal (DGS&D) in the Government of India and "Stores Purchase Departments" at the State level, helped the governments in procuring goods through a process of "rate contracts" wherein rates for different items to be purchased as well as the suppliers are fixed periodically and then all government departments and agencies place orders on such suppliers directly. The General Financial Rules (GFR) provide the procedural framework to be followed for purchase of goods and services by government departments. The State governments have their own financial rules which are generally similar to the GFR, while Central Public Sector Units (CPSUs) have internal policies that broadly mirror the basic principles of the GFR. The CAG and the Local Fund Audit Departments of State Governments are the primary oversight agencies to ensure accountability. The Central Public Accounts Committee and the State Public Accounts Committees examine the reports of the CAG. The CVC, a statutory authority also issues guidelines in regard to procurement and has powers of oversight in the case of criminal misconduct and corruption on the part of public servants involved in public contracts. The Civil Courts and the High Courts and the Supreme Court provide judicial remedy in matters involving irregularities in procurement. The CSO's and the media also play a part in bringing corruption in public procurement to light.' Indeed, one should add more to this list—the Delegation of Financial Powers Rules, the Manual on Policies and Procedures for Purchase of Goods/Services, the Defence Procurement Manual, the Defence Procurement Procedures and even some clauses in the Competition Act.

With this background, the World Bank report was fairly clear. 'The basic framework of rules and procedures require open tenders, open to all qualified firms without discrimination, use of non-discriminatory tender documents, public bid opening and selection of the most advantageous tender taking all factors (preferably pre-disclosed) into consideration. Restricted or limited tenders are permitted if the value is small or only limited suppliers are available and single tenders are permitted in the case of urgency, small value, and proprietary and in other exceptional circumstances. In this respect, the basic procedural framework is no different from World Bank Guidelines or UNCITRAL Model Law or the GPA of WTO and other good models of public procurement. In the past two decades, the procedures have been further influenced by the World Bank and the Development Bank and the tender documents used by the better agencies are modelled on their documents. Thus, there is a reasonably good framework of rules, procedures and documents and a few good practitioners as well.'[7]

Notwithstanding this, in the World Bank's diagnosis, there are several problems:[8]

1. Absence of a dedicated policymaking department on public procurement.
2. Absence of a legal framework, that is, something like a public procurement law.
3. Absence of a credible complaint/challenge/grievance procedure.
4. Absence of standard tender documents.
5. Preferential treatment in the procurement process.
6. Negotiations as part of the procurement process.
7. Delays in tender processing and awards.
8. The two-envelope system.
9. Specific issues with works contracting.
10. Records management.
11. Competence, skills and training of officers and staff.

While some problems (3, 4, 7, 9, 10 and 11) focus on a need to streamline the process and make it more efficient, others (5, 6, 8) actually involve value judgements and if social costs/benefits deviate from private costs/benefits, may or may not be desirable. In that sense, they belong in a different basket. The remaining two (1 and 2) are unclear. Also while these are 'problems' associated with procurement, their correlation with corruption is even more tenuous. Even if one desires to reduce corruption, taken individually, each of the eleven is neither a necessity nor a sufficient condition.

Building on the World Bank's report, the report of the ARC stated the following. 'The generic measures or integrity pillars can be categorized as follows viz. an effective criminal justice system which punishes the wrong doers; effective administrative supervision and management control systems inherent in the system of governance; an efficient civil service system with well laid down code of integrity and conduct; right of access to information; effective audit to ensure value for money by an independent audit authority; anti-corruption commission and investigative agencies to ensure effective enforcement; independent ombudsman to investigate high level corruption; and strong laws relating to corruption, whistle-blower and witness protection and civil remedies to secure compensation for loss sustained. These generic measures need to be supplemented by specific remedial measures for misconduct in relation to procurement. Some of the specific measures are: All procurements should be after competition between suppliers. The specifications should be so designed that there are always a few suppliers who could meet the requirement. All States and the Union should have a "Transparency in Procurement Act". This law should stipulate the methodology for procurement, lay down the authorities for procurement decisions, stipulate an appellate mechanism to look into irregularities etc. The terms and conditions governing the procurement process should be clearly spelt out without any ambiguity. It should be ensured that all bidders are informed about these terms and conditions, and their doubts, if any, should be clarified before the bidding begins. Information about decisions made and the reasons thereof should be placed in the public domain. The criteria for evaluation of the bids should be laid down before the bidding begins and it should be made known to all bidders. Under no circumstances should the criteria be changed mid-way. Evaluation of bids involving large amounts should be carried out by committees. Procurement wings of departments should carry out market research to arrive at reasonableness or otherwise of the bids. Increasingly recourse should be made to Information Technology in order to make the procurement process transparent and efficient. Only officials with proven integrity should be involved in the procurement process. Payments to the suppliers should be settled promptly. Integrity pacts should be made use of in purchases of high value. The tender contracts should include a condition making it possible for the government to forfeit payments if bribery is detected.' With the exception of the recommendation about passing laws, everything else is in the nature of a motherhood statement. Perhaps that is the reason why people tend to get fixated on a piece of legislation. It is something tangible; conveying the impression that something is being done.

The ARC did acknowledge there were such statutes in Tamil Nadu and Karnataka. 'Several measures have been taken by the Union and State Governments to reduce the scope of corruption in procurement. A beginning has been made by the Governments of Tamil Nadu and Karnataka to provide a formal legal framework to regulate public procurement for the first time in the country in the late 1990s, the pioneering effort in this context being by the Tamil Nadu Government when it enacted the Tamil Nadu Transparency in Tenders Act, 1998. This was followed by the Karnataka Transparency in Public Procurement Act, 1999.' This was an echo of the World Bank's sentiments. 'Even among the States, some are better performers than others. Of the three states selected as representative samples, the southern states of Tamil Nadu and Karnataka were better than the northern state of Uttar Pradesh. In Tamil Nadu, pursuant to a high level committee recommendation[9], the State passed an Act of the legislature (law) called "The Tamil Nadu Transparency in Tenders Act 1998" (which came into effect only in 2000) complimented (*sic*) by a unified Rules of Procedure, which inter alia mandated the open (advertised) tender system and publication of tender notices and tender decisions in weekly bulletins, and introduced an appeal procedure. Karnataka followed suit soon after and enacted "The Karnataka Transparency in Public Procurement Act 1999" complimented (*sic*) by Public Procurement Rules. These measures have enhanced transparency and will hopefully improve public confidence.' Measured by perceptions, out of the three States gauged, Tamil Nadu and Karnataka may have been perceived to be superior to Uttar Pradesh. But one cannot statistically control the existence or presence of a piece of statute. In any event, the World Bank's survey in the three states was conducted in 2001. The expectation that changes between 1998 and 2000 have an instantaneous impact in 2001 is a shade too optimistic.

Consider e-procurement initiatives, including ones through the Directorate General of supplies and Disposal (DGSD). The DGSD's GeM now has 1,429 registered buyers, 3,733 registered sellers and 110 service providers.[10] This did not require any legislative change. There was indeed a Public Procurement Bill that was introduced in Lok Sabha in 2012, meant for the Union government (with some exceptions). This drew on the 2001 recommendations of a Committee on Public Procurement, a separate 2011 Bill on Public Procurement drafted by the former Planning Commission, UNCITRAL and GPA.

Rule Framework in India

The GFR, the primary source of rules on procurement at the Union level in India, are 'a compilation of rules and orders of the Government of India to be followed by all when dealing with matters involving public finance'.[11] These are executive instructions which are binding on all central government departments, as well as attached and subordinate bodies. They do not have statutory backing, but having been first issued in 1947, have the authority of more than seventy years of custom and practice. Violation of the GFR is taken seriously, especially by the CAG and anti-corruption agencies. Conscious or outright violation of the GFR is extremely rare. It does not apply to Community and Public Sector Unions, which make their own procurement policies. However, these policies are often aligned in their essential aspects with the GFR. This is for two reasons. Firstly, government officials are invariably represented on the boards of public undertakings and they tend to encourage alignment with the government's own rules on the assumption (not always valid) that the government's time-tested rules are the best. Secondly, the CVC does have jurisdiction over government companies and corporations—its Chief Technical Examiner and his staff are generally drawn from the ranks of central government departments such as the Central Public Works Department, and therefore, tend to view the GFR as a benchmark.

State governments have their own financial rules, sometimes referred to as 'financial codes'.[12] These are similar to the GFR though, until the recent revision of the GFR in 2017, some of them were arguably more advanced in their coverage of procurement than the GFR.

Procurement Laws

Procurement laws fall into a special category of laws intended to restrain the government rather than the citizenry (other examples being fiscal responsibility acts, debt ceiling acts etc.). Such laws are more common in countries with a separation of legislature and executive (like the USA), where the legislature uses the law to restrain the executive, and less so in parliamentary systems where the government can typically pass financial legislation at will.

In the United States—a federal polity like India—the federal government has enacted laws on federal government procurement. The federal laws (Federal Property & Administrative Services Act 1949, Federal Acquisition Reform Act 1996, etc.) are broad 'framework laws'. The *bulk of the law is delegated legislation*, viz. the FAR (Federal Acquisition Regulations), thereby providing the Executive a lot of flexibility. American states have their own laws. In practical terms, this is not too different from the Indian situation.

The UNCITRAL produced a revised 'Model Law on Public Procurement' in 2011, a revised version of a similar Model Law issued in 1994. This 'contains procedures and principles aimed at achieving value for money and avoiding abuses in the procurement process. The text promotes objectivity, fairness, participation and competition and integrity towards these goals. Transparency is also a key principle, allowing visible compliance with the procedures and principles to be confirmed.'[13]

Effects of a Procurement Law

It is important to understand the benefits of a law as compared to a mere executive instruction. Firstly, the law could provide for, and make mandatory, the following of principles and procedures for fairness and transparency. Secondly, by putting those principles and procedures into a law, it becomes more difficult for government to circumvent rules like the GFR, which can theoretically be relaxed through ministerial or cabinet approval (and this may not be possible with a law except to the extent the law itself allows it). A third benefit is that the law could provide explicit remedies to aggrieved tenderers who feel the procurement process has been unfair. The UNCITRAL model provides for a challenge procedure. Procurement laws may also provide for a 'standstill' period for representations by losing tenderers. A fourth benefit is that such a law could provide for penalties for violation, thereby deterring wrongdoing.

On a close and rigorous examination, it is not clear that these benefits hold up *in the Indian context.*

Judicial interpretation in India has already made it essential to follow the basic principles of fairness which are part of, say, the UNCITRAL Model Law. Indian courts have unambiguously held that government cannot be arbitrary in its procurement decisions and needs to follow principles of fairness. The GFR, too, require the observation of these principles. There is little evidence that government officers or departments deliberately flout the GFR.

The Indian Constitution already provides a writ remedy—where citizens including tenderers can take the government to court even where there is no contractual right—and the courts have widened it by interpretation to cover all possible scenarios. Unlike many of the countries where such laws have been enacted or proposed, Indian courts do not go by the strict wording of the law and readily entertain challenges even if there is no explicit provision therefor. Many tenderers can and do challenge tender awards and even obtain stays on the tendering process. In Indian conditions, explicit provisions of new remedies in addition to the existing ones are likely to delay the completion of procurement and encourage vexatious litigation.

Deterrent penalties for procurement irregularities or failing to follow procedure (even the procedure contained in executive instructions) are already present in practice because India's anti-corruption laws are very strong and there is little a new law can usefully add. Indeed, it has been credibly argued that India's anti-corruption law is counter-productive because it punishes even honest decisions if, by hindsight, it can be shown that a tenderer or other private party gained by a decision.[14]

In short, in a country like India where judicial review and anti-corruption laws are already very strong, the marginal benefit of a law in these respects—mandating principles of fairness, providing remedies and prescribing penalties—is limited.

Of the four benefits mentioned above, the only real advantage that remains to be considered is the second one: that unlike executive orders such as the GFR, a law can bind not only low-level officials, but even the highest levels of the government. In examining this further, it is necessary to distinguish between parts of a 'law' that can be modified through delegated legislation and those which can only be modified with approval of the legislature. To the extent the 'law' is contained in delegated legislation (most of the US procurement law is in this form), it is almost as easy for the government of the day to modify it as it is to issue executive orders. However, delegated legislation has to be placed in Parliament whereas mere executive orders do not. This means, both in theory and in practice, there is a slightly but distinctly greater level of rigidity attached to rules. Portions of the law that require legislative approval are of course difficult for the executive to modify in the short run. Greater rigidity, i.e. *reduced ability of government to relax procedure*, is the only real difference between procurement law and executive instructions.

However, this very rigidity can be a cause of inefficiency. As it is, the requirements of transparency and fairness put the government at a disadvantage versus a private buyer in a game-theoretic sense. Information is power. The government is not allowed to conceal information and under the RTI Act can be compelled to disclose everything it knows sooner or later. It must follow a pre-set procedure. It cannot act unfairly. A private buyer, on the other hand, can simply refuse to deal with a vendor it dislikes for reasons of past bad performances in order to induce a better price or indeed on a mere whim, and is not required to state reasons. A private vendor to the government is not required to disclose anything beyond what is asked for and is not expected to be transparent about its costs. Nor is it, as a private citizen, held to any norms of fairness. A vendor to government can litigate repeatedly without becoming ineligible for future procurement. Poor performance is very difficult to establish to a judicial standard of proof, and judicial processes often take years. If public administration were totally honest and competent and there were no risk of corruption (and if the notion that 'fairness as a good thing in itself' is ignored), transparent and fair public procurement procedures could actually end up costing the taxpayer money by weakening the bargaining power of the taxpayer's agents.

Greater rigidity in procedure (the one true benefit of a law over instructions) can worsen this competitive disadvantage. It would raise the bar in terms of government's obligations to show adherence to procedure. While price is quantifiable, quality differences between suppliers often cannot be 'proven' objectively to a judicial standard; suppliers may produce quality 'good enough for government'. Substantiating poor or delayed execution to a judicially acceptable standard is also difficult and therefore, suppliers feel they can provide bad service *without* suffering in future procurement. Rigid rules can create difficulty in responding to changing circumstances or special situations. It was the absence of rules that enabled President Thomas Jefferson to purchase in 1803 (on a negotiated basis with no 'transparency') 828,000 square miles of land from France (the so-called Louisiana Purchase) doubling the size of the then United States, a decision which was questioned at the time.

Thus, while rigidity may reduce scope for abuse, it can also be a constraint on acting in the best interest of the public. If, to avoid rigidity, a provision for relaxation is included in the law, it allows for genuine cases, but also lends itself to misuse for improper reason and gets one back to the situation with executive instructions—a paradox which cannot be easily resolved

Moreover, sophisticated forms of corruption are based on manipulation without procedural deviation and can coexist with a good law. Few of the instances of corruption in procurement have involved violations of procedure. Barring the very early laudatory reference from the World Bank a year after the law came into force in Tamil Nadu, there is no evidence—empirical or anecdotal—that corruption in procurement in Tamil Nadu or Karnataka is significantly less than at the central level or in states without a procurement law. Indeed, in conversations with the authors, civil servants who have worked in those states and in the Government of India stated that they do not see procurement in those states as less corrupt than procurement in the Government of India or other states.

In practice, therefore, the existence of a procurement law is neither a necessity nor a sufficient antidote to corruption. In India, where existing rules are quite sophisticated, corruption coexists with sophistication and typically occurs without violation of rules.

Benefits Unrelated to Fighting Corruption

There are certain other benefits which a procurement law might bring, which are not related to the issue of corruption. To the extent it introduces new and modern forms of procurement not common in the country; a law can have a beneficial impact on improving the knowledge base and acceptability of these new forms. For example, the use of framework agreements—well known in India for decades as 'rate contracts'—is not as widespread as it should be. Till recently, the GFR did not have explicit provisions for electronic tendering. The revision of the UNCITRAL Model Law was mainly done to allow for modern electronic means of procurement. Such new procedures could well be introduced through executive instructions, but a law may have some advantage insofar as it reduces the likelihood of a new procedure being challenged in the courts.

Another advantage of a law could be that it would cover not only government departments but also government companies and corporations. An Act with good rules could thus promote procedural standardization which could reduce transaction costs. Once again, this is possible without legislation.

A major problem in Indian public procurement is the inability to exclude bidders who are known to have performed badly in the past (especially in terms of delay) or who are unduly litigant. This allows poor performers to go unpunished and continue to win new tenders. Theoretically, executive instructions could be issued to establish a system to rate vendor performance and exclude bad suppliers. Nevertheless, an explicit statutory provision for this may make it easier to enforce such a system and reduce the likelihood of judicial challenge. Rating of vendors will inevitably involve some discretion and thus could potentially be abused by a corrupt executive; therefore it is desirable that all disqualifications be approved by a credible group of experts.

Lack of Procedural Clarity

The real problem that has plagued procurement in government is not that the rules of the game are merely rules, not a law. The issue has been the absence of clear procedures for procurement that fall outside the traditional nineteenth and twentieth century tendering framework of 'goods' or 'public works'. Till recently, the GFR had many gaps:

1. They did not adequately provide for procurement of services where non-price considerations are crucial, and where 'quality' is not a pass–fail test but something to be optimized.

2. They did not contain provisions dealing with electronic means of procurement.
3. They were not adequately supported by practical guidance or 'good practice notes' that could enable procuring personnel to apply and implement broad principles correctly and consistently, when dealing with complex projects in a modern economy.

States like Tamil Nadu and Karnataka, where there are procurement laws, had an advantage in this respect. Many of the ambiguities in the central GFR had been made clear by the rules under these laws, since those rules were issued much more recently than the GFR. However, this beneficial impact did not stem from their statutory backing—it arose because they had updated their practices.

Recently, the central government has moved to rectify the weaknesses in procurement policy and practice. The GFR were thoroughly revised and re-issued in 2017 with greater clarity and with explicit provisions for modern methods of procurement. They were accompanied by both a Manual for the Procurement of Goods and a Manual for Procurement of Consultancy and Other Services.

The Key Problem—Disposal Rather Than Procurement

As mentioned earlier, many high-profile scandals or controversies do not relate to procurement—they relate to the sale or disposal of valuable rights by government. The use of the term 'procurement' in the title of most procurement laws, and the definitions of procurement given, may lead to judicial challenge on the applicability of a procurement law to disposals, especially of abstract rights. Some East African countries (under UNDP guidance—Uganda, Kenya and Tanzania) have covered 'disposals' also under the law, but the provisions are sketchy. The draft Bill introduced in 2012 in India had some rudimentary provisions which would not have effectively covered sophisticated rights like spectrum or mining.

The Government of India appointed the Committee on the Allocation of Natural Resources, which recommended a series of measures for fairness and transparency in natural resource allocation.[15] The Supreme Court has also clarified the broad principles applicable to allocation of certain types of natural resources.[16] The Court recognized that different circumstances would require different approaches. A general law relating to disposal would be extremely difficult to draft and implement unless it were at the level of very general principles, in which case its anti-corruption effect would be insignificant.

In Indian conditions, a procurement law is unlikely to produce any major impact on probity and, unless kept at the level of broad principles, can hamper efficiency. Its effects on sophisticated forms of corruption are likely to be negligible; on corruption, the main effect is thus cosmetic. Further, a procurement law will not necessarily address issues relating to disposal or sale of tangible or intangible rights.

If enacted as a set of broad principles of universal application with the details either given in regulations or left to the implementing agencies, a procurement law may possibly have some beneficial impact towards modernization and efficiency. However, with the possible exception of making it easier to penalize poor quality suppliers, nearly all of these benefits could be obtained without legislation. If an Act is found to have merit, it would have to be very short. As an example, the whole edifice of the All India Services stems out of a one-page Act. The merit has been the flexibility to deal with changes over half a century.

Procurement and disposals are core executive functions; they require discretion in the proper, judicially approved sense of careful application of mind to relevant criteria in public interest. These functions cannot be reduced to rigid rules especially in the midst of rapid technical change, without seriously impairing the efficiency of governance. Introducing rigidity will not solve the problem of probity but will create new sources of delay and buck-passing in an already risk-averse and slow system.

Thus, a public procurement law does not offer a magic wand or simple solution. Good guidelines with good intentions have the best chance of working—the best law with bad intentions will unfortunately not prevent corruption.

References

1 http://www.oecd.org/gov/public-procurement/

2 http://www.oecd.org/gov/ethics/OECD-Recommendation-on-Public-Procurement.pdf

3 4th Report, 'Ethics in Governance', http://arc.gov.in/4threport.pdf. The discussion is in Annexure VII(1).

4 'India: Probity in Public Procurement', https://www.unodc.org/documents/southasia/publications/research-studies/India-PPPs.pdf

5 This presumably refers to defence, railways and telecom.

6 "India Country Procurement Assessment Report, World Bank, December 2003.

7 UNCITRAL is United Nations Commission for International Trade Law and GPA is Government Procurement Agreement. The GPA is a plurilateral agreement, in existence since the Tokyo Round (1979). India has not signed the GPA, but has been an observer since February 2010.

8 Note that these are 'problems' associated with the public procurement system and they don't belong in the same basket.

9 Knowledgeable insiders point out that this came after the election of 1996 in which corruption was seen as the factor which decided the result.

10 https://gem.gov.in/

11 'General Financial Rules 2017', Department of Expenditure, Ministry of Finance .

12 See for instance the 'Tamil Nadu Financial Code', partially available at http://www.tn.gov.in/documents/dept/9/2010-2011

13 'UNCITRAL Model Law on Public Procurement 2011', United Nations Commission on International Trade Law, Vienna, http://www.uncitral.org/uncitral/en/uncitral_texts/procurement_infrastructure/2011Model.html

14 See for instance, Box 2.2 in the 'Economic Survey 2015-16', Ministry of Finance, Government of India, pp. 48–49.

15 'Report of the Committee on Allocation of Natural Resources', Cabinet Secretariat, Government of India, May 2011.

16 Supreme Court of India, Natural Resources Allocation, In re, Special Reference No.1 of 2012; (2012) 10 SCC 1.

◆

Bibek Debroy is Chairman of the Economic Advisory Council to the Prime Minister and Member of NITI Aayog.

Dr T.V. Somanathan is a 1987 batch IAS officer and a former Joint Secretary at the Prime Minister's Office (PMO).

16

Cooperative Corruption

RANVEER NAGAICH

Driving in India follows a set of unwritten rules, which of course are at odds with the actual rules. Many may even confuse the right of way as a constitutional right, judging by the anarchy one witnesses on the streets. As it turns out, in a prevailing culture of corruption, individuals find it easier to bend the rules, rather than follow the prescribed norms. Insights from game theory tell us that individuals act in a manner to maximize their return. This implies that our incentives are aligned towards bending the rules rather than following them. We constantly blame corrupt politicians and bureaucrats. However, many of us don't realize that our collective actions as a society let corruption persist and even encourage it. Insights gained from behavioural economics suggest that corruption in India is encouraged by individuals seeking to further their self-interests. In certain situations, the costs involved in acting according to the prescribed rules are often greater than the costs involved in bending the rules. Thus, corruption in India can be thought of as a collective action problem. With pervasive and persistent corruption, the incentives for individuals to act in a non-corrupt manner are diminished greatly, whereas the incentives to follow the 'rules of the game' are greater. Not only does corruption result in a transfer of resources, it also has the effect of distorting allocations.

In a recent survey of corruption in Delhi[1], nearly one-third of the households sampled had paid a bribe over the past year, whilst 26 per cent of the households had first-hand experience of corrupt practices at the regional transport offices (RTOs). An interesting result was that first-hand experience was nearly negligible in utilities such as LPG, gas and water supply. Another disturbing result was that the highest service denial rate was in driving licenses. Service denial means that a public service has been denied over non-payment of bribes. Even the Union Transport Minister Nitin Gadkari has termed RTOs as 'hotbeds of corruption who have looted more than Chambal dacoits'.[2] He further stated that nearly a third of the licenses issued in India are fake. Some studies have attempted to explore the link between poor driving and corruption. Comparing World Health Organization's 2013 data on road deaths per 1,00,000 and scores on Rule of Law by the World Justice Project, James O'Malley finds a strong correlation between the two.[3] Countries scoring low on Rule of Law had more road deaths per 1,00,000 than those which scored higher.

Corruption and Social Outcomes

Corruption is generally viewed as a transfer of resources from citizens to bureaucrats.[4] However, Bertrand et al.[5] show that it distorts allocations as well. Studying the allocation of drivers licenses in New Delhi, the authors are of the opinion that policies, too, are distorted with prevalent corruption. In their experiment design, drivers seeking licenses were divided into three different groups—a comparison (base) group, a bonus group and a lesson group. Drivers in the bonus group were offered a cash prize if they managed to obtain a permanent licence within thirty-two days of securing their temporary licence. The base group were asked simply to obtain a license and appear for a follow up survey, for which they were paid ₹800. Drivers in the bonus group received ₹800 and a ₹2,000 cash prize. Those in the lesson group were simply offered free lessons. The results obtained were quite startling. Over 70 per cent of those in the bonus group were able to obtain licenses, whilst the number stood at 48 per cent for the comparison group. Furthermore, 74 per cent of those in the bonus group did not bother to learn how to drive. An interesting result is also that approximately 80 per cent of drivers in both the comparison group and the bonus group employed agents. Furthermore, of those that hired agents, only 23 per cent went through the prescribed driving test, whilst 89 per cent of the comparison group took the test. In order to test whether corruption in the licensing process put more unsafe drivers on the road, the authors administered a surprise driving test at the time of the follow up survey. Over half of the bonus group failed the driving test, indicating that hiring agents is the main channel through which bad drivers are able to obtain licences.

The above is an example of how corruption has led to an increasing number of unsafe drivers on the road. Individuals acting in their self-interest hire agents to expedite the process of obtaining licenses. The agents, acting in collaboration with bureaucrats are able to 'simplify' the process of obtaining a license. However, with such individuals acting in their best interest, society as a whole is worse off, as there are more bad drivers on the road. This study was undertaken after agents were banned at the New Delhi RTO, in a move to curb corruption. However, as we have seen, corruption seems rather pervasive.

The root of such behaviour can be explained by game theory. Mishra[6] examines the extent through which 'corruption as an individual norm of behaviour can sustain itself in the long run'. The author is able to show that corrupt behaviour tends to be self-sustaining against other forms of behaviour. The key argument rests on a standard cost–benefit analysis. If the benefits of engaging in corrupt activities exceed the cost, then we may have pervasive corruption. Similarly, if the costs involved in following the rules are greater than not following the rules, then corrupt behaviour may become the norm.

The costs are not necessarily monetary, but intrinsic as well. An oft-repeated phrase is 'Time is Money.' The time taken to act in a compliant manner tends to be far greater than the time taken to act in a non-compliant manner. The evidence presented by Bertrand et al (2007) confirms this hypothesis. The bonus group was able to obtain licenses in a much quicker time frame than the comparison group. Anecdotal evidence also points towards a similar conclusion. A routine matter with the income tax department could take weeks to be sorted, including multiple visits to the office. However, this time could be easily saved by providing the correct 'incentives' to the concerned officers. When faced with such a choice within an atmosphere of prevailing corruption, a compliant individual weighing up his or her choices will end up picking the non-compliant option, as the payoff is higher.

Social Cooperation

The classic stag hunt game can be thought of as an analogy of social cooperation. Imagine the following scenario: Two individuals go for a hunt; where they can each hunt for a stag or a hare. Here's the catch: neither knows what the other will do. The stag is a more desirable option for a meal. However, it will take two of them to trap the animal. Individually, both are able to catch a hare each, but will remain unsatisfied. Does each player think the other will join the hunt for the stag? Or does each of them expect the other to go for the hare? This situation is illustrated below. As it can be seen, if both players hunt the stag, then each receives a payoff of 3. If both hunt the hare, then each receive a payoff of 1.

Player 2

	Stag	Hare	
Stag	3, 3	0, 2	Player 1
Hare	2, 0	1, 1	

One would think the best option for both hunters would be to pool their resources. However, this would require that the two hunters trust each other. Expectations as to how the other player would act play a key role in the hunters' decision-making. If both trust the other to join the hunt for the stag, then we would have a socially optimal outcome. On the other hand, if one hunter decides to go for the stag and the other for the hare, then the first hunter remains hungry. Rather than going hungry, each hunter could be expected to hedge their bets and pick the safe option with the hare.

Extending this analogy, imagine the situation in any RTO in India. A person seeking a license has two options: go through an agent or go through the correct channels. By going through an agent, the person is likely to obtain a license quicker, and may not have to go through the driving test. On the other hand, going through the proper channels would require an investment in time. Now, in deciding what path to take, this person is likely to consider how others in the same position had acted. If everyone went through proper channels and cleared their driving tests, then Indian roads would be much safer to drive on. However, if each player in this game expects others to pay an agent and not go through the driving test, then why would he bother spending his time in going through the right channels? This example can be extended to the delivery of many public services in India. Are we better off paying the traffic policeman a bribe or paying the fine? Is it better to bribe the income tax official to get your file approved or fight through proper channels? These are just some of the strategic decisions faced by many Indians every single day.

This situation can also be described through a simple public goods game. Here's the scenario: in a room full of people, each person is asked to secretly contribute some money to a public fund, to be divided equally. The total pool will be multiplied by a factor greater than one, but less than the number of people. How would you play this game? Even by not contributing anything, by virtue of being a part of the group, I will still receive an amount equal to the rest of the group. However, by not contributing my share, the size of the pie will be smaller. This game can be further illustrated by the income tax situation in India. Recently, in his Budget speech, the Finance Minister stated that tax evasion had become a way of life, with the burden largely falling on the honest.[7] By not disclosing their income, these individuals do no contribute to the public pool that pays for infrastructure, healthcare and education. Hence, society as a whole is worse off, whilst those not paying taxes reap the benefits of public goods. The key takeaway from this discussion is that my actions are dependent on my beliefs as to how others would act. If I believe others to act in a cooperative manner, then I will contribute money. However, if I believe a majority of the group to consist of free-riders, then my contribution will be limited as well.

Corrupt Coalitions

In the earlier example of driving licenses, it may be useful to imagine the agents outside the RTOs and officials inside as being part of a coalition, where they coordinate their actions. By colluding, both are able to extract larger payments from people seeking licenses. RTO officials, by virtue of being part of the coalition, could possibly make it harder for a person seeking a license independently. At its core, a coalition involves (i) a binding agreement, (ii) a pooling of resources and (iii) distribution of these resources in a specified manner. So one can reasonably expect that the agents and RTO officials are in some sort of agreement, to pool the bribes and distribute them accordingly in a specified way. Anecdotal evidence also supports this view. Whilst applying for my license years ago in Kanpur, a single payment was made to an agent, rather than individual payments to RTO bureaucrats. How would one act in such a situation? Does one become part of the nexus by joining the coalition? With knowledge that such a coalition exists, the phrase, 'if you cannot beat them, join them', is quite relevant. It would make more sense for me to join this coalition by paying a 'fee'.

Expectations and Culture

The previous section showed us that when thinking strategically, the actions of individuals are dependent on their expectations as to how others would act. So how are these expectations formed? Several authors have established the hegemony of a culture governing our actions. For example, studying corruption in post-communist countries, Sandholtz & Taagepera[8] find that corruption is not only a result of economic incentives, but also of cultural orientations. Their key hypothesis is that communism left behind a culture that encouraged corruption. This hypothesis could potentially be extended to the case of India. As we know, until the early '90s, we were a largely command-and-control type of economy, with the license raj reigning supreme. In the years prior to liberalization, corruption became institutionalized within India. Echoing the words of the finance minister, tax evasion had become a way of life in India prior to demonetisation. Not just with tax evasion, corruption was evident in every sphere of public services.

The observation that the perception of how others act influences individual behaviour finds further support with Dong, Dulleck & Torgler[9]. The authors postulate individual corruption to be conditional on the behaviour of others. There are two key hypotheses to their paper: first, individuals find corruption to be more acceptable if they perceive their societies to be more corrupt. Second, corruption is contagious; a society with a prevailing high level of corruption is likely to witness increased levels of corruption in the future as well. Exploring how norms affect corrupt behaviour through an experiment, Kobis et al.[10] find that societal norms are a predictor of corrupt behaviour. Descriptive norms are those that convey information regarding how people act in certain situations. The authors designed an auction, where two players were each given a budget of 50 credits for a total prize of 120 credits. In case of equal bids, the prize is split equally between the two participants. As game theory tells us, the optimal approach for each player would be to bid 50 credits each and receive 60 back. Both players would be equally well off. However, the authors introduce an aspect of bribing within the game as well. The third player is an official who allocates the prize and with whom one of the participants can collaborate (bribe) to tip the scales in their favour. The prize is then split between the player and the official. The game is set in such a way that only one player has the option of bribing. How would this player react, given the knowledge that such behaviour is prevalent? As it turns out, according to their regressions, the authors find that descriptive norms of corruption influence individual behaviour. With the knowledge that such behaviour is commonplace, the students selected for the experiment were more likely to take up the option of bribing the official.

One can see how the above two hypotheses characterize the corruption situation in India. With corruption being both pervasive and prevalent, the incentives for individuals to act in a non-corrupt manner are diminished greatly, whereas the incentives to follow the 'rules of the game' are greater. Thus corruption should not be viewed through the narrow lens of the classic principal–agent problem.

Individual crusades against corruption are thus unlikely to bear fruit as well. Until society reaches a 'critical mass' of individuals willing to act in a cooperative manner, corruption will remain prevalent and persistent within our society.[11] Corrupt collaboration as Weisel, Ori & Shalvi[12] call it, is widespread when there is equality in profit sharing from corrupt acts and is more frequent than individual dishonest behaviour in a similar setting.

Behavioural economics can also be used to explain individual corrupt behaviour. Gachter & Schulz[13] designed an experiment to measure intrinsic honesty in a simple die rolling game. The authors also developed a countrywide index on prevalence of rule violations (PRV). The game was simple: students would be paid $1 for rolling a one, $2 for rolling a two and so on; however, the payout was zero if they rolled a six. Only the students were allowed to see the actual rolls; the experimenters were not. The authors found that students from countries with high scores on the PRV index tended to act in a more dishonest manner than students from countries with low PRV scores. According to the authors, if all students were perfectly honest, the average claim would be $2.5, and the average claim if everybody was dishonest would be $5 (since it was the highest payout). Thus, being brought up in a corrupt environment tends to corrupt the individual. What makes the claims of this paper rather strong is that the PRV index developed by the authors is based on data from 2003, whilst the study was conducted in 2016. Thus the students who were selected for the survey would not have influenced the PRV index. This allowed the authors to maximise the distance between the measurement of PRV and the time the experiment was conducted. So the relationship becomes unidirectional. It is the PRV index affecting student behaviour, not the other way around. This makes the results more robust. This hypothesis holds in another setting as well. Studying whether diplomats from more corrupt countries received more parking tickets in New York[14], the authors found a positive correlation: the more corrupt a country the diplomat came from, the higher number of parking tickets he was likely to receive.

Exploring the link between values and corruption, Lipset & Lenz[15] state that social systems set cultural goals and objectives, and the approved means of attaining them. The authors investigate the link between values and corruption through two different lenses. In the first, citing Merton, they postulate that societies that place a high value on economic success, but prevent access to achieving these goals will have prevalent corruption. Thus according to this theory, corruption stems from social pressures that result in violation of norms. On the other hand, citing Banfield, the authors introduce the concept of amoral familism. This theory claims that people are motivated solely by the well-being of their family members and may sacrifice the greater good by acting in such a way. That humans are driven by their own motives as well as societal norms is something that is echoed by Lambsdorff[16] as well. His hypothesis is that it is the power of reciprocity that sustains corrupt networks.

In a related study, Uslaner[17] explores the relation between corruption and trust. According to him, more trusting societies are generally less corrupt. However, this relationship depends on how one defines trust. There are two types of trust that are of main concern to the author: strategic trust and particularized trust. Strategic trust is based on our day-to-day interactions with specific people. Particularized trust, as the name suggests, means that we have faith only in people like ourselves. According to the author, corrupt networks exhibit both types of trust. In our example of driving licenses, the RTO officials trust each other not to be whistle-blowers (an example of particularized trust), whilst their trust with agents is based on their strategic interactions on a day-to-day basis.

Combating Corruption

Does the game theory offer solutions to this menace as well? If we were to believe the results obtained from game theory, then we would never see an honest public official, or a public movement against corruption such as the one led by Anna Hazare. Time and again, corruption has been viewed through the narrow lens of the classic principal–agent problem. Resultantly, most anti-corruption programmes, as the one described above, fail to meet their objectives. Working with interview data in Kenya and Uganda, Persson, Rothstein & Teoril[18] find they cannot presume the existence of 'principled' individuals willing to hold corrupt officers accountable. Their hypothesis that the benefits of corruption depend on the number of people in the same society willing to act in a corrupt manner was also echoed by Mishra. Thus the equilibrium solution, in game theory jargon, depends on expectations as to how others would act. So the success of any anti-corruption measure centres on altering beliefs of individuals. Corruption should be thought as 'rules of the game'. Bending the rules is normal, and anyone following the actual rules will have a hard time.

Kaushik Basu proposes a radical idea in one of his papers[19]: for a certain set of bribes[20], the act of paying the bribe should be made legal. The key idea behind his paper is asymmetric punishment[21]. The bribe-taker should be more heavily penalized than the bribe-giver. According to the PCA, both parties are equally liable for punishment for a bribe. Imagine the following situation: you are due an income tax return, but you cannot access these funds without a bribe. Thus, to get your return expedited you pay a bribe. You also cannot report the bribe, as under the law, you are equally liable to be punished. How does one control bribery (or corruption) then?

One of the oldest approaches to controlling corruption suggests a combination of monitoring and punishment.[22] On the other hand, monitoring at local levels has also been gaining traction in the literature. By being members of a community programme, such people are likely to have better incentives for monitoring the successful completion of a project. Olken[23] designed a field experiment in Indonesia to examine both these views. Each of the 608 villages selected for the experiment were about to start building a road as part of a nationwide village-level infrastructure project. Three different interventions were planned. In the first group of randomly selected villages, they were told that the probability of government audit would be raised from 4 per cent to 100 per cent. In the second group, invitations were sent for accountability meetings, where public officials would account for the funds being spent. The third group was provided with anonymous feedback forms, to be sealed in a drop box with the results being presented at these accountability meetings. Thus, the second and third experiments sought to quantify the effects of community monitoring, whilst the first experiment measured public (government) monitoring. In order to determine the cost of these roads, the author contracted an independent team of engineers and surveyors. Their estimates of the costs involved would be compared to the data provided by the villages. The difference in these costs, termed missing expenditures by the author, could be thought of as a measure of corruption. Missing expenditures could either constitute missing labour costs or material costs.

The results strongly supported public monitoring. The author found that missing expenditures were reduced by around 8 per cent with government audits, whilst community monitoring resulted in insignificant reductions, despite increased community participation in these meetings. However, the variability within groups is of interest as well. In the villages with government audits, it was found that a substantial number of jobs were given to family members of project officials, suggesting one form of corruption has been substituted by another. Furthermore, in community-monitored villages, missing labour costs were substantially reduced, with no effect on material costs. These results indicate that since labour was sourced from the villages directly, citizens had better incentives to monitor the payment of wages rather than material costs. We can infer that the free-rider problem still exists. The results from this experiment provide us with an important observation: there is no one golden way to fight corruption. The approach to fighting corruption must take into account the form of corruption being fought. Thus, in programmes where the benefits are accrued directly to the end consumer, like the public distribution system, each citizen has an individual interest in ensuring compliance. However, in the case of public goods, such as roads, individual interest seems to wane.

This behaviour can again be explained by game theory. By monitoring only wage payments, villagers in Indonesia are looking after their own best interests and not the society's as a whole. In the public goods game, those who honestly contributed money will notice that not everyone contributed equally, whilst not knowing the identities of the free-riders. In the next iteration of the game, they might reduce their initial contribution, based on the knowledge of how others have acted in previous rounds. However, there have been experiments that have shown that if the identity and contribution of each player is revealed, then contributions tend to be higher.[24] With their identity and contribution being revealed, the free-riders of the group are exposed to social sanctions. This result supports the notion that social norms may enforce cooperation in public good situations.

How did social cooperation emerge in such a situation? Corrupt societies would tend to be less trusting.[25] However, by revealing identities and contributions, my beliefs as to how others act have been altered. Thus, any effective anti-corruption programme must have the effect of altering my beliefs regarding the behaviour of others. How would making bribe-giving legal induce a reduction in demand for bribes? By altering the law and making it known to both the bribe-seeker and the bribe-giver that the bribe-giver will have immunity and receive his bribe back, the interests of the two parties are no longer aligned. I now have the knowledge that not only will I not be prosecuted, but I will also receive my money back. Thus, it would now be in my best interest to report the bribe, without fear of sanction. With this knowledge, the bribe-taker will be less inclined to accept a bribe as well.

We encourage corruption within the system by pursuing our self-interests. However, it is due to a prevailing culture of corruption that our self-interests and the interests of the society have been misaligned. The key insight from game theory is that the best strategy for us to play is to act in our best interest. The costs involved with us following the rules are greater than those in not following rules. Corruption in such instances is further exacerbated when coalitions are formed between groups/individuals with shared interests. In a nutshell, corruption should not be viewed through the lens of the classic principal–agent problem any longer. It should be viewed as a collective action problem and strategies to combat corruption must take into account insights from behavioural economics and game theory.

References

1 CMS-India Corruption Study 2015.

2 http://www.financialexpress.com/india-news/rto-most-corrupt-body-loot-more-than-chambal-dacoits-nitin-gadkari/177177/

3 http://www.citymetric.com/horizons/streets-bucharest-how-road-behaviour-correlates-trust-government-2015

4 J. Svensson. 2005. 'Eight questions about corruption', *The Journal of Economic Perspectives*, 19(3), 19–42.

5 M. Bertrand, S. Djankov, R. Hanna & S. Mullainathan. 2007. 'Obtaining a driver's license in India: an experimental approach to studying corruption', *The Quarterly Journal of Economics*, 122(4), 1639–76.

6 A. Mishra. 2006. 'Persistence of corruption: some theoretical perspectives', *World Development*, 34(2), 349–58.

7 http://indiabudget.nic.in/ub2017-18/bs/bs.pdf

8 W. Sandholtz & R. Taagepera. 2005. 'Corruption, culture, and communism', *International Review of Sociology*, 15(1), 109–31.

9 B. Dong, U. Dulleck, & B. Torgler, B. 2012. 'Conditional corruption'. *Journal of Economic Psychology*, 33(3), 609–27.

10 Köbis NC, van Prooijen J-W, Righetti F, Van Lange PAM. 2015. 'Who Doesn't?—The Impact of Descriptive Norms on Corruption,' PLoS ONE 10(6): e0131830. doi:10.1371/journal.pone.0131830.

11 O. Weisel & S. Shalvi. 2015. 'The collaborative roots of corruption'. Proceedings of the National Academy of Sciences of the United States of America, 112(34), 10651–56. http://doi.org/10.1073/pnas.1423035112

12 W. Ori & S. Shaul, Corrupt Collaboration (May 18, 2015). Inequality, Trust and Ethics Conference: London 2015. Available at SSRN: https://ssrn.com/abstract=2607507)

13 Gächter Simon & Jonathan F. Schulz. 2016. 'Intrinsic Honesty And The Prevalence Of Rule Violations Across Societies', *Nature*, 531(7595), pp. 496–99, doi:10.1038/nature17160.

14 Fisman & Miguel. 2010. 'Economic Gangsters', as cited in Shalvi et al.

15 S.M. Lipset & G.S. Lenz. 2000. 'Corruption, culture, and markets'. *Culture matters: How values shape human progress*, 112, 112.

16 J.G. Lambsdorff. 'Behavioral and Experimental Economics as a Guidance to Anticorruption. 279–99 in: D. Serra, L.D. Serra, L. Wantchekon (eds.). *New Advances in Experimental Research on*

Corruption: Research in Experimental Economics. 2012. Emerald Group Publishing.

17 E.M. Uslaner. 2004. 'Trust and corruption.' *The new institutional economics of corruption*, p. 76.

18 A. Persson, B. Rothstein & J. Teorell. 2013. 'Why anticorruption reforms fail—systemic corruption as a collective action problem', *Governance*, 26(3), pp. 449–71.

19 K. Basu. 2011. 'Why, for a Class of Bribes, the Act of Giving a Bribe should be Treated as Legal', Working paper, Government of India.

20 Harassment bribes are those that people have to pay to obtain something they are legally entitled to.

21 K. Basu, K. Basu, & T. Cordella. 2016. 'Asymmetric Punishment As An Instrument Of Corruption Control'. *Journal of Public Economic Theory*, 18(6), pp. 831–56, doi:10.1111/jpet.12212.

22 G.S. Becker & G.J. Stigler. 1974. 'Law Enforcement, Malfeasance, And Compensation Of Enforcers' *The Journal of Legal Studies*, 3(1), pp. 1–18, doi:10.1086/467507.

23 B.A. Olken. 2007. 'Monitoring Corruption: Evidence From A Field Experiment In Indonesia', *Journal Of Political Economy, 115(2)*, pp. 200–49, doi:10.1086/517935.

24 M. Rege & K. Telle. 2004. 'The impact of social approval and framing on cooperation in public good situations'. *Journal of public Economics*, 88(7), 1625–44.

25 See Uslaner (2004).

◆

Ranveer Nagaich is a Young Professional at NITI Aayog working on areas such as Macroeconomics, Public Finance and Trade.

Acknowledgements

On the trail of the Black would not have been possible without the contributions made by an eclectic mix of professionals who share a common passion to see India free of corruption and black money. The diverse set of expertise our contributors bring on board has helped us stitch together a holistic action agenda against this challenge.

Special thanks to Maninder Kaur Dwivedi, Anna Roy, T.V. Somanathan and Alok Kumar for supporting us with their contributions. This book has benefitted immensely from their rich perspectives, honed through years of experience in policymaking and implementation. We also wish to thank Suparna Jain, law professional, and Dhiraj Nayyar, economist, for undertaking in-depth assessment of issues within their respective domains and sharing insightful solutions. Grateful for the time and efforts each of them invested, despite busy schedules.

Another feature of this book is that it includes perspectives of promising young professionals who not only dream of a corruption-free future for India, but also wish to contribute in the making of it. We would like to thank Sonal Badhan, Aparajita Gupta, Shashvat Singh, Swati Saini, Shambhavi Sharan, Bhavana Kohli, Ranveer Nagaich, Kheya Melo Furtado, Ritika Aghi, Sneha Palit and Alok Kumar Dubey. Their well-researched and thorough analysis of their respective areas shows how India's youth see and perceive corruption and how keen they are to eliminate this challenge.

Special gratitude to Kapish Mehra, Managing Director, Rupa Publications, and his team for giving us this opportunity and supporting us all along the process. In particular, thanks to

Yamini Chowdhury, Senior Commissioning Editor, and Prerna Mathur, Copy Editor, for their diligent efforts in providing editorial inputs and giving the book its final shape.

Finally, we dedicate this book to the Prime Minister of India, Narendra Modi. It is after a long time that we, as a nation, are witnessing a decisive commitment of the highest office to dismantle the institution of corruption. One of the first actions he took after assuming office in 2014 was to set up a Special Investigation Team on this. Since then, a series of steps have been taken, several documented in this book, and they show that he is serious about cleansing the system. Demonetisation, one of the boldest policy actions ever taken, demonstrates that the Prime Minister does not shy away even from potentially unpopular measures. We have been profoundly inspired by his unwavering commitment against corruption and black money. This book is an expression of our gratitude towards him in this fight.

Finally, to the reader, we hope that this book reignites a dormant urge within all of us to rid India of the disease of corruption and black money. It's only when citizens play their part pro-actively and work in tandem with the government that this malaise can be overcome.

Bibek Debroy
Kishore Arun Desai

Index

www.ingramcontent.com/pod-product-compliance
Lightning Source LLC
Chambersburg PA
CBHW030808310726
48980CB00006B/419/J

9788129149220